PORTRAITS IN AN ALBUM

Jenny Glanfield

LONDON NEW YORK SYDNEY TORONTO

This edition published 1997
By BCA
By arrangement with Victor Gollancz
An imprint of the Cassell Group

First Reprint 1997

CN 3677

Typeset by Rowland Phototypesetting Ltd
Bury St Edmunds, Suffolk
Printed and bound in Great Britain by
Mackays of Chatham PLC, Chatham, Kent

For my brother Tony and all the friends of our childhood
– and for Kirstie –
With love

PROLOGUE

He woke abruptly. The bedroom was pitch dark. There was not even a moon to shed a glimmer of light.

For a few moments, he hovered in that strange half-world between sleeping and waking, still caught in the sweet, warm spell of his dream. Then he became aware of a branch beating against the window and realized that outside – in direct contrast to the stillness of his dream – a gale was blowing, battering against the house walls and rattling the ill-fitting window in its frame.

The branch beat louder and more persistently against the glass. Somewhere inside the house, a door slammed, jolting him into full wakefulness. Living in such an exposed spot, he was used enough to winds and storms, usually sleeping through them. But after such a dream, it was impossible to sleep again.

He got out of bed, dressed and made his way downstairs, quietly, so as not to disturb the other sleepers. He needed no light to guide him. Each bare floorboard was familiar to him, each uncarpeted tread of the staircase, each flagstone in the passageway.

A dim glow illuminated the kitchen, for the old range was stoked up every evening, so that it should last the night. The soot-blackened kettle, filled with water, stood beside the hob and a breakfast tray was laid in preparation.

But he was in no mood for indulging in creature comforts. The walls of the house were crowding in on him. He craved the solitude of the hills, the sting of the wind against his face, the ozone tang of the air on his lips. He put on his old donkey jacket and hobnail boots, then opened the back door, only to have it nearly wrenched from his hand by a gust of wind.

An electric excitement coursed through him, making his heart pound and his nerve ends tingle. When he was a boy, storms had frightened him, but no longer. He had lived so close to nature that he had become a part of it.

Closing the back door carefully behind him, he set off up towards the open hills. He needed no torch to guide him through the darkness. So often had he gone this way over the years that every step of the ground was familiar.

The wind was a south-westerly, the prevailing wind in those parts. It struck chill, but only because of its extreme strength and because he was walking into it. It tugged at his skin, drawing it taut across his face, making his eyes stream and blowing his thick mane of hair out behind him. He revelled in the feeling of pitting his might against the wind's, of leaning into it and forging forwards.

In the paddock, the oak tree was being buffeted this way and that, its leaves ripped from its branches and tossed through the air like huge pieces of confetti. But he felt no more concern for the oak tree's safety than he did for his own. Its roots reached deep into the earth. It had stood for centuries before he was born and would stand for centuries more after he was gone.

Then he was up on to the hillside and experiencing the true force of the wind. He could scarcely stand upright against it now, let alone move forward. Suddenly, a gust blew him almost from his feet and he found himself driven in the direction the wind selected for him – away from the bare hilltops and towards the wood.

Perhaps this was better, for the tree trunks created a barrier of sorts against the wind, although, like the oak tree in the paddock, they were bending and twisting in agonized contortions, their leaves torn from them, their boughs creaking and groaning in distress.

How different from that summer day, only weeks ago, when he had walked here with her and she had murmured reverently, 'It's so quiet. And the way the trees arch overhead – it's like being in a cathedral.'

'I love trees,' he had told her. It had been a confession of faith. Each tree in the wood was a living entity to him. He knew them all more intimately than any of his fellow human beings. Many of them he had planted himself . . .

The wind was gathering in strength, assuming a demonic personality of its own, screaming and howling in a savage frenzy, as it rampaged between the trees, whipping up fallen leaves, twigs and dead undergrowth, whirling them round in the air, then flinging them down on the ground.

Suddenly, it abated. There was a lull and, for a moment, he thought the storm might have exhausted itself. Then, screaming in triumphant fury, the wind returned with renewed vigour. The tree tops crashed confusedly into each other, like medieval armies wielding staves and pikes.

The wood provided little shelter now, but that was of no import. This wind was evil, nihilistic, hell-bent on havoc and destruction. To leave his trees alone to face its wrath would be to desert friends in their hour of direst need.

For himself, he felt no fear. Already the details of his dream had faded, but still the sensation of it lingered and, with it, the overwhelming conviction that, in one thing, he had not been misled. She cared for him. And armed with this knowledge, he had become invincible. Whatever fate might hold in store for him, he was invulnerable . . .

With shrieks of manic rage, the wind pitched itself, again and again, against the trees. Then, directly above him, he heard the rending crack of a breaking limb.

The wind had claimed its first victory.

Chapter 1

'Lot 58, a period mahogany bureau-bookcase and miscellaneous books,' the auctioneer announced, his eyes scanning the room. 'Three hundred pounds to start.'

Seated at the back of the room, Sebastian Devere did not move. He had not even examined the piece before the sale because, with his reputation, he knew that if he showed undue interest in it, it would acquire additional value to other dealers before the bidding began. The mere fact that he was present at the Worthing auction had already aroused curiosity. He was conscious of heads turning to glance at him – a slim and distinguished figure in a Savile Row suit and Gucci shoes, appearing younger than his fifty-three years despite the threads of silver in his dark hair.

Provincial auctions tended to be a waste of time for top London dealers such as himself, although, as a matter of course, he subscribed to all the catalogues and occasionally – as in this instance – sent off for condition reports. House clearance sales on the Costa Geriatrica did sometimes yield unexpected bargains, even though television programmes such as *Going for a Song* and *The Antiques Roadshow* had alerted the public to the potential value of family heirlooms.

This secretaire-bookcase, erroneously described by the auctioneer as a bureau-bookcase, was just such an example. It could, of course, be a fake. Without examining the inside of the drawers, the rabbets, the veneer, the condition of the wood and the direction of the grain, it was impossible to be one hundred per cent certain. But after more than thirty years in the business, Sebastian had developed a sixth sense. There was something about its appearance which showed it to be a family piece, used and cared for over the centuries. Chippendale, 1750 to 1760, he would say, judging by

11

the rather stiff architectural cornice and the astragal bead on the bookcase doors.

'Eight hundred and fifty. Nine hundred. Nine hundred and fifty.'

This last offer was made by a middle-aged woman against whom Sebastian had found himself bidding on previous occasions. She owned a shop in the Lanes at Brighton and was one of those types he most disliked, who succeeded in combining elegance, intelligence and charm with an astute business mind. Even though he was exceeding his own reserve, he raised his thumb.

'One thousand at the back of the room,' the auctioneer intoned. 'Anywhere else now?' The Brighton dealer nodded. 'One thousand and fifty. Anywhere else for one thousand one hundred?'

Sebastian raised his thumb again.

'One thousand one hundred. Anywhere else now?' The auctioneer looked queryingly at the Brighton woman, who shook her head. Nobody else bid.

'Sold for one thousand one hundred at the back of the room.'

Not the bargain he had hoped for, Sebastian reflected, but still not bad. It should fetch at least a couple of grand in his South Kensington showroom. This trip would pay for itself.

He skimmed down the catalogue through his half-rim reading spectacles. Although furniture was his speciality, he was always interested in silver and glass — 'smalls', as they were known in the trade — which brought furniture alive in the showroom. Lot 79, some early Victorian silver, which included some rather nice candlesticks, might prove worthwhile, but apart from that there was nothing else in his line.

However, once the bidding topped four hundred, he let the silver go to the Brighton woman. Unless she already had a buyer, she'd find it hard to shift.

He glanced at his Rolex: just past two. The auction had gone more briskly than he had expected. He would be back in London at a reasonable hour.

He paid for the secretaire-bookcase in cash and an elderly porter helped him out with it to the Range Rover. 'Don't forget your books, sir,' the man said, after they had loaded the piece of furniture carefully and covered it with a blanket.

The books appeared to be a miscellaneous collection of anthologies, classics, dictionaries, encyclopaedias, art and history books, and Sebastian doubted very much that they had any value, but they formed part of the lot and he had to take them away. 'Shove them in the back,' he ordered. His assistant, Michael Ashton, was a bookworm: he could sort through them.

A few moments later he was heading through the slow, erratic Worthing traffic towards the A24 and London. It was early January and the day was already drawing in. Many cars had their sidelights on. The hump of the South Downs rose ahead of him, bleak and forbidding. A clump of trees on the ridge was silhouetted against a steel-grey sky.

An Austin A30 emerged from a side road heedless of any right of way, causing him to step hard on the brakes and thump the horn. The driver, a bald-headed old boy with a wispy fringe of white hair and heavy spectacles, pottered along in the middle of the road at somewhere between fifteen and twenty miles an hour, before abruptly turning right without signalling, narrowly missing a van coming from the opposite direction.

The houses stopped, the road turned into a dual carriageway and climbed over the South Downs. Sebastian put down his foot on the accelerator. There was nothing worth listening to on the radio. The afternoon play on Radio 4 was centred around a mining community in Wales, while Radio 3 was playing Birtwistle or Tippett, and he was too far from London to pick up LBC.

His glimpse of the driver of the Austin A30 lingered in his mind. There was something about that face and the expression on it – that blissful obliviousness to his surroundings – which reminded him of Professor Berkeley . . .

Although Sebastian made a living – and a very reasonable one – by dealing in the artefacts of the past, he was not prone to indulge in reminiscences of his own past, particularly his childhood.

But the Professor was among his good memories. To remember the Professor was to experience a little glow of warmth that counteracted the grey chill of the outside world. For if there had been one overwhelmingly important influence on his life, it was that old man, who had found endless time for a bewildered and lonely little boy, to listen to his troubles and to give unstintingly of his sympathy. And, when the Professor had died, he had felt a sense of loss such as he had not experienced when he had learned of the death of his own father.

For that matter, he owed all the Berkeleys an immense debt. Without them he would not be the man he was today. Adam Berkeley, the Professor's son, and his wife Eve had taken him in, an orphan of the war, and included him in their family. He and their son Elliott – born within a few months of each other – had grown up together like brothers, once Elliott had overcome his initial suspicion of the intruder. They had attended the same schools, done their military service together, gone up to Oxford together and now they worked together . . .

In his mind's eye, Sebastian saw himself back in the Professor's sitting room at Hill House, with the Professor, a shortish, rather tubby figure in a rough tweed jacket, ensconced in his armchair beside the fire, and himself, a young schoolboy in short trousers, knee-length woollen socks and lace-up shoes, sitting on the hearthrug at his feet, watching the sparks jump up the chimney, while the flames cast flickering shadows over the room.

The Professor's sitting room had been his sanctuary and the Professor his guardian angel, especially in the first few months after his arrival at Puddlescombe at the beginning of the war, when he had been so unutterably unhappy in his strange new surroundings. Never had the Professor been censorious: never had he urged him to 'learn to grin and bear it' or 'take these things like a man', as his housemaster and Matron did at school. But neither had he always taken Sebastian's part nor tried to buffer him against the harsh realities of his new existence.

Instead, once his tears had abated, the Professor had allowed him to examine some of the souvenirs he had brought back from his travels as an archaeologist – in Greece and Egypt and India and China – to hold in his hands a scarab carved from red stone, an ivory model of an elephant, ostrich feathers, a bronze statuette of Apollo, an oil lamp looking just like the one from which the genie appeared in *Aladdin* and a fragile sheet of papyrus inscribed with hieroglyphics.

Then he would light his pipe, pour himself a tot of whisky, and tell Sebastian about ancient kings, ancient tombs, ancient rites and ancient gods, mighty kingdoms and the mighty wars which had destroyed them. And Sebastian would lose himself in another world and forget the troubles besetting him in this.

How fortunate he had been that the war had put a stop to the Professor's travels – although, of course, the Professor had been getting on in years by then. Not that he had ever stopped working. Right up until his death, he had continued writing, making lecture tours and the occasional trip abroad to an important new dig.

During the school holidays, he had taken Elliott and Sebastian around the Dorset countryside to Iron Age forts, to Turnworth Down and Hod Hill, to see the massive figure of the Giant carved into the hillside near Cerne Abbas, to look for fossils in the cliffs and search among the flintstones in ploughed fields for shards of pottery, arrowheads and Roman coins.

For Elliott, those expeditions had merely been a diversion, for he had never shared his grandfather's and Sebastian's all-absorbing interest in ancient civilizations. Whereas Sebastian had read Classics up at Magdalen and spent most of his spare time in the Bodleian, Elliott had read English and idled away the hours on the river and at parties. After graduating, Elliott had become a car salesman in a swish Mayfair showroom, while Sebastian went to work as an assistant curator at the Victoria & Albert Museum, where an interest in furniture had become a passion.

Then the Professor had died. That was in 1958, when they were both twenty-five. The Professor's library and his collection of antiquities had gone to a museum, but he had left a substantial sum of money to Sebastian and Elliott, with the request that they should use it to set up in business together. For Sebastian an antiques shop was the obvious choice and Elliott was happy to go along with it. The money, though not a fortune, was enough to obtain the lease on a shop and buy some stock.

Yes, he had a lot for which to be grateful to the Professor . . .

Wearing olive-green corduroy trousers and a thick Aran fisherman's sweater, Elliott was standing in the lamplight outside the showroom in the cobbled South Kensington mews, admiring a gleaming red Jaguar SS100 1939 3.5-litre sports two-seater, when Sebastian drove in.

As he switched off the Range Rover's engine, Elliott sauntered across, the eternal cigarette dangling between his fingers and a broad grin on his face. '*Age cannot wither her, nor custom stale her infinite variety*,' he quoted. 'Isn't she beautiful?'

Sebastian got out of his own car and, shivering in the cold air, walked over to the Jaguar. The number plate seemed familiar. 'Surely it's not . . . ?'

'It most certainly is. The very same vehicle. My first car. The parents gave her to me for my twenty-first in 1954. For six years, she was my only true love. Then dire and dreadful circumstances drove us apart . . .'

Over thirty-two years ago, Sebastian thought incredulously. How time does fly. We had just completed our National Service then and were in our freshman year at Oxford. Yet Elliott's hardly changed since he was an undergraduate. He's scarcely put on any weight, there isn't a grey hair on his head and he still exudes the same boyish charm. He even wears the same style of clothes as he did when he was a student, except that then his sweater had been black and his corduroys purple.

'As I recall,' he interjected drily, 'you got Barbara in the family way, had to get married, and sold the Jag for four hundred pounds.'

Elliott grimaced ruefully. 'I would prefer to erase such banalities from my memory. Gaze upon her and admit that she is as bewitchingly lovely and desirable as ever.'

'It certainly looks in good condition,' Sebastian conceded. 'But not exactly practical at this time of year.'

'Your problem is that you have no soul, Sebastian. To you a thing of beauty is not a joy for ever, but an object of trade and barter. In your eyes, this car merely represents a means of transportation, while for me she is a transport of delight.'

'Am I to assume you've bought it back again?'

'I chanced to be walking past the vintage car showroom in the Brompton Road and her headlights gazed mournfully at me through the plate glass window. How could I resist?'

'May I enquire how much you paid?'

'She was a mere bargain at a hundred and twenty grand,' Elliott replied nonchalantly. 'But what is money?'

'What I slave for day and night and everyone around me disposes of with depressing ease.'

'Better than giving it to the taxman. However, worry not, old chap, she did not come out of the company's profits, but my own pocket.'

'Out of your pocket?'

'Recently I suffered a tragic bereavement. You were possibly so busy that I did not mention it at the time, but my Great-aunt Jessica passed away at the age of one hundred and one, and very generously left me a small legacy. Well, not so small, I suppose . . .'

'So that's why you kept dashing down to Bournemouth! You were coffin-polishing again!'

'You do have such a crude turn of phrase. Think of the happiness I gave an old lady in the last lonely years of her life.'

'I'd rather not.' He glanced into the showroom. 'Where's Michael?'

'Gone to the post office.'

'When he comes back, I'll need him to give me a hand with my latest acquisition.'

'So you, too, have been in spendthrift mode.'

'The secretaire-bookcase I have purchased is stock – not an attempt to recapture my misspent youth . . .'

Elliott gave a sigh of exasperation. 'Have you developed second sight or something? You can't have known I've had Barbara on the phone.'

Sebastian's feet felt as though they were turning into lumps of ice. 'I'm perishing. Let's get inside.'

They went into his office. Elliott sat down behind the desk, which was littered with several empty coffee cups and an overflowing ashtray. Leaning back in the chair – a fine example of Sheraton's craftsmanship, made of rosewood and inlaid with brass, which Sebastian was keeping for his own use until a suitable purchaser should materialize – he said, 'Barbara rang to tell me that Donald has decided to get spliced. Stupid idiot. You'd think he'd know better with my example before him, wouldn't you? And Barbara has hit upon the wonderful idea that his real daddy should be present on the auspicious occasion.'

Sebastian crossed the room, felt the jug on the filter coffee machine, found it still lukewarm and poured himself a cup. 'And so you should. If and when my daughter gets married, I sincerely hope to be present.'

'The circumstances are rather different. You only have Pippa.'

'How many times do I have to ask you not to call her Pippa? Her name is Philippa.'

'But she prefers being called Pippa.'

'What she calls herself is up to her. However, as you well know, I no more approve of her being called Pippa than I like being called Seb myself.'

'But Seb doesn't suit you. Whereas Pippa does suit her.'

Sebastian grunted and sipped his coffee.

When he and Valerie had married, he had not wanted children, which was understandable in view of everything he had gone through in his own childhood. But Valerie had been the maternal type and it was not as easy then as now to take precautions. In fact, if Valerie hadn't made a mistake about the time of the month – whether deliberately or not, he would never be certain – it was unlikely that he would ever have chosen to become a parent.

However, overtaken by fate, he had found himself with a daughter, whom he had come swiftly to adore. A good-tempered baby, Philippa had grown up into an attractive, intelligent and sweet-natured girl, endowed with a lively imagination. She was the one weakness in his life, the sole chink in his armour. Not that he had spoiled her or was blind to her faults, but he had done everything for her good that it was humanly possible to do. Above all, he had never knowingly shirked his parental responsibilities. How could he, with the example of his own mother before him?

Philippa had been privately educated – but not as a boarder. Having suffered that fate himself, he would never have inflicted it upon anyone else, certainly not his own child. Most of her teenage enthusiasms had been indulged and, for her eighteenth birthday, he had given her her own car, which allowed him and Valerie peace of mind and Philippa independence.

From an early age, she had shown a talent for drawing and painting – which was certainly not inherited from himself or Valerie – so it had come as no great surprise when she had announced, upon leaving school, that she would like to go to art college. Rather against his better judgement – art students, in his own youth, having enjoyed a notorious reputation for being a wild bunch – he had agreed, with the proviso that she continued to live at home. But the friends she had made at college were all very respectable, taking their studies surprisingly seriously, so he had had to revise his opinions somewhat.

'Returning to my situation, however,' Elliott was saying. 'I have had four wives and six bloody kids.'

'For which you have only yourself to blame,' Sebastian retorted sharply.

Elliott grinned. 'Well, it seemed fun at the time. But it's over twenty years since Barbara and I split up. Donald and I scarcely know each other.'

'He's still your son.'

'In name only. Cecil must have had far more a paternal influence on him. Talking about names, how could any woman marry a man called Cecil?' Elliott lit another cigarette and leaned even further back in the Sheraton chair, so that it balanced precariously on two legs. 'In any case,

Donald's apparently been living with the girl for two years. If they must get married, why not do it discreetly in a registry office? Why go for the full white wedding?'

'Perhaps the bride's parents . . . ?'

'Probably. Barbara, too, no doubt. And it would appeal to her vanity to have two husbands to show off. A sort of status symbol. Well, I'm not going and that's that. If I go to this one, I'll have to go to all the others. No, I refuse to set a precedent. I'll send Donald a cheque. I'm sure he'd prefer a present to my presence.'

'You could offer the Jaguar to take the bride to the church,' Sebastian suggested, only slightly facetiously.

'Could I hell! Well, enough of all that. Let's unload your spoils and take her out for a quick spin. We could go down to the river. There's that pub at Isleworth . . .'

A quick spin to Isleworth in the Jaguar, probably – knowing Elliott – with the hood down, held little appeal, particularly since it was bound to turn into a long – and extremely alcoholic – evening. Home beckoned more welcomingly. 'Sorry,' he said, 'we've got people coming to dinner.' Not true but it was an acceptable excuse. 'And you know what Valerie's like.'

Elliott nodded soberly. 'OK. We'll leave it for another day.'

Sebastian heard the note of disappointment in his voice. 'Well,' he relented, 'just once round the block.'

Elliott grinned. 'I knew you wouldn't be able to resist. But on your head be it. I'd hate to be held responsible for the soufflé sinking.'

Sebastian never entered the drive of his home without feeling a burst of pride. Considering his start in life, he had done well for himself and his family.

First he had had the good fortune to meet Valerie. She was the sister of Malcolm Blyth, who had been at school with him and Elliott, and her father was a leading Harley Street heart specialist.

Elliott had not approved of her. 'It was a woman like Valerie Blyth whom Milton had in mind when he wrote "Virtue and the conscience of her worth",' he had warned. 'You mark my words, she'll turn into a domestic drag – and she has wide child-bearing hips. I sincerely hope you're not intending to marry her.'

But the very characteristics which Elliott had so deplored were exactly what had attracted Sebastian to her. Indeed, if he was honest, she had been rather plain, with a roundish face and plumpish figure. But there was an intrinsic niceness and old-fashioned modesty about her which had appealed to him – and which he had respected throughout their long courtship.

She had been his first and only girlfriend. They had become engaged during his second year at Oxford and married the year after the Professor's death, at which point she had given up her job as a receptionist at her father's consulting rooms.

Despite his dire warnings, Elliott had been best man. And, unlike Elliott's own attempts at wedded bliss, their marriage had worked out well. Of course, there had been the occasional disagreements: but the good times far outweighed the bad. Most importantly, whilst Valerie might not be the most glamorous or intellectual of women, she had proved unerringly faithful to him and a devoted mother to Philippa.

They had had four homes since they were married. The first had been a flat in Tooting. After Philippa was born, they had moved to a semi in Worcester Park and then, as his fortunes had improved, had come a detached house in Barnes. Dulwich was the epitome of all his dreams.

It resembled Hill House as nearly as it was possible for a mock-Georgian house in Dulwich, standing in a mere half-acre of garden, to resemble a real Georgian house in the middle of the Dorset countryside, set in two acres of grounds, with fields beyond. Since neither he nor Valerie was a keen gardener, he did not regret the lack of land. All he needed was a little privacy from the neighbours and a safe place for Philippa to play with her friends when she was small. He employed a man to do the necessary digging, weeding and mowing two mornings a week, just as he had a boy come in to wash the Range Rover, Valerie's Volvo Estate and Philippa's Metro every Saturday, and a daily woman to do the cleaning.

It was a big house, with three reception rooms and five bedrooms, larger than they needed, but, like all families, they expanded to fill the available space. Valerie used one of the spare bedrooms as a sewing room, for as well as being an excellent cook she was a keen needlewoman, making many of her own clothes and doing the most intricate embroidery and patchwork.

Philippa had been given the room adjoining her bedroom as a study and, for his part, Sebastian had taken over one of the downstairs rooms as an office, which provided a useful bolt-hole when Valerie was having one of her coffee mornings.

He had paid only thirty thousand for the house, ten years ago, in 1977, and a couple of months ago their neighbour opposite had sold his place for three hundred thousand. So his own should fetch at least three fifty. Whatever else one thought of Margaret Thatcher, one had to give her credit for the booming economy her government had created. Not that he was thinking of selling yet, but when Philippa left home – as she presumably would, in the not too distant future – then it might be wise to consider making a move. After all, prices couldn't continue going up for ever. At some point, the market had to peak.

As he let himself in the front door, Valerie emerged from the kitchen, her face flushed from the heat of the stove, her mascara slightly smudged, and wearing a peach leisure suit beneath her cook's pinafore that did not flatter her over-full figure. From behind her wafted an appetizing smell of baking pastry with a tang of herbs.

They gave each other a perfunctory, routine kiss, followed by the ritual questions and answers. 'Have you had a good day?'

'So-so. And you?'

'Not bad.'

'Philippa home?'

'No, not yet.'

'Working late again?'

'I assume so.'

Sebastian pursed his lips. When Philippa had decided, at the end of her first year at college, to specialize in photography, little had he realized what she would be letting herself in for.

He had assumed that, after three years at college, she would emerge fully qualified, in a position to take on commissioned work. Instead of which, a year and a half later, she was still what was termed an assistant but, in fact, little more than a general dogsbody. She worked an incredibly long day, much of which seemed to be spent making coffees and clearing up the studio, and quite often weekends as well. And for all her hard labour, she was paid a hundred pounds a week, which, calculated at an hourly rate, was less than Valerie paid Mary, their cleaning woman.

To make matters worse, Philippa's relationship with Richard White, the photographer she worked for, was not purely professional. How intimate it had become Sebastian did not know, nor did he really want to. But since Richard's work involved trips to far-flung parts of the country and even abroad, necessitating overnight stays in hotels, and Philippa always accompanied him, he could not help but fear the worst. And even when she was working at his studio, sometimes she did not come home at all at night.

'Dinner's nearly ready,' Valerie said.

He relegated the problem of Philippa temporarily to the back of his mind. 'Something smells good.'

Valerie gave an appreciative smile. 'It's salmon *en croûte*. I've found a new recipe.'

While he was having his pre-dinner Scotch and Valerie her dry Martini, he told her about Elliott's 'coffin-polishing' and the old Jaguar.

She did not find the story amusing. 'Typical,' she snorted. 'You're out buying stock and he's buying a very expensive car that he can't afford and doesn't need.'

Sebastian shrugged. 'You know what they say. The difference between men and boys is men have more expensive toys.'

Valerie sighed. 'Why must you always stick up for him? Just once in a while you could admit that he has failings. Take today as an example. You were doing all the work and he was having all the fun.'

'That's not entirely true. He's the salesman. Without him we wouldn't have a business.'

'Rubbish! Without you, he'd have gone bust years ago.'

'Well, there you are. We both contribute in our different ways.'

His relationship with Elliott was something Valerie would never understand. There was no one to whom she was as close as he was to Elliott. It was not just his and Elliott's nearness in age and their shared upbringing. It was also their essential differences. They complimented each other: his own caution counterbalanced Elliott's charm and wit, while Elliott's enthusiasm inspired him to venture into unknown territories. They were a perfect team.

CHAPTER 2

A few days later, when Sebastian returned from an auction preview at Christie's, he found Michael kneeling on the floor at the back of the showroom, surrounded by piles of books, old periodicals and other junk. 'It's been so quiet all morning, I decided to clear out the storeroom,' he explained.

The weather wasn't encouraging people out of their homes and offices. Snow was causing traffic chaos in London and blocking roads in country areas. It had taken him the best part of an hour to make the short journey from Dulwich to Kensington this morning. It was quite ridiculous how just a little bit of snow brought the country virtually to a halt.

He was looking forward to going on holiday. Once Philippa had grown too old to accompany them, he and Valerie had started taking their annual holiday in the early spring, to recharge their batteries after the long winter months. Last year they had gone to Florida and both hated it, but this year they were flying to Nassau and cruising for a fortnight round the Bahamas.

Left to his own devices, he would have preferred a more intellectually stimulating holiday but Valerie wasn't too keen on ruins and museums. For her, the pleasure of travelling lay principally in meeting new people. So, since they both enjoyed the sun, they had reached a compromise. And Sebastian consoled himself that, on board a reputable cruise ship, he wouldn't have to worry about whether the plumbing worked or whether he was going to get food-poisoning or be pestered by street beggars, as would happen if he went to, say, Egypt.

'These books here are the lot you bought in Worthing,' Michael said.

'Good grief! I'd forgotten them.' The secretaire-bookcase had sold almost immediately, at an even better price than he had anticipated, which was probably why the books had completely slipped his mind.

'I assume there's nothing of any value?'

'No first editions, though there's a set of Trollope I wouldn't mind having. And some books on photography and some kind of album which Pippa might be interested in.'

Michael turned to the inside cover of a leather-bound photograph album, which, at a quick glance, could be mistaken for a book. Written in a precise hand was the name 'Edith Spencer'. He flicked through the pages, every now and then pausing at full- or half-plate black and white portraits, which judging by the sitters' clothes and hairstyles had been taken in the 1930s.

Sebastian shrugged. 'I suppose so, though I doubt it. They look rather old-fashioned. But I'll take them home tonight. As for the rest, call Peter Simpson. If he doesn't want them, throw them in the bin.'

Pippa burst into the lounge while he and Valerie were having their pre-dinner drinks. 'It's wicked out there,' she exclaimed, dropping her anorak, scarf, gloves and a bulging canvas bag on to the floor just inside the door. A bit shorter and very much slimmer than Valerie, she was wearing trainers, sweatshirt and figure-hugging blue jeans. Her fair hair was tied back in a pony-tail, from which curly tendrils had escaped, clinging damply to her forehead and the nape of her neck. She wore no make-up, for her smooth complexion needed no help from cosmetics and her big, long-lashed eyes – blue, with unusual hazel flecks in them – shone with a natural vitality.

'You're home early,' Valerie remarked.

'We finished on time for once.'

'Are you going out again?'

'No.' A little frown momentarily creased her forehead. 'I fancied an evening in for a change.'

'In that case I'd better do some extra vegetables.' Refilling her glass, Valerie hurried off kitchenwards.

Pippa perched herself on the arm of Sebastian's chair and kissed him on the forehead.

He glanced at her affectionately. 'You look tired.'

'Yes, I am a bit.'

'I'm not surprised, with the hours you work.'

'It's not that so much. It's . . . Oh, it doesn't matter.' She stood up. 'I'll go and have a wash and change. I'll feel better then.'

'Want to take a drink with you?'

'I wouldn't mind actually. Can I have a whisky, too? But you'd better water it down. I haven't eaten all day.'

During dinner, Philippa said little and seemed unusually subdued, leading her parents to suspect that something had gone wrong during the day. But they knew better than to ask. As they had learned the hard way, parental concern was all too often misinterpreted as interference.

When they had finished eating, Sebastian suddenly remembered Edith Spencer's books. 'I've got something for you,' he said, going out to the hall, where he had left the bag. 'I don't know if these are of any interest. They're rather old, so they're probably not of much use.'

Pippa cast a quick eye over the titles, then noticed the photograph album. She opened it on her knee and, after a few moments, stopped at a portrait and asked, 'Who took these pictures?'

'Since the books belonged to a certain Edith Spencer, I assume she did.'

'She was obviously a professional photographer. It's strange her putting the prints in an album like this. You'd think she'd have mounted them properly. Hey! Who's this?'

Valerie peered over her shoulder. 'It looks like King George the Fifth.' She turned to the next page in the album. 'And here's another famous face! Howard Redmayne. Have you ever heard of him? He was a film star, a real heart throb. He was killed during the war.' She sighed nostalgically and turned the page again, this time to a rather shy-looking young woman, seated against a muslin background. 'She looks familiar, too. But I can't think . . .'

The next picture was of a woman's body, naked under a sparse covering of leaves, emerging out of the bole of a tree and apparently flying up into the clouds.

'How on earth was that done?'

'It's a montage,' Pippa explained. 'You shoot all the different parts and then print the relevant bits of the negatives on to a single print. It's extremely difficult to do well.'

Sebastian grunted in embarrassment. Nudity disturbed him. Philippa had a couple of photographs in her portfolio of friends wearing no clothes, which he found extremely disconcerting. The only woman's body he had ever seen naked was Valerie's and he would never have permitted her to be photographed in that state, even by himself.

Valerie moved to the next photograph, that of a girl's head amid a mass of waterlilies, her skin pale as the waterlily blossoms, her hair swirling to the same form as their leaves. 'How uncomfortable. Why is she floating in a pond?'

'Where did you get this album, Dad?' Pippa asked.

'At an auction. The books were making up a lot.'

'Is this the only album?'

'So far as I'm aware. You'd have to ask Michael, he sorted through all the books. Why?'

'Because I think these pictures are simply brilliant.' She went back to the beginning of the album, gently extracted the portrait of George V from the photo corners and turned it over. On the back was a photographer's stamp. 'Gawaine Devere, FRPS,' she read, '10 Porter's Place, London.'

For a moment, all three of them were silent. Then Pippa turned excitedly to her father. 'Do you think he is – was – related to us?'

Sebastian slowly shook his head. It was most unlikely. He supposed he must have had some relations, even if they were very distant. But they had never tried to find him – and he had never gone in search of them.

'Gawaine was one of the Knights of the Round Table,' Valerie said. 'I've always thought those old Celtic names were so romantic. When I was little, I used to wish my mother had called me Guinevere. Though perhaps it was a good thing as it turned out. Guinevere Devere would be a bit of a mouthful . . .'

Pippa ignored her. 'Are you sure, Dad?'

'As sure as I can be,' he said brusquely.

She looked again at the photographer's stamp. Finally, she said, 'You never talk about your father, so I've never liked to ask you before, but what did happen to him?'

'He died.'

'Yes. I know that. But I mean, was he ill – or did he have an accident?'

'He was killed early in the war. I don't know the exact circumstances. I was only seven at the time.'

'Was he a soldier?' Pippa asked.

'I'm sorry, but there's no point in asking me about him, because I don't know any more.'

Though it sounded improbable, it was true. Presumably, if he asked them, Adam and Eve could fill in more of his family background, but he did not want to know about his parents. He never had and he never would.

'And what happened to your mother?' Pippa asked.

'She – er – disappeared.'

'That's why Dad was brought up by Uncle Adam and Aunt Eve,' Valerie interjected.

'Oh, I see.' Philippa bit her lip. 'Poor Dad, how horrid.'

Sebastian shrugged. 'Things like that happened in wartime. But from the little I know about my family, I think it's highly unlikely that Gawaine Devere has any connection with us.'

His tone invited no further questions.

Sitting at the desk in what was still referred to as her studio, but which had been woefully neglected since she had finished college, Pippa was studying the photograph album.

Apart from the prints, it contained some snapshots and a few press cuttings and exhibition reviews, all relating to Gawaine Devere.

'*The exhibition currently being held at the Burlington Gallery establishes Gawaine Devere's position among this country's greatest living photographers,*' a review from 1932 stated.

An article from a magazine the following year began, '*Gawaine Devere's portrait of Howard Redmayne has been selected by the Royal Photographic Society . . .*'

'*Society photographer Gawaine Devere has been commissioned to take a portrait of His Majesty King George V to mark the Silver Jubilee . . .*'

'*With his surreal portrait of the actress Lily Waters, Gawaine Devere has returned to the visual inventiveness which established his success at the Burlington Gallery in 1932 . . .*'

Setting aside the cuttings, she turned to the snapshots. They lacked Gawaine Devere's professional touch and had, Pippa guessed, been taken by Edith Spencer herself. Two buildings featured among them. One was an imposing house in a city street – 10 Porter's Place? – the other an old country house set amid beautiful gardens. Several were of people, but presumably they had been so familiar to Edith Spencer that she had felt no need to identify them. One showed a photographer peering into a camera on a tripod, whom she assumed to be Gawaine Devere, but his face was in shadow and his features indistinguishable.

Gawaine Devere . . . Devere was an unusual name. And a photographer too. Was it possible that he was a relation? Wouldn't that be wonderful? One way and another, she had a decided shortage of relations. Compared to her friends, especially those who came from broken marriages and had a host of half-brothers and -sisters, as well as step-mothers and -fathers, she had a meagre supply. In fact, since the deaths of her mother's parents, all she really had were her mother's brother, Uncle Malcolm and his family, who had emigrated to Canada not long after she was born.

There were Uncle Adam and Aunt Eve, who had always been like grandparents to her. And Elliott, of course. But they weren't real family. There was strong affection between them, but no ties of blood, no feeling of kinship, no sense of a common identity. She couldn't look at Aunt Eve or Uncle Adam and think, 'I must have inherited this or that trait from them.'

It was strange how little her father knew about his parents. On the other hand, if he had been only seven when his father died, perhaps it was not so surprising. How much could she remember of the first seven years of her life? Not a great deal. She could remember, very distinctly, falling down the stairs when she was four, because she had broken her arm and had to go to hospital. But, apart from that drama, she had no personal memories of living in Worcester Park. For that matter, she had only hazy ones of Barnes. Presumably, nothing out of the ordinary had occurred to her, so there were no milestones in her memory of those early years.

Books were what she remembered most about her own childhood, books and the fantasies she had spun as a result of the stories she had read. Books had become her companions long before she went to school and made human friends. Her mother had always been an avid reader and, although her father's reading tended to be limited to newspapers and trade magazines, he had been strict about the amount of television she was allowed to watch when she was small. So, unlike most other children of her generation, books had provided her entertainment and fed her imagination.

She had absorbed all the children's classics – Beatrix Potter, Enid Blyton, *Swallows and Amazons, Heidi, The Wind in the Willows* and the *Enchanted* books. As she had grown older, she had read her way through the children's section in the library, then explored her mother's bookshelves, discovering such old-fashioned, romantic authors as Daphne du Maurier, A. J. Cronin, E. M. Forster and Mary Webb.

Inevitably, then, she had discovered poetry and even written some herself, although she had never shown it to anyone. Poetry was a very private thing. Short stories, however, at which she had also tried her hand, were less personal. By attributing your own emotions to fictitious characters, you were not directly laying open your soul. However, her few attempts to get her stories published in magazines had met with rejections. Concluding that writing was not the career for her, she had turned instead to art, for which she had been fortunate enough to show a natural flair. Unconvinced that she wanted to spend the rest of her life painting and drawing, during her foundation course at art college she had become increasingly fascinated by photography.

She turned her attention again to the photograph album and to Gawaine Devere's prints. John Heartfield, Man Ray and Angus McBean were among those who had influenced her student work. On and off during her college years, she had tried to create her own photomontages by combining up to ten juxtaposed images in a single print and she had experimented with Man Ray's solarization techniques.

But this was the first time she had ever held original prints from that era in her hand, been able to gaze at them through a magnifying glass and see where they had been 'spotted' to remove a skin blemish or an unwanted highlight. These weren't reproductions: they were real. These were the actual prints which had been handled by the photographer, his printer, his retoucher – and now they belonged to her.

In the corner of the room stood her portfolio case, unlooked at since she had gone to work for Richard. She opened it and leafed through the laminated prints. There were a couple of photomontages from her first year, one featuring her schoolfriend Deborah, who had gone on to study textile design, depicting her amid various pieces of fabric and the tools of her trade – a loom and a weaving machine, scissors, yarns and threads. The other, sepia-toned, showed Caryn, who had been at college with her, crouching naked inside an apple. This had earned lewd comments from their male fellow students.

Then came pictures from her second-year project on architecture: Battersea Power Station on a misty morning; a room in a recently converted warehouse apartment in Docklands; a stark view across the Barbican; an exterior shot, looking upwards, of the Lloyds building lift, all metalwork and angles; an office interior, all squares and rectangles. Finally, there was the ceiling of a church crypt, which she had hesitated about including, because her tutors had complained at the time that it didn't fit in with the others. But she was pleased with it: the pattern of the architraves still fascinated her and she liked to think she had successfully captured the calm, cool atmosphere of that subterranean chapel.

Her third-year project had been a series on people at work: a watch-mender with his eyeglass, surrounded by the circular faces of clocks and watches; a granite-browed stonemason wielding his chisel; a greasy-haired, oily-fingered mechanic under the bonnet of an old car; an ancient museum curator, looking like one of the mummies he was guarding, asleep in his chair in a beam of light filled with shimmering particles of dust; and Pippa's favourite, a woman vet, with a thin face, long nose and shoulder-length blonde hair, giving an injection to an Afghan Hound that could almost be her double.

They had been fun to shoot. And not particularly difficult, for the shots had basically been set up for her. The background and the props were already there. All she had needed to do was add a touch of lighting and catch the sitter with the right expression.

She would have liked to do much more portraiture, but her college had only had three studios and limited equipment. There had been fifty students in the third year alone, about a dozen of whom had been specializing in still life, for which a studio was necessary. She had tended to spend most of her time on outside locations, particularly since she had shown a flair for landscapes and aspects of buildings, which her tutors had encouraged her to develop. When she had managed to get the use of a studio, she had found the blank space intimidating and felt nervous of using a large format camera.

That had changed since she had been working for Richard. Now, she felt quite at home in a studio environment and was familiar with virtually every format of camera. However, assisting a photographer was different from taking photographs oneself. Although she often set up the camera and lights for Richard, he was the one who actually shot the picture.

Theoretically, she should have been continuing to take pictures in her free time and improving her portfolio. But that was easier said than done, even though Richard was happy for her to use his studio and equipment when it was free. Being an assistant, however, was not only one of the worst paid jobs there was, but one of the most demanding in time and energy.

Of course, she was in many ways her own worst enemy. Because she and Richard not only worked together but were having an affair, their business and personal lives overlapped − or, rather, were a continuation one of the other. And the last thing Richard wanted to do was to spend the weekend taking more pictures. He needed to relax and recharge his batteries.

When she had first got to know him she had thought she was finally meeting her soulmate. He had been so different from any of her previous boyfriends. Quite different from James, whom she had met while in the sixth form at school and who had been the first serious love in her life. James had been the very opposite of herself. Outgoing, party-loving, he had come from a large family and possessed a huge collection of friends. She had lost her virginity with him and believed him when he said he loved her. Then she had discovered that he was seeing not just one but two other women at the same time.

After him had come Matt, who had been in her year at college. An only child like her, Matt was single-minded about the things which interested him most. Wildlife photography was his speciality. He would stay up all night to photograph badgers and rise at dawn to photograph birds. He and she had gone on hiking holidays in the Lake District and on the Yorkshire Moors, burdened with heavy rucksacks and weighed down with camera equipment. Every few yards they had stopped to record flowers, insects, birds and animals.

Through Matt, a hitherto unknown world had been opened up to her, for, London born and bred, the countryside had been a mystery until then. But, before long, she was growing impatient of him. He did not see the landscape, only the rocks, trees and plants which formed a habitat for the creatures he wanted to photograph. He was by nature a scientist and a technician − she was a romantic.

Then she had met Richard. It had been love almost at first sight. He was thirty and she twenty-three, although she had never felt conscious of an age gap between them. He had long black hair tied back in a pony-tail, and deep brown eyes under straight, thick eyebrows. He shared her interest in literature and the arts in general and introduced her to classical music and traditional jazz.

When she had started working for him, he was already making quite a name for himself in advertising: her college friends were all envious when they heard who she was going to work for.

His problem was, however, that he was so intense he literally wore himself out. Every job he did – no matter how small – had to be completed to the very highest degree of perfection. And while his attitude was laudable, it was also exhausting, particularly when it spilled over into their personal life. An introvert, he took any criticism of his work seriously to heart. Sometimes they had spent all night reshooting a picture quite unnecessarily, merely because an art director had passed a flippant comment about the positioning of a reflector.

He was a possessive lover. He kept asking her to move in with him, but so far caution – as well as fear of her father's reaction – had prevailed. At least by living at home she retained a vital degree of independence. She could still mix with her own friends, people like Deborah and others she had remained in touch with from college. Not that she saw them as often as she would like, but if she lived with Richard she could imagine that they would fade out of her life altogether.

His jealousy she had found flattering to begin with – now it was wearing her down. If he caught another man laughing and joking with her, he immediately assumed that she fancied him, which inevitably led to a scene later that left them both emotionally drained. In fact, all too often now she felt like his prisoner. When she left the studio it was as if she was entering the free world.

Career-wise she wasn't making the progress she wanted either. Without any shadow of doubt, Richard had taught her a lot. However, if she worked for him for another eighteen months she would find herself little further forward. Much of his work was still life, room sets or abstract images. Probably because he wasn't very good at directing, few of his pictures involved people, which was what she most wanted to do.

She put her own pictures back into their case and returned her attention to Edith Spencer's album. Gawaine Devere's photographs were technically expert and visually striking. They were beautifully composed and yet the end results were classically simple. These were the sort of images she had hoped to create when she had started studying photography. This was the kind of work she would still like to do . . .

Next morning, she took Edith Spencer's album with her to the studio. Richard was in one of his dark moods. Another photographer had been given a job which he had assumed would come to him. For a couple of hours she had to listen to him criticizing the other photographer's work.

Hoping to distract his attention she showed him the album. He made only the smallest pretence of interest in it and scarcely seemed to register the coincidence of Gawaine Devere's name. When she looked up Porter's Place in the *A–Z* and found that it was in nearby Chelsea, she suggested that they went to look at number 10 at lunchtime, but he said he had too much to do.

So she went on her own. But disappointment awaited her. Porter's Place was a select square with a railed garden in the centre. Although some of the houses were Regency, like the one in Edith Spencer's snapshot, a couple of them were considerably more modern in style. Number 10 was one of these. A brass plaque announced it to be a doctor's surgery.

She rang the bell and a middle-aged woman opened the door. Pippa briefly explained her quest, but the woman shook her head. She had never heard of Gawaine Devere and all she knew about the building was that it had been bombed during the war and rebuilt some time in the 1950s.

Rather than return immediately to the studio, Pippa walked down to the Embankment. Leaning her elbows on the railings, she propped her chin on her hands and let her glance wander along the river from Chelsea Harbour to her right down towards the Houses of Parliament and Big Ben. London was so lovely on a day like this, it reminded her of a Turner painting.

Had Gawaine Devere been inside 10 Porter's Place when the bomb fell on it? Had he been killed? Was that why Edith Spencer, whoever she was, had kept his photographs in her album? Or had he been away and returned to find his home razed to the ground?

These were questions to which it seemed unlikely that she would ever learn the answer. And, in the meantime, she had other questions of more immediate importance.

Did she love Richard? She had loved him and he had loved her. But now? Did she want to spend the rest of her life with him? The mere fact that she was asking herself these questions and not coming up with a spontaneous, emphatic 'yes' was an answer in itself.

So where to go from here? Did she let the situation drift on in the hope that things would improve? Or was it time for a change?

A big black cloud suddenly covered the feeble sun and an icy breeze blew up the river. Pippa shivered and set off at a brisk pace back to Fulham.

CHAPTER 3

Because she had finally admitted to herself that she was unhappy in her job and in her relationship with Richard, Pippa found herself growing increasingly critical of him. It was strange: she felt quite detached, almost as if she were standing outside their situation, observing it as a stranger. Yet, at the same time, she could not help but remain involved, with the result that she grew irritable with him, snapping at him and doing little things which she knew would annoy him, simply out of contrariness. The effect of this, of course, was to upset him, so that he made mistakes he would not otherwise have made, that in turn made him bad-tempered.

It was a state of affairs which could obviously not continue for much longer. If only she didn't work for him . . . Then it would be possible for them to take a break from each other and assess things from a distance. But their circumstances rendered this impossible. With Richard, it had to be all or nothing.

She decided to talk things over with a friend and went out for a drink after work with Caryn, who had given up full-time employment to become freelance.

She was aware that she must be careful what she said. She and Caryn were close but not that close. Caryn might suspect that she and Richard were having an affair, but she did not know for certain. Neither did Pippa intend to tell her. She didn't want gossip flying round the photographic community. However, concern about her career was perfectly legitimate.

Caryn heard her through without interruption. Then she said, 'I honestly don't know how you've lasted this long. Still life and room sets would have sent me out of my mind by now. All that fiddling about, moving an object a quarter of an inch and then back again – I simply couldn't stand it. You've been with Richard for eighteen months. It's time for a change, Pippa. You have to move on.'

'Yes, that's what I've decided. But how on earth do I find another job? Nobody ever advertises for an assistant.'

'Because it's all done through word of mouth. And that's another problem you've got with Richard. You live such an insular existence. You're stuck in that studio all day long – you never meet anybody else in the business. I'm always being invited to parties and meeting new people.'

Pippa smiled. 'No reflection on you, but I don't really want to go freelance. I'm sure it's good experience, but at the risk of sounding horribly boring, I rather like some security.'

'I'm not suggesting you go freelance. But you should move to a studio where there's more happening. Would you like me to send out a few feelers?'

'Why not? But what about Richard? I wouldn't want to leave him in the lurch.'

'For God's sake, Pippa. He'll find someone to replace you before you've finished telling him you're going. You must have assistants ringing up every day, looking for jobs.'

The following Sunday, Caryn rang her at home. 'Now how's this for fate taking a hand? You must have heard of Tim Collins? He does a lot of work for the *Sunday Times* and *Tatler* – portraits and fashion – and he does, oh, things like record sleeves—'

'Of course I've heard of Tim Collins,' Pippa interrupted impatiently.

'Well, his assistant's leaving him.'

'But he wouldn't consider someone like me. I haven't got the necessary experience.'

'Don't put yourself down. In any case, he prefers assistants he can train himself. I've told him all about you.'

'What? You know him?'

'I met him at a party last night. He seems a really nice guy. Anyway, he gave me his home number and said you should ring him. Have you got a piece of paper and a pen? Right, well, it's 622 . . .'

'Caryn, you're a star.'

When she put down the phone, Pippa hugged herself. There was no guarantee that, since they had been at a party, Tim Collins would remember his conversation with Caryn and certainly not that he would offer her a job, but at least things were moving. And, if she no longer worked for Richard, perhaps their personal relationship would be given a new lease of life?

To her delighted surprise, Tim Collins not only recognized her name but suggested she came round to see him the following evening.

She liked him at first sight. He was in his late thirties, maybe forty, tall, slim and quite good-looking, with longish, wavy brown hair and a neatly trimmed beard. His voice contained a hint of a Yorkshire accent.

His studio was in an attractive, oldish building on a small industrial estate in Clapham, much nearer to Dulwich than Richard's premises in Fulham. It was surprisingly untidy, cluttered with rolls of paper and painted canvas backgrounds, trestles, table tops, stands, lights and other photographic paraphernalia, not to mention magazines, empty wine bottles, dirty mugs and overflowing ashtrays.

'It's been a bit of a hectic day,' he explained. 'We've been photographing a rock band called Mortal Men. Interesting shoot, but not my kind of music, I must admit.'

Pippa smiled. 'I'm not really into heavy metal either.'

'What kind of music do you like?'

'Most things – everything from Duran Duran to Beethoven.'

'Don't tell me you actually listen to classical music?'

'Afraid so. Not all the time, but sometimes.'

'Don't be afraid. I'm delighted. My present assistant, Simon, has never progressed beyond Radio One and the Pogues. I'm sorry you can't meet him. He had to rush off early. So, now, tell me a bit about yourself. I think Caryn said you're working for Richard White at the moment. I've never met him but I know his work, of course. He's excellent.'

She had scarcely opened her mouth when two young men ambled in. 'Hi. Sorry to interrupt,' one said, putting a couple of bottles of wine on the table. 'This is to thank you for the use of your studio, Tim.'

'And I was hoping I could borrow your Polaroid back,' the other said.

Tim grinned and turned to Pippa. 'This is Dominic Wilkinson. He was my assistant before Simon. He's just gone freelance. And the other poser is Nick Edwards, who was my assistant before him and now has a studio just behind mine. And this is Pippa.'

Nick eyed her portfolio case. 'What do you do? Are you a make-up artist or a stylist?'

'No. An assistant.'

'You're not thinking of working for Tim?'

'We've only just—'

'Pippa had only been here a few minutes before you two barged in,' Tim explained. 'I haven't even seen her work yet.'

'Then let's all have a look,' Nick announced.

'It's mainly college stuff,' Pippa said, as she opened the case. 'I know it sounds feeble but I haven't had much opportunity to do any work for myself since I've been assisting.'

'I'm not surprised if you're working for Richard White. He has a reputation for being – what shall I say? – single-minded. Still, let's see what you were up to at college.'

The three men went through her prints, occasionally asking what camera or lighting she had used. 'I like this one,' Dominic said, when he came to the museum curator, and Tim laughed aloud at the woman vet and the Afghan. 'This is great! I'd be quite proud to have taken this myself.'

'I'm disappointed,' Nick announced.

Pippa looked at him in apprehension.

'There are no graveyards, no tattooed torsos and no oil refineries belching smoke into a filtered sunset.'

'Oh, Nick, shut up!' Dominic said. To Pippa, he explained, 'He's being sarcastic. It's just that those three shots tend to appear in one form or another in most student portfolios.'

Tim sucked in his breath. 'Tell you what, Dominic. Why don't you open one of those bottles? The corkscrew's around somewhere.'

'Looks like I'd better wash up first.' Dominic began gathering up the dirty glasses.

'Can I help?' Pippa offered, rising to her feet.

Dominic grinned. 'Feel free. The sink is this way.'

As they returned to the studio, Pippa could hear Tim's voice saying, 'But that's my point, Nick. She'd never cope with—'

He stopped as they came in.

'I couldn't help overhearing,' Pippa said. 'What do you think I wouldn't be able to cope with?'

In reply, Tim pointed to an electronic flash power pack, the size of a suitcase. 'Things like that. I work a lot on location and take loads of equipment with me. I've always had male assistants until now, for the simple reason that I don't think it's fair to expect a girl to lug heavy gear about.'

Pippa might be small but she was deceptively strong. You had to be to survive in a studio. Richard hadn't pampered her. He had expected her to pull her weight – literally. But rather than argue the point, she went over to the flash pack, ensured that it was not plugged in, picked it up and carried it down to the end of the studio.

Dominic laughed. 'That would seem to put paid to that argument.'

Tim handed her a glass of wine. 'So why are you leaving Richard White?'

'Well, it's nothing against him personally. I've learned an awful lot from him. But I really don't want to be a still life photographer. I want to photograph people.'

'Why? Because you think it's glamorous meeting celebrities?'

'No, not that at all. It's something I enjoy and I think I could be good at.' She turned his question back on him. 'Why do *you* like photographing people?'

He grinned. 'Because it's fun.'

Two hours later, when she left his studio, both bottles were empty. It could hardly have been described as a formal interview on either side, more a case of getting to know each other. And she certainly knew quite a lot now about Tim, Dominic and Nick. She knew, for instance, that Tim was married with two children, a girl and a boy, and that his wife Janet was a freelance financial journalist. Neither Dominic nor Nick was married, although both apparently led busy social lives and Nick had been much ragged about his friendship with a page three model called Suzi.

The two younger photographers clearly adored Tim and it was obvious that they relied on him for advice as well as for the use of his studio and equipment, which indicated that, despite his being such a well-known photographer, he had not let success go to his head.

When she asked why Simon was leaving, he told her that he didn't believe in assistants staying at any job longer than two years. After that, they got comfortable, with the result that they became complacent. Simon had been with him just under two years and was now off to New York – with his blessing.

At the end of the evening, Tim offered her a job – what was more, it was at fifty pounds a week more than Richard was paying her. As she got into her car, Pippa felt as though she were walking on air.

Telling Richard of her decision was a less pleasant experience. Unfortunately, it was one of those days when the phone never seemed to stop ringing and one thing after another went wrong with the shoot they were doing. First, the product was late arriving, then the art director turned up and changed the brief and, finally, just when they seemed to have it in the can, the lab rang to say that the technician had dropped one of their rolls of film and scratched it. To make matters worse, one of their bikers had broken down in Chiswick, while the other had been delayed in Battersea, so they wouldn't be able to get the film over to them for at least an hour. Unsure which roll had been damaged, they had little alternative but to reshoot the whole lot.

It was nearly nine o'clock when the art director left, complete with transparencies which he was going to work on overnight before attending a client meeting first thing in the morning.

'This is a ridiculous bloody business!' Richard grumbled. 'Panic, panic, panic. Why don't they give themselves more time? And then that bloody lab!'

It was hardly the most propitious moment to make her announcement. On the other hand, tomorrow might be just as bad.

'Richard,' she said firmly, 'I've got to talk to you.'

'Does it have to be now?'

'Yes, I'm afraid so.'

He was silent for a few moments, then he said, 'You're leaving me, aren't you?'

'Well, not exactly. But I've been offered another job.'

'Who with?'

'Tim Collins.'

'Ah, I see. And how did this occur? Did he just happen to ring you up and ask if you would like to work for him?' He had turned his back on her. His voice was very cold.

'No, of course not. I heard he was looking for a new assistant, so I went to see him.'

'Why didn't you tell me?'

'Because . . . Oh, Richard, please don't be difficult. This is a tremendous opportunity for me. You know I've always wanted to do portraiture.'

'Why didn't you tell me?' he repeated.

'It won't make any difference to us, except that we won't be working together, which will make things better, in fact. We see too much of each other at the moment, that's the problem.'

'I wasn't aware that there was a problem.'

'Surely you've realized . . . ?'

'No, all I've realized is that you've been behaving in a most peculiar fashion during the past few weeks.'

'Well, I haven't meant to. It's just that . . .'

'Pippa, it's been a long day. Say what you have to say.'

'I've said it. Tim Collins has offered me a job and I'd like to accept it.'

'Then you'd better do just that.'

'We can still go on seeing each other.'

'I don't see how.'

'Most couples don't work together.'

'Most couples have trust between them.'

'Richard, I do still love you.'

'At least do me the favour of not lying. I'm not a fool, Pippa. I know you're not happy. I know you haven't been happy for quite a while.' He spun round to look at her, his face very pale but expressionless. 'It seems simple to me. If you love me, you'll want to be with me. If you don't love me, you'll want to be somewhere else. Well, you've made your decision. So there's nothing left to discuss except when you intend starting your new job.'

She could feel tears stinging behind her eyelids, although whether of remorse or anger she was unsure. She bit her lip to force them back. 'I don't want to leave you in the lurch.'

'Professionally, though it pains me to say so, I doubt that I shall have much problem in replacing you. Emotionally, I'm sure I shall survive. So I suggest you leave here at the end of the week.'

Had she done the right thing or not, Pippa wondered miserably, as she drove home. But the die was cast now and it was too late for second thoughts. It was also too late to call Tim Collins – that would have to wait until the morning. If necessary, she would ring him from a telephone box.

No, of course she had done the right thing. Richard's reaction proved that. Still, that didn't stop it hurting. Eighteen months was a long time to write off in a few minutes. He could at least have shown some regret – and concern for her career. His reaction seemed to indicate that he'd never really cared about her . . .

To her great relief, when she arrived home her parents were out. A note from her mother on the kitchen table said that they had gone to dinner with friends, but that there was a meal ready in the micro-wave.

She wasn't hungry, so she put the dish in the fridge and made herself a mug of coffee, which she took up to her room. She felt exhausted but too on edge to hope to sleep.

On the table were the old photographic books which had come with Edith Spencer's album. In her excitement about the album, she had all but forgotten them. Without thinking, she picked up one of the volumes. It was inscribed in gold lettering on a dark green cover: *The British Journal of Photography Almanac 1933*. To begin with, as she flicked through its pages, it appeared as unexciting as its title – over a hundred pages of advertisements followed by a list of contents such as 'Lantern Slides: Simplified Thiocarbamide Developer'.

She was going to put the book back, when it fell open at a full-page illustration. The photographer's name hit her eye immediately: Gawaine Devere, FRPS. The picture was entitled 'Woman in the Moon' and depicted a beautifully lit, seated nude, clasping her knees in her arms, forming the same shape as a huge three-quarter moon in the background.

It was precisely the kind of image she had been trying to achieve with Caryn and the apple. But she did not need to compare the two to recognize how miserably she had failed.

However, the reason the book had opened at that page was that inside it, acting as a bookmark, lay a small envelope addressed to Miss E. Spencer, Chanctonbury Lodge, West Parade, Worthing. The letter it contained was written on a cheap, lined sheet of paper in a hasty, rather old-fashioned hand:

Dear Edith,

*Thank you for your letter and your concern. Although
I am naturally extremely upset by what B said about me, I
am endeavouring to keep things in perspective. You are
probably right that jealousy was the motive. Fortunately,
there always seems to be something that needs doing around
the house or in the grounds, so my mind is kept occupied.
Jethro suffers badly from lumbago and cannot get about as
well as he would like, but Millie is fine and Ted has
grown into a strapping lad. I am sure you will be glad to
hear that I have had no further trouble with the Authorities
or violations to my land.*

Trusting this finds you as it leaves me,
Yours,
G.G.D.

Pippa looked again at the envelope, but the postmark had smudged and
the only clue as to the date was the stamp, which was pre-decimalization.

Eagerly she searched through the other books, all of which had been
published in the 1930s, but although she found various slips of paper
marking pages, including another two Gawaine Devere photographs, there
were no more letters. The most recent of the pictures appeared in the
1939 *Almanac* and was a disturbing portrait of a wild-eyed, dishevelled yet
still very beautiful young woman against a grey sky. It was entitled 'Despair'.

For a long time she stared at this portrait, so spontaneous, so much less
stylized than the rest of Gawaine Devere's work. This was, she felt, a very
personal picture, in which the photographer had let down his guard and
for once revealed part of his innermost soul.

And at that moment, for some strange reason, she knew, with absolute
conviction, that she was doing the right thing in leaving Richard. She had
loved him, but now she loved him no more. It was like having had an
illness and starting to recover from it. Of course one felt weak, but after
a few days the pain would lessen and eventually it would become a distant
memory.

In the meantime, there was the future to look forward to, a whole new
world opening up. With Tim Collins she would be doing the type of

work she really wanted to do. She would be learning again and, who knew, maybe one day she would produce pictures as good as those of Gawaine Devere.

As she had anticipated, the next three days could hardly be described as pleasant. Richard treated her almost as a stranger. Fortunately, however, they continued to be busy and most of the time there were other people in the studio, so they were not forced into making polite conversation with each other.

The question of her successor was swiftly resolved, in the same way as she had found her own new job with Tim Collins – by personal recommendation. Interestingly, Richard chose to replace her not with another girl but with a male assistant, a rather serious young man a year out of college and with an impressive still life portfolio.

As for herself, Tim was – not surprisingly – taken aback to hear that she could start with him so soon. 'Simon doesn't go to New York for another fortnight and I assumed you'd have to give a few weeks' notice,' he said. 'Listen, I tell you what, why don't you take a bit of holiday and join me in a fortnight's time? That way you'll have had a break and be starting fresh and bright. How does that sound?'

Apart from the fact that it was not the time of year she would have chosen for a holiday, it seemed a sensible suggestion. In any case, an idea was already forming in her mind as to how to spend at least one of those days.

CHAPTER 4

Pippa woke early and left home before the rush hour, so that the South Circular Road was still relatively free of traffic. On the M4 the cars were bumper to bumper, heading into London. She was filled with a queer, light-headed sense of freedom and escape, as great as though she were in one of the planes that was taking off from Heathrow Airport, their engine roar loud as they set off for destinations unknown.

She had worked for the last time with Richard. They had said their goodbyes. She had cried herself to sleep on Friday night, then woken up on Saturday morning with the knowledge that today was different, that today was the beginning of the rest of her life.

Now it was Monday and, instead of being in Fulham with a man she no longer loved, doing a job she no longer wanted to do, she was on the trail of Gawaine Devere. She had her day fully planned. First she would go to Bath, to the Royal Photographic Society, and then to Puddles to see if Adam and Eve could throw any light on her father's family background.

Not that she had told them that was the reason behind her visit. When she had rung them she had merely said that she was going to be in their neighbourhood and asked if it would be all right if she popped in. Quite apart from the fact that they might feel upset if they thought she had any ulterior motive, she didn't want them talking to her father before her arrival.

Adam had answered the phone. 'Why, Pippa! What a lovely surprise. And how are you, my dear?'

'I'm fine, thank you, Uncle Adam. And you and Aunt Eve?'

'I'm flourishing and Eve's just darning her fig-leaf.'

He had paused and she had obligingly laughed. Adam never tired of referring to the extraordinary coincidence of his wife's name. He had a

45

little repertoire of such quips. He liked to say that he had fallen for Eve because of the apple she had given him. And at their wedding reception he had told the assembled guests: 'To put your minds at rest, we shan't be calling our house Eden and nor will our children be called Cain or Abel, although doubtless they will need caning and I trust they will be able.'

These oft-repeated anecdotes were an essential part of Adam, which it was impossible to resent. He was such a pet, the last thing you wanted to do was upset him in any way. It was difficult to imagine him ever having been a lawyer, specializing in criminal cases, although her father maintained that he had been strict with him and Elliott when they were boys and it was Eve – who seemed rather daunting to Pippa – who had been the more lenient of the two.

She drove past Windsor Castle and Eton, past industrial Slough and commuter-belt Maidenhead, then Reading and finally into the countryside. On an impulse, with only herself to please, she turned off the motorway at the Newbury junction and took the A4. The fields were rimed with frost and when she reached Savernake Forest the tall, dark pines gave her an impression of not being in England at all but in Bavaria or even the Alps, for the banked clouds on the horizon were shaped like mountains and tinged with pink.

At the Royal Photographic Society she struck unexpectedly lucky. An exhibition of British war photography was currently being staged and in it were some of Gawaine Devere's pictures taken in Germany during the final months of the Second World War.

The booklet accompanying the exhibition gave brief details about the photographers whose work was being featured. Of Gawaine Devere, it said: 'Born in 1907, he became a Fellow of the Royal Photographic Society in 1932. A leading society photographer in the 1930s, he was employed during the war by the Ministry of Information. His portraits convey the tragedy of war and the pathos of those who suffered as a result of it, regardless of which side they were on.'

The first of his photographs that Pippa came upon was of a group of women inmates of Belsen concentration camp, sitting and lying on some grass. A few yards behind them was a heaped pile of naked corpses. The next picture showed a man carrying a skeletal corpse on his back in the same way as he might have carried a sack of coals. The third was a head and shoulders portrait of an emaciated man, his head shaved, standing behind barbed wire. Then came a pair of pictures, both of children. One was of two little girls, with huge, glittering, dark eyes. The caption under them read: 'Typhus sufferers. Belsen, April 1945.' The other was of two small boys, blond and sullenly defiant, with the caption, 'Hitler Youth. April 1945.'

She continued round the rest of the exhibition and found two more Gawaine Devere images. One was entitled 'German refugees' and showed a crowd of people moving slowly along a roadway, on foot, bicycle and by horse-drawn wagon. The other was of a German soldier with only one arm, his feet bound in rags, asleep on the forecourt of a Berlin railway station.

Like many of her generation, Pippa's knowledge of the Second World War was hazy. She had learned about it at school but because it had no personal relevance to her, she had retained only a sketchy impression of its events.

The pictures from Belsen were not, of course, the first she had seen of the harrowing sights that had met the eyes of British troops when they liberated German concentration camps. But the fact that these photographs had been taken by Gawaine Devere lent them a previously unknown sense of immediacy.

In her bag was Edith Spencer's album. The same man who had shot the pictures in that album had taken the photographs she was looking at now. The same man who had taken the portrait of the girl he had entitled 'Despair'.

Deeply moved and ashamed of her own ignorance of the events depicted, she left the gallery. On her way out, she asked the attendant whether she knew if Gawaine Devere were still alive. The woman was not sure, but suggested she went upstairs to the library. There, the librarian pointed her in the direction of the archives, but two hours later all Pippa had discovered was that Gawaine Devere had retired from the Royal Photographic Society in September 1945. The last address given for him was 10 Porter's Place, London.

Hungry by then, she had a quick lunch, then drove across country to Puddles. Puddles, it suddenly occurred to her as she saw the signpost to Puddlescombe, was the only abbreviation of a name her father ever used. She thought of herself as Pippa and her mother and all her friends called her that, but to her father she was always Philippa, just as her mother was always Valerie and never Val. But, for some reason, Puddles was the exception to her father's rule.

She drove up the steep main street to Hill House, aptly named as it sat on top of its own little knoll. As always, she was struck by the classical stateliness of the finely proportioned, red-brick Georgian house, with its pillared porch, sweeping drive and striped lawns. It made her think of horse-drawn coaches, debauched squires, saucy serving wenches, powdered wigs and hooped dresses.

The front door opened and Aunt Eve appeared, graciously elegant as always in a cream, polo-necked sweater and Liberty skirt, her immaculately groomed hair tinted a discreet silvery blonde. She was leaning slightly on a stick, and Pippa recalled that she had had a hip replacement not so long ago. Aunt Eve was a person who remembered every little detail about other people and expected them to do her the same courtesy in return.

A labrador bounded out of the house, ecstatically waving its stubby tail and totally ignoring Eve's cries of 'Bertie! Stop it! Come here, Bertie!' Uncle Adam followed, in twill slacks, open-necked shirt and olive-green V-necked sweater. A comfortable lifestyle had thickened his figure, a fondness for claret had reddened his tubby cheeks and his head was now almost completely bald, yet considering he would be eighty that year he was amazingly sprightly for his age. Hurrying down the steps and across the gravel drive, he kissed her avuncularly, squeezing her shoulders and declaring, 'Well, Pippa, my dear. How very nice to see you.'

'I'm sure you're gasping for a cup of tea,' Aunt Eve said.

'Thank you. That would be very nice,' Pippa murmured.

'I'll make it, dear,' Adam said. 'You and Pippa go into the drawing room.'

'Would you like to powder your nose?' Aunt Eve asked.

'No, I'm fine, thank you.'

Whenever she came to Hill House, Pippa found it easy to understand where her father had picked up many of his habits and turns of phrase, although why they had stuck to him and passed Elliott by was less readily comprehensible.

'So how are you, Pippa? I must say, you look very well.'

'I am, thank you, Aunt Eve. And you? How about your hip?'

'How sweet of you to remember. I'm making good progress, I'm glad to say. The doctors are very pleased with me. The miracles of modern medicine . . . And your father? Is he all right?'

'Yes, busy as always. He and Mum are going on holiday next week. To the Bahamas.'

Uncle Adam wheeled in a tea trolley, which had clearly been ready and waiting, with everything on it except the pot of freshly made tea.

'Now tell us what you're doing here on a Monday, instead of being at work,' he said, as Eve did what she called 'the honours'.

'Oh, I'm between jobs. I've got a fortnight off.'

'Then you could have gone on holiday with your parents,' Eve said.

'Not really. Everything happened in a bit of a rush. But I'll probably take them to the airport.'

'And what's the new job?' Adam asked.

To her surprise, they recognized Tim's name.

'We see his pictures in the *Sunday Times*,' Adam said. 'Well, that does sound a step forward for you. You'll be meeting a lot of famous people, there's no doubt about that.'

'Talking about famous people,' Pippa said, delving into her bag, 'I've got a little mystery that I'm hoping you may be able to help me solve. About a month ago, Dad went to an auction in Worthing. And as part of a lot, he bought – this.' She pulled out Edith Spencer's album and opened it at Gawaine Devere's portrait of King George V. She couldn't help noticing Adam's astonished expression when he saw the photograph and glanced swiftly in Eve's direction, but she attributed his surprise to the subject of the portrait.

'Yes, it is,' she told him. 'It is George the Fifth. And it is an original print. But this is the *really* extraordinary bit. You'll never guess the name of the photographer!' She took the print from its photo corners and turned it over. 'Look! Gawaine Devere!'

Adam spluttered into his tea and Eve cast him an exasperated look before handing him a napkin.

'Well, I'm sure you've already guessed what my next question is,' Pippa continued, once he had recovered himself. 'Of course, I want to find out if Gawaine Devere is related to us. I've asked Dad but he doesn't seem to remember anything about his family. Since his father died when he was only seven and his mother disappeared during the war, I suppose that's not altogether surprising. But I wondered whether you knew anything. I mean, how did he come to stay with you?'

Eve raised her cup to her lips, her little finger delicately crooked. 'He was evacuated here.'

'Yes, but . . .'

Adam wiped his mouth on his napkin. 'Naturally parents – and the government – were greatly concerned for the safety of children during the war. If my memory serves me right, about one and a half million children were evacuated from London and other major cities to country areas like Puddles during the first three days of the war, and thousands more after that. People like ourselves, who had spare rooms, were expected to accommodate them. Ours was not to reason why – or who.'

'But surely Dad must have talked about his family?'

'I'm sure he did. But you have to remember all this happened nearly fifty years ago and, with the best will in the world . . .'

Pippa nodded understandingly. 'Yes, of course. But do you know if his parents were already dead when he came to Puddles?'

'No, they were still alive. His father died about a year later.'

'Pippa, dear, do have some shortcake,' Eve said.

Pippa dutifully took a piece and nibbled on it. Then she said thoughtfully, 'I suppose Dad must have a birth certificate somewhere. That would show his father's name, wouldn't it?'

'Under normal circumstances, yes. But unfortunately, it was lost. That's something I do remember – as a former solicitor, such little details stick in the mind. As Sebastian's guardian, I was also responsible for getting him properly registered with the authorities. There was a lot of bureaucracy during the war.'

'But it's possible to get a copy of a birth certificate, isn't it?'

Adam sucked in his breath. 'Pippa, may I give you a little advice? Your father's separation from his parents was an extremely traumatic experience for him. He didn't understand the reasons and blamed them for sending him away. He felt they had abandoned him and, to this day, he's never really forgiven them. Now I know you are intrigued by this Gawaine fellow and the coincidence of your names but, please, be wary of resurrecting old ghosts.'

Pippa tried to imagine herself in her father's shoes and acknowledged that she, too, would probably feel bitter towards her parents in such circumstances.

'Didn't his parents visit him or write to him after he came to Puddles?' she asked.

'You have to remember there was a war on,' Adam replied. 'People couldn't do just as they pleased. Family considerations had to take second place to duty – and national security. In your father's case, the main thing was that he was safe and well. And I'd like to think that he was happy here at Puddles, once he overcame the initial shock of being uprooted from his own home. We always tried to treat him and Elliott as equals, and not show any favouritism. Whatever Elliott had, Sebastian had too.'

'Oh, Dad's very fond of you and Aunt Eve, that's obvious,' Pippa assured him, 'even though he doesn't talk much about the past. But then, Dad isn't a sentimental sort of person. Men aren't as a rule, are they?'

Adam chuckled. 'I'm not so sure. But I do think we're less competent at expressing our feelings. It's all part of the stiff upper lip syndrome that was knocked into us from our schooldays on. It's accepted that women are weak, emotional creatures, but men are expected to put a brave face on everything, with the result that we bottle up our feelings inside ourselves, instead of having a damn good cry every now and again, which would do us a power of good.'

'And you don't believe it would do Dad good to talk about his parents – and get it all out of his system?'

'It could well be cathartic,' Adam agreed. 'But I think you should beware of playing the amateur psychologist and doing more harm than good.'

'There must be some other way to find out more about Gawaine Devere,' Eve remarked.

'Yes, I thought that, too,' Pippa said and told them about her visit to the Royal Photographic Society.

'The exhibition made me realize how shamefully ignorant I am about the war,' she went on. 'I suppose if you don't know anyone who was in it, then it's something you never discuss.'

Adam nodded. 'To your generation the war is history. Whereas to us and most of our contemporaries it was the most eventful period in our lives. We could go on talking about it for hours.'

Before seeing Gawaine Devere's photographs and learning of the mystery surrounding her father's family, Pippa would probably have smiled politely at that remark and changed the subject. Instead, she asked, 'And do you mind telling me what you did during the war?'

'Not in the slightest, though it was nothing as adventurous as your namesake there, I'm afraid,' Adam replied, pointing at Edith Spencer's album. 'As well as continuing in the legal profession, I was a major in the Home Guard. Do you ever watch *Dad's Army*? Well, that was us. And we were laughed at and ridiculed even then.'

'And most unfairly,' Eve said sharply. 'Uncle Adam volunteered for active service the day war broke out,' she told Pippa. 'But he was turned down because he had a fibrous lung.'

Adam grimaced. 'That was actually a mistaken diagnosis. It gave me quite a shock at the time, of course, and I consulted a specialist. He told me it was just scar tissue from a bad chest illness I had when I was a little boy. And since I've survived this far, despite an unhealthy fondness for Havana cigars, I think he must have been right. However, I was short-sighted as well, so that ruled me out of active service.

'Our house was the local Home Guard headquarters. We had Nissen huts in the garden and the loft above the stables was where all the weapons and ammunition were stored, ready for the German invasion. Hasn't your father ever told you about our armoury?'

Pippa shook her head. 'No, as I said, he hardly ever talks about his childhood.'

'They were a couple of rascals, those boys. Let me see, they must have been seven or eight when the Home Guard was set up. And they believed that the country was in grave danger with its defences left to an old codger like myself, particularly as – in their opinion – I spent far more time in meetings than stomping and shouting on the parade ground and generally behaving like a proper major.

'I was issued with books with titles like *How to Kill the Enemy*, which they got hold of, of course. They used to patrol the neighbourhood in the hope of catching Germans dropping in by parachute or making their way inland having swum ashore from a submarine. And needless to say, they devised dire and dreadful booby traps to deal with them.'

'You can laugh,' Eve said, 'but it wasn't funny at the time. I'll never forget the day PC Andrews brought them home, having discovered them in some hideout in the woods, both armed with sten guns. I was horrified. I had no idea that they were able to get into the armoury.'

'Neither had I until then. Should have known better, I suppose. They just helped themselves to my key when I was out. After that, I had to find a new hiding place every couple of days – and then remember where I'd put it.' He shook his head, lost in reminiscences. 'Do you remember, Eve, when Elliott shot the cockerel you were saving for Christmas dinner?'

'No I do not. I must have assumed it died of old age or a heart attack.'

'And what about when Sebastian nearly put paid to the Obliger?'

'I'm certain I never knew about that. Which Obliger? Not Mrs Fagg?'

'Think it was, actually. Sebastian objected to her name. The boys had just started at senior school.'

'So that's why she suddenly refused to come here any more! And I always blamed your father, because he wouldn't let her tidy his room. Instead of which, it was the boys. I should have known.'

Uncle Adam's eyes twinkled behind his glasses. 'I wouldn't be surprised if my father didn't put them up to it. He and the boys were thick as thieves,' he explained to Pippa, who was listening in rapt fascination.

'I'm sorry you never met my father,' Uncle Adam continued. 'He was an archaeologist, as you're probably aware, and extremely well respected in his field. Elliott was named after him. The Pater was very good with the boys, which was a godsend for Eve and myself, as you can imagine, especially during the school holidays. He used to take them out on treasure hunts, looking for Roman coins and Iron Age weapons. That's how they became interested in antiques. They gave him a new lease of life and made up for his disappointment in me.

'He'd always hoped that I would follow in his footsteps, you see. When he came back from the Valley of the Dead to the land of the living at the end of my freshman year at Oxford and discovered I'd switched from History to Law, he was very upset. Not that I've ever regretted my decision. I've done very well by the legal profession . . .'

'Don't forget cricket,' Aunt Eve cut in.

'Ah, yes, the Pater was a keen cricketer as well. I regret to say that I was not in the least sporty.'

'I was thinking more of all those broken window panes.'

'That was Sebastian, I'm afraid. The Pater tried and tried to school him in the art of the slow spinner, but he was a real butterfingers when it came to throwing or catching a ball. However, he wasn't a bad batsman and, give him his due, he could sprint like an antelope.'

'The problems I used to have,' Aunt Eve sighed. 'The Professor simply refused to recognize that there was a war on. He didn't – or wouldn't – understand that it was virtually impossible to buy glass. And the trouble I used to have getting him to observe the blackout. However, there was one good thing about him. Rationing didn't worry him at all. He didn't care what he ate, so long as he had tobacco for his pipe and a tot of whisky every evening.'

'So that's where Dad acquired his fondness for Scotch.' Pippa laughed. 'Oh, thank you so much for telling me all this. I've never imagined Dad being – well, naughty.'

Eve frowned. 'No, that's the wrong word to describe him. Elliott was naughty. But not your father. When your father got into scrapes it was nearly always because Elliott led him on. And the unfortunate thing was that people didn't realize this. Elliott was so charming and looked so angelic that it was hard to credit him with some of the pranks he got up to. And he always had some explanation ready. Whereas Sebastian was painfully honest and so determined to be brave and face up to his punishment like a man that he used to get caned while Elliott escaped scot-free.'

'Now, steady on. Elliott didn't pull the wool over my eyes,' Adam objected. 'He felt the sole of my slipper on countless occasions.'

'Oh, you and I saw through him. But at school he got away with murder, while poor Sebastian was always in detention or doing lines. In fact, I've often suspected that Sebastian used deliberately to shoulder the blame in order to protect Elliott.'

'Well, at least neither of them were bullies or cowards or sneaks,' Adam commented. 'And I don't think Sebastian's experiences did him any harm in the long run, although, with hindsight, I think Elliott might well have benefited from a little more discipline. However, it's easy to be clever after the event – and who could have foretold that our son would turn out to be such a ladykiller?'

Eve pursed her lips. 'That reminds me. It had clean escaped my mind. Barbara rang me while you were playing golf this morning. Donald's getting married and apparently Elliott has refused point-blank to go to the wedding. She is terribly upset.'

'Can't think why,' Adam said. 'She hated his guts when they got divorced. I've seldom known a woman to be so vindictive.'

'And can you blame her after the way Elliott behaved?' Eve turned to

Pippa. 'Don't get me wrong. I love Elliott dearly. But I have tried never to allow my love to blind me to his faults. Nor to Adam's, for that matter.'

'Faults?' Adam demanded jocularly. 'I don't have any faults. Like all men, I'm perfect. However, before Eve tries to prove me wrong, let me change the subject. You're not thinking of driving back to London this evening, are you, Pippa?'

'Well, I was intending to.'

'Nonsense. Unless you have a pressing engagement tomorrow morning, you must stay the night.'

There was nothing in London to call her back. 'Well, if you're sure.'

'Of course. We don't see enough of you, do we, Eve?'

'No, we certainly don't.'

'Good, that's that settled. You'd better give your parents a ring, so they don't start worrying about you. And I expect there's a spare toothbrush in the guest room. And now you don't have to drive anywhere, let me offer you a drink. I don't know about you ladies, but all this talking has made me thirsty.'

The guest room was very pretty. It had a cream carpet and was hung with a delicate pink wallpaper bearing a faint Regency stripe, with the curtains and bedspread made from fabric in a matching shade. The dressing table, chest-of-drawers and wardrobe were white and gold, in the style of Louis XVI. Opposite Pippa as she lay in bed were two watercolours in gilt frames: one showed a landscape of rolling hills, the other a view of an old-fashioned cottage garden. They were not subjects she herself would have chosen to paint, but they were executed in her sort of style. When she examined them more closely, she found they were signed in the bottom right-hand corner with a *K* and dated August 1932.

When Adam brought her a cup of tea the following morning, she said, 'I've been lying here looking at those paintings. I don't remember seeing them before.'

Adam glanced at them. 'Really? They've always been there.' He crossed the room to draw the curtains. 'I'm afraid it's another grey old day. Did you sleep all right?'

'Like a log, thank you.'

'Good, good. Aunt Eve said to tell you that if you'd like a bath there's plenty of hot water. And what would you like for breakfast? We usually

55

just have some cereal and toast. But you can have what you like.'

'That sounds great. I don't usually have time for breakfast.'

'Well, you have time today. There's no hurry for anything.'

Over breakfast, Eve asked, 'You will stay for lunch, won't you?'

'Well, if it's not too much trouble.'

'It's no trouble at all. Adam, would you mind going down to the butcher's? We'll need an extra chop.'

Pippa wondered whether she should, after all, have said no.

'And while you're in the village, could you buy me some stamps?'

'You'd better make me a list,' Adam said.

'Do you have a supermarket near here?' Pippa asked.

'There's one in Shaftesbury,' Eve replied. 'We go there about once a month to buy things like dog food and washing powder. But we like to support the local shops. And Adam enjoys the walk down to the village.'

'I could drive down there if you like,' Pippa volunteered.

'I could drive myself for that matter,' Adam said. 'But it does Bertie and me good to stretch our legs.'

At the sound of his name, Bertie, who had been asleep on a rug beside a radiator, suddenly pricked up his ears and wagged his tail.

'Would you like me to come with you?'

'No, you stay and keep Aunt Eve company.'

'Running a house this size is such a lot of work,' Eve sighed, as she and Pippa put the finishing touches to Adam's bed, 'even with Gladys coming in to help during the week. I suppose, one day, we'll have to consider moving, though I must confess it would be a wrench to leave Hill House.'

'Have you lived here ever since you were married?' she asked.

'Yes. The house belonged to Adam's parents, of course. I was a London girl myself and I must admit that the idea of living in the country didn't appeal much to me, especially since it meant moving in with my in-laws. However, my mother-in-law was a dear soul – I grew tremendously fond of her and was very sad when she died. And, of course, the Professor was abroad a lot. It was only during the war that he was home for any length of time.'

'How did you and Uncle Adam meet if you lived in London and he lived in Puddles?'

'The same way as most young couples met in those days. At a party. He had a lot of friends in town. He was part of a set who had all been up at Oxford together . . .' Eve's voice tailed off and she paused in the middle of folding Adam's pyjama trousers to gaze out of the window. Then she collected herself and said briskly, 'Well, that was a long time ago.'

They moved on to the guest room. 'I do like those paintings,' Pippa commented, as they stripped the bed.

Eve cast her a strange look. 'They were a wedding present.'

'They're lovely.'

'Hmm.' Eve sounded less certain.

'Don't you like them then?'

Eve did not reply. Then she sat on the edge of the unmade bed and said, 'I don't know whether I should tell you this or not. Those pictures were painted by your grandmother – by Sebastian's mother.'

Pippa turned to her in astonishment. 'By my grandmother? So you knew her then?'

'Yes, we knew her.'

'Then why . . . ? Last night . . . ?'

'Yes, I know. But I'm afraid you took us both a bit by surprise, coming out with all those questions about your father. We were unprepared.'

So many more questions were racing through Pippa's mind that she did not know which to pose first, so she let them just tumble out. 'Does Dad know that you knew her? Did you know Dad's father, too? And Gawaine Devere? *Was* he a relation?'

Eve gave a strained smile. 'I'm sorry, Pippa. I've already said more than I ought.'

'But you *must* tell me more.'

'No, I can't.'

'Then Uncle Adam—'

'No, please don't say anything to him. He'd be very upset if he knew that I'd betrayed a confidence.'

'Then why did you say anything at all?'

'Because – because I suppose I feel you have a right to know.'

Pippa tried to stifle her impatience. 'But you haven't told me anything yet, except that you knew my grandmother and she gave you these pictures.' She glanced at the date in the corner of the paintings and did some rapid calculations. 'If these were done in 1932 and Dad came here when the war started – in 1939? – and he was six or seven then—'

57

Eve shook her head vehemently. 'It's no good, Pippa, I'm not going to say any more. It's not my place to. It's up to your father.'

'But you know Dad won't tell me. And yesterday evening you explained why. Listen, I don't want to hurt him.'

For a long time Eve sat in silent contemplation of the two paintings, as if in the hope that they would solve her dilemma. Finally, she murmured, 'Yes, why not?' She turned to Pippa. 'I think the best person to answer all your questions is your grandmother herself.'

'You mean she's still alive?'

'Very much so.'

'Does Dad know?'

'Yes.'

'Then why did he say . . . ?'

Eve eased herself off the bed, putting her hand to her hip. 'Her name is Kitty Pilgrim. She remarried, although she's a widow now. She lives in Arundel, in Sussex. I have her full address downstairs. I'll give it to you, on one condition – that you say nothing to anybody else until you've seen her and heard what she has to say. Is that a promise?'

Pippa nodded. 'It's a promise.'

'You did what?' Adam demanded.

It was mid-afternoon. Pippa had left again for London and Adam and Eve were sitting in their respective armchairs, opposite each other, on either side of the fire.

'I gave Pippa Kitty's address,' Eve repeated.

'But what on earth possessed you to do that?'

'I'm not really sure. We were in the guest room and she mentioned Kitty's watercolours . . .'

'Yes, she said something about them to me when I took her her cup of tea in bed this morning. I ignored her remark.'

'Yes, you would. In your eyes Kitty can do no wrong.'

'That's not true!'

Eve gazed into the fire. 'Something in me just snapped suddenly. I don't know why. Perhaps it's because now Pippa's older, she's growing to look more and more like Kitty. And it all came back to me – that day when Kitty returned after the war. It was a Friday afternoon, because I know I was waiting for the boys to come home from school. You weren't in –

presumably you were in court. I think the Professor must have gone away for the weekend, because he certainly wasn't around.

'I shall never forget opening the door and finding Kitty on the doorstep. She looked so small and pathetic in her thin, travel-creased coat and dusty shoes, carrying a battered little suitcase. I took her up to the guest room and sat on the bed, while she washed her face and brushed her hair.

'Her first questions were about Sebastian. Then she told me how much she had appreciated your letters during the war. And then she started talking about Leo and Piers and that woman who ran the school – you know who I mean. And I know it sounds silly, but she didn't ask about me. She just took me for granted and went on talking about herself.

'Then I heard the boys come in, so I hurried downstairs, telling Kitty to follow when she was ready. Of course you know what happened then.'

She paused and Adam said, 'Sebastian was only twelve, Eve. You can't blame him for reacting as he did.'

'No, I don't blame Sebastian at all,' Eve responded sharply, looking him full in the eyes. 'I blame Kitty. Kitty has been totally and utterly selfish and irresponsible all her life. And I think it's about time that she faced up to the truth. That's why I told Pippa about her.'

'But it wasn't your decision to make.'

'I disagree,' Eve replied in a clipped voice. 'From the moment I met you, Kitty has haunted my life. Do you think I don't realize that you were in love with her then – and that you have gone on being in love with her ever since? You only married me because you had no hope of marrying Kitty. I was your second choice.'

'Eve, darling, you're talking utter nonsense!'

He looked so shocked that, for a few fleeting seconds, she wondered if she might have misjudged him these many years. Then all those instances came flooding back, when Adam had rushed to Kitty's help and Kitty's defence, and she knew she had not been mistaken.

'No, I'm not. If Kitty hadn't already been married, you wouldn't have married me. Not if there was hope that she might change her mind and fall in love with you. And then, when she went off with Leo, don't pretend that you weren't heartbroken. Why else did you rush off to see her before the war started? It wasn't for Sebastian's sake. It was for Kitty's. You weren't intending to bring Sebastian back on his own. You wanted Kitty. But having Sebastian here during the war made you feel closer to her . . .'

'Eve, that's simply not true!'

'It doesn't actually matter now whether it's true or not. When you first brought him here, I admit that I resented him. But I realized that it was wrong to inflict the sins of the parents upon the child. I grew to love him. I grew to think of him as being as much my own son as Elliott. In some ways, if I'm honest, I loved him more than Elliott, because he was so much more in need of love. Elliott was always so self-sufficient, whereas Sebastian . . .

'Then Kitty returned. I can still see you looking at her with such adoration in your eyes, hanging on her every word, and saying to me afterwards, "Poor Kitty, what a terrible time she must have gone through." Oh, yes, poor Kitty . . .

'And, to add insult to injury, you wanted her to stay here, to live in my home, the reason you gave being, of course, that she should be near Sebastian. That was when I put my foot down.'

She stopped and for a long time they were both silent. The only sound in the room was the crackling of logs in the fireplace.

Then Adam went across to the sideboard and poured them both a drink. As he handed Eve hers, he said ruefully, 'I suppose I should tell you more often that I love you, but, after fifty-five years, I assumed you knew.'

'I do know,' she assured him. 'Otherwise I wouldn't have stayed with you.'

'Then why all this about Kitty?'

'It's the difference between loving and being in love. You and I are like a pair of comfortable old slippers – we have moulded ourselves to each other's shape over the years. Without wishing to sound self-pitying, you take me for granted. I have always been here when you needed me – and you know I always will be. Kitty, on the other hand, is like an elusive butterfly that you have been chasing across a meadow, always tantalizingly just out of reach. And you have been so long bewitched by the bright colours on her fluttering wings that you cannot see the shallowness of the personality underneath.'

Adam shook his head uncomprehendingly. 'I admit that I was, once, in love with Kitty. But that was a very long time ago, before I met you. Now, all I feel for her is a sort of brotherly affection, I suppose. I certainly don't have any idealized image of her.'

Eve held up her hand, aware of how childish her outburst had been.

One always thinks of love as being the prerogative of the young, she thought, yet here I am, nearly eighty years old, and still capable of jealousy, still in need of reassurance. 'It's all right. You don't need to say any more.'

'But I want you to know,' Adam insisted. 'It's important. You always have been and always will be the greatest love in my life.'

She nodded, even though she knew his avowal wasn't entirely true and that he was fooling himself while hoping to convince her.

'But to come back to Pippa,' she said. 'I don't regret telling her about Kitty. I do believe, very strongly, that she is entitled to know about her family background. She's not a child any more. She's old enough to form her own conclusions about people. So, in case you were thinking of ringing Kitty and warning her, may I suggest that you don't? Sebastian is her son and Pippa her granddaughter. It's up to them to sort things out between them.'

From the expression on Adam's face she knew that he had indeed been intending to telephone Kitty. And she also knew that, as a result of what she had said, he wouldn't. And, for once in her life, she had the satisfying sense of having triumphed over her rival.

The following morning, Adam took Bertie for a much longer walk than usual. He was still feeling stunned and perplexed by Eve's revelations. Who would have imagined that, over all these years, she was capable of harbouring such resentment? Eve, of all people . . . Eve, who was always so rational, so untemperamental.

Yes, he had been in love with Kitty, madly in love with her. He had adored her from the moment he first set eyes on her, dressed in a pair of the gardener's cast-off trousers, riding bareback across the paddock, her hair flying out in the wind, her cheeks glowing and those huge blue eyes of hers shining with excitement. She had been little more than a child then, totally unaware of the effect she was having on him.

Then she had gone away to finishing school in Switzerland and, when she returned, it had been like the proverbial ugly duckling turning into a swan. He could visualize her still, in a short-skirted dress, patent leather shoes and the most beguiling of cloche hats, sitting in a deckchair in the shade of a tree. Her German friend, Sonja, had been with her . . .

That was in the summer of 1928, for the Pater had just given him his first car, a red Cowley, as a twenty-first birthday present. During the war,

61

he had been lucky enough to run a Jaguar Mark V. Funny, when he thought about it, all the major stages in his life were marked by the cars he had been driving at the time.

Elliott's passion for Jaguars had started during the war, which was why they had given him the red SS100 for his twenty-first. What a fluke that Elliott had found that car again and been able to buy it back.

He couldn't remember what they had given Sebastian for his twenty-first. It wasn't a car, that he did know, because Sebastian didn't have a car until after he was married. But he must have been offered one, for he and Eve had been scrupulous about treating the boys as equals. No, Sebastian must have said he'd prefer money instead. Yes, that was it. He had met Valerie about that time, so they were probably already saving up for the deposit on a house.

Now, what had he been thinking about? Yes, that was it. His old Cowley. He had let Kitty drive it. There had been a road leading down from Beachy Head to Eastbourne, which was a series of hairpin bends. Kitty had careered down it, doing well over forty. What a madcap she had been! Several times two of the wheels had been over the edge and he was sure they would end up in the sea.

And what a dancer . . . That was the summer when West had bought the portable gramophone. The summer the Charleston was all the rage. Every evening they had danced, and far too often he had ended up with Sonja as a partner.

But finally he had managed to get Kitty out on her own in the garden. He had thought he was being immensely sophisticated. He had pointed upwards to the new moon and, when she had followed his gaze, he had kissed her. And then she had laughed.

He had been wearing dinner dress and, as she had tilted back her head and raised her eyes to his, the moon had reflected in his spectacles and, with his lips slightly parted, he had – she said – reminded her of a rather surprised penguin.

No, that wasn't entirely true. She hadn't said that at the time. But later, when he had refused to accept that she did not love him, she had blurted out the truth. She had not intended to be cruel, of that he was convinced. She was far too sensitive to inflict wanton pain: and even though she had not loved him, she had been immensely fond of him.

He prided himself on having been man enough to make a joke of her words, even though he had felt terribly hurt. He had repeated a favourite quip of his uncle Hamilton's, who used to say that the most glamorous girls married ugly men with big bank accounts, but the nicest girls fell for good-looking men who made them laugh.

Just weeks after he had kissed her, she had announced her engagement. Fortunately, he hadn't been present at the time. The Pater had arrived home from one of his expeditions and summoned him back to Puddles, after which he had returned to Oxford for his final year. He hadn't seen Kitty again until her wedding.

Then, in due course, he had met Eve, who had proved far more suitable a wife. If he had married Kitty, the marriage wouldn't have lasted. Kitty had not been cut out to be the wife of a provincial solicitor. She had never been the twinset and pearls type and would have failed miserably with the county set, into which Eve had fitted so well. The people with whom he mixed would have bored her stiff. She would have become restless and had an affair with someone like Leo. And then she would have broken his heart . . .

As if she hadn't done that anyway.

He returned abruptly to the present, suddenly conscious of not having seen Bertie for some while. He called and whistled, then continued his walk. Bertie knew their route. He would catch up or come back, now he realized he was not being ignored. But Bertie was his own dog. He would return to his master when it suited him.

Yet, when it came down to it, wasn't everyone the same? Didn't everyone – be they man, woman, child or dog – basically follow the dictates of their own heart and mind? Having set their sights on a goal, however nebulous or questionable, that was what they would aim for.

Take Pippa. *Look! Gawaine Devere! Well, I'm sure you've already guessed what my next question is. Of course, I want to find out if Gawaine Devere is related to us.*

What should he do – if anything?

And then Eve: *Kitty has been totally and utterly selfish and irresponsible all her life. And I think it's about time that she faced up to the truth.*

He had always tried to do his best for Kitty. Rejected as her lover, he had remained her friend. She had always known where to find him and he had always been there to comfort her in her moments of despair, to be a tower of strength in her times of need. Eve, thank heavens, was unaware of quite how much he had done for her over the decades.

Or was she? *So, in case you were thinking of ringing Kitty and warning her, may I suggest that you don't?*

If Pippa turned up on Kitty's doorstep, how would she react? It would be a shock, of course. But Pippa was a sweet, kind-hearted girl and not insensitive to other people's feelings. And it wasn't as if Kitty was unaware of her existence. He had kept her informed of all the major developments in Sebastian's life, by letter and, occasionally, when he could find an excuse to leave Puddles, in person.

Eve was right. Sebastian was Kitty's son and Pippa her granddaughter. He had done his bit. Now it was up to them.

Bertie suddenly appeared through a hedge, trotting towards him with a stick in his mouth. After a brief, friendly tussle, Adam took the stick from him and threw it high into the sky, so that it twisted as it flew through the air. Barking joyfully, Bertie tried to anticipate where it would land. Adam gave a thin smile. How simple life was, if one was a dog.

CHAPTER 5

A week later, Pippa was at Gatwick airport, seeing her parents off to the Bahamas.

'Now, I've left Mary's money in the usual place in the kitchen,' her mother said. 'And I've also left a couple of cheques for the milkman, if you could remember to put them out on Saturday.'

'Mum, don't fuss. Everything will be all right.'

'And you won't forget to switch on the burglar alarm whenever you go out?' her father added.

'Of course not. Don't worry.'

Fortunately, they had been too preoccupied with their holiday preparations to pay much attention to her during the past few days. Her father, as always when he left the business for any length of time, was worried about how Elliott and Michael would manage without him, while to her mother had fallen the chores of organizing clothes, packing and ordering currency, as well as making sure that all the domestic arrangements continued to run smoothly in her absence.

Otherwise, they would certainly have noticed that something out of the ordinary had happened.

'I suppose it's worth it,' her mother sighed, looking exhausted.

'Of course it is,' Pippa assured her. 'You'll really enjoy yourselves once you're on board ship.'

'Yes, I'm sure we shall.'

To Pippa's relief, their flight was called promptly and they set off towards passport control and the departure lounge. She waved them goodbye, then they disappeared from view and the rest of the day belonged to her.

She hurried across the concourse and along the corridor to the short-term car park, where she had left the Metro. On the way, she passed a telephone booth and wondered whether to ring the number she had obtained from directory enquiries for her grandmother. But there was no point. If her grandmother wasn't at home, then she would go on to Worthing and see if she could find Edith Spencer at Chanctonbury Lodge. She had the photograph album with her in her bag, just in case.

And if she could get to see neither her grandmother nor Edith Spencer, then she would come home again and send them both letters, which had been her original intention after Eve had given her Kitty Pilgrim's address. But, under the circumstances, it was probably much better to introduce herself in person. Letters could so easily be misinterpreted.

However, her initial interest in Gawaine Devere had diminished somewhat since Eve's astonishing revelation that she had a grandmother she hadn't known existed. What would her grandmother be like? She tried to form a mental image of her. Tall and rather handsome, like her father, she decided. But beyond that, she could not visualize her. And what kind of woman was she, who had deserted her own son? Eve clearly did not like her. On the other hand, Eve had said that she ought to meet her and listen to what she had to say . . .

Soon, she was heading south and the ridge of the South Downs was rising ahead of her. Although it was so near to London, Sussex was not a county with which she was at all familiar, apart from going to Brighton a few times. Being in unknown territory added to her feeling of excitement.

She skirted the back of Worthing and eventually came to Arundel, with the castle looming high on her right and the cathedral ahead. Her grandmother lived in Rose Cottage, Pannet's Row. Not having the slightest idea where that might be, she drove into the car park, just past a little hump-backed bridge over the River Arun, and made enquiries at the tourist information office. The girl there gave her a map and suggested that, since parking was difficult elsewhere, she leave her car where it was.

Arundel, Pippa decided, as she went up the High Street, was a picturesque if rather touristy town, with lots of arts and crafts shops and quaint tearooms. The roads leading off it were very narrow, little more than lanes, and many of the old houses fronted directly on to the road.

When she reached Pannet's Row, however, she discovered that she could have parked there, for it was rather wider than some of the other streets and had no yellow lines. It was set on the hillside, with a lovely view across the rooftops and along the Arun valley to the distant silver rim of the English Channel.

Rose Cottage stood at the end of a terrace, with a grassy bank in front of it, massed with snowdrops and crocuses. It was not difficult to guess why the house was so named. The entire front wall was covered with climbing roses, which Pippa could well imagine must be an absolute picture in the summer.

She stopped, feeling suddenly nervous, very much aware of what she was about to do. Was she a fool walking in where angels feared to tread? Should she go away now, before it was too late, before she stirred up a hornet's nest, which might have untold repercussions? Yet Kitty Pilgrim was her grandmother and, as Eve had said, she had a right to know about her. On the other hand, her father must have a reason – and presumably a good one – for breaking all contact with her.

At that moment, the decision was taken out of her hands. The door of the next cottage opened and an elderly man emerged, with a clipped white moustache, ruddy cheeks and pale, watery eyes. The Yorkie he had on a lead was tugging him in Pippa's direction. 'Good morning. Can I help you? Are you looking for someone?'

'Er, yes, I've come to see Mrs Pilgrim.'

'Well, you've come to the right place.' He paused and peered at her curiously. 'Excuse me asking, but are you a relative of hers?'

'Umm, yes, I am actually.'

'Hah! Thought you must be. Extraordinary resemblance.'

If it were not for the thought that her grandmother might be looking out of the window, watching this encounter, Pippa would have liked to ask him more. As it was, she said, trying to inject her voice with a confidence she did not feel, 'Well, I'd better find out if she's at home.'

'I'm sure she is. Saw her in the garden earlier. If she doesn't answer your knock, that's probably because she's still out there. She won't have an electric bell, you know. In fact, I expect the door's open.' He lifted the latch. 'Hah, yes, I thought so! Usually is. I'm always warning her against burglars, but she won't pay any heed.' Then he called, 'Mrs Pilgrim! Are you there? You've got a visitor!'

It was not the entrance or means of introduction Pippa had intended but perhaps, she reflected fleetingly, her meeting with her grandmother might be less awkward if it took place in front of a stranger.

Just inside the front door was a hallway, with polished wooden floorboards, furnished with an old wooden settle and a most unusual coatstand, inlaid with mother-of-pearl and inset with a mirror. To the right, a staircase led upstairs and to the left a couple of small steps led down into what appeared to be, through the partially opened door, a living room.

From the far end of the hall, a voice replied, 'I'm in the kitchen. Just one moment.'

A small figure appeared in the passage and hurried towards them. 'Ah! Colonel Wakehurst! And . . . ?'

Pippa stepped forward, then stopped abruptly, understanding why Colonel Wakehurst should have remarked upon an extraordinary resemblance. When she became old, this was how she might look: with a thick mop of unruly white curls and big blue eyes – her grandmother's eyes even had the same hazel flecks in them as her own – in a pointed face, with a neat nose, rounded cheeks and a rather obstinate little chin.

Her own astonishment was reflected on the other woman's face. 'Why, surely – you must be . . . are you Philippa?'

Pippa nodded.

He grandmother stood shaking her head incredulously. Then she seized both of Pippa's hands in hers and said tremulously, 'Oh, my dear, you have no idea . . . What a wonderful, wonderful surprise. All these years I've hoped and imagined but I never dreamed—'

The Colonel cleared his throat in embarrassment. 'Must be getting on with my constitutional. Ladies, I wish you a good day, grumphh.'

Still holding one of Pippa's hands in hers, her grandmother led her down the hall into a large room, white-painted, low-ceilinged and hung with dark oak beams. A radio was softly playing classical music. A tabby cat was asleep on a chair in a ray of sunshine; the flagstone floor was littered with cat bowls, various footwear and gardening paraphernalia; the sink was full of unwashed crockery; a large Welsh dresser was a-clutter with plant pots, trays of seedlings and nursery catalogues; and on the table lay a box of watercolour paints, a palette and an open sketchpad, with a half-completed picture of some roses.

'I'm sorry you find me in such a mess. If I'd known you were coming, I'd have had a tidy up. Oh, this is such a wonderful, wonderful surprise! I simply can't get over it. Please, do sit down and make yourself comfortable. Let me move Tabitha. She always chooses the most comfortable chair.'

'Don't disturb her. She's lovely.' Pippa stroked the cat, who rolled over on her back in a rather undignified but ecstatic pose to have her tummy stroked.

Her grandmother smiled fondly. 'I can see you like cats.'

'Yes. But I've never had one of my own. I'd love to, but . . .' Pippa was about to explain that her father didn't like animals, when it occurred to her that this was neither the best way nor the opportune moment to introduce him into the conversation.

'I was very fortunate when I was a girl,' her grandmother said. 'I had lots of animals, including a dog – and a pony.'

'How wonderful! I would have loved to have learned to ride. But living in London, it's not very easy. Of course you can ride in the parks, but it's not the same as in the country.'

'I know. I lived in London for a while. But what am I thinking of? Here I am chattering away and I haven't even offered you a cup of tea. Though having said that, I think the occasion warrants more than tea. We really ought to have champagne, but I'm afraid I don't keep any in the house. However, I should have some sherry.' She scurried across to the fridge and took out a bottle of Tio Pepe. Filling two glasses, she handed one to Pippa and raised the other in a toast. 'Philippa, to you. And thank you so much for coming to see me.'

Pippa clinked her glass against her grandmother's. 'Could I ask you to call me Pippa? Only Dad calls me Philippa.'

'Why, my father was just the same! He always insisted on calling me Catherine, whereas all my friends called me Kitty. Do you know Robert Browning's poem, "Pippa's Song"? Let me see, how does it go?

'The year's at the spring
And day's at the morn;
Morning's at seven;
The hill-side's dew-pearled;
The lark's on the wing;
The snail's on the thorn:
God's in his heaven,
All's right with the world!'

Pippa gazed at her with wondering delight.

'Yes, I think Pippa's a lovely name,' her grandmother went on, putting down her glass and moving some of the things from the table on to the dresser. 'Oh, all this gardening junk! I really ought to have a greenhouse, but my garden is much too small.'

Pippa glanced out of the kitchen window into a tiny walled garden, as meticulously maintained as the interior of the cottage was disorderly. Just outside the back door was a little patio, and a birdtable, heaped with seed, from which were suspended nets of nuts and two half-coconuts, thronged with small birds. Beyond that, a paved path led a winding trail under a rose arch and across a small lawn edged with flower beds.

'It looks the perfect size for a garden to me,' she said. 'However, going back to names, what would you like me to call you? Mrs Pilgrim is much too formal and Grandma is . . .'

'Much too staid – and not exactly suitable,' her grandmother agreed. 'I think you ought to call me Kitty, too.'

'Thank you – Kitty.'

She removed a pile of papers from a chair, at which moment Tabitha jumped down on to the rug. 'Now, if that isn't typical of cats! Always contrary. Well, now at least we can sit down.' However, although Pippa took a seat, Kitty continued to clear the table. 'I really should have taken you into the living room, but it's very chilly in there in the mornings and I haven't lit the fire yet. I tend to spend most of my time here in the kitchen – as you can see. It faces south, so it gets the sun most of the day. It used to be two rooms, but when I bought the house I had the dividing wall knocked down.'

Pippa realized that Kitty was far more nervous than she was. 'How long have you lived here?' she asked.

'Oh, a long time. Nearly thirty years.' Kitty lifted up the sketchpad, peering at the paint to see if it was dry.

Pippa seized her opportunity. 'That's really lovely. The texture of the petals is like velvet.'

'Oh, do you think so? Thank you. I'm doing it from a snapshot I took during the summer. I prefer painting from life, but in the winter it's not always easy. And this winter has been so cold, I'm beginning to wonder if spring will ever arrive.'

'It's actually because of your paintings that I found out about you.'

'Because of my paintings you . . . ? What do you mean?'

'Well, you see, I didn't even know you existed until a few days ago. That sounds awful, but it's true. I was down in Puddles, staying with Adam and Eve. They have two of your paintings in their guest room. I admired them and Aunt Eve told me about you. Well, she didn't actually tell me anything very much about you but she gave me your address.'

Kitty replaced the sketchpad on the table and sank down on Tabitha's vacated chair. 'And until then you didn't even know I existed?'

Pippa shook her head. 'If I had, I'd have come to see you before.'

'But . . . what . . . ?'

She looked so upset Pippa wished she could retract what she had said and phrase it less bluntly. 'So, what did you think had happened to me?' Kitty asked eventually.

'Well, Dad told me . . .'

'Please, don't be nervous, tell me what he said.'

'Well, that his father died during the war and that you – umm – disappeared.'

Kitty nodded slowly. 'In a way, he was right.' Then, in a brisker one, she continued, 'But I'm very glad that Eve told you the truth. I have always feared that I would die without meeting you, although I've often felt that I knew you. Adam's kept me in touch with your family news. He's been such a dear, good friend to me over the years.'

Pippa longed to ask her to expand on her first statement but she did not dare to. This was not the right moment. Perhaps later in the day, when they had got to know each other a bit better, there would be another chance.

'Do you paint at all?' Kitty asked, moving them back to safer ground.

'I used to, but I haven't done any for years, not since my first year at college, in fact. I did art, design and photography for my foundation course. Then I decided I liked photography best, so I took my degree in that.'

Kitty put the caps on her tubes of paint and closed the box. 'That's right, I remember Adam telling me that you are a photographer.'

'I'm not actually a photographer yet. I'm still an assistant. In fact, I'm between jobs, which is why I've got today off. I start working for a new photographer next week. His name's Tim Collins. I don't know if you've seen his work? A lot of the newspapers use his pictures.'

'I'm afraid I seldom buy a newspaper. I don't know about you, but I

71

find the news generally so depressing. And I see no point in getting upset about events over which one has absolutely no influence. Whether or not you're aware of them, politicians will continue squabbling, disasters go on occurring and people will still kill each other.'

'Yes, I know what you mean.'

Kitty shot her a quick, birdlike glance. 'What sort of pictures do you enjoy taking most?'

'I like everything really. The last photographer I worked for did mainly still life. But portraiture is what interests me most. That's why I'm really looking forward to my new job.' Pippa wondered, fleetingly, whether she could mention Gawaine Devere but, equally quickly, she sensed that it would be wrong.

'You said you are an assistant. What does that mean?'

'Basically, an assistant does everything from making coffee to loading film for the photographer. But at my new job I shall be doing quite a bit of production as well, making appointments and organizing make-up and stylists.'

'It sounds fascinating. I must say I rather envy you. My father wouldn't allow me to train or study for a career. Nice girls didn't work when I was young.'

She paused, in such a way that Pippa thought she was going to add something more. Instead she said, 'Your glass is empty. Would you like some more sherry?'

'Well, yes, please.'

'And you will stay to lunch, won't you? Not that I have anything exciting to offer you. I live a very simple life – and I'm a vegetarian. Now, let me see. There's cheese, eggs, salad . . . or we could have pasta. No, I know! We'll have a Spanish omelette.'

'Please don't go to any trouble,' Pippa begged.

'Oh, I do so wish I had known you were coming. I hate being unprepared. And what you must think of this mess, I simply don't know.'

'I don't think it's a mess. I think it's lovely. Our house is more like a page in *Homes and Gardens* than a home.'

Kitty began chopping cold potatoes, tomatoes, onions and garlic. 'Would I be right in assuming your father's still in the antiques trade?'

'Yes, he's in partnership with Elliott – Adam and Eve's son. But, actually,

Dad and Mum have gone on holiday today to the Bahamas. I took them to Gatwick before I came here.'

'So you have a car?'

'Oh, yes. But it's only a Metro.'

'I don't know how I'd survive without my dear old Morris Minor. Did you see it outside? Oh, I'm finding this so strange. You must forgive me. We have *such* a lot to talk about and so many years to catch up on . . .'

'I know, but what I think is really, really amazing is that we have so many things in common, like painting and poetry. Ever since I found out about you, I kept wondering what you were going to be like.'

'And how did you visualize me?'

'I don't know any more. I can't imagine you any different from how you are.'

'Well, I had the advantage over you. I knew what you looked like from Adam's descriptions and I had quite a good idea of your personality.'

'And am I how you thought I would be?'

'Much, much better,' Kitty said warmly.

She lit a gas ring on the stove, tipped a little oil into a frying pan and put it on the hob. 'We could almost turn this into a sort of question and answer game. For instance, do you like cooking?'

'Not particularly. Mum's a cordon bleu. She doesn't like anyone else working in her kitchen. And you?'

'I'm afraid I've never been a very domestic person. And cooking for yourself is certainly more of a chore than a pleasure. However, this gas stove was my seventy-fifth birthday present to myself, last year, together with a gas central heating boiler. Before that, I had a solid fuel Aga, on which I used to cook and which heated all the water and the radiators. Then I decided that I simply couldn't be bothered any more with carrying coal and emptying ashes, although I still have an open fire in the sitting room. I must admit that gas has made a great difference to my life. It's so clean and easy, I don't know why I didn't do it years ago.'

She tipped everything on her chopping board into the frying pan, gave it a quick stir and began to lay the table. 'We never used to eat in the kitchen when I was a girl. That was considered very much a working-class habit. And my father hated cooking smells.'

'What did your father do?' Pippa asked.

'He was a vicar. As you may have gathered, I didn't like him much. He was very strict and authoritarian.'

She beat some eggs in a jug and poured them over the vegetables.

'Did you live in Dorset then?'

'What, when I was a girl? No, we lived in Sussex. Now then, what's missing? Oh yes, bread. And something to drink. I'm afraid I don't have any wine. But I could pop up the road and get some.'

'No, please don't bother. Water will be fine.'

She cut some bread, put it in a basket and served up the omelette. 'There, I hope it's all right.'

'It looks delicious.'

Kitty took her place and Tabitha jumped on her lap. Pippa guessed that this was a little ritual that happened every mealtime. They ate in silence for a few moments and she became aware of the radio which had continued to play quietly in the background. 'You like classical music?' she asked.

'Immensely. I keep my radio tuned in to Radio 3.' Kitty cocked an ear. '*L'après-midi d'un faune*! One of my favourite works. Do you play any instrument?'

'I'm afraid not.'

'Your father used to play the piano.'

'Really? I didn't know that.'

Finally, they were starting to move in the right direction.

'Yes, he was very musical. Still, I suppose . . . Please help yourself to some more bread. Our local baker is excellent. Now, please, tell me more about yourself. Adam is a faithful correspondent, but he doesn't always give me the sort of detail I like. For instance, whenever I meet a person for the first time, I always want to ask them what they read.'

Pippa laughed. 'So do I! Unfortunately, all too often I find they don't.'

'What? They don't read? So what *do* they do?'

'Watch television.'

'Well, I do watch a certain amount of television myself, I must admit. I like nature programmes and I enjoy some of the old films. But there really is nothing to beat a good book.'

Needless to say, they shared similar tastes in reading.

Kitty shook her head bemusedly. 'It's quite amazing. Not only do you look like I used to look when I was young, but you like the same things. What surprises me just as much, though, is that you have such old-fashioned tastes. I thought that modern girls only read – what do they call them? – sex and shopping books.' She tempered her query with a smile.

'Oh, I read those too, sometimes,' Pippa told her. 'But, basically, when you've read one, you've read them all. I like a book I can get my teeth into.'

'I couldn't agree more. Now, have you had enough to eat?'

'Thank you, I'm full. That was delicious.'

Kitty put her plate – with a few titbits arranged in the centre – on the floor. The cat jumped down with alacrity. 'Tea or coffee?' she asked, getting up and filling the kettle. 'I'm afraid I only have instant.'

'That's fine by me.'

Kitty rinsed two mugs under the tap. 'I'm getting very lazy in my old age. I tend to wash up only once a day, in the evening, after supper.'

Pippa giggled. 'Tabitha's making such a good job of your plate, I'd leave the washing up to her.'

At that moment, there was a loud knock on the front door. 'Now, who on earth can that be?' Kitty asked.

She was quite, quite wonderful, Pippa thought, as her grandmother left the kitchen. So alert and sprightly. And not at all the sort of woman who would deliberately abandon her son. A million and a half children had been evacuated in the first three days of the war, Adam had said, so it wasn't as if her father were the only child to be sent away. Even if he was upset at the time, surely, now he was older, he must realize that? So why had he never forgiven her? Something else must have happened. But what? And had Kitty ever tried to heal the breach between them? If so, how had her father reacted? Presumably negatively. But why?

However, these were not the sort of questions one could ask at a first encounter, even though she was convinced that Kitty was as aware as she was of the figure of Sebastian standing – almost tangibly – between them. But before that touchy subject could be broached, absolute trust had to be established.

In any case, for the moment at least, the past did not really matter. The main thing was that she and Kitty were getting to know each other – and that they liked each other. Her father wouldn't be back for two weeks. There was time enough to decide how to deal with him.

'Now, isn't that kind?' Kitty said, returning to the kitchen with a jar in her hand. It had a red and white checked cotton top, tied round with a bow. 'That was Colonel Wakehurst. He's such a dear, well-meaning man. He was in the army and spent a lot of time in India.'

Pippa was just wondering whether there might be a budding romance between her grandmother and the Colonel, when Kitty continued, 'And this is a present from Mrs Wakehurst. Some home-made strawberry jam for my granddaughter's tea. Though what it will taste like is another matter. Poor Mrs Wakehurst isn't the best of cooks. They always had servants, you see. When they first moved in, Mrs Wakehurst didn't even know how to empty a Hoover bag and I had to show her.

'But I shouldn't laugh. I'm very fortunate to have such good neighbours. They keep an eye on me, but they don't interfere. We don't live in each other's pockets. Now, is that kettle boiling yet?'

Later, after tea – with Mrs Wakehurst's surprisingly good strawberry jam spread on granary bread – Kitty asked, 'You haven't, by any chance, brought any of your photographs with you, have you?'

They had moved into the living room by then, where she had lit the fire. It was a cosy room, cluttered with little tables and glass-fronted cabinets containing old china and ornaments, on the top of which stood indoor plants, many of them in bloom. One entire wall was lined with bookshelves and the others were closely hung with pictures.

By that time, they had become sufficiently relaxed in each other's company for Pippa to dare to show her Edith Spencer's album. 'I'm afraid I haven't. But I have got something else I'd rather like you to see.' She reached towards her bag. 'A few weeks ago, Dad went to an auction in Worthing and as part of a lot, he bought some old books and a photograph album. The album contains some amazing pictures – some of really famous people and some of a beautiful old house.'

'And you have this album here?'

'Yes.' She delved into her bag. 'When Dad first showed me everything, I assumed the pictures had all been taken by the woman who had owned the books, but—'

Kitty got up from her chair. 'You'll have to excuse me a moment. I must go and get my reading glasses from the kitchen.'

While she was gone, Pippa took out the album and leafed through it until she came to the snapshots of the house. Hearing Kitty's footsteps return down the hall, she continued, 'In fact, in a funny way, the house reminds me of here. I think it's called Yondover, because I found a letter in one of the books addressed to Edith Spencer. That's the woman whose name is at the front of the album.'

The footsteps stopped and Pippa looked up. Her grandmother was fumbling in her handbag.

'But this is where we come to the really incredible bit.' She turned to the portrait of George V and carefully extracted it from its photo corners. 'Look. This is King George the Fifth and the photographer's name is . . .' She paused, then said, 'Devere – Gawaine Devere.'

It was at that instant that Kitty fell.

She was just coming down the steps into the living room and, presumably because she was paying more attention to the photograph Pippa was holding up than to where she was going, she lost her balance and tripped, knocking against a tall, narrow, glass-fronted cabinet on rather spindly legs just to the left of the door, which came crashing over and knocked her, face forwards, on to the floor.

There she lay, absolutely still.

Pippa dropped the album and rushed over to her. 'Kitty! Are you all right? Kitty!'

But her grandmother neither moved nor replied.

Pippa lifted the cabinet away from her. Some of the panes of glass had broken and the china in it smashed.

To her relief, Kitty was still breathing, although her breath was very shallow. Her eyes were closed and remained so.

Panic-stricken, she looked around for a telephone, then remembered seeing one in the hall. Minding the step, she ran from the room and called for an ambulance.

It was evening when Pippa returned to Rose Cottage from Arundel Hospital. Mercifully, the ambulance had arrived very quickly and the ambulance men had carried the still unconscious Kitty out on a stretcher and borne her away, with blue lights flashing and sirens blaring, leaving Pippa to follow under her own steam, after looking for the house keys and finding them eventually in Kitty's handbag, locking up, and obtaining directions to the hospital from Colonel and Mrs Wakehurst, who were agog to know what had happened.

'Oh, poor soul,' Mrs Wakehurst had sympathized. 'I do hope it won't turn out to be anything too serious.'

'She may have had a stroke,' the Colonel had said. 'That's how they happen, you know. A friend of ours – your grandmother met him when he came to tea with us a couple of months ago – he was just going to have a bath, when . . . Still, he's recovering very well. Can't use his left hand properly yet and he's a bit tottery on his pins, but then aren't we all?'

'Or maybe a heart attack,' Mrs Wakehurst had added.

A stroke? A heart attack? Pippa had looked at them aghast. 'She just fell, she tripped down the step into the living room,' she said.

At the hospital, however, she was told much the same thing. Kitty had already been taken away for X-rays and other examinations by the time Pippa arrived, having had to retrieve her car from the car park by the castle. After giving a clerk as much information about her grandmother as she was able, she had sat, biting her nails and leafing sightlessly through magazines, as the minutes ticked past and the frustrating rituals of hospital waiting rooms were enacted before her, until she was eventually summoned to the presence of a doctor.

'We'll need to keep Mrs Pilgrim in while we carry out tests to make sure she hasn't suffered any brain damage and to find out what caused her to fall,' he said. 'She may have had a black-out and, if so, we must find out why. For that matter, this may not be the first time it's happened.'

'Hasn't she regained consciousness yet?' Pippa asked fearfully.

'Oh, yes, she's come to.'

Pippa felt a great surge of relief. 'Can I see her?'

'Better not. What she needs most now is rest. She's still very woozy and will be for quite a while. She's been quite badly concussed. As well as hitting her head, she has bruised her ribs and has a nasty gash on her shoulder, which we've stitched up. We've given her some pain-killers, which will also help her to sleep.'

'You'll be able to ask her, won't you, whether she's ever fallen before?'

'She may well not remember. Concussion often causes amnesia. It could be several days, even weeks, before she remembers the more recent events in her life and it's probable that she will never remember what happened to her today. It's quite common for at least the last twenty-four hours before a person is concussed to disappear totally.'

'How long will she have to remain in hospital?'

'That depends upon the speed of her recovery and what our tests show up. Does she live alone?'

'Yes, I just came to see her for the day.' Pippa decided against explaining that it was the first time she had ever met her grandmother. That was an added and unnecessary complication. 'But I could stay on,' she added. Apart from not having any spare clothes or overnight things with her – and that was easily remedied – there was no reason for her to rush back to London, provided she returned by Monday to start her new job.

'It might be a good idea. Does she have any other relations nearby?'

'No. She has friends, of course.'

'The first twenty-four hours tend to be critical in a case like this. We have your grandmother's telephone number and we'll let you know if there is any change in her condition overnight. Of course, you're welcome to ring the ward sister whenever you like to check on her progress. But the best thing you can do is go home and get a good night's sleep yourself. You look worn out.'

She felt absolutely drained. 'It must be shock. If only I hadn't distracted her attention . . .'

'You don't know that that's what caused her fall. Don't forget she might have fallen when you weren't there and lain for hours before anyone found her.'

'When can I see her?'

'I suggest you come along tomorrow afternoon during visiting hours.'

'Will it hurt if I talk to her about her accident?'

'Not at all. In fact, she'll undoubtedly be curious about it. But go gently with her. Concussion can leave people – especially old people – very confused and disorientated. She's had a bad jolt, mentally and physically.'

Back at Rose Cottage, Pippa had not even opened the front door before Colonel Wakehurst emerged from his house.

'Saw you get out of your car. Wondered how Mrs Pilgrim is.'

Pippa told him what the doctor had said and he nodded knowingly. 'The first twenty-four hours are always the most critical. Once she's got through those, then we'll all be able to relax a bit more. Now then, the Memsahib said that I was to ask you if there's anything you need.'

'No, I don't think so, thank you.'

'Don't hesitate to call on us if there's anything we can do. We're very fond of Mrs Pilgrim. Such a dear, good-natured lady. We've always wondered . . .' He cleared his throat. 'But it's none of our business, of course.'

No, Pippa thought, it isn't. And, what's more, I don't know the answers myself, so even if I were so inclined, I couldn't satisfy your curiosity.

She gave a sweet but tired little smile. 'I'm sorry, it's been a very long day . . .'

'Yes, yes, of course. We can have a longer chat another time. Well, grummph, I'll wish you a good night. And remember, we're only next door.'

'Thank you. And good night.'

On entering the house, she was met by a highly indignant Tabitha, who led her to an empty bowl. After peering into various cupboards, Pippa found a store of cat food and opened a tin. Not hungry herself, she made a coffee, washed up after the lunch that now seemed so long ago and cleared up the debris in the living room, discovering to her surprised relief that less had actually been broken than had at first appeared. Finally, she made the bed in the spare room, had a bath and washed out her underwear, putting it in the airing cupboard to dry. Then, aware that she must keep an ear open for the phone, she clambered into bed and drifted into an unsettled sleep.

CHAPTER 6

Kitty opened her eyes to find herself in a dimly lit room, with a ceiling she did not recognize, which seemed to approach and recede in a most extraordinary fashion. She could hear distant noises which were not the sounds of home – the mumble of unfamiliar voices, the shuffling of feet, the scraping of chair legs on vinyl flooring and the faint rumble of people snoring. And there was a pervading odour of disinfectant and antiseptic. She moved and an excruciating pain shot through her head, shoulders and down her back, making her feel sick and giddy, so that she closed her eyes again.

Footsteps approached. Cool fingers gently clasped her wrist. A female voice asked, 'Mrs Pilgrim, can you hear me?'

She gave a grunt, which did not seem to come from her at all.

'I've just checked your pulse and now I'm going to take your blood pressure,' the voice said. 'You just lie still. It won't take a moment.'

Where was she? Why was this disembodied voice checking her pulse and taking her blood pressure? She must be in hospital. But why? And how? The effort was too great to form the words. She tried to think back, but the last thing she could remember was – yes – looking at a rose, a very beautiful rose, with perfectly formed, pink petals . . .

The rose was one of a mass of blossoms on a bush far taller than she was. Ahead of her was a high, flintstone wall, up which another rose was clambering, spreading itself in lavish abandonment, its trunk thick with age, its furthermost tendrils intertwined with a creamy honeysuckle. Around her were more roses, interspersed with mallows and lace-cap hydrangeas, paeonies and lilies, all laden with extravagant pink and cream blooms,

81

underplanted with clumps of old-fashioned pinks, carnations, thrift, scabious, love-in-a-mist and delicate Japanese windflowers.

'When I inherited the place upon my father's death, this was a mass of brambles, thistles and nettles,' she heard West's voice saying. 'Originally, it was part of the farmyard, but any goodness there might have been in the soil had seeped away long ago. We had to bring cartloads of topsoil up from the village.'

In the strange way one could sometimes see oneself in dreams, she saw herself as a girl of thirteen, in a short cotton dress, her hair hanging loose to her shoulders. But in an equally strange way, she could not see West, only hear his disembodied voice.

She let go the rose and wandered along the path until she came to a couple of steps, which led up and through a small open gateway, from the crevices of which sprang white and pink valerian, and on which an old door, unshut for decades, leaned slightly askew, overgrown by a crimson-leaved vine. Passing through the gateway she entered another garden, utterly different in colour and character from that which she had just left, as vivid and vibrant as the other had been pastel and gentle.

'And over there was a barn,' West's voice said. 'Although the roof had fallen in, the walls were still sound. The flowers here are at their best in the late afternoon and evening, when their colours reflect the glowing embers of the setting sun.'

Here in the walled garden, the roses climbing up the walls were carmine, mingling with a clematis of so azure a blue as to make the sky above seem almost insipid. The deep beds were massed with the spikes of butterfly-laden buddleias, blue and purple delphiniums, multi-hued hollyhocks, red-hot pokers, mullein, silver-leaved, blue-headed globe thistles, plumed astilbes, fluffy liatris and fragrant tobacco plants; with giant, golden sunflowers, crimson paeonies, scarlet and orange poppies, yellow, black-eyed daisies, coral flowers, potentilla, bergamot, asters and cornflowers.

On the far side was another gateway, broad and high enough to give access to two horses yoked abreast bringing in a cartload of hay. On it valerian again grew rampant. Here she came to a divergence of ways. To her right, steps led down to a broad walk lined with azaleas and cotinus, soft green now, but in spring and autumn blaze with flame-coloured flowers and leaves.

Beyond that could be glimpsed the orchard, where the lean figure of the Gurneys' grandson, Jethro, could be seen scything with steady, even strokes. 'Jethro always claims that if he had his way, the whole garden would revert to pasture,' West's voice laughed. 'He maintains that flowers are a frivolity. You should hear him going on when the bulbs are out. The orchard is a picture in spring – carpeted with golden buttercups and vaulted with fruit blossom.'

Behind the orchard, the ground rose slightly to the paddock, in which several horses grazed in the shade of an ancient oak tree, swishing their tails to keep away the flies. 'That tree's a miracle of nature,' West's voice mused affectionately. 'It was fully grown when my grandfather first came here and since then it's survived gale and storm.'

Where the paddock ended, West's wood began, only the very edge of it visible from where she stood, although to the east it went down the hillside to the river and northwards it crossed the Lewes highway towards the railway line.

She wandered between beech and hornbeam, oak and birch, over a sun-dappled carpet of last autumn's leaves, beechmast and bracken, between the tall, brown cusps of early summer's foxgloves.

'I planted most of these trees myself,' West's voice said. 'The original wood, down by the road, is very old, but I extended it up the hillside to obliterate the view of the railway.'

And then: 'I have never understood why most Christians worship God one day a week and ignore Him the other six. I'm accused of being an atheist because I don't attend church, but to me God is around us all the time.' In the branches of a beech tree arching above them, a thrush was pouring out its own rhapsodic song of praise. 'Why go to church when one can worship here in God's cathedral?'

In the absence of a stream running through his wood, West had created a river of blue and white flowers that twisted and tumbled its way between boulders.

Ahead of her, a wooden gate was set into the clipped yew hedge surrounding Gurney's vegetable garden and for a few moments she leaned over it, gazing at the neat, marshalled rows of plants, such a contrast with the riotous exuberance of the flower gardens she had just left: at tall, scarlet runner beans, climbing up wigwam-like stakes; giant, purple-headed artichokes; tomatoes, massed with luscious ripe fruit; spiky onion leaves; plump, green and yellow striped marrows peeping out from under broad, protecting leaves; crisp lettuces; creamy cauliflowers; cabbages, green, purple and red; cloches for cucumbers; terracotta pots sprouting rhubarb; netting sheltering strawberries; a compost heap; and a scarecrow which could have been Gurney himself, tall and spare with sparse, straw hair sticking out from beneath a flat cap, a morose expression on its sacking face, its trousers secured round its waist with a length of string.

He hadn't known whether to laugh or be angry when she had made that scarecrow, nor when, the following spring, a robin had nested in its hair . . .

She smiled and turned to her left, where the path led under the mossy northern shadow of the barn wall to open into Fanny Gurney's sunny herb garden. She stooped to breathe in the aroma of the herbs, before passing on into a flagged, horseshoe-shaped courtyard, flanked by the wisteria-hung kitchen wing of the house, a row of stables, in and out of which swallows flitted, and the old dairy. On the wooden cover of the well in the centre of the yard a ginger cat lay outstretched, asleep in the sun.

From the kitchen came the clatter of dishes and the mouth-watering, yeasty scent of baking bread, and she peeped in through the window for a glimpse of Fanny's kingdom. On the hob a sooty kettle was whistling, while various copper pans simmered and steamed. In pride of place on the mantelshelf stood the cup Gurney had won for growing a prodigious marrow.

And there was Fanny herself, rolling pastry on the scrubbed, wooden table, dressed in black bombazine, covered with a starched white pinafore, as short and round and cheerful a figure as her husband was tall and lean and dour, her white hair drawn back in a bun under her old-fashioned lace cap, her cheeks rosy and her brown eyes twinkling just like a robin's. Rolling pin in flour-covered hand, she came to the door. 'Ah, Miss Kitty, just in time for a slice of my seed cake . . .'

At that moment, Rafe came racing past Fanny's skirts, ecstatically waving his plumed, black and white tail. He bounded ahead of her as she followed the drive round the side of the house, past the open French windows leading into West's music room, planted to either side with night-scented stocks. A broad shaft of sunlight fell over the cream carpet to the foot of the grand piano. On the walls were paintings of shimmering landscapes.

Although nobody was playing, strains of Liszt and Schubert seemed to hang on the air.

The drive continued across a stretch of velvety, daisy-studded lawn, through a gate set in another flintstone wall, until it reached the ridge of the hill, where it disappeared to twist down the steep escarpment in the direction of the village.

She turned, and there before her stood Yondover, its glinting, silvery grey walls wreathed with roses, clambering in profusion right up to and around the upper storey casements, where curtains billowed gently in the breeze. On the roof some doves were perched and the air was filled with their soft cooing, the twittering of swallows, the chattering of sparrows, the drowsy drone of bees – and heavy with the perfume of roses.

'Lovely old place, isn't it?' West's voice said. 'This was the original farmhouse and dates back to the 1600s. The kitchen wing is more modern. My father added that in the middle of the last century, when he refurbished the house. It wouldn't have surprised me if he had put on a hideous mock-Gothic extension, but he didn't, thank heavens.'

Then she was indoors, wandering through low-ceilinged, oak-beamed rooms, with dark oak floors, white lath and plaster walls and deep-silled, small-paned windows. The sitting room, furnished with faded, chintz-covered settees and armchairs, had a huge, inglenook fireplace piled on either side with logs, the space between hearth and mantelshelf lined with blue and white Delft tiles. The dining room, its walnut refectory table polished every day by Fanny Gurney so that its surface shone like water, smelled of pot-pourri and beeswax polish. The homely confusion of West's study invited her to browse among the rows of leatherbound books of his library.

Then, finally, she was mounting the twisting, wood-panelled staircase, hurrying past the first-floor bedrooms, up to the attic where the servants had slept back in the days when Yondover had first been built. Now it formed one long room, with a ceiling so low she was the only person in the household who could stand upright in it.

'This used to be my nursery,' West's voice said. 'It will always be my favourite room.' With a little sigh of contentment, she leaned her elbows on the window sill and gazed out across the gardens to the great hump of

Uffing Down, whose lower slopes seemed to embrace Yondover like the arms of a mother around an infant on her lap, reassuring, protective and benign.

CHAPTER 7

Again, fingers were clasped on Kitty's wrist and a band fastened round her upper arm for her blood pressure to be read, arousing her from her deep, comatose sleep. With great difficulty, she opened her eyes to find a pretty, dark-haired girl with brown eyes, wearing a nurse's uniform, bending over her.

She felt a huge surge of disappointment. 'Oh, I thought I was at Yondover.'

'Yondover?' the nurse asked, smiling. 'Where's that?'

But Kitty's mind was too muzzy to formulate a reply.

'You must have been dreaming,' the nurse went on.

Dreaming? Oh, no! It had been too real to be a dream.

'If it was a nice dream why don't you go back to it? I shan't be disturbing you again for a while. Just close your eyes and remember where you were . . .'

Or perhaps this was the dream and the pretty little nurse was a figment of her imagination? Yes, that must be the case, for now the nurse was moving out of her vision, was going out of focus, had quite disappeared – and the ceiling of the hospital room was turning into an infinite blue expanse of sky, in which seagulls were wheeling and crying, and a lark was spilling out its jubilant song, a scarcely visible speck between earth and heaven . . .

They were lying on the close-cropped turf, the dog Rafe with his nose on his paws, and Catherine, her chin propped on her hands, her bare arms warm on the wiry, tufted grass, sweet with the scent of wild thyme, studded with scabious, yellow lady's slipper and big, purple thistles. Behind her, across several miles of rolling hills, where sheep grazed, rabbits scampered and butterflies danced, the gently undulating slopes patterned by occasional

87

small copses and dappled by the shadows of tiny white clouds scudding across the sun, was the sea – a distant, silvery shimmer.

Yesterday, the air had been clear and a thin sharp line on the horizon had seemed to mark the beginning of the French coast, but today it was as if the water merged into the sky and went on for ever in a blue haze.

Looking towards the north provided a sharply contrasting aspect. Where, in a steep escarpment, the South Downs ended, the Sussex Weald began: a rich patchwork of meadows and woods, rivers, railways and roads, farm-steads, villages and towns, stretching as far as the eye could see, across the Ashdown Forest to the misty hump of the North Downs and, beyond them, London.

Immediately under the lee of Uffing Down, where the hill's northern flank jutted out into the plain, lay the village of Kipwell. From her vantage point, Catherine had a clear view of the village street, lined with flintstone cottages. Children – minute figures, seen from this great distance – were playing on the small village green, around which stood the school, St Peter's Parish Church and the Vicarage, a red-brick Queen Anne building, stand-ing apart and aloof from the other houses.

Her father, in dog collar and surplice, his bald head glowing in the sun, was making his deliberate way across the churchyard, and in the Vicarage garden her mother, Prudence, dressed as always in muted pearl-grey, her face shielded by a straw hat, was giving orders to Polly, the housemaid, trim in white frilly cap and apron, as she hung out freshly laundered linen.

Beyond the village was Kipwell Grange, home of Sir Hector and Lady Maude Pugh, its entrance guarded by two unicorns rearing up on their hind legs. Soon after their arrival in Kipwell, the Pughs had invited them for drinks at the Grange. Lady Maude had studied her critically. 'Girl looks a bit peaky,' she had commented. 'You should get her a pony. This is marvellous country for riding – and hunting, of course.'

The stuffed stags' heads in the great hall had stared down on them from glassy eyes and Mrs Fellowes had replied timidly, 'Coming from London, Catherine has never learned to ride. In any case, I don't know that I should feel at all happy about her being out alone on horseback. She's only thirteen . . .'

Lady Maude had given an impatient, equine snort. 'I rode almost before I could walk. But for that matter, there's nothing wrong with walking. Not making the best of life, of course, but better with a dog. One of the sheepdogs at the Home Farm pupped at the beginning of the summer and we've still got one left. He's your daughter's if she'd like him.'

Later, back at the Vicarage, she had overheard her father telling her mother, 'It would have been most unwise to refuse Lady Maude's offer. She and Sir Hector are extremely influential in the neighbourhood. And I'd rather Catherine was out walking with a dog than mixing with the village yokels.'

Beyond the Grange lay the railway, where a train was snaking its way towards the station, perhaps the very same train that she and her parents had travelled on when they had moved here from London. It appeared tiny, the billow of steam from its funnel a mere wisp of cotton wool.

Catherine gave a deep sigh of contentment. This wasn't a dream. She wasn't going to wake up and find herself back in Finchley. Kipwell was her home now.

The train left the station again and, running parallel to the Downs, crossed the little River Kip to continue its journey towards Hastings, and she shifted position slightly to watch it until it disappeared from sight. Then she moved a bit more, so that her gaze followed the line of the Kip, meandering lazily under a hump-backed bridge and through a gap in the Downs towards its estuary, temporarily disappearing behind the thick sloping woods belonging to Yondover.

At this point, Yondover itself came into view, a tantalizing glimpse of roofs and chimneys above trees and high flintstone walls, and the drive – scarcely more than a cart track – leading away from the house in its sheltered dip, over the brow of the hill, to emerge in the village between the church and the Vicarage.

'Eccentric's the word to sum up Westrup Lambourne,' Lady Maude Pugh had stated that Sunday when she had given her Rafe. 'As a person, I'm fond enough of him, I suppose. And he has a good eye for a horse, I'll grant him that. But as a neighbour, I deplore him. He encourages every kind of varmint to flourish. I'll warrant there are more rabbits, foxes, badgers and pigeons at Yondover than there are in the whole of the rest of Sussex. He won't allow fishing in his stretch of the Kip, shooting in his woods or the hunt to cross his boundaries. For that matter, he even kicks up a shindig if he finds hikers on his land.'

'Can't say I blame him for that,' Sir Hector had interjected. 'Walkers are the farmer's greatest pest, treading down crops, leaving litter . . .'

'Westrup's no farmer,' Lady Maude snorted. 'He lets our sheep graze on his land, but that's simply in order to keep his grass down.'

'At least he doesn't charge us for the privilege,' Sir Hector pointed out.

'He doesn't need to. Westrup may be lacking in common sense, but not in money.'

The Vicar's eyes had lighted up. 'So he's a gentleman of means?'

'Quite considerable means,' Sir Hector replied drily. 'His father was the railway baron, Samuel Lambourne. He was a director of the London–Brighton South Coast Railway and largely influential in the building of the East Coast line between Lewes and Hastings. It's thanks to him that Kipwell has its own railway station.'

'Though I'd agree with Westrup there – whether the station is a bane or a blessing is a moot point,' Lady Maude remarked. 'But Westrup's certainly done nothing to increase the family fortunes. On the contrary, he must have squandered thousands on his fancy ideas for Yondover . . .'

'Is he married?' the Vicar had enquired.

'Was, for a short time. Rather a tragic story. His wife left him – she was a Scot, y'know – and took their baby daughter with her. The girl married quite well – a diplomat I think her husband was. But they both perished on the *Titanic*.'

The Vicar had clucked sympathetically.

'There's a grandson who's at Harrow,' Sir Hector had added. 'Lives with his grandmother. Comes to stay at Yondover sometimes during the school holidays. Nice enough looking boy – takes after Westrup in appearance – but a bit namby-pamby.'

Catherine was just going over this conversation again in her mind when Rafe espied the rabbit. A farm dog, he knew better than to chase sheep and cattle, but, as if to prove his early upbringing under the influence of Lady Maude, he possessed one great weakness: he merely had to catch sight of a rabbit for all his baser instincts to be aroused.

The rabbit bobbed across the grass and Rafe simply could not control himself. Catherine called to him to stop but he paid no attention, disappearing in hot pursuit down the steep hillside. She had no alternative but to follow him, her feet scarcely touching the springy turf, her arms outstretched, her hat dislodged and her hair flying out behind her.

The rabbit found refuge in a burrow, but girl and dog continued their precipitous dash until they burst through a little copse and found themselves on the edge of a meadow in the presence of an elderly man painting at an easel. He wore a floppy hat pulled down over his ears, a worn tweed jacket and baggy plus-fours, and had a short, white beard and deep-set brown eyes under bushy white eyebrows. He peered at them over a pair of gold-rimmed spectacles set halfway down a rather long nose.

Rafe bounded forward, his tail wagging and tongue hanging out. The man stroked him, then turned to Catherine, who was standing breathless and dishevelled, her cheeks flushed, her clothes awry. 'I was just thinking that I needed a central figure,' he said, quite as if they were old friends and this was not their first encounter. 'Go on, both of you, run through the field, just as you did coming down the hillside.'

Catherine hesitated, but Rafe, barking joyfully, charged into the long grass, and she somehow felt compelled to follow him.

'Stop there!' the man ordered. 'Now make the pup jump up to your hand.'

This they did several times, then he called, 'That's enough.'

Catherine caught Rafe up in her arms and returned to the artist. 'May I look at your picture?'

'If you're interested.'

She stared in perplexity at the crude daubs of paint on the canvas, the bold brown-green of the grass splashed with the vivid scarlet of poppies and yellow of tansy, the intense blue of the sky, the indistinct impressions of herself and Rafe. Then instinct made her move back and narrow her eyes and she realized that this was how the meadow had appeared to her at first glance as she had raced out of the copse, before any of the detail had impinged itself upon her consciousness.

'So what do you think?' he enquired.

'It's how the field looked when I came out of the trees, out of the darkness into the sunshine again.'

His surprise was evident. Then he gave a pleased laugh and added a few more brushstrokes, so that Rafe's black, plumy tail became more defined and her own shapeless, navy blue, cotton dress seemed to swirl above her black lisle stockings.

Rafe jumped down and wandered off, nose to the ground, on a wonderful journey of discovery, to investigate the scufflings and whisperings of the little creatures inhabiting the edge of the wood and the meadow.

Catherine watched the artist as he dabbed some white paint on the previously dull ochre of her hair, so that it suddenly shone like gold. After a while, he asked, 'Those trees in the background. What do you think? Do they need a bit more emphasis? Some more black?'

Semi-closing her eyes again, she looked at his palette with its tantalizing kaleidoscope of colours. 'Not black . . . ,' she replied hesitantly, 'but maybe brown and orange?'

'Ah, yes.' After another short silence, he asked, 'You like painting?'

'We're not allowed to paint like this at school. We have to do still lives and portraits, and they must look exactly like the subjects. Mine never do. I usually come bottom in the class.'

'I have the same problem, as you can see,' he laughed. 'But don't make the mistake of thinking that what I'm doing is any good. I love pictures, particularly those of the Impressionists. I even tried to earn my living as an artist for a while, until I realized that an ability to enjoy other people's work did not mean that one had talent oneself. Now I paint simply for my own pleasure.'

Catherine watched a white butterfly with orange tips to its wings settle on a stinging nettle, then said obstinately, 'I still like your painting.'

'Thank you.' They were both silent for a while, then he said, 'Are you new to these parts? I've only recently noticed you up on the hills.'

'We've just moved here. We used to live in London.'

'It's grand on Uffing Down, isn't it? As if you're on top of the world. I used to spend every free minute on the Downs when I was a boy.' His eyes glazed over. 'I remember my father once asking me what I thought about while I was up there and caning me when I said that I didn't really think about anything. Everything my father did had to have a purpose.'

'My father's rather like that, too.'

'He never understood how a boy could lie on his back for hours, just looking into the clouds. Do you ever do that – see mountains and islands and deserts in the sky? And buildings – fairy-tale castles and ancient ruins. For that matter, I still see people up there – ogres, cherubs, beautiful ladies in trailing dresses – even people I have known . . .' He paused for a moment, then quoted, ' "Qu'aimes-tu donc, extraordinaire étranger?"

' "J'aime les nuages . . . les nuages qui passent . . . là-bas . . . là-bas . . . les merveilleux nuages." Do you know Baudelaire?'

She shook her head.

'But you do speak French?'

'A little . . .'

He sighed. 'But your teachers are too busy ramming the subjunctive down your throat to allow you to read the works of the immortal poets. Did you understand those lines?'

'Oh, yes. You said, "What do you love, extraordinary stranger? – I love the clouds . . . the clouds which pass . . . over there . . . over there . . . the marvellous clouds." But it sounded much better in French.'

For the second time, she could tell by his expression that she had surprised him, but all he said was, 'Of course. French is the most elegant language in the world.'

He added a few more splashes of colour to his canvas, then asked, 'Are you fond of reading?'

'Mmm, but I always seem to be in trouble for reading when it's time to go to sleep or time to get up or when I'm supposed to be doing my homework.'

He nodded sympathetically. 'We seem to have quite a lot in common, you and I.' Then, squinting at the sun, he said, 'The light's changed too much to do any more today. Time to stop. You live in Kipwell? Then we may as well go back together along the drive.'

Since the only drive in the vicinity was the track between the village and Yondover, Catherine had to assume he meant that. 'Oh, no! Everyone knows Mr Lambourne doesn't like people walking across his land.'

'That's true. But in this case it wouldn't be trespassing. I am Westrup Lambourne.'

He was so different from the mental image she had conjured up of him that this possibility had simply not occurred to her. The blood rushed to her cheeks and she stammered, 'Oh, I didn't know – I'm sorry, Mr Lambourne.'

'Why are you sorry? Do people make me out to be such an ogre?'

She bit her lip.

'It doesn't matter. However, you could at least return the compliment and tell me who you are.'

'My name is Catherine Mary Fellowes, Mr Lambourne.'

'For God's sake, girl! You've been talking to me perfectly naturally. Why are you now suddenly calling me "Mr Lambourne" at every opportunity?' He stared at her over his spectacles, his eyes seeming to bore into her skull, as if he were trying to see what went on inside her head. Finally, he said, 'Your big, round eyes remind me of a kitten's. I'm going to call you Kitty. And since we're to be friends, you can call me West . . .'

'Catherine, are you awake?' The voice was strangely familiar, although it did not belong to Yondover. It seemed to come from a great distance, yet at the same time be very close. 'Catherine, can you hear me?'

Who was calling her Catherine? It was a female voice, but not that of her mother, the only woman persistently to have called her Catherine.

Fingers grasped her wrist. 'Mrs Pilgrim, can you hear me?'

Blearily, she opened her eyes and found herself lying in a dimly lit cubicle, with a pretty little nurse, whose face she vaguely remembered, placing a thermometer under her armpit. The girl smiled.

'That's better. And how are you feeling now?'

While she had been asleep she had felt fine, but now she was awake she felt dreadful. 'Where am I?' she asked.

'In Arundel Hospital.'

'Why? What's the matter with me?'

'You had a bad fall.'

A fall?

'Where did I fall?'

'I'm sorry, I don't know. I wasn't on duty when you were brought on to the ward.'

The nurse was looking at the watch pinned to her uniform. Next to it was a name badge, but the letters kept moving, so Kitty couldn't read what they said.

She intended to ask the girl's name, but instead she asked, 'What time is it?'

'Just gone five o'clock.' The nurse pursed her lips. 'Your temperature is rather high. I'll give you some pain-killers.' Gently, she lifted Kitty up on the pillows.

'What have I done?' she gasped, as a shaft of pain seared through her.

'You've been concussed and you've got some quite bad bruises.' She held the glass of water while Kitty swallowed the tablets. The simple exercise left her pouring with perspiration and utterly exhausted.

The curtains parted and another nurse entered, wheeling a trolley. 'I'm sorry to disturb you, Mrs Pilgrim, but we need to take another blood sample, so that Doctor can see the results of the test before he does his morning round,' she explained briskly, wiping the crook of Kitty's arm with a cold, damp swab. 'This won't hurt.'

Vaguely Kitty was aware of a needle prick in her arm. She closed her eyes. It was simply too much effort to keep them open.

'There, that's all done,' the nurse said, tucking the blanket back over her. 'Now you can go to sleep again.'

To sleep . . . Oh, yes, please. To dream again and be back at Yondover . . .

And where the nurses had been standing, there was West, perched up a ladder, cutting the dead heads off roses on the front wall of the old grey farmhouse.

It was the morning after their first encounter and Catherine was returning with her father, who had insisted upon satisfying himself that Westrup Lambourne was a suitable person for his daughter to associate with.

As they drew up in the trap, West descended from his ladder and strode across to them, wiping his hand on his trousers before extending it to the Vicar. 'Mr Fellowes, I assume? Good day and welcome to Yondover. Wasn't expecting you or I'd have been better prepared. My gardeners are excellent fellows, but they have no feeling for roses, so I insist upon looking after them myself. I'm sure you sympathize.'

'My daughter said you had invited her to Yondover again, after she so rudely intruded upon your privacy yesterday, Mr Lambourne. I felt it incumbent upon myself to ascertain that this was so.'

'Yes, indeed. She's a charming and most intelligent girl. A credit to your upbringing, Vicar.'

Her father nodded complacently, then looked around him curiously. 'A fine place you have here, if a little off the beaten track.'

'It suits my simple tastes.'

'I understand from Lady Maude Pugh that you are a keen gardener.'

West beamed. 'Aha! Do we share this interest in common? In that case, I'm sure you will admire my *Ipomoea rubrocaerulea*. A healthy specimen, would you not agree? I grew it myself from seed and it has now survived several winters.'

'Yes, er, very fine . . .'

'But an unattractive name for such a beautiful plant, don't you think?'

'Yes, er, quite so,' the Vicar mumbled.

'Such a pleasure to meet a fellow enthusiast,' West exclaimed. 'But what am I thinking of? Allow me to offer you some refreshment, while we continue our fascinating discussion. Some of Mrs Gurney's excellent rose-hip tea − or mint tea, perhaps?'

The Vicar paled. 'Most kind, Mr Lambourne, but I don't want to put you to any inconvenience.' He drew his watch from his waistcoat pocket. 'And unfortunately, er, my time is a little short. I have an appointment . . .'

'Oh dear, what a pity. But in that case, I mustn't hold you up.'

And her father had little alternative but to take his departure.

Catherine waited until the trap had disappeared out of sight, then asked, 'What is *Ipomoea*?'

'That,' West replied, pointing to a plant twining its way over the front porch, covered in a mass of huge, sky-blue trumpets. 'Gurney calls it convolvulus, but to me it can only be morning glory.'

'Morning glory.' She repeated the name slowly. 'Oh, that's the perfect name for it. Convolvulus sounds much too complicated, and *Ipomoea* sounds rather like an infectious disease.'

West laughed. 'It certainly had the effect of sending your father scurrying off in a hurry.'

Catherine found herself saying something she would never have dreamed of saying aloud before. 'Yes, he hates it when somebody talks to him about a subject he knows nothing about.'

'That must make conversation with him extremely limiting,' West commented with a wry smile. 'However, I don't think he'll disturb us again for a while. Now then, Kitty-Cat, back to gathering rosebuds. I take it you'd like to help?' He handed her a pair of clippers. 'By taking off the dead blooms, we are encouraging the rose to put all its strength into its flowers and not into producing hips. Be careful not to remove the leaves, for they enable a plant to produce its food.'

As a result of West's influence, gardening had always remained for her a mixture of poetry and practicality. Photosynthesis, as a biological process, was still as great a mystery to her as the workings of the internal combustion engine. She had never learned Latin appellations and always needed to look them up when ordering from catalogues. Species too exotic to possess a folk name she never even attempted to grow, sensing there could be no affinity between herself and so rarefied a plant.

Most people believed that all plants needed in order to flourish was food and water, but West had known that plants, like people, needed affection as well as attention to their everyday, practical needs.

She herself had been like a plant. And at Yondover she had developed from a pale, spindly weed into a flower — not into anything as exquisite as a rose, of course, more a humble pansy or poppy, but none the less cherished by those who cared for her, by West and Fanny and Gurney.

The Gurneys . . .

'Came to me as a stable lad did Gurney,' West had told her. 'All he could think of in those days was horses — and horses remain the greatest love of his life. Talk to him about cars and he'll reply in terms of horse power. Talk to him about gardening and he'll talk about horse manure. I've never known him so upset as when his son, Frederick, went to work on the railway.

'Fanny joined me a couple of years after Gurney. She was a pretty girl, but to judge by Gurney's reaction, you'd have thought she was a hellhag. Yet she succeeded in getting him to propose to her. Or maybe she proposed to him. Either way, they've been married over fifty years.'

From their first meeting, Catherine had called Fanny by her first name. But her husband was always Gurney. Nobody, apart from Fanny — not even West — called Zachariah by his Christian name. It was not an easy name to get the tongue around and Gurney was not the sort of man to be called by a pet name, any more than his son and grandson were. In the village Zachariah was known as old Gurney, Jethro as young Gurney and Frederick was simply the Station Master.

Although she had soon endeared herself to Fanny Gurney's motherly soul, she had found it much more difficult to penetrate Zachariah Gurney's tough old shell and she never really felt at ease with Jethro.

'They're unused to strangers,' West explained. 'They see Yondover and myself as their own personal property. Give them time, Kitty-Cat. Once they realize you're not a threat, you'll become friends.

'Jethro was badly injured on the Somme,' he had continued. 'He came back to England a gibbering wreck, physically and mentally. Seventeen years old and he looked more like seventy, poor fellow. As soon as he was released from hospital, we brought him up here to convalesce — and here he has stayed ever since. But to this day, the mere sound of a gun being fired is sufficient to plunge him back into a state of shock.'

Even more than he resented Catherine, Gurney resented Rafe. 'Never known a dog as spoiled as that un,' he would grumble. 'There be mice and rats and rabbits enough around for she to catch 'er own food, but no, she has to be fed best marrow bones. If Oi ever find 'er in among my vegetables, Oi'll have 'er guts for garters. Lady Maude only give you 'er because she was runt of litter and she 'ad no use for 'er on farm. Now my ol' Rover, she were a real dog – best ratter in 'ole of Sussex. Nineteen, she were, last spring, when she died.'

It took Catherine some time to realize that Gurney, Sussex born and bred, referred to all creatures – male and female – as 'she'.

Horses were to provide the key to Gurney's heart. Although Catherine would not admit it even to West, she shared her mother's nervousness of horses. Indeed, it was possible that her father was also afraid of them. Certainly he never rode and probably drove a trap only because he could not afford a motor car and pride forbade him to ride a bicycle – that was for the likes of Tom, Padden the Grocer's errand boy, and Jethro Gurney.

From a distance, horses were marvellous to look at but, close to, so tall and unpredictable in their movements. As for those big, yellow teeth . . .

There were three horses at Yondover – Conker, West's glossy chestnut mare, Pegasus, his grandson's black gelding, and Captain, the carriage horse. First thing each morning West would ride Conker over the Downs, sometimes taking Pegasus on a leading rein, but usually leaving him for Gurney to exercise.

West was dealing with some papers in his study, Jethro was in the orchard, Fanny in the kitchen, and Gurney – as Catherine thought – busy among his vegetables, when she went up to the paddock one afternoon, her pockets full of apples from the loft above the stables, determined to overcome her secret fear.

Leaning over the fence, she called to the horses and eventually Conker forsook the shade of the oak tree and ambled towards her. She held out the apple between finger and thumb.

'An' what mischief be you up to now?' Gurney's voice broke in on her and he snatched the apple from her hand. 'Doan't you know better than to give an 'orse an 'ole apple like that? Why, that could stick in old Conker's gorge and choke 'er to death.' Deftly, he broke the apple into quarters, then, placing one of them on the palm of his hand, held it out to the mare, who took it gently in her velvety lips.

When all four pieces of apple were gone, Conker looked consideringly at Catherine, then reached her head over the fence down towards her pocket. She backed away and Gurney said, 'So you've more than the one apple, 'ave you? She knows, you know. You can't fool 'er. Not our Conker. An' 'ere come the others. They're not wantin' to be left out, neither. Well, fair's fair, an' now you've seed 'ow it's done, you'd better be givin' them their treat, too.'

She split the apple as Gurney had done and, with a hand that trembled only slightly, held up a segment to Pegasus, then to Captain. Their breath was hot and moist on her skin, rather like Rafe's nose when he licked her.

'Always keep your 'and flat,' Gurney said and his voice was suddenly less rough. 'They doan't mean no 'arm, but sometimes they fergit theirselves. Mebbe as 'ow they thinks fingers is carrots or summat. Is that right, Conker, me ol' lovely?' He stroked the white star on Conker's forehead.

Catherine took a deep breath. 'Mr Gurney,' she asked, 'will you teach me to ride?'

From his great height, he stared down on her suspiciously. 'Teach you to roide?'

'I'd really like to learn.'

'Aye,' he said slowly, 'stands to reason as you would. But not on these horses, you doan't.'

She bit her lip.

Then Gurney continued, 'No, Miss Kitty, you grow a bit more, then we'll see about learnin' to roide.'

After that, his attitude towards her mellowed, so that she was soon even allowed to help him in his vegetable garden, picking beans, cropping autumn fruiting raspberries, lifting potatoes, carrots and turnips, plaiting the withered leaves of onions and hanging the ropes in the scullery. Under his tuition, she learned to prune back raspberry canes and currant bushes, to burn off the old straw over strawberries, to hoe and rake and mulch and spread manure and prepare the soil for new crops of winter spinach, spring cabbage, broccoli and radish.

Thus her first summer at Yondover passed, one perfect day merging into another. Her face, arms and legs became deeply tanned, the soles of her feet hard from walking barefoot, and she grew wise in country lore.

Not all her days were spent in the garden. Often, she and West and Rafe would take to the hills, walking for miles and miles and never encountering another human soul, except perhaps a shepherd. Over Firle Beacon and Mounts Harry and Caburn they would go; or across to High and Over, along the Cuckmere Valley to the sea, over the Seven Sisters – of which she counted eight – to Beachy Head, and home over Windover Hill, where the Long Man of Wilmington was carved into the hillside.

As they walked, West would tell her the old Sussex legends: tales of smugglers and witches and buried treasure – of the knight in golden armour buried under Mount Caburn and the Roman in a gold coffin beneath the Long Man; stories about the Devil, Old Scratch, as he was called in Sussex, who tried to drown the churches by digging the Dyke behind Brighton but mistaking an old lady's candle in a cottage window for the rising sun, abandoned his work before it was completed. 'Our own Uffing Down,' West told her, 'was formed from the earth Old Scratch removed from his dyke.'

Several mornings they spent trying to restore a dewpond, tamping down wet clay with their bare feet to catch and hold the early morning dew. Gurney said that dewponds were fed by rainwater, that dew evaporated in the sun. But West and Catherine walked the Downs when the sky was a river of crystal light and the grass beneath their feet a sea of diamond dew. They knew that those droplets needed only a container and there could be preserved a nectar fit for the gods.

She learned, too, the names of the downland flowers, and those which blossomed by the riverside, in wood and field. She found out about nuts and berries, those which were safe to eat and the animals which fed on them. She became familiar with different types of gull, hawk, crow and wader, as well as the more common hedgerow birds. She knew the heady excitement of spotting a rare large blue butterfly, of coming across a viper basking in the sun, and waiting upwind of a badger sett or fox earth in the evening, until mother and cubs cautiously emerged to hunt and play, secure from the barbaric crimson-coated huntsmen and baying hounds West so deplored.

She came also to know the old legends attached to plants and beasts. So, for instance, she never picked stitchwort, in case she was kidnapped by fairies, but would always pluck the first primrose, because she might come upon a castle with an iron-studded door which, if she touched it with the primrose, would fly open to reveal a pile of primroses, under which would lie buried treasure – hers, so long as she replaced the flowers.

And fern seed she would try to catch as it fell to carry in her pocket, in the hope that it might render her invisible.

West put never-to-be-forgotten rhymes in her head so that she could soon forecast the weather as accurately as her father, but far more poetically. He would see the barometer falling and predict, with gloomy satisfaction, 'We're in for a chilly spell.' And more accurately than Gurney, who would say, 'Swallows be flying low — that means rain.'

She would see wispy clouds in the sky and remember:

> Trace in the sky the painter's brush,
> Then winds around you soon will rush.

Even when the portents were bad, the pretty words lent an edge of magic, making the wind or the rain or the storm ahead seem something to be looked forward to, not a dreary meteorological fact.

It was on Uffing Down that she learned to love thunderstorms, late one afternoon, when she and West were returning from the sea. Black clouds were rolling up and the first raindrops pattering down.

'When I was a little boy, my nanny told me that rain was the tears of angels, crying for all the sad people on earth,' West said. Then over the Weald lightning flashed, followed by a rumble of thunder. 'But no,' he continued, and there was a note of excitement in his voice, which took her by surprise, 'the angels have taken shelter today. We are about to witness a drama on a bigger scale. The celestial giants are about to do battle.

'Imagine the clouds as platforms, Kitty-Cat, on which the giants are preparing their weapons — blunderbusses, cannon, mammoth water pistols and immense buckets of water to hurl at each other. They are battling for — but how can we mere mortals know what they are fighting for?'

The sky grew dark as night, to be illuminated by a vivid fork of lightning, immediately followed by a crash of thunder. Heavy drops of rain turned into a torrential downpour. West lifted his face to the heavens and held out his arms, as if in supplication, and Catherine followed suit, feeling the water stream down her hair and face, soaking into her clothes, moulding them to her body.

Then West said, his voice scarcely a whisper against the din of the storm, 'Now we have made our obeisance, we had better be going home.'

A bedraggled Rafe raced ahead as, hand in hand, they returned down the slippery chalk track, while the battle continued to rage above them.

Then came the day when her mother started packing her trunk in readiness for her to go away to her new boarding school in Hove – St Margaret's School for the Daughters of Clergymen and Missionaries.

'It won't be long till Christmas and then you'll be back again,' Fanny Gurney consoled her.

'Oi've been thinking about that dog of your'n, Miss Kitty,' Gurney said. 'Moi feelin' is as 'ow Vicar be'n't too fond of animals. 'Appen young Rafe won't be welcome at the Vicarage when you're away. Moight be best if she stayed 'ere. Moi woife misses ol' Rover something bad. Rafe 'ud be company for 'er.'

On her last afternoon, she and West went to the river and sat on the bank. Rafe waited for a few moments, his tongue hanging out, then, when they did not continue their walk, he set off, tail wagging and nose to the grass, on one of his endlessly satisfying journeys of discovery.

Dragonflies skimmed over the scarcely moving surface of the water, at the edge of which grew bulrushes and tall yellow water irises. The air was heady with the scent of meadowsweet.

Suddenly, West exclaimed, 'Kitty, look!' There was a flash of turquoise and gold and a kingfisher swooped across the river to perch momentarily on an overhanging branch of willow. Then a vole plopped into the water and the brilliantly coloured bird was gone again.

'I don't want to go to St Margaret's,' Catherine burst out. 'I wouldn't mind school if I could stay in Kipwell, but I don't want to go away.'

'And I wish to God you could stay!' West exclaimed. 'What you have learned this summer is of far more importance than the useless knowledge they will cram into you at school. Boarding schools are like prisons: they confine the body and restrain the mind. As for schoolteachers, all they do is confuse and contaminate, moulding their pupils to their own ideals, suppressing their innate spiritual self. They will try to chain you to convention, Kitty, fetter your imagination, blinker your vision and stifle your spontaneity . . .'

He turned to her with almost painful intensity. 'I have tried to do for you what I wanted to do for my own daughter. I have wanted you to glimpse a vision of the world beyond that made by men, to be free and wild, to see, as Wordsworth described, "into the life of things". I have wanted you to know what he called "the hour of splendour in the grass, of glory in the flower".

'Please, Kitty, whatever else you do, don't let them destroy your inner spirit. Don't let them rob you of your natural self.'

Kitty was abruptly awoken by a plump, officious-looking nurse – very different from the pretty girl who had attended to her during the night. The new nurse studied the chart at the foot of her bed, felt her pulse, took her temperature and checked her blood pressure, then added some notes to her chart.

'Am I all right?' Kitty asked.

But the nurse merely gave one of those infuriatingly superior smiles employed by the medical profession to indicate that patients cannot be entrusted with details about their own health, and continued to the next bed.

After that, the hospital day commenced in earnest. First came breakfast, for which she had no appetite, although she felt extremely thirsty and would gladly have had another cup of tea, had it been offered to her. Then the curtains were pulled round her bed and another nurse examined her ribs and a wound she apparently had on her shoulder. It hurt when she removed the dressing, but Kitty tried hard not to show it.

'That's good, there doesn't appear to be any infection,' the nurse said approvingly.

'Will I be able to go home today?' Kitty asked.

'I'm sorry, dear, Doctor is the only person who can decide that.'

After that, she took her turn with her fellow patients to go to the bathroom, although, to her great dismay, her legs were so weak and her head so dizzy that she needed a nurse to support her on the short journey.

Upon her return, however, she was told she could sit in her chair while the cleaners set to work with mops and vacuum cleaners. Just this small effort had tired her out. She sank back against the pillows in the chair.

The woman in the next bed glanced at her sympathetically. 'Had a fall, have you, dear?'

Kitty nodded.

'Nasty things, falls, particularly when you're our age. Really shake you up. Lucky you didn't break your back. That's what happened to me. I was bed-ridden for months. Never been the same since. That was six years ago and I've been in and out of hospital ten times since then.'

Kitty knew they were heading for the type of conversation guaranteed to make her run a mile when she was fighting fit but, confined to her chair, there was no escape.

Kitty's eyelids drooped and she made no effort to raise them.

'. . . The doctor said he'd never seen one like it. The nurse told me afterwards it was as big as a tennis ball . . .'

She had been dreaming during the night, such a lovely dream, one of those sweet, warm dreams which seem so real it is hard to believe they are only a dream, the kind of dream she used to have when she was young, when she would wake impatient for the day ahead – days when elusive sunbeams had for ever lit up flowers, when hope was strong and at the rainbow's end had surely lain a crock of gold.

'. . . thirty stitches. You should see the scar. Of course, I'd had a hysterectomy years before . . .'

In her dream, she had been at Yondover – with West.

People said that, when you grew old, childhood memories became clearer than those of more recent years, in much the same way as childhood summers seem to have been perpetually sunny. There must have been times during those long ago days with West when the skies above Yondover were grey and clouded, but in her memory, apart from the occasional thunderstorm to clear the air – those spectacular battles of the celestial giants – Yondover had basked from dawn to dusk in a golden sheen of sunlight.

Or was it simply that first impressions were the most lasting? Was that why West's words remained so indelibly etched upon her mind? There was nothing particularly original in his thoughts. Indeed, considering he had then been about the same age as she was now, his observations seemed romantic and almost incredibly naive.

West had been a dreamer. He had never completed anything. For years, the painting of herself and Rafe in the meadow had stood, unfinished, on his easel. The dewpond, she was sure, still leaked. West had dabbled with art and gardening, as he had dabbled with marriage. As he had dabbled with life . . .

But his life had not been an empty dream, nor the grave its only goal. Right to the end he had been filled with youthful energy and enthusiasm, far too involved in life to worry about death. He, of all men, had acted within the living present and, after his departure, left behind him footprints on the sands of time.

His influence upon her had been immense. She had, of course, been at a most impressionable age. But it had been West, far more than her parents or schoolteachers, who was responsible for the person she would become: West to whom she owed her deep, abiding affinity with nature; West who had first stirred her soul with music; West who had opened wide the windows of the world and set her spirit free; West who had imbued her with the courage to be independent; West who had given her the gift of love.

Had he known how grateful she was for everything he had given her? Had he known how much she loved him? Or had the realization of all he had done for her come too late for her to tell him? Had she been so immersed in herself that she had been oblivious to the fact that, despite his youthfulness of mind, he was an old man and death was, even then, hovering in the wings?

Yet how could she have been otherwise? She had been young and had taken him, as she had the Gurneys, for granted. Only when circumstances had separated her from her own son had she fully understood how greatly she must have helped fill the still aching gap left in West's life by the departure of his wife and child. Only when she was older had Fanny confessed how she had once longed in vain for a daughter, and Gurney admitted how deeply she had touched his heart with her enthusiasm for the things dearest to his own. As for Jethro – but no, she had never won Jethro's trust, although for a short while it had seemed as if she might.

Certainly, at the time, it had never occurred to her that she might be as important to these four people as they were to her. She had merely sensed that they brought a hitherto unknown warmth to her life, that they were the family she would have liked to have. She had no way of knowing that, until her arrival, they had been almost as lonely as she was. It had never even crossed her mind that old people would be lonely.

For that matter, she had had no idea that she was herself lonely. An only child, whose parents discouraged her from friendships with other children, she had always been used to making do with her own company . . .

*   *   *

105

It was Christmas – the most wonderful Christmas of her life. Her first term at St Margaret's was over and she was racing up the steep path and across the wild, windswept, winter grasslands to Yondover, and there was Rafe bounding towards her, and behind him West, and beyond them dear, familiar Yondover, blue smoke spiralling up from its chimneys. And West was reaching out his arms to her, folding them around her, holding her to him and murmuring, 'Kitty-Cat! Oh, Kitty-Cat.'

And now West was taking her out to the stables and hanging on one of the stable doors was a horseshoe-shaped garland of holly, ivy and Christmas roses. And inside the stable, when she unlatched the top door, was the prettiest pony she had ever beheld, a pale, warm brown in colour, with a cream mane and forelock.

West reached in his pocket for a carrot, which he gave to her, and the pony moved forward eagerly, its breath warm and moist, as it took the carrot from her hand.

'What's its name?' she asked.

And West replied, 'That's for you to decide.'

'You mean . . . ?'

'Yes, he's yours. He's my Christmas gift to you.'

For a few moments, she simply stood there, stunned. Then she threw her arms round his neck and kissed him. 'Oh, West, thank you!'

'Don't just thank me, thank Gurney. He and Lady Maude joined forces to find him.'

'That's enough a that,' Gurney grumbled, as she kissed him as well. 'First thing you've got to do is learn to groom she – and muck 'er out.'

'The first thing she must do is learn to ride,' West laughed, opening the lower half of the stable door. 'Come in and give him a hug, too. I'm sure he'd like that, wouldn't you, old chap?'

She put her arms over the pony's thick mane and nuzzled her face against his. 'I'm going to call him Honey,' she announced.

Then she was indoors, in the sitting room, where a log fire was roaring and candles were flickering on a Christmas tree glittering with tinsel, and Fanny was handing her a bulky package. 'This is a little gift from me.'

She undid the ribbon and tore off the paper to reveal a black, velvet riding jacket and light beige breeches.'

'Go and try them on and put us all out of our misery,' West ordered.

'Fanny's been driving us mad ever since she started making them, wondering whether they're the right size.'

It was as she was changing that Catherine realized that whilst she had sewn her mother a pinafore and knitted her father a scarf, she had nothing for West and the Gurneys. The jacket and breeches were a perfect fit, but her face was long when she returned to the sitting room wearing them.

However, Fanny was too concerned with the results of her handiwork to notice her expression. 'There, I said you didn't have to worry,' West told her.

Fanny let out a satisfied sigh. 'It's the first time I've ever made britches for a girl. I weren't sure . . .'

Before Catherine could stop it, a tear trickled down her cheek, followed by another.

'Here, what's the matter?' West demanded.

Catherine bit her lip and shook her head.

'Come on, out with it, Kitty-Cat. Don't you like your presents?'

Misery welled up in her. 'Of course I do. They're wonderful. But I haven't anything to give you.'

'Bless you, child, don't upset yourself, we didn't expect anything,' Fanny told her. 'We're glad to have you back here again at Yondover. We've missed you while you were away at school. Isn't that so, Zachariah?'

Gurney gave the fire a vicious poke and cleared his throat.

West reached out his hand. 'Fanny's right, Kitty-Cat,' he said gruffly. 'You bring us joy – and that is the best gift of all.'

CHAPTER 8

The sun was streaming into the room and the clock beside the bed read seven when Tabitha uncurled herself from where she had been sleeping in the small of Pippa's back, stretched and positioned herself on her chest where, gazing myopically into her face, she purred so loudly that she woke her up. For a few moments, Pippa lay yawning, then, recalling the events of the previous day, leaped out of bed and flew downstairs to ring the hospital.

The ward sister seemed reassuringly surprised to receive her call. Mrs Pilgrim, she said in the tone of one who had more urgent matters on her mind, had passed a comfortable night, although she was naturally still a big groggy as a result of her concussion. Of course, Pippa was welcome to come and see her during visiting hours. If she could bring a change of nightclothes for her grandmother, toothbrush, toothpaste and so on, that would be appreciated.

Light-headed with relief, Pippa filled the kettle. Now she realized that in the back of her mind had been lurking the fear that Kitty might have suffered brain damage, be paralysed or, worst of all, not even have survived the night.

With a reproachful 'miaow', Tabitha clawed at the carpet, plainly indicating it was time for her breakfast. Almost like an oblation to the gods, Pippa opened the most expensive can of cat food she could find and heaped Tabitha's dish high with biscuits.

It was during her own breakfast – a mug of coffee and a couple of slices of toast – that Pippa was struck by the quietness of Kitty's existence compared to the chaos usually reigning at this hour in Dulwich, with Dad snarling, Mum snapping, herself rushing round losing things, and all three of them getting under each other's feet and on each other's nerves.

There was the contrast, too, of Kitty's old-fashioned kitchen to the extremely expensive fitted one which was her mother's pride and joy in Dulwich. Nothing here was modern, except the gas stove and even that was old-fashioned in style. The washing machine was a twin-tub. There was no freezer and the fridge not only contained very little but was decidedly antiquated. The radio, too, was a museum piece – 1950s Bakelite. And when Pippa, out of curiosity, turned on the portable television set in the living room, the picture was black and white. Who needed a television, though, when the birds provided a far more entertaining spectacle at the birdtable – and when there was Kitty's delightful, half-finished watercolour painting and other pictures by her on the walls?

But why was everything so out of date? Was it because her grandmother could not afford labour-saving modern appliances – or because she didn't like them? *She won't have an electric bell, you know . . .*

Well, these were all questions to which she would learn the answer in due course. In the meantime, how was she going to spend the morning? Remembering the sparse contents of Kitty's fridge, the ward sister's request and her own need for basic toiletries and a change of clothing, Pippa decided that shopping should take first priority.

Just as she was leaving the cottage, Colonel Wakehurst emerged from his front door to enquire after Kitty and she repeated what she had been told by the hospital.

He nodded in satisfaction. 'And how about yourself, young lady? Did you spend a comfortable night?'

'Yes, thank you.'

'Is there anything you need?'

'No, I'm fine. I'm just going shopping for a few odds and ends.'

'Mrs Wakehurst likes to go into Worthing or Chichester for her shopping. Arundel doesn't have such a wide selection of shops – although what we do have are very good,' Colonel Wakehurst added loyally.

'I'm sure I shall find what I'm looking for.'

'Well, don't hesitate to call on us if there's anything you think we can do. As I told you last night, we're very fond of Mrs Pilgrim.'

'I'm going to visit her this afternoon. I'll tell her you've been asking after her.'

'If she has to stay in for any length of time, we'll visit her ourselves.

But we don't want to tire her out. I know what it's like when you're in hospital.'

Pippa smiled. Colonel Wakehurst was undoubtedly a well-meaning man, but she was thankful he was not her neighbour. She glanced pointedly at her watch. 'I'm sorry, but I ought to be getting along.'

'Grummph, yes, of course. Didn't mean to hold you up.'

'It's very nice of you to be concerned.'

Colonel Wakehurst's mention of Worthing reminded Pippa of Edith Spencer. She didn't want to go too far from the cottage this morning in case Kitty suffered a relapse and she was needed urgently at the hospital, but maybe tomorrow . . .

Kitty was dreaming when yet another voice broke in on her. 'Wake up, Mrs Pilgrim, it's lunchtime.' Oh, why did they have to keep waking her? Each time she fell asleep they woke her up again. She seemed to have spent most of the morning being wheeled from one part of the hospital to another and having needles jabbed into her and people poking and prodding at her and feeding her pills and talking about her over her head and asking her questions she could not answer.

Why could they not leave her in her dream? She was so tired and confused. But when she was asleep and back with West at Yondover, everything was straightforward and nothing hurt.

She forced open her eyes to find herself confronted with a plate of shepherd's pie and cabbage, swimming in gravy.

From the next bed her neighbour was complaining loudly. 'What's this, nurse? I didn't order an omelette.'

Grimacing as her bruised ribs and bandaged shoulder reminded her yet again of their existence, Kitty righted herself in her chair and returned to the present world. 'I don't eat meat,' she said. 'If you'd like to swop with me . . .'

'Don't eat meat? No wonder you're so tired. Well, thank you, that's more like it. Though I'd rather have a nice juicy fillet steak. Mind you, with the price of meat nowadays, that's a rare treat. My boys love steak – and you should see them. Both well over six foot and broad with it. And their sons are the same. Peter, he's my eldest grandson, is six foot four and I'd swear he's still growing . . .'

Kitty consoled herself with the thought that stories about the woman's grandsons were better than the gory details of her medical history. And soon, when she had finished the rubbery omelette, she would be able to escape again, back to the world of her dreams.

'Mrs Pilgrim, wake up. You have a visitor.'

A visitor . . . Not a nurse or a doctor, but a visitor.

'Hello, Kitty, how are you feeling?'

She opened her eyes and seemed to be confronted by her own self, fifty years ago.

The young woman smiled. 'Do you remember me? I'm Pippa.'

Pippa . . . ? Where did Pippa fit into everything? Pippa was Sebastian's daughter. Adam had written about her in his letters.

Pippa sat down on the chair beside the bed and, taking her hands in hers, said gently, 'Do you remember? I came to see you. I was with you when you fell.'

Kitty shook her head. 'I can't remember anything.'

'We were in your sitting room.'

Kitty screwed up her eyes in concentration. 'My sitting room?'

'Yes, your sitting room at Rose Cottage.'

'At Rose Cottage?' Yes, of course, Rose Cottage. She lived at Rose Cottage now. Not at Yondover.

'We'd just had tea.'

'When I woke up this morning, I was sure I'd been on horseback.'

'On horseback? No, nothing so energetic. You must have been dreaming.'

'I suppose so. Yet it seemed so real . . . So tell me exactly what happened.'

'Well, I came to see you. You made me some lunch and we talked about all sorts of things. Then we were in your living room and you went to get your glasses from the kitchen and you tripped on the step from the hall.'

Why could she not remember that Pippa had come to see her? Such a momentous event and quite forgotten . . .

'I simply can't remember a thing. Isn't that ridiculous?'

'Don't worry about it. The main thing is that you're all right.'

'I think I am, although I do feel rather bruised and battered.'

'Anyway, in case you've been worrying, everything's fine at home.

111

Tabitha spent the night on my bed and woke me at the crack of dawn this morning.'

'Tabitha!' Kitty sat upright with shock. 'Oh, how dreadful, I'd forgotten all about her!' Then she grimaced. 'Ouch! I shouldn't have done that. Whenever I move it seems to hurt in another place.'

'Do you want me to call the nurse?'

'No, all she'll do is give me another pill and I'm already so full of pills that I'm sure I'd rattle if I was shaken, particularly after all the blood they've taken.'

'The doctor explained to me that they have to do tests to find out what caused you to fall. They're worried in case you fainted or blacked out.'

'Yes, he said the same to me. He kept asking me all sorts of questions . . . Oh, I feel so stupid. But tell me about Tabitha.'

'Well, as I said, she spent the night on my bed. In fact, I've come to the conclusion that she's outrageously spoiled and decided that if I'm reincarnated, I'm going to come back as your cat.'

'Ever since Rafe I've treated my pets more like human beings than animals. But they've always seemed like family to me.'

'Who was Rafe?' Pippa asked.

'Why, don't you remember? He was my first dog.' Then Kitty gave an exasperated little snort. 'But of course you wouldn't know. Oh, I am so confused today. Now, you were telling me about Tabitha . . .'

'Just to say she's absolutely fine. I found her food OK and gave her some fresh milk. So don't worry about her. Now, look, I went shopping this morning and bought you some bits and pieces – a new toothbrush, a comb, some eau de cologne wipes – I thought they would be refreshing – and Sister said to bring a nightie. I don't know if this is the right one?'

'Please explain. Are you staying at Rose Cottage?'

'Yes, I hope you don't mind. But I didn't want to leave you.'

'Of course I don't mind. I just don't understand . . .' Kitty leaned back against the pillows and closed her eyes again. She felt as though she was juggling three separate existences, of which Yondover seemed the most real but apparently had no connection at all with her present life. No, hospital was real. Rose Cottage was real. And Pippa was real . . .

The woman in the next bed asked Pippa, 'Is she your nan? Yes, I thought so. You look like her. Nasty things, falls, especially when you get old. Really shake you up. Lucky for her she's so skinny. When you've put

112

on a bit of weight, like I have, you fall heavier. I broke my back. They told me I'd never walk again. But I proved them wrong.'

After ten minutes listening to every gruesome detail of the woman's accident and ensuing operations, Pippa was thankful to spot an orderly trundling in with a tea trolley.

Kitty woke again, just as the tea lady reached them. 'Ah, tea, that's good. It's so hot in here. Now, tell me, please, how you come to be in Arundel.'

Pippa hesitated. Then she said, 'I went to see Uncle Adam and Aunt Eve in Puddles. Aunt Eve gave me your address.'

'Oh, I see.'

'You do know who Adam and Eve are?'

'Yes, I know who everybody is. I just can't remember anything about my accident. I don't remember you coming to Rose Cottage.'

'Well, what happened was that, a few weeks ago, Dad went to an auction in Worthing and bought some old books on photography as part of a lot. Because I'm a photographer – well, a photographer's assistant – he gave them to me. Among them was a photograph album.'

Kitty felt that goosefleshy sensation Fanny Gurney used to describe as 'somebody walking over my grave' – an unaccountable presentiment of danger. 'A photograph album?'

'I was about to show it to you yesterday afternoon, when you fell. It contains some amazing pictures, which I assumed to begin with had been taken by the woman whose book it was – Edith Spencer.'

Somebody was treading very heavily over her grave. Edith Spencer . . .

'However – this is the most amazing part – the photographer was actually called Gawaine Devere. He used to have a studio in Chelsea and he lived – or lives – in a house called Yondover. Naturally, I couldn't help wondering if he might be a relation.'

It felt to Kitty as if, for a few seconds, her heart stopped beating. Small wonder if, after a shock like that, she had fainted. Even now, although the ward was almost intolerably warm, she could feel herself breaking out in a cold, clammy sweat. She imagined herself going down the little step from the hall into the living room and suddenly hearing those names. If she had not actually passed out, then certainly the shock would have been sufficient to make her forget where she was going.

With an unsteady hand, she reached for her teacup and took a few sips.

'Dad said he had never heard of him, so I thought I would ask Adam and Eve. Then Eve told me about you . . .'

For the first time in her life, Kitty experienced what it was like to be totally bereft of speech. All she could do was mutely shake her head.

Fortunately, Pippa took her negative gesture to mean that Gawaine Devere's name signified nothing to her. 'I didn't really expect him to be. And it doesn't really matter. Not now I've met you. That's far more important.' She stopped and gazed anxiously at her grandmother. 'Kitty, are you all right? You look very pale suddenly.'

No, she was not all right. But she must not alert Pippa's suspicions any more than she had already. Above all else, Pippa must not realize that Gawaine Devere and Yondover meant anything more to her than names and pictures in a photograph album casually acquired in a Worthing auction room.

From somewhere she found the strength to speak. 'I'm fine. Just very, very tired. My head . . . It's all so confusing.'

'Oh, I'm sorry.' Pippa was full of contrition. 'I shouldn't have told you.'

'I'm glad you did. But I don't think I can take in any more at the moment. Can we talk about this matter another time?'

'Yes, of course.'

Then it suddenly occurred to her that Pippa did not live in Arundel. 'But don't feel you have to stay on here. If you have to go back to London, I shall quite understand. I'll be perfectly all right, I promise you.'

'There's no problem. I'm on holiday all this week. I start a new job next Monday.'

'And what day is it today?'

'Only Tuesday.'

Tuesday of what month and what year? But it didn't matter . . .

Pippa bit her lip. 'Would you like me to go now, so that you can sleep?'

'It might be best, if you don't mind.'

'I'll come and see you again tomorrow.'

'That would be very nice.'

'Is there anything else you'd like me to bring in? Something to read?'

'Yes, a book – and my reading glasses.'

Pippa leaned over and kissed her. 'Please take care and get better quickly.'

'Mmm. I'll certainly do my best . . .'

*   *   *

After Pippa had gone, Kitty closed her eyes, but sleep evaded her. She understood now why, ever since she had been in hospital, her thoughts had centred so much on Yondover. Her subconscious mind had latched on to what Pippa had been telling her and, like a tongue playing with a loose tooth, kept returning to it, to West, the Gurneys, her parents . . .

But never Gawaine Devere. No, each time her thoughts had verged on him, her mind had shied away again, baulking at the prospect of that which it could neither accept nor resolve, fleeing the dark, gaping chasms opening up before it.

Oh, if Edith Spencer's album had to be found, why did it have to be found by, of all people, Sebastian? And why was Pippa so interested in Gawaine Devere?

But, of course, Pippa's name was Devere and she was a photographer. That was the link. Had Gawaine Devere been anyone other than a photographer, Edith Spencer's album would have been left to gather dust on a shelf, until the pictures in it had faded and its pages disintegrated with age. Instead, by a cruel stroke of fate, her own life had come round in a full circle, and the things she had hoped to leave behind were catching up with her again . . .

Photographs. Photographs, framed and hanging on a wall. Black and white prints, soft images, which gave the same impression of shimmering light as West's paintings.

'This is Mr Westrup and this one here is of Zachariah and Jethro in the garden, though it's a bit fuzzy,' Fanny's voice was saying. 'He's very keen on photography, is Master Giles. Mr Westrup gave him a camera one Christmas and they had a rare time, taking pictures and making prints in the darkroom they set up alongside Mr Westrup's studio in the old dairy.

'We're always pleased to see Master Giles at Yondover,' Fanny went on. 'He usually spends the school holidays with his grandmother, Mrs McDonnell, in Edinburgh. His parents went down in the *Titanic*, you know. Poor Master Giles, orphaned at the age of five. But for all her sins, his grandmother is a big-hearted woman and she lets Mr Westrup see Master Giles . . .'

Then the scene changed and she was no longer at Yondover but in the Vicarage kitchen, drinking her bedtime milk. It was Christmas, possibly the same Christmas that West had given her Honey – but no, it must have

115

been the following one, for she was no longer a novice on horseback, but able to canter and gallop and jump hedges and ditches.

Cook said, 'I hear Master Giles is back at Yondover for the holiday. That will please Mr Lambourne. He's right fond of that lad.'

'I saw him being driven up from the station,' Polly sighed. 'He's grown ever so handsome. I wish I had a young man who looked like him.'

'You count yourself lucky to have a young man at all. Bob Ireland's a very good catch for someone in your position.'

Polly pulled a face. 'But he's hardly romantic. Imagine what it would be like to be kissed by Master Giles. Ooh, it makes me feel all shivery just to think of it.'

'You mind your talk and get on with the dishes,' Cook scolded sharply. 'And you, Miss Catherine, it's high time you were in bed.'

As Catherine left the kitchen, she heard Cook demanding, 'What were you thinking of, putting ideas like that in the child's head?'

She lingered in the passage to hear Polly's response. 'I wasn't much older than her when I first started walking out with Bob,' she retorted defensively.

'But you'd already left school and were working for your living. Miss Catherine's not a forward little hussy like you.'

Then the sitting-room door opened, a bell jangled in the kitchen and Catherine was forced to move away.

But her thoughts, as she lay in bed that evening, were not following the same lines as Polly's. Far from considering Giles in any romantic aspect, she saw him as a threat. Ever since Sir Hector Pugh had spoken of West's grandson – 'Nice enough looking boy . . . but a bit namby-pamby' – she had wondered about him.

Even in his absence, reminders of Giles were everywhere at Yondover. His photographs on the walls of his bedroom. Pegasus, his horse. A tree house West had built for him when he was a child. A swing in the orchard.

She had grown to feel that she belonged at Yondover, that she was as much a part of it as West and the Gurneys, but now she found herself doubting whether they would still want her if Giles were there.

She was in this same state of apprehension when she went to Yondover the following morning. There was a hoar frost and the sun was hanging low in the sky, a huge orb casting an orange glow over the white grass. The house came into sight and no West was waiting to meet her, no Rafe racing towards her. Yes, it was as she had feared – now Giles was back, she was unwanted.

Despondently, she went back along the track, scrambled over a hedge and clambered up Uffing Down, going to the far side of the hill, where she sat down on a fallen fence post, out of sight of Yondover.

Then she heard a horse's whinny, a dog's bark, and West's voice exclaiming, 'Kitty! What are you doing up here?' Rafe leaped on top of her, pushing her to the ground, his tail wagging in frenzied excitement, smothering her face and arms with rapturous kisses. She heard West laughing. 'Rafe, you daft ha'p'orth, stop it!'

She thrust the dog away and sat up, only to find Honey's velvety nose nuzzling her face and blocking her vision.

'I wish we had the camera with us!' West laughed. He took Catherine's hand and pulled her to her feet. 'Come on, you disreputable-looking urchin, you'll catch your death of cold. There's someone waiting to meet you.'

Only then did she realize the significance of that 'we'. Slowly, she brushed the hair out of her eyes and looked past West to where Giles was perched, high above her, on Pegasus's back. Tall and slight in build, he had straight, dark hair, deep-set brown eyes, an aquiline nose and a delicate mouth.

He nodded towards her and something about the way he looked at her – the rather aloof tilt of his head, the slight frown creasing his brow – made her feel very small, childish and inelegant. Despite what Polly had said, she had not expected him to be quite so grown-up and good-looking.

'We saw you coming over the hill,' West went on. 'Then you disappeared.'

'When you weren't waiting, I thought . . .' Her voice tailed off.

He gave her shoulder a quick squeeze and for a brief moment she felt close to him, not just physically but in spirit. 'We were saddling up in the paddock so that we could ride out to meet you,' he explained. 'We've been at sixes and sevens ever since Giles arrived yesterday. He sent a telegram, but it must have gone astray.'

She moved away to where Honey was now standing, finding reassurance in the familiar feel of the pony's shaggy mane under her fingers. Giles had turned his head and was staring into the distance, in the direction of the sea.

117

West glanced from one to the other of them, then swung himself up on to Conker's back. 'Well,' he announced briskly, 'let's get moving.'

They set off, but as her pony cantered and she tried to keep up with the two men on their trotting horses, she felt increasingly like a child, trailing along behind its elders. They were talking about Oxford, where Giles was going in the autumn. 'G–grandmother wants me to read P–politics, Ph–philosophy and Economics,' Giles was saying. 'She'd l–like me to be a d–diplomat like F–father.'

Their conversation seemed to be taking place on another plane, way above her head in every sense. Then they, too, broke into a canter and she was left behind.

On the next ridge they stopped and waited for her to catch up. 'I'm sorry, Kitty,' West said, 'I forgot Honey only has short legs.'

'It doesn't matter,' she replied, in a stiff little voice, trying to conceal her hurt.

After that, they matched their pace to hers, but their conversation lagged and she was certain that Giles resented her being there and blamed her for holding them back, while West seemed almost oblivious to her presence.

When they reached the cliffs, disturbing a colony of gulls which took off, crying plaintively, over the silver sea, Giles came to a halt. For a long time he gazed out across the water, then, in a curiously soft voice, he said, 'It is wonderful to b–be back again, West. I've m–missed all this so much.'

His use of West's pet name, which she had believed to be hers alone, and the fact that he had ignored her, made her feel all the more excluded.

Honey ambled over to a clump of long grass, put his head down and grazed. When Catherine looked round, she saw West and Giles, with Rafe in attendance, moving off slowly in the opposite direction. For a few moments she waited, undecided what to do, then she turned Honey round and set off back towards Yondover. Neither West nor Giles seemed to notice her departure. Once or twice, she glanced over her shoulder and saw they were following at a gentle walk. She urged Honey into a gallop.

While she was unsaddling in the paddock, Gurney trundled over with a wheelbarrow of hay. He reached in his pocket for an apple for the pony and commented, 'Seen you flying along like a bat out of hell.'

Tears stung at her eyes and she brushed them away with her glove, hoping he would assume they were caused by the freezing air.

Gurney emptied his barrow of its load then, squinting into the light, looked towards Uffing Down, where the two men had just topped the brow of the hill. Then he said, 'Jethro be sawing logs and Fanny wants spuds for dinner. I could do with an 'and diggin' she up.'

Not trusting herself to speak, she followed him in the direction of the vegetable garden.

She was just emerging into the back courtyard, having delivered a basket of freshly dug potatoes to Fanny, when she was confronted by West. She gave him what was meant to be a nonchalant smile, but West was not deceived. Taking her hand, he led her into his studio. 'Come on, Kitty-Cat, spit it out.' She stared mutely at the floor, but he put his hand under her chin, tipping her face up, so that she was forced to look at him. To her dismay, although she tried to fight them back, tears again rose to her eyes.

He sighed. 'It's Giles, isn't it?'

'Yes . . . No . . .' Then she burst out, 'Now he's here, you don't want me.'

'Kitty-Cat, remember, this is his first day. He would have been disappointed if I hadn't paid him any attention.'

But did that have to be to the exclusion of her?

West read her mind. 'Don't be jealous of Giles, Kitty, because there's absolutely no reason to be. On the contrary, if you feel anything it should be pity. I know he gives the impression of being arrogant, but he isn't at all. That's what psychoanalysts call a defence mechanism. You must have noticed his stammer when he talks? Well, that comes on when he's feeling nervous.

'You don't know how lucky you are, Kitty-Cat. You will never experience the full horrors of the British public school system. Oh, I know you resent your lack of freedom at St Margaret's and that if you're naughty you get lines or you're even put in detention. But that's nothing to the purgatory Giles has to go through. Boys are much crueller than girls and schoolmasters much more vindictive than their female counterparts. As an example, because Giles's first two initials are G.G., he's always been nicknamed "Horsey". Even the masters call him that. Do you know the song "Horsey keep your tail up!"? That's how the sports master taunts him, if he misses the ball playing rugger. And, unfortunately, Giles is not very good at sport.'

She blew her nose. 'Why doesn't he just kick them and live up to his name? Well, maybe not the master, but the other boys?'

West could not contain a smile. 'Giles doesn't have your spirit. He isn't a fighter, Kitty-Cat. I wasn't either at his age. In fact, to this day, I still hate upsetting other people.'

'So do I. I'd much rather be friends than enemies.'

'I know. And that's why I hope you'll be generous in your attitude towards Giles and make allowances for his behaviour. Please, Kitty – you will try and be friends with him?'

Slowly, she nodded. 'I'll try,' she promised.

For West's sake, she tried. But it was not easy, although Giles's passion for photography helped pass what would otherwise have been very long days, for the weather turned dismally rainy and he went down with a bad cold, which lasted most of his stay.

West's former attic playroom was set up as a makeshift studio and, although Giles continued virtually to ignore her as a person, Catherine found herself in demand as a model, being photographed in a variety of strange costumes or even draped around with curtains, adopting uncomfortable, classical poses, while he and West discussed composition and exposures. But no matter how hard she tried to follow his stuttered directions, the sessions usually ended in him falling into a brooding silence, while she felt increasingly awkward and tongue-tied in his presence.

It was with a feeling of relief that she would hear Jethro being instructed to pump water into the darkroom tank, so that they could wash their prints. They would be busy in the darkroom for some time. Then she would escape to canter over the Downs on Honey, or walk through the woods to the river with Rafe. But when she returned, it was to hear Giles complaining, 'K-K-Kitty's no good as a model. Nobody ever looked less like a n-n-naiad,' and West saying consolingly, 'But I like the lighting, Giles, and the effect of printing through glass is very interesting. Perhaps if you increased the exposure a little more . . .'

Then came the afternoon when rain drove in sheets across the Downs, the clouds so low and dark it was almost like night. With no light by which to take photographs, they went to the music room, where Fanny had pulled the curtains and lit a fire. West sat at the piano and, rather to Catherine's surprise, instead of taking an armchair, Giles settled near her on the hearthrug with Rafe at their feet, his knees hunched in his arms.

And as the room filled with the sublime music of Schubert, Scriabin, Chopin and Liszt, so the squally rain buffeting the windows seemed to recede and, with it, the tensions between herself and Giles were dispelled.

After the last, lingering notes of a Schubert sonata had faded away, Giles murmured, without a hint of a stammer, '*Music, when soft voices die, Vibrates in the memory . . .*'

Catherine glanced at him and, in the firelight, his features appeared softened, a smile curving his lips and in his eyes a tranquil, faraway glow.

'*And so thy thoughts, when thou art gone*,' West continued, in the same dreamy tone, '*Love itself shall slumber on.*'

He rose from the piano stool and came to sit on the sofa behind them, resting his hands on both their shoulders, drawing them to him. Catherine leaned her head against his knee and his fingers stroked her hair. And suddenly she knew, with absolute certainty, that he was telling her that she and Giles were equally precious to him, and she had the strong sense of his love, Schubert's music and Shelley's words binding the three of them together into futurity.

CHAPTER 9

It was a cold, cheerless evening when Pippa arrived back at Rose Cottage. She lit the fire in the living room then, feeling unusually hungry, went into the kitchen, fed Tabitha, made herself a pot of tea and spread some bread with Mrs Wakehurst's strawberry jam. She carried her little meal on a tray into the living room and placed it on one of Kitty's occasional tables. Then she drew an armchair up to the fire, which was already starting to cast some heat. If I'm not careful, I'll become quite like an old lady myself, she thought, as Tabitha jumped on her lap.

After tea, she set about choosing some books to take Kitty in hospital. In Kitty's situation, what would she feel like reading? Nothing too intellectual or demanding. And not a thriller or a detective story. No, something sweet and warm and romantic . . .

Her eyes roamed along the titles on Kitty's bookshelves. *Anna Karenina*? No, that was much too heavy and had an unhappy ending. *Wuthering Heights*? No, the print was too small, Kitty would find it hard to read. What about *Frenchman's Creek*? Or, better still, *Rebecca*. Right, that was one. Now, another author. There was a whole set of books by Francis Brett Young, a writer unfamiliar to her but obviously a favourite with Kitty. She selected *This Little World* because the title appealed to her.

Then her glance fell upon *Down the Garden Path* by Beverley Nicholls. That seemed a safe bet for a keen gardener. And one more. What about E. M. Forster? *A Room with a View*? No, one of her own favourites, *Howard's End*.

She put the books on the coatstand in the hall, so that she wouldn't forget to take them with her next day, then embarked upon the even more pleasurable task of finding a book for herself. The huge selection spoiled her for choice. She was in the throes of deciding between *Rogue*

Herries and *Frenchman's Creek* when her eyes lit on a set of slim, matching volumes, each bearing the title *The Enchanted . . .*

With a delighted little smile, she pulled out *The Enchanted Mountain*. The *Enchanted* books by Katherine Fountain had been among her favourite reading when she was a child. But it was years since she had last seen that distinctive cover with its pen and ink drawing of a snow-capped mountain, delicately tinted in watercolours. Presumably, once her parents considered her to have outgrown them, they had thrown them out or given them away.

She carried her tea tray out to the kitchen, washed up, then returned to the living room and prepared to indulge herself in a luxurious bout of nostalgia.

Once upon a time, there was a little boy called Roman, who lived with his Mummy and Daddy in a house built out of logs, halfway up a mountainside. The house stood all alone in a big meadow, which was full of golden buttercups in the summer and white with snow in the winter.

Roman had his own bedroom in this house, a loft room with a pointed ceiling, right under the steep roof, and his bed was beside the window, so that when he went to sleep at night, the moon shone on him, and when he woke up in the morning, there was the sunlight pouring in. If Roman looked out of his window, he could see right down to the village of Sonntag in the valley below and, in the other direction, up to the top of the Greiskopf.

The Greiskopf was aptly named. 'Greis' means old man and 'kopf' means head – and in the mountain at which Roman gazed every day it was easy to see the features of a venerable old man. Its rocky summit was rounded and snow-covered, like locks of white hair. Then came a steep cliff, like a forehead, with snow-covered ridges, like eyebrows, underneath which were hollows, like eyes. An outcrop of boulder formed the nose, another snowy ledge the moustache, and a glacier the old man's flowing white beard.

Pippa turned the page to another of those delightful drawings, this one showing an alpine chalet, with a little boy looking up at the clearly recognizable Greiskopf.

The first thing Roman did, when he got up, was to say good morning to the Old Man in the mountain. Occasionally, however, he would wake to find the Old Man had disappeared from view. His Daddy explained that this was because the Old Man was very tired and had pulled the bedclothes over his head, but Roman was not convinced by this. He believed the Old Man went away sometimes on secret journeys.

One day, when he awoke to find that even the cows, with their soft brown eyes and jangling bells, could no longer be seen on the meadow, Roman slipped out of bed, pulled on his clothes, padded very quietly out of the house and set off to find out where the Old Man went to.

Here there was a picture of a bare-footed small boy in leather shorts, with braces decorated with flowers, wearing a Tyrolean hat and carrying an alpenstock, walking up a stony path into a swirling mist. Engrossed, Pippa turned to the next page.

First Roman had to pass through the forest, where squirrels scampered and shy little deer gazed curiously as he passed, then the track he was following opened on to the bare mountainside. Still he could see little more than a few yards ahead, but he was not frightened or worried about losing his way, because he had often been up here with his parents. However, he did begin to feel hungry and was glad there were plenty of berries for him to eat and streams to drink from to quench his thirst.

On and on he clambered, until finally he reached the top of a ridge and suddenly – looming majestically above him, bathed in sunshine – there was the Greiskopf. Never before in his life had Roman experienced anything so wonderful. At his feet were the fluffy, pink tops of clouds. Of the forest, his home and the village in the valley, he could see no sign. He had entered into another world.

'Good morning, Old Man!' he called joyfully, and, to his amazement, for this had never happened before, the Old Man winked . . .

Arundel had long been asleep when Pippa, with a deep feeling of contentment and regret that she had come to the end, put down the last of the *Enchanted* books. She had savoured every word and taken in every detail of the illustrations. Even though she was no longer a child, she still found the stories absolutely charming and the pictures spell-bindingly beautiful. No wonder they had captured her imagination when she was a little girl! No wonder that she had identified with Roman going up into that enchanted world above the clouds, meeting the magic snowman in the enchanted village, gliding on a deer-drawn sledge across the enchanted lake, meeting the Wizard in the enchanted forest and being taken by the Sunflower Fairy through the enchanted garden . . .

With a final glance at the cover illustration of *The Enchanted Garden*, she put the books back on the shelf. There was something about the style of Katherine Fountain's drawings, something so familiar. But it was probably simply because they had been engrained in her consciousness since childhood . . .

'Hello, Mrs Pilgrim. And how are you feeling tonight?' The pretty little nurse was back on duty again and studying her chart.

'Much better, thank you.'

'Good. You're looking much brighter, I must say. Well, let's see what's happening to your temperature.'

Kitty opened her mouth for the thermometer and peered at the nurse's name badge but the lights in the ward were too dim to make out the letters. When the thermometer was removed, she asked, 'What is your name?'

'Sonia Willis.'

'Sonia . . . How extraordinary. That's the name of my best friend. You even look a bit like her. But I expect your name is spelled with an "i", whereas hers is spelled with a "j" – Sonja.'

'That's unusual.'

'It's the German spelling. She was born in Germany, although she lives in New York now.'

'So you can't see each other very often.'

'Unfortunately not. But we keep in touch by letter.'

'I'm afraid your temperature's still a bit high.'

'I'm not altogether surprised. I've had quite an exhausting day.'

Nurse Willis smiled. 'Hospitals are very tiring places. Well, I shouldn't have to disturb you again for a while. Go back to sleep now.'

A sweet little thing, the same age as Pippa probably. Both of them so kind and well-meaning . . .

Sonia. Sonja . . .

It was Sonja who had told her that one needed only nine friends throughout one's life – those people one would choose to stand around one's death-bed . . .

They had been on the mountainside above Vevey, looking across Lake Geneva to Mont Blanc, one glorious afternoon in late autumn, when the mountains were at their most lovely, their peaks capped with snow, their slopes mauve with heather and rock-roses. Nearby, a stream cascaded towards the valley below, from where came the melodious tinkling of cowbells. On the lake, a steamer hooted as it pulled in to the pier. A weasel darted out of the trees and stopped just a few feet from the two girls, standing on its hind legs, its nose twitching. Above, a hawk hung motionless in the sky.

Catherine had listed the names of her friends. 'West, Fanny, Gurney, Jethro and, of course, you, Sonja. With Rafe and Honey, that makes seven.'

Sonja had turned to her, joy lighting up those dark, sloe-shaped eyes in the delicately moulded face, framed by sleek, long, black hair, tied back loosely in a ribbon. Seizing her hand fervently, she had said, 'Oh, thank you for including me, Kitty. But you are fortunate. Although I have very many acquaintances, I have only four friends – my parents, Felix . . . and now you.'

Yes, Sonja had been the first friend she had ever had of her own age. At St Margaret's, she had made no bosom pals. Not that she had been unhappy at school, apart from missing Yondover, and West's dire apprehensions about its effects upon her had proved unfounded. Because she was naturally obedient, she was seldom in trouble, and whilst never top of the class, neither was she bottom. Her performance in sports was unspectacular and she was included in neither school nor house teams. Although she got on well with her fellow pupils and was reasonably well liked in return, nobody had asked her home with them for the holidays, nor had she invited anyone back to Kipwell.

Her friendship with Sonja, however, begun sixty years ago at Madame Valentin's *Internat* in Vevey, lasted to this day. It was a friendship between opposites: herself, a shy, gauche tomboy; Sonja, the only daughter of fifth-generation German Jewish bankers, a refined, sophisticated city girl. A friendship which had not only surmounted the barriers of nationality and religion, but stood the test of time, continuing despite both their marriages and surviving immeasurably long periods of separation.

What an enlightened woman Madame Valentin had been, viewing he girls entrusted to her to be 'finished' as considerably more than potential husband-fodder, determined to deliver them back into the world not merely instructed in etiquette, deportment, grooming and the art of polite conversation, but able to type and take down shorthand, fluent in languages other than their mother tongues, sensitive to cultures different from their own – in short, as cultivated and integrated young Europeans.

She had recognized the individuality of each of her pupils, seeking to enhance their basic attributes and develop their existing talents. In Catherine's case, she did not try to crush her artless spontaneity, but guided it so that it became part of her charm, encouraging her natural gift with words, her feeling for art and music, so that when Catherine left the *Internat* at the end of two years, she was fluent in French and German and spoke passable Italian, had painted some watercolour landscapes which were considered good enough to be exhibited in the local art gallery and could play the piano sufficiently well to give pleasure to others as well as herself.

Even West could not help but approve Madame Valentin's vision, and although he and Catherine saw less of each other while she was in Vevey than at any other time, he never gave her to feel that he resented her absence, as had been the case while she was at St Margaret's. Even when she compared Uffing Down disparagingly to the towering alpine peaks with which she had fallen in love, he had not been hurt, but smiled with tolerant understanding.

Neither had he, as she had feared, resented her friendship with Sonja. But, of course, she had been full then of childish insecurities, too young to know that jealousy and possessiveness were characteristics of the emotionally immature. She had not perceived the wisdom which was already West's, that it is the lot of every human being to have and to hold, and in time to let go. That hard lesson had come later – if indeed she had yet fully learned it . . .

Nor had West uttered any criticism when she had chosen to spend an entire summer holiday with Sonja in Berlin and returned home full of wonder at the Liebermanns' superbly appointed and luxuriously furnished villa, with its inner courtyard, countless salons and amazing gallery hung with costly tapestries, old masters and carvings; the intimate *thés*, intellectual *soirées* and elegant *dîners* she had attended, mixing with the cream of Berlin society; the avant-garde art exhibitions, theatre and opera productions and concerts she had been to; the bohemian artists and poets she had encountered in pavement cafés; and the week she had spent at the Liebermanns' magnificent country home, on a lakeside, deep in the forests of Pomerania.

West had recognized Berlin as a vital part of her education, trusting her to be neither overwhelmed nor corrupted by the experience.

She still had the diary she had kept while she was in Berlin, in the little attaché case under her bed at Rose Cottage, with the other most precious souvenirs of her life. At the time it had seemed important because it recorded the first occasion she had seen Leo. Only later had she realized it documented a way of life which had disappeared for ever, even before Berlin itself was devastated by Allied bombs and Russian tanks during the Second World War and Pomerania shut off behind the Iron Curtain.

With hindsight, however, the most astonishing thing was that her father, with his fear and hatred of foreigners, should have sent her abroad to finishing school in the first place, let alone allowed her friendship with Sonja to develop. But he had wanted her to acquire the necessary social graces to attract a wealthy, well-born husband; Madame Valentin's *Internat* had been highly recommended by the headmistress of St Margaret's; and neutral Switzerland, a favourite holiday destination for the British, must have seemed safe enough. It had probably never even occurred to him that her room-mate would be anyone other than a Protestant English girl.

Which had upset him most about Sonja – that she was German or that she was Jewish? Although the 1914–18 war had then been over some eight years, the Reverend Thurston Fellowes had neither forgotten it nor forgiven the 'war-mongering Huns' for starting it. And by 'Huns', as Kitty had later realized to her cost, he meant all German-speaking peoples, not least the Austrians who had been the first to declare war, after the Austrian Archduke Franz Ferdinand was assassinated in Sarajevo.

Never mind that the Vicar himself had ignored Kitchener's call to arms, deeming God's need of his services to be greater than his country's. Never mind that Sonja's father, being a Jew and therefore regarded in Germany as a second class citizen, was not considered worthy of joining the élite forces of the Kaiser's Army, even had he so desired. The Vicar, being British, had God and Right on his side. Herr Liebermann, being German and Jewish, had consigned his soul to the Devil before he was even born.

Sonja, although of a different sex and a younger generation, had been damned on both counts, too.

When, the summer following her own visit to Berlin, Sonja had come to stay with her in Kipwell, the Vicar had, quite deliberately, stigmatized her in front of his entire congregation, basing his sermon on that verse from St Matthew which went, *Except ye be converted, and become as little children, ye shall not enter the kingdom of heaven.*

Catherine had been mortified. Not once during her visit to Berlin had the subject of religion been raised. The Liebermanns had not questioned her beliefs and certainly had made no attempt to convert her to their own. Sonja had asked politely if she would like to go to church, but the Liebermanns themselves had not attended synagogue nor observed any orthodox practices.

After the service, Catherine had let fly in an angry tirade, the first time she had ever openly opposed her father. When she had finished, absolute silence had reigned, then her father had stalked, white-faced, from the room, slamming the door behind him. Laying her napkin on the table, her mother had apprehensively followed him.

Catherine's hands had trembled as she turned to Sonja. 'I'm sorry,' she said, speaking in German to emphasize her words. 'I'm sorry for the offence he's caused you.'

Sonja had shaken her head. 'I wish you hadn't spoken to him like that. It's his job to bring people to the Christian faith.'

Darling Sonja, so generous, so forgiving, so quick to see the other person's point of view. And perhaps there was justice in the world after all, for her friend had survived Hitler's barbarism, whereas her father had fallen victim to a Luftwaffe bomb.

In order that Sonja's visit should not be ruined, she had apologized to her father, after which he had treated Sonja with stiff civility. But following Sonja's return to Berlin, such a generous donation had arrived from the Liebermann Bank towards the fund for a new village hall that, in typically hypocritical manner, the Vicar had found it possible to overcome all his prejudices, racial and religious. Yes, at the final count, greed had been the dominating impulse in her father's life.

And mine, Kitty wondered, as she tried to move her complaining body into a slightly more comfortable position on the unyielding hospital mattress, what was my guiding principle?

But that was simple. It was love, of course. Love had governed her thoughts and ruled her heart for as long as she could remember, even when her experience of it was limited to houses, dogs, horses, hills and mountains and, of course, that very deep, special feeling towards West . . .

'Who needs an alarm clock with you around?' Pippa grumbled, as Tabitha repeated her performance of the previous morning. But she wasn't really cross. She felt rather touched by the relationship developing between the cat and herself.

Again, the first thing she did was to ring the hospital and this time the ward sister seemed very surprised indeed to hear from her. Apart from still running a slight temperature and feeling rather stiff, Mrs Pilgrim continued, she assured Pippa, to make excellent progress.

Finally convinced that Kitty was off the danger list, Pippa decided to pick up the trail of Gawaine Devere and spend the morning in Worthing.

West Parade proved easy to find, for it formed part of the seafront, and Chanctonbury Lodge was a big, modernish block of flats, each with its own glassed-in balcony. Finding a parking space was more difficult, for the promenade was lined with cars, many of them occupied by elderly people reading newspapers or asleep. Why drive to the sea, Pippa wondered, and not get out of the car and enjoy it?

Eventually, she parked in a side street, took the bag containing the photograph album and Gawaine Devere's letter from the boot and walked back. Overhead, gulls wheeled and cried, and from the beach drifted the pungent but not unpleasant salt smell of seaweed.

Outside Chanctonbury Lodge, a board announced: 'Retirement flats with resident warden'. A bent old lady, wearing carpet slippers, was shuffling down the path between the immaculately striped lawns with the aid of a walking frame. Pippa smiled and murmured, 'Good morning,' but the old lady continued on her laborious way, apparently unaware of her presence.

What if she was Miss Spencer, Pippa thought, in sudden horror. How on earth could she explain her mission to someone like that?

Resolutely, she went through the revolving door and approached the grey-haired woman sitting behind the desk in the foyer. 'I'm trying to find a Miss Edith Spencer,' Pippa explained.

'Miss Spencer?' The woman lowered her voice. 'I'm sorry, my dear, Miss Spencer passed away earlier this year.'

'Oh, I'm sorry, too.'

'You're not a relative by any chance? Oh, for a moment I thought . . . It always seems so tragic to me when people get old and none of their family . . .'

'I'm a photographer,' Pippa explained. 'A few months ago, my father bought some items at an auction in Worthing and among them were some photographic books which belonged to Miss Spencer. There was a letter in one of them with this address, from which it appears that she knew a photographer called Gawaine Devere. I was wondering if she ever mentioned him?'

'Gawaine Devere? That's an unusual name. I'd remember that.' The lift door opened and another old lady emerged, this one with blue-rinsed hair and leaning on a cane. 'Good morning, Mrs Fortescue,' the woman behind the desk called in a loud voice. 'Going out for a breath of sea air?'

Mrs Fortescue merely glared at them both.

'Deaf as a post and refuses to wear her hearing aid,' the woman sighed, when she had gone.

'Did Miss Spencer live here long?' Pippa asked.

'Let me see. She was eighty-five when she died, so I suppose she must have been here about fifteen years. But she was a very reserved lady, kept herself to herself. She had her own table in the dining room – she didn't even play whist. But just a moment, what am I thinking of? The person who may know something about the photographer you mentioned is Mr Kingsley, Miss Spencer's solicitor. His office is in Liverpool Gardens, just behind Bentall's.'

'Thank you, I'll try him. I'm sorry to have troubled you.'

Pippa made her way out into the welcoming sunshine. How, she wondered, could Miss Spencer have borne to live fifteen years at Chanctonbury Lodge?

Mr Kingsley turned out to be a rather jovial, elderly man, who, conveniently, was able to see her without an appointment. 'The weather is fine, so nobody wants to make a will,' he chuckled. 'When it snows, they're queuing at my door! So, Miss Devere, how can I help you?'

She repeated her story and showed him the photograph album and letter.

'Ah, and you're wondering if Gawaine Devere may be a long-lost relation.'

'Even if we're not related, I'd like to find out more about him. I think his pictures are wonderful.'

'You do surprise me! I'd have thought his work would be considered very old-fashioned in this day and age.'

'You know of him then?'

'Certainly, although I've never met him. My late client, Miss Spencer, used to be his – now let me see, what is the term? – yes, his retoucher – back in the days before the war, when he had a London studio.'

'So that's why she kept these prints. They were her work as much as his!'

'I suppose so. I'm sure she'd be pleased they have found a good home.'

'Do you know if Gawaine Devere is still alive?'

'He is as far as I'm aware, although he stopped working as a photographer years ago. Must be getting on a bit – eighty, if he's a day.'

'You haven't any idea where he lives? The letter only says "Yondover".'

'Yes, I assume he's still there. Are you familiar with Sussex?'

'Not really. My grandmother lives in Arundel, but . . .'

'I assume you've already told her about your little quest and she knows of no family connection?'

Pippa explained how Kitty's fall had prevented her from pursuing her enquiries.

Mr Kingsley clucked sympathetically. 'Dear, dear, the problems of getting old. Now, if my memory serves me right, Gawaine Devere's place is the other side of Lewes, near a little village called – sleepy-sounding name – yes, that's it, Kipwell. Let me have another look at that letter. "I am sure you will be glad to hear that I have had no further trouble with the Authorities." Hmm, that's right, it's coming back to me now. The house is set in a lot of land and there was some problem or other with planning permission – can't remember any details, just that there was a dickens of a row which even made the national press. But that was years ago, probably before you were even born.'

'There are some pictures of a house in the album. Do you think they are of Yondover?'

'I wouldn't recognize it if I saw it. My knowledge of Gawaine Devere is limited to the little I learned from Miss Spencer.'

'They apparently kept in touch, even though they no longer worked together, so presumably they were good friends?'

'Ah, I think I see which way your mind is working. Well, if you're wondering whether there was any sort of romantic attachment between Miss Spencer and Gawaine Devere, I think you're barking up the wrong tree.'

'Do you know who B is?'

'I'm sorry, I don't. Again, Miss Spencer must have known. It's a pity you weren't able to meet her. She would have enjoyed talking to you about her work. Ah well, time's wingèd chariot . . .' He reached under his jacket and pulled out a pocket watch on a gold chain. 'Talking of which, it's nearly time for my lunch.'

He stood up and reached out his hand. 'I've enjoyed meeting you, Miss Devere. I hope your grandmother's soon up and about again. You may even find that your investigation will be therapeutic and help take her mind off her own troubles. Old people like thinking back to the old days.'

'Kitty, how are you feeling today?' Pippa perched herself on the edge of the bed, swinging her jeans-clad legs.

'I feel fine,' Kitty assured her from the bedside chair.

'You do look much better actually. And your bruises?'

'I don't think they hurt nearly so much as they did.'

'Has anyone given you any idea when you can come home?'

'No, the nurse said . . .' Was it really only this morning? 'Let me see, what did she say? Oh, yes, that I have to wait for the doctor to see me again.'

'Well, in the meantime I've brought your glasses and some books. I hope that one of them will suit your mood.'

'I'm sure you'll have chosen well. So what have you been doing with yourself since yesterday? I do hope you haven't been too bored. Arundel is hardly the most exciting place on earth.'

'I think it's a rather nice town. But in fact I went to Worthing this morning.'

'Worthing?'

'Yes, do you remember yesterday I was telling you about the photograph album Dad bought as part of a lot?'

Kitty's heart seemed to miss a beat. She nodded.

'Well, I had Miss Spencer's address – she was the woman whose name was in the front of the album – so I drove to Worthing in the hope of seeing her. But at the home where she used to live, they told me she died earlier in the year. However, the warden was able to give me her solicitor's address, so I went and saw him. Apparently, Gawaine Devere *is* still alive. And, even more of a coincidence, he lives in Sussex – near a village called Kipwell . . .'

Somehow Kitty managed to get through the rest of Pippa's visit, although she took in little of what Pippa said as she babbled on cheerfully about Tabitha, the birdtable, the Wakehursts, people in cars on the seafront . . .

Then supper arrived and Pippa took her departure. Kitty had no appetite. She pushed the food around on her plate, then gave up on it.

An orderly came to take away her tray. 'Don't you like your supper, dear?'

'I'm sorry, I'm not hungry.'

Moments later, Sister bustled up. 'Now then, Mrs Pilgrim, what's the matter? I understand you haven't eaten anything. Are you in pain?'

In pain? No, not the sort of pain Sister meant. Not the pain of a gashed shoulder and bruised ribs.

'Let's get you back into bed.' The curtains were pulled. Sister gently helped her from her chair and settled her against the pillows. Then the rigmarole of pulse, temperature and blood pressure. 'Hmm, your temperature's still up and your blood pressure's a bit high. We'd better keep an eye on you. Ah, I see your granddaughter's brought you some books. Do you like reading?'

'Yes, very much.'

'Then maybe you'd like to read for a while? Let's see what she's brought along. *This Little World* by Francis Brett Young. I don't know that. *Howard's End* by E. M. Forster. Didn't he write *Passage to India*? That was a lovely film. *Down the Garden Path* by Beverley Nicholls. Are you keen on gardening? Oh, and *Rebecca*! Now why don't you read that?'

Pippa's selection was perspicacious. Yet in the wake of the bombshell she had let fall, how ironic her choice.

She took *Rebecca* and opened it at the first page, to that perhaps most famous of first lines: *Last night I dreamt I went to Manderley again . . .* Her eyes skimmed the familiar words, the description of a beloved house in ruins and a garden returned to nature. She turned the pages. *I am glad it cannot happen twice, the fever of first love . . .*

Sister pulled back the curtains. 'I'll come and look at you again in a little while. If you want anything, just ring.'

The nurses were all so kind. Everyone was so kind . . .

Kitty let *Rebecca* fall on her lap and closed her eyes.

'You place too much importance upon love,' Sonja had once said. It must have been at the time when Sonja had become engaged to Felix, for they had been talking about marriage. Yes, that was it, Sonja had been telling her that she ought to marry Adam.

Felix Arendt had been the son of one of Herr Liebermann's banker colleagues, but Sonja had denied that it was a marriage of convenience, assuring Kitty that Felix was the only man with whom she wanted to share the rest of her life.

'Passion is not the criterion on which to base the rest of your life, Kitty,' she had insisted. 'Affection, trust, respect, companionship – these qualities are far more important in a marriage than romantic love. You read too much poetry and too many novels. The heroes of whom you dream – Count Vronsky, Heathcliff – such men do not make good husbands. If you persist in your foolish fancies, you will create a great unhappiness for yourself.'

And Sonja and Felix's marriage had worked out well – as Adam's had. Doubtless they had experienced their ups and downs, but their marriages had lasted – both couples had celebrated golden anniversaries. But whilst remaining married to the same person for half a century represented a feat of endurance, was it not a similarly overrated achievement to attaining extreme old age? Longevity in itself had little to commend it. What was important was not the length of one's days, but the quality of one's living.

No, at the final count, she was not sorry that she had followed her heart

135

and not her head, even though Sonja would claim that her worst fore-bodings had been justified. For love, as she had known it, had proved to be ephemeral, a dream and maybe an illusion . . .

CHAPTER 10

She had fallen in love with Giles. How could she fail to? He was West's grandson, bone of his bones, flesh of his flesh. He had West's features – the same eyes, nose and mouth. Like West, he was artistic and he possessed West's sensitivity of soul. Yes, that above all. For what Sir Hector described as being 'namby-pamby', she recognized as an extreme delicacy of feeling.

Never mind that he remained as apparently uninterested in her as he had been on their first meeting. Never mind that during subsequent visits to Yondover he never said anything to her beyond common politeness, such as thanking her when she passed the salt. Adam – when he came to stay, after Giles met him at Oxford – joshed and teased her, yes, and West took pains to include her in their conversations. But Giles ignored her.

No, never mind that he did not love her. That, she was convinced, would come later, when she was older, less gauche and awkward, and the four-year age gap between them no longer seemed so wide. In her mind's eye, she saw them wandering along rain-washed paths through dawn-shone trees, and, on the top of Uffing Down, gazing in silent communion across the yellow-lit hills to the silver rim of the sea. Then, in a cataclysmic explosion of feeling, transporting them both beyond and above the everyday world, so that they soared *from earth to ecstasies unwist*, their love would be revealed to him.

That was the dream which sustained her through her last year at St Margaret's, as she underwent the painful confusion of adolescence, developing physically and changing mentally, still happiest when she was making bonfires with Gurney, climbing trees and riding Honey bareback round the paddock, yet desperately wanting to be regarded as a young woman.

That was the dream which inspired her during her two years at finishing school in Vevey, so that when she returned to Kipwell, it was as an ugly duckling transformed into a swan.

That was the dream which led her to compose those poems in the attaché case under her bed at Rose Cottage, poems which nobody except Sonja had ever seen. No, not even West – and certainly not Giles – had read those poems, for they described, even more than her diaries, her most intimate thoughts.

No wonder Sonja had been apprehensive on her behalf. For Sonja, although of the same age, possessed a wisdom beyond her years. She could see that Catherine was so young and inexperienced – but so ripe for love – that she was intoxicated with the sheer notion of love, seizing impulsive hold of it and moulding it into the substance of her dreams, without ever once considering that the man she loved might be nothing but a figment of her imagination.

Yet even Sonja, when she met Giles, could find nothing concrete with which to fault him, except to say, 'Poor Giles, I feel sorry for him. I have met several young Englishmen like him. I am sure he is quite at ease when he is among men, but with women . . . Ach, the British educational system is so barbaric! Your schools are like convents and your universities like monasteries! They teach many facts, but so little of life.'

Or had Sonja sensed more than she had liked to express? Was that why she had cautioned her against following the romantic impulses of her heart and urged her to encourage Adam's attentions?

As Sonja was her own first friend of her own age, so Adam was Giles's. Both were Magdalen men and they roomed together in the quaintly named, eighteenth-century New Buildings. Not that Giles ever spoke much about his experiences at university, except in a photographic context, for he had joined the university camera club and his letters to West always contained examples of his latest pictures.

Not until he brought Adam to stay at Yondover at the end of their freshman year were she and West aware that his nickname had accompanied him to Oxford, although Adam – apparently known as 'Curly' because of his already thinning hair – always referred to him as G.G. and never Horsey.

It was from Adam, too, unwitting as they all were of what lay ahead, that they heard for the first time of Boy Tate.

Adam was as articulate and outgoing as Giles was reserved and withdrawn. 'Oxford,' he had explained, 'is dividing itself into two groups, the athletes and the aesthetes: those who row and those who read; those who drink beer and those who sip sherry; those who eat in hall and those who dine out; those who sport tweed jackets, college pullovers and grey flannel trousers – and those who wear silk ties, pink trousers and lilac shirts. G.G. and I like to count ourselves among the aesthetes, but neither of us can hold a candle to Boy, who is so aesthetic as to be almost effete.'

West had raised an eyebrow. 'Boy?'

'Constant Tate, sir. He's the oldest son of Lord Blendon.'

How that connection had impressed her father, even though Lord Blendon was poor as a church mouse and mad as a hatter. Not that Tate had ever come to Kipwell, thank God – there was nothing in that little backwater to titillate his particular tastes . . .

'There's a topping photograph G.G. took of Boy during the OUDS production of G.B.S.'s *Saint Joan*. If you didn't know, you'd never realize he wasn't a woman. G.G., do you have that picture of Boy with you?'

Giles shook his head and West commented drily, 'I can survive without seeing it. But it does occur to me that you young fellows seem to devote rather more time to pleasure than to study. Judging from Giles's letters and listening to you talk, Adam, nobody would believe that any of you were preparing to follow in your respective fathers' illustrious footsteps.'

Again Adam laughed. 'Oh, I think our fathers are all doomed to disappointment. Boy doesn't intend to spend the rest of his life vegetating in the far northern wastes of Yorkshire, looking after the ancestral home – he's going on the stage. As for G.G., his grandmother may cherish dreams of him becoming a diplomat, but photography's the only career for him. You must be aware of that yourself, sir, since you've encouraged him.'

'And are you kicking over the traces, too?'

'Yes, sir. I'm switching from History to Law next term. But you see, it's not what you know, but who you know that makes the difference in life. Examinations and qualifications aren't as important as the formation of friendships which will endure long after Oxford's dreaming spires have become but a whispering memory.'

He had been right. When he and Giles had left Oxford, there had been a ready-made clientèle awaiting them among their fellow graduates, embarked upon their own careers in politics, the arts, the sciences, the military, the City and the Church, buying property, getting married and divorced, suing and being sued, making wills and inheriting estates – becoming famous or infamous, all requiring portraits of themselves, their fiancées, families and débutante sisters. As for Boy Tate . . .

But no, that had all still lain in the future. First had come the summer of 1928: the summer she and Sonja had left Vevey; the summer Sonja had stayed at Kipwell and the Vicar had vented his spleen upon her; the summer that Adam's father had given him his first car and she had driven at breakneck speed down the horseshoe bends from Beachy Head to East-bourne; the summer that she had danced the Charleston with wild abandon; the summer Adam had kissed her and she had laughed in her confusion, then made things worse by explaining that he had reminded her of a surprised penguin . . .

But those events, though important, had counted as little at the time compared to Giles. For Adam had not arrived alone at Yondover in his red Cowley. Giles had been there, too.

In her mind's eye, Kitty visualized them sitting on the lawn at Yondover, sipping drinks in the late afternoon sunlight, Giles's face wearing that aloof expression she remembered so well and her own heart aching with unrequited love. As in the past, it was left to Adam to carry the conversation forward and it was he who informed them that Giles had graduated with a first class honours degree. Giles shrugged off their congratulations, gazing away into the distance as Adam prattled on cheerfully. Because he had changed courses, there was still another year ahead of Adam before he went down. 'Things won't be the same without G.G.,' he said in a mock-tragic voice, 'but no doubt I shall manage to struggle by.'

'What happened to that other fellow – Tate, wasn't it?' West asked.

A shadow passed over Adam's face. Then he replied, 'Oh, Boy left before taking his degree.'

'Sent down?'

Adam glanced quickly from Giles to the two girls. 'Er – yes. A rather unfortunate incident. I'd rather not go into details, sir.'

Later, of course, she had learned the full story. But then, Boy Tate had been nothing but a name, to be instantly forgotten, irrelevant to her own life.

Then, the only thing to matter to her was Giles.

Oh, that summer, that halcyon summer . . . During the daytime they had walked or ridden over the Downs. They had driven to the beach to swim and sunbathe. They had lounged in the garden, talking about art, music, politics, places they had visited and all the things they intended to do with their lives. And in the evenings, they had danced to the new wind-up gramophone West had bought – and Adam had kissed her.

Only after Adam's departure, summoned to Puddles by a telegram announcing the return of his father from Egypt, did it become apparent how he had held the four of them together with his easy-flowing chatter and ready humour. When he was gone, Sonja's balanced poise seemed to desert her, Giles's stutter became more pronounced, and Catherine herself was seized by an unutterable shyness in his presence.

West came to the rescue by suggesting that Giles took some photographs of the two girls.

'No! It won't work!' was her own vehement reaction, remembering the disasters of the past. 'You know I'm not photogenic.' But when West pleaded with her at least to give it a try, she gave in.

The first session took place in the attic room and required Catherine to lie on some black velvet, with Sonja kneeling above her, so that her long, dark hair formed a backdrop, and both their profiles were reflected in a mirror.

'Sonja, look a bit more pensive and avert your face so that you're looking past Kitty,' Giles's voice came from under his darkcloth. 'Your mind is far away. You're thinking about Berlin and Felix. Kitty, open your eyes wider. Don't look so tense. Relax! Sonja's your friend. She won't bite you! That's it! Now, don't move.' The camera shutter clicked. 'And again.'

Catherine found herself falling under the spell of his voice, as he asked them to shift position slightly, this way and that, while the camera shutter continued to click and he changed slides.

The resulting photographs were a dramatic testimony to his direction, sense of composition and lighting, this latter particularly since – there being no electricity at Yondover – he had to rely on daylight coming through the windows and more carefully positioned mirrors and white boards to act as reflectors. He had arranged the girls in such a way that Sonja's dark beauty contrasted starkly with Catherine's fair hair highlighted against the black velvet, while the effect of their mirror images – leading the viewer to wonder which was real and which the reflection – was oddly disturbing.

Sonja looked tranquilly, almost tragically beautiful, but Catherine was surprised to discover a luminous, even ethereal quality to her own features, accentuated by the bright halo of her thick, bobbed hair.

Giles was so pleased with the experiment that there followed several more sessions, all of them studies in light and dark, as he photographed the girls perched on the lowest branch of the oak tree in the paddock, their faces peering through tufts of out-of-focus leaves; on horseback, silhouetted against the sunset; as water nymphs, among the rushes on the banks of the Kip; and wearing black evening dresses, among white boulders, against the white chalk cliffs at Birling Gap.

This last shot was the most ambitious they had tried and attracted several curious spectators while they were shooting. Since Giles had discouraged even West from being present at their previous sessions, Catherine expected him to be disconcerted by this audience, but so immersed was he in what he was doing that he was oblivious to everything around him.

Then she realized the change which took place in him while he was working. So long as he was able to talk about his favourite subject, he was completely at ease. Of his stammer there was no hint. Of that disdainful twist to his mouth there was no sign. As for the relationship between the three of them, now they were a team, joined by a common interest, they were getting on famously together.

When he declared himself satisfied with the shot and began dismantling his equipment and packing it away in its case, the onlookers drifted away. Sonja made her way up the steps to the top of the cliff, where Jethro was waiting in the trap, for Adam's departure had left them with no car.

'Let me carry something for you,' Catherine offered.

Giles handed her his tripod and, as he did so, their fingers met. She looked up at him and, for a moment, his eyes gazed into hers.

Had it not been for that moment of silent communion, she would have been concentrating more as she followed in Sonja's wake up the rickety staircase. As it was, several treads up, she tripped on the hem of her long skirt and – conscious that, whatever else, she must not drop Giles's tripod – she tumbled backwards, landing in an ungainly heap on the shingle.

She was not injured but she did feel extremely stupid, and the suddenness of her fall, together with the weight of the tripod against her chest, had left her slightly winded. For a few seconds she lay where she was, then she heard Giles's voice asking anxiously, 'I say, Kitty, are you all right?'

He took the tripod from her and reached down to help her up. She made to reply that yes, of course she was all right, when she noticed a strange expression on his face and her words remained unuttered. Taking his hand, she rose slowly to her feet, but when she was standing he still did not let go her hand and for a long moment, their eyes remained locked. For that instant, she forgot all about Sonja and Jethro and even the plash of the waves on the pebbles seemed to cease, so that she had the feeling of the two of them being quite alone in a silent world in which time had stood still.

Then, further along the beach, a dog barked and a child called to its mother. A seagull cried and the waves resumed their gentle breaking. A flush coloured Giles's cheeks, which had nothing to do with the hot sun. He released her hand and looked away from her. The moment was gone.

Next day, West announced that Gurney was driving himself and Sonja into Lewes, where he had some business to conduct and Sonja wanted to buy some gifts to take home. Both insisted that they would complete their tasks more speedily without hangers-on. Since Fanny had decided to take advantage of their absence to give the house a thorough clean and declared she did not want Catherine and Giles 'getting under her feet', they found themselves thrust into each other's company. At Giles's suggestion, they rode up on the Downs.

The weather was very close and, so as not to over-exert the horses, they went at a gentle pace to the top of Uffing Down, then across to Long Barrow and down to the Kip, where they dismounted to let the horses rest and drink. Until then, they had ridden in virtual silence but now Catherine recognized the need to say something. 'What are you going to do with all the pictures you've taken?' she asked.

'My g-grandmother has agreed that I should have a b-bash at making a c-career of photography. After the holiday, I'll go up to L-London and show them and others in my p-portfolio to various magazines in the hope

143

of picking up some c-commissions.' His stutter had suddenly, inexplicably, returned.

Catherine had no doubt as to his ability, but it puzzled her as to how he could expect to be paid for taking his particular type of photograph. 'What kind of magazines?'

'*V-vogue*, the *T-tatler*, *New S-society Arts* . . .'

'But surely they aren't going to buy pictures of Sonja and me?'

'N-no,' he admitted, 'but they will g-give an idea of m-my style of photography. And they will g-get me n-noticed.'

For some while after that they relapsed again into silence, then Giles asked, 'W-what are you intending to do?'

The subject of her future had not been raised at home since her return, but she had no reason to doubt that her father still had his heart set on a suitable marriage, while her mother kept hinting that she was expecting her to share in the running of the household and assist with various parish duties: taking meals to the elderly and infirm, helping with the Young Mothers. 'I'm not really sure,' she prevaricated. 'I'll make a decision once Sonja's gone back to Berlin.'

'You're not thinking of taking up a c-career, are you? Personally, I think it's all right for women to have h-hobbies and interests, but they shouldn't try to be equal with men in the professional world, certainly not when they are m-m-married. It's not fair on their f-families. Being a w-wife and m-m-mother is a full-time occupation.'

Rafe chose that instant to cause a diversion by plunging into the river and setting off in hectic pursuit of a water rat. By the time she had chased downstream after him and persuaded him to relinquish his hunt, dragging him in a soaking and bedraggled state to the bank and herself not much better, the sky had grown overcast, a wind had picked up and the sun was concealed behind lowering thunderclouds.

Ever since that first battle of the celestial giants with West on Uffing Down, Catherine had revelled in thunderstorms. Among the most wonderful of all her experiences at Vevey had been the electric storms in the mountains, during which, to Madame Valentin's dismay and the amusement of the other girls, she would rush out into the grounds and dance, barefoot and bare-armed, in the rain.

Giles apparently did not share her enthusiasm. 'We'd b-better be getting b-back,' he said.

However, they had only just reached the wood when the rain began and a great shaft of lightning rent the sky, followed almost immediately by an ear-splitting clap of thunder, which reverberated across the Weald. Other than giving a nervous twitch of the ears, Honey did not react, but Pegasus − possibly infected by his rider's fear − rolled his eyes and reared up in fright, almost throwing Giles.

Catherine brought Honey to a halt, jumped down from the saddle and raced over to grab hold of Pegasus's bridle. Taking care to avoid the horse's thrashing hooves, she hung on grimly, all the time murmuring soothing words of reassurance, until Pegasus calmed down sufficiently for Giles to dismount. Then she went over to where Honey was waiting and, looping his reins over her arm, returned to stand beside Giles.

It was curiously unreal in the woods, for although the booms of thunder were deafeningly loud and the blue forks of lightning blindingly brilliant, the foliage prevented most of the rain from reaching them. She had the sensation of being a spectator in a sheltered auditorium, with the trees as her fellow members of the audience and the sky and the Downs forming a huge outdoor arena. More than anything, she was aware of a feeling of suspense, an almost palpable, electric excitement, which made her heart pound and her nerve ends tingle. Even the hushed trees seemed to be holding their breath, waiting, with her, for the high point of the drama to occur.

After some five or ten minutes, the storm moved inland and the sky began to brighten in the direction of the sea. The rain continued, but the lightning flashes became more sporadic and the thunder a distant rumble. At ease again, Pegasus lowered his head to graze on some blades of grass. Catherine let go of Honey's reins and walked to the edge of the wood, lifting her face, shutting her eyes and stretching out her hands to receive the benison of the rain.

'Th-thank you,' Giles said, shakily. 'You s-saved my life j-just now.'

She shook her head, knowing she had done nothing so dramatic.

After a long silence, Giles went on, 'You are a very unusual g-girl. The st-storm didn't frighten you at all.'

'Why should it?' she asked, and her voice seemed to come from far away, as if it did not belong to her. 'Storms are wonderful.'

145

'Most w-women would . . .' His voice tailed off and then he said, 'I wish I had my c-camera. I'd like to photograph you like that.'

Then he wasn't saying anything more, but had taken her in his arms and was kissing her wet, upturned face.

Being kissed by Giles was very different from being kissed by Adam. Whereas Adam had kissed her with the ease of one who had done the same thing at least once before, she was instinctively aware that she was the first girl Giles had ever kissed. His lips were clumsy as they sought hers, and his body shook as he held her to him.

And when he released her, there was nothing even vaguely ridiculous about him, although the rain was dripping down his face and his wet hair was plastered flat against his head. Only one adjective could describe him and that was – beautiful. His lips still trembled from their kiss and his eyes gazed back at her like dark, bottomless pools, so that she felt she was seeing right into the depths of his soul.

'I'm s-sorry,' he stammered. 'I shouldn't have d-done that.'

'Oh, Giles, no, please don't apologize . . .'

'I know that you and A-Adam . . .'

'No,' she cried in anguish, dreading that he should have found out about that episode in the garden. 'There is nothing between myself and Adam – except friendship.'

'And there is n-no one else?'

'Nobody,' she assured him vehemently.

He grasped her hands, squeezing them so tightly that she thought her bones would break. Several times he made as if to speak, only to stop before the words came out. Then he burst out, 'I love you, K-kitty.'

And at that instant, the rain stopped and from behind a bank of cloud the sun exploded, flooding the hills with rays of golden light, dazzling in their brilliance. Catherine's heart was filled with a sense of joy so over-whelming that for a moment she was powerless to speak. Then she said, 'And I love you, too, Giles.'

By the time they finally reached Yondover, West and Sonja were back, full of the excitement of the storm, which had started when they were just leaving Lewes. Gurney had insisted upon driving through the down-pour but, as they had reached Kipwell, lightning had struck an elm tree by the entrance to Kipwell Grange, causing it to fall across the road within feet of them. 'I have never seen such a thing before,' said Sonja, still in a slight state of shock. 'If we had been just a few seconds earlier, it would have fallen on us.'

'I wonder what other damage the storm's caused,' West said. 'There may be trees down in the wood.'

'No, I don't think so,' Giles told him. 'K-kitty and I were there. We w-would have known.'

West turned on him. 'You were in the wood during the storm? That was a damnfool thing . . .' Then his words died on his lips, as he realized that Giles and Catherine were standing very close together, their hands interlocked. A slow smile replaced his tense expression. 'Ah,' he murmured, 'so, at last, you two young things have come to your senses . . .' He placed his hands on their shoulders and drew them to him. 'I could ask for no greater happiness.'

Sonja was due to return to Berlin a couple of days later and, before she left, Giles went to the Vicarage to ask the Reverend Fellowes for his daughter's hand in marriage, after which the Vicar sought an interview with West. The outcome of these meetings was that her father duly summoned the young couple to his study and announced, 'It gives me great pleasure to grant my permission for your union. In my opinion, it's an eminently suitable match, bringing together the interests of two local families. Furthermore, Mr Lambourne owns a property in London – a house in Porter's Place – which he is giving you as a wedding gift. And he has agreed to settle a most generous allowance on Giles, to enable him to set up his photographic studio.'

It did not escape Catherine's notice that her father was more concerned with the financial arrangements than with her and Giles's happiness. Her mother, however, in a rare show of emotion, cried with joy at the news, until the Vicar instructed her to 'stop making an exhibition' of herself. Once she had sufficiently recovered, she began planning shopping expeditions for the trousseau. 'Just the two of us, dear. We'll go to London. Now, what colour dresses for the bridesmaids? Pink, I think . . .'

But most important to Catherine was that West and the Gurneys should approve – and of this there was no doubt. Fanny hugged them both to her capacious bosom, while Gurney shook them fervently by the hand, congratulating them gruffly. Jethro said nothing immediately, but went into the garden and returned with a bunch of red roses, which he shoved into Catherine's hands, muttering, 'To wish you 'appiness.'

Determined to establish himself in his profession as quickly as possible, Giles immediately moved into Porter's Place and embarked upon its refurbishment. By the time Catherine and her mother made their first shopping trip to Harrods, the builders had already started work.

Naturally, Giles's first priority was his studio and to accommodate this, he was having the dividing wall demolished between two of the spacious ground-floor reception rooms. The cloakroom was destined to become an office. The breakfast room already housed a collection of photographic equipment, background canvases, properties and lights, and the scullery was being converted into a darkroom.

Of the original downstairs rooms, only the kitchen, dining room and a sitting room would remain for her own and Giles's private use. As for the first floor, one of the bedrooms and a bathroom were to be set aside for the use of his clients.

Then there were the servants' quarters and, in due course, the servants themselves, regarding whose appointment Catherine had no more say than she did about the alterations to and furnishing of the house.

When she and her mother made their final visit to Porter's Place before the wedding, it was to find a married couple, Mr and Mrs Forsyth, installed as butler and housekeeper, and a cook presiding over the kitchen. A trim little housemaid relieved them of their coats and shopping bags and a parlourmaid served them their tea.

Two male assistants were employed in the studio and, in the office, a Miss Edith Spencer had taken up occupancy. Miss Spencer, with her straight, bobbed hair, tweed suit, white blouse and black brogue shoes, presented a formidably businesslike appearance, even though she was probably only a few years older than Catherine herself. According to Giles, Miss Spencer lived in Putney and had to work in order to support a widowed mother and spinster aunt.

It was only when Catherine learned this that the implication began to dawn on her of Giles's words beside the Kip that morning before the thunderstorm, when he had stated that he did not believe in married women having a career. What, she could not help wondering, would she find to do in this household which, well before she was installed as mistress, was apparently already running itself?

But she did not dwell on this thought. Of far greater importance was that Giles was happy and that fortune was smiling on him from the outset of his career, even though he complained of having to bow to convention in the style of his portraits more than he would prefer. Not only were the magazines to whom he showed his portfolio so impressed by his ideas that they were giving him a lot of work, but commissions were pouring in, as Adam had predicted, through acquaintances from Oxford.

CHAPTER 11

Kitty woke abruptly, her mind startlingly clear, almost as though she had spent the past few hours or days – she had lost all sense of time – in a sea mist, which had suddenly lifted and dispersed.

It was night again, for the curtains were drawn and the lights dim. Judging by their snores, the five other occupants of the ward were sound asleep.

She sat up, knowing from experience that she would be unable to go to sleep again. Insomnia was a familiar if unwelcome acquaintance, but over the years she had come to terms with it. If she were at home, she would go downstairs to the kitchen, make herself a pot of tea, then listen to some music until dawn broke, when she would go out for a walk and shake off the dark dreams which had disturbed her slumber.

But she was not at Rose Cottage: she was in hospital. And, in hospital, one could no more wander off to the kitchen in the middle of the night and make oneself some tea than go out for a walk. However, one could quite legitimately make a trip to the bathroom.

Gingerly, she eased her legs over the side of the bed, felt for her slippers and stood up. Her shoulder still felt stiff and her ribs ached, but the pain was nowhere as bad as it had been. She hoped she would soon be allowed to go home.

She padded up the ward, her legs still stupidly weak, but considerably stronger than they had been.

'Mrs Pilgrim, are you all right?' It was Nurse Willis, hurrying out from the little office behind the ward sister's desk.

Kitty found herself feeling rather like a schoolgirl caught leaving the dormitory. She gave a penitent smile. 'I've done nothing but sleep since I came in here and now I think I must finally have outslept myself.'

'How about a cup of tea?'

'Oh, that would be nice.'

'Well, after you've been to the bathroom you get back to bed and I'll bring you one.'

When Kitty returned to her bed, Nurse Willis was already there with the promised cup of tea and the ubiquitous thermometer. But her temperature, when measured, was back to normal.

'You work such long – and very unsocial – hours,' Kitty remarked, her voice low, so as not to disturb the other patients. She wanted to keep the nurse with her for a while and to talk about something different – something to divert her thoughts from Giles.

'Yes, but I don't mind. I enjoy my job. And, of course, I don't always work nights.' In an unconscious motion, she twisted a ring on the third finger of her left hand between the thumb and forefinger of her right.

Kitty noticed the movement. 'And what does your boyfriend think about it?'

'My boyfriend? Oh!' Nurse Willis glanced down at her hand. 'I shouldn't really be wearing this ring while I'm on duty. But we only got engaged last weekend.'

'Congratulations. Or I should really congratulate him. He's a lucky young man.'

'Thank you.'

'What does he do for a career?'

'He's a research chemist at Beecham's in Worthing.'

'So you both come from Sussex?'

'No, funnily enough, we don't. I was brought up in Guildford and Jamie is from Edinburgh. He'd like to go back there after we're married, but I'm not so sure. I like Scotland but it always seems to rain when I go there.'

The conversation was not serving its intended purpose at all. Instead of diverting her mind, it was leading her back down the very paths she had been seeking to avoid.

'I've only ever been to Edinburgh once. That was in the winter. It was snowing then.'

'I like snow.'

'Mmm, provided there's not too much of it.'

The nurse laughed. 'I think it's different when you're young.'

Kitty gave a rueful smile. 'That applies to most things. Not just snow. But I mustn't keep you any longer. I'm sure you have lots of things you ought to be getting on with.'

'Do you think you'll be able to go back to sleep now?'

'I'll try.'

'Let me arrange your pillows to make you a bit more comfortable. There, that's better. Now lie down – and sweet dreams.'

Obediently, Kitty lay back and closed her eyes.

Edinburgh . . . Marion McDonnell . . . Giles . . .

She had gone to Scotland with Giles so that she could meet his grandmother, for it had naturally been important to him that they should know and like each other. And West, too, had encouraged her visit – strange though it had seemed to her at the time, for she had still been very young – only just eighteen – and divorce, like death, was outside her experience, and it had not occurred to her that two people might still care for each other, even though they could not live together.

As vividly as though it were yesterday, she could see Marion McDonnell, a tiny woman – smaller even than herself – who had been dwarfed by the winged, high-backed armchair on which she perched. Her hair was pure white, framing a neat-featured little face, and she was dressed entirely in black, the sombreness of her attire relieved only by a gold watch hanging from a chain around her neck.

She had motioned Catherine to take a seat on the pouffe beside her and after the maid had served tea, asked in a pleasant, lilting, Scottish accent, 'Now tell me, how is Westrup?'

The directness of her question had taken Catherine aback. Not knowing how to respond, she had given a rather embarrassed smile.

Mrs McDonnell had patted her hand. 'Because we are divorced does not mean that I'm not still fond of Westrup. As you know, my grandson used to stay with him during the holidays, so I have been kept reasonably well informed about life at Yondover. But Giles is like all young men – so wrapped up in his own affairs that he is scarcely aware of the world around him. I should value your opinion, my dear. Is Westrup well? Does he seem happy?'

'He's extremely well and he seems very content,' Catherine had assured her, determined to stand up for West at all cost.

'I am sure your friendship has made a great difference to him. It is good for old people to have young people around them.'

'But I never think of West as being old!' Catherine had exclaimed.

Mrs McDonnell's smile could have been nothing other than genuine. 'Oh, I'm so glad to hear you say that! Whenever I think of Westrup, I think of him as still being young – like he was when I first met him.'

There was such warmth in her voice that Catherine was suddenly convinced that she spoke the truth when she said she was still fond of West. Encouraged by her manner, she had ventured to ask, 'Please, would you mind telling me – what went wrong in your marriage? Why did you leave West?'

Mrs McDonnell was not offended. She took a few sips of tea, then replaced her cup on the tray. 'Yes,' she murmured, 'perhaps you, of all people, should know the whole story . . .'

For a few moments she was silent, collecting her thoughts, then she began: 'My people were simple, country folk from a small village near Fort William. My mother was a cook at a big house and my father a gamekeeper on the same estate. Myself, I was a nursemaid when Westrup and I met. He and my employer had been at school together. My employers must have been very generous and liberal-minded people, for they allowed me a lot of free time while Westrup was staying with them. I remember we walked for miles over the mountains and as we walked Westrup told me about all the dreams he had for his life. He was quite a bit older than me and so handsome . . . Never had I met anyone like him before. He seemed so – yes – so romantic. When he proposed, what could I have said but yes?'

She gazed into the roaring log fire, as though looking back through the years, to the time when the flame of love had burned as brightly in her heart.

'He took me back with him to Yondover, so that I could meet his father. Ah, what a tyrant he was, that old man. I can see him now, standing with his hands tucked under his coat tails, barely suppressed rage suffusing his features as, in answer to his questions, I told him about myself and my family. Later, after I had retired to my room, he ordered Westrup not to marry me. When Westrup defied him, he disinherited him.'

'He disinherited him? But why?'

'Because I came from the wrong class.'

'What do you mean?'

'Has Westrup ever spoken to you about his family?'

'I only know his father was something to do with the railway.'

'Yes, that's where he made his money. But he was born in the East End of London. He was a Cockney, born within the sound of Bow Bells.'

'Then I don't understand. It wasn't as if he came from a grand family.'

'Ah, my dear, what a lot you have to learn about people. If Samuel Lambourne had been a born aristocrat, he might still not have approved of me, but he would probably have been more compassionate.'

'So what did you do?'

'To begin with, we were so much in love, we didn't care what happened to us. Westrup's father owned the house you and Giles are going to live in in Porter's Place, but he would not allow us to live in it, so we rented a small cottage in Kensington. We lived very simply, yet even so our money soon ran out. Westrup was a fine artist and tried to get commissions for portraits. However, they were slow coming in – and Westrup really did not enjoy painting them. Then Elizabeth was born and we had another mouth to feed. For two more years we struggled on, getting ever deeper into debt, and Westrup's health and nerves began to suffer.

'Sometimes he would talk yearningly of Yondover and I was sure he was wondering whether he had made the right decision in marrying me. Many times I thought of seeking an interview with his father, but even had my pride permitted me to go begging to him, I knew what his answer would be.

'Eventually, I realized there was only one option open to me. I was the obstacle to Westrup's happiness. If I left him, his problems would be resolved. He would be restored to his father's favour and when the old man died, he would inherit Yondover. So I pawned my engagement and wedding rings to buy a railway ticket and returned to Scotland. I wrote to Westrup that I had met someone else. And, in due course, I did indeed marry Hugh . . .' Her voice tailed off.

Everything had started to fall into place. Marion McDonnell had sacrificed her own happiness for West's. But in that case why, when Samuel Lambourne had died, had she not returned to him? Unless, of course, she was already in love with Hugh McDonnell.

'How soon after you left West did his father die?' Catherine asked.

'Oh, not very long – only a year or two.' Mrs McDonnell paused. 'I know what you are wondering, my dear, and I will do my best to answer your unspoken question. I did not leave Westrup because of Hugh, nor was he the reason that I did not go back to Westrup after his father's death.'

Absently, she smoothed the black material of her dress. 'I had known Hugh for a long time – we were children together. He was very kind to me and treated Elizabeth like his own daughter. He was heartbroken when she died . . .' Her eyes clouded at the memory. 'Yes, we were married for thirty-three years. But I was never in love with him in the way I was with Westrup.'

'Then why . . . ?'

Marion McDonnell turned to the cyclamen in blossom on the low bookshelf beside her. 'Love is like an exotic hot-house flower,' she said slowly. 'It needs to be very carefully nurtured to survive the cruel elements. And the love which Westrup and I knew was more fragile than most. For a short span, it was very bright and very strong. But in an atmosphere of cold and hunger and extreme poverty, it withered and died.'

'But that's not true,' Catherine insisted. 'You still loved West and he still loved you. He must have done. He never married anyone else.'

'No,' the old lady corrected gently. 'He fell in love with a dream. He created an image of me which had no bearing to reality. By leaving him, I was able to restore to him the one true, enduring love of his life, a love which would never fail him – Yondover.'

Kitty hovered in that strange half-world between waking and sleeping, when the mind seems to detach itself and view with quite abnormal clarity a situation which becomes hazy when the sleeper awakes.

Had Marion McDonnell been trying to warn her? Had the old lady seen deeper into her heart than she had realized? *He created an image of me which had no bearing to reality . . .*

But at the time, she had recognized no personal relevance in Marion McDonnell's story. Why should she have done? Although she had been in love and soon to be married, her father, tyrannical though he might be in other respects, had not opposed her choice of husband. She had not been faced with the stark prospects of poverty and hunger. Her love for Giles, she had been convinced, was not a fragile flower which would wither and die, but a powerful tree, like the oak in the paddock at

Yondover, which would withstand all adversities, growing stronger and ever stronger.

Back at Yondover, she had found a pretext to ask West about his father.

'Yes,' he had said, 'my father spent the first fifty years of his life in London. He didn't come to Yondover until 1850, just before I was born. He began life as one of ten children in a slum tenement in the East End. Not that I ever met my grandparents or any of my uncles and aunts. He had distanced himself totally from them by the time I was born.

'He left school when he was twelve to be apprenticed on the railway. He was lucky. He was in the right job at the right time – a railway engineer at the beginning of the railway boom. From the day he started work he invested his wages in the railways. With the income from his investments, he bought more shares – all in companies connected to the railway.

'Imagine, Kitty, he never spent a penny on anything other than bare necessities! He amassed a fortune but never gave a sou to his family. He never wasted money on fashionable clothes, fine food, theatres or women. If he travelled, it was free of charge on the railway. His only indulgence was to buy Porter's Place – and even that was an investment, for the property increased dramatically in value during his own lifetime.

'He bought Yondover for much the same reason. It was just a derelict farmhouse when he acquired it, but it possessed a lot of land. When the East Coast line was built from Lewes to Hastings, guess whose property it crossed? He used to boast that he received more in compensation than he'd paid for the entire estate and, as part of the deal, he stipulated that the company should build a railway station for his own convenience. Then, having skimmed off the cream – and allowed a beautiful piece of countryside to be ruined – he sold the land he didn't want to the Pughs, at an exorbitant profit, of course.

'He didn't marry until he was over fifty – after he had bought Yondover, in fact – and then he chose for his wife the daughter of one of the partners in the joint-stock bank which financed the London–Brighton South Coast Railway, so that he could further his business interests.' He paused for a moment, a far-away expression on his face. 'I never knew my mother. She died giving birth to me . . .'

Eventually, he continued with uncustomary bitterness, 'My father was a mean, money-grubbing tyrant, who did his best to ruin my life. It was

156

my father who drove away my wife and, because of him, my daughter grew up a stranger to me. When he died, I very nearly renounced my inheritance, I hated him so much. I hadn't made the fortune I stood to inherit. It wasn't my money. I didn't want it. But there was Yondover. And I loved Yondover . . .'

He gazed towards the house. 'Finally, I decided to turn my legacy into beautiful things – into pictures and music, flowers and trees. Money is a currency, Kitty. It shouldn't be left to grow stagnant or used simply to make more money. It should be allowed to flow – and to create beauty.'

Yes, she and West had shared a lot in common. There had not been much to choose between the Reverend Thurston Fellowes and Samuel Lambourne. Both had been utterly selfish and totally lacking in Christian charity, unscrupulously prepared to sacrifice their children's happiness for the sake of their own dogmatic principles and ruthless ambition.

What a saint her mother must have been to put up with such a husband: always remaining blindly loyal to him; putting wifely duty before maternal instinct; suffering a joyless marriage and a colourless existence without a single word of complaint; ignoring the fact that he had chosen her because she was a Dean's daughter and hoped, through the Dean's influence, to gain preferment – ambition of such a kind being, according to St Paul, perfectly acceptable. For had not the Apostle written, *If a man desire the office of a bishop, he desireth a good work?* And, although the Reverend Thurston Fellowes had not risen as high as he might have hoped in the ecclesiastical hierarchy, the Church had provided him with an easy living, amid the most comfortable of surroundings.

Her father had been a fervent adherent of St Paul, holding the same misogynous opinion of women and unyielding attitude towards children. *For if a man know not how to rule in his own house, how shall he take care of the church of God?* had been one of his favourite quotations.

What a bigot he had been, what a bully, what an unmitigated snob and what a hypocrite. She remembered standing with her mother at the church porch, while her father greeted his parishioners as they trooped out of church after Matins, nodding aloofly to the poor tenants of rented cottages, who could afford only to put farthings on the collection plate, but bowing ingratiatingly towards Sir Hector and Lady Maude, involving them in conversation, so that he could later quote them in company: 'As my friend Sir Hector says . . .' 'As I told Lady Maude . . .'

He had revered the aristocracy almost more than he did God and worshipped money as an even more omnipotent power, yet clothed his hypocrisy under a mask of piety. For he had claimed that it was not money but the love of money which St Paul had condemned when he wrote that it was the root of all evil.

Furthermore, the labourer was worthy of his reward. The Vicar had taken to himself Paul's directive to Timothy to charge those that are rich in this world not to trust in uncertain riches, and sought constantly to persuade them to give of their wealth to the Church – and thus augment his own stipend.

That, of course, was why her father had encouraged her friendship with West from the beginning. He had learned from Sir Hector and Lady Maude that West had inherited a fortune and his first glimpse of Yondover had proved that money was not lacking for its upkeep. Then Giles had provided an additional incentive, so that even though the only occasion West was ever to enter St Peter's was in his coffin, the Vicar had continued to overlook his eccentricities.

CHAPTER 12

Again it was horribly early when Tabitha woke Pippa. Now Kitty was well on the mend, she had no particular reason to get up immediately, but she was too wide awake to go back to sleep. That's what came of going to bed before ten, she thought. But, after carrying out her various chores the evening before, she had found her eyes closing as she sat at the kitchen table eating her supper of baked beans on toast. Talk about early to bed and early to rise – if this continued, she should be very healthy, wealthy and wise. And she felt ravenous. A mug of coffee and slice of toast wouldn't go far this morning. Once she had rung the hospital and had a bath, it was bacon and eggs and to hell with any extra inches.

In fact, after the ward sister had informed her somewhat testily that of course Mrs Pilgrim was all right, Pippa had the feeling that she was considered rather a nuisance and decided not to ring any more in the mornings. Although her telephone calls were prompted by the best of motives, she did not want her concern to be misinterpreted and, least of all, conveyed to Kitty, who might be led to think that her condition was worse than it actually was.

By nine o'clock, her own and Tabitha's appetites satisfied, Pippa was well on her way to Kipwell and although, because of the rush-hour traffic in Brighton and Lewes, the drive took longer than she had anticipated, it was still only just gone ten when she saw a signpost stating: KIPWELL VILLAGE ONLY.

She turned up a lane towards the Downs, slowing when she reached a wrought-iron gateway which she thought might be the entrance to Yondover but discovered instead to belong to a property called Kipwell Grange. A little further on, she entered the village street, lined with pretty cottages and a single, bow-windowed shop – PADDEN'S THE GROCER, its fascia board

159

announced – with a jutting red and yellow sign showing it also to be a post office.

Beyond was a green, around which stood a pub, the church, a Queen Anne house which she assumed to be the Vicarage and another which looked as if it had once been a school, beside which was a kissing gate and a track leading up the hillside, with a signpost indicating a public footpath to Uffing Down.

The road then entered an overgrown wood, securely fenced off with barbed wire and dotted with PRIVATE PROPERTY notices. After a short distance she passed under some high voltage electricity cables, then found herself back on the A27. She drove along it, past a signpost to the right pointing to Kipwell Station and, soon afterwards, the lane she had first taken to Kipwell village. Outside Kipwell Grange, she encountered three people ambling along on horseback, then she was in the village again. She parked in front of the church, taking care not to obstruct a driveway barricaded by a five-barred gate, set back somewhat, so that she had not noticed it originally, padlocked and topped with barbed wire and bearing a board stating: PRIVATE PROPERTY – TRESPASSERS WILL BE PROSECUTED.

A middle-aged woman and a labrador emerged from the gate to what she saw was indeed the Vicarage, and set off at a brisk pace up the footpath to Uffing Down. As she got out of the car, the woman began to climb up the steep hillside, her dog bounding on ahead of her.

There must be a brilliant view from the top. But although, as always, she had her camera with her, she hadn't come to Kipwell to take pictures. Another time, perhaps . . .

She crossed the green to Padden's. A bell jangled as she opened the latched door and, for a moment, she thought she was entering a traditional, old-fashioned village grocer's, but that illusion was swiftly shattered when she saw a pile of wire baskets and realized that Padden's had succumbed to the mini-market syndrome.

The post office counter was at the far end, where several elderly people were queuing, clasping pension books in their hands and gossiping with the easy familiarity of old friends. All eyes turned to her as she approached.

'I'm in no hurry – you go before me,' the man ahead of her said. He reminded her of Colonel Wakehurst.

'Thank you, but actually all I want is to find out where a certain house is,' Pippa explained.

'House? Should be able to help you there. What's the name?'

The chatter died down and everyone stared at her expectantly.

'Yondover,' Pippa replied.

The Colonel Wakehurst look-alike gave a short, barking laugh. 'I can tell you where Yondover is. Beside the church is a gate. If you go through there and follow the drive over the Downs, you'll come to Yondover.'

Pippa's heart sank. 'Is that the gate with barbed wire and a sign saying private property?'

'That's the one. I wouldn't advise going up there unless you have an appointment. "Dynamite" Devere doesn't take kindly to trespassers.'

'Dynamite Devere?' she queried. 'I'm actually looking for Gawaine Devere. He used to be a photographer, back in the 1930s.'

'Photographer, eh? Possible, I suppose. Devere's got up to enough other strange things in his life.' The Colonel type turned to the counter and bellowed, 'Mrs Taylor, Dynamite Devere, is his first name Gawaine?'

The post office clerk reached for the next pension book and mumbled something inaudible behind the glass, which seemed to be an affirmative.

'So at least he's still alive,' Pippa murmured.

'Unless he's died and none of us have heard,' the Colonel type said. 'That would never surprise me. Devere's a recluse. I've lived nearly twenty years in Kipwell and so far as I'm aware he's never left Yondover in all that time. I for one have certainly never set eyes on him.'

Pippa could not help thinking that if he was typical of Gawaine Devere's neighbours she did not altogether blame him for shutting himself off from them.

'Well, thank you for your help,' she said and, with a general smile to the curiously staring faces, left the shop.

As she went, the Colonel type was saying, 'Photographer, eh? Never knew that. Just goes to show . . .'

Outside, Pippa stood for a moment in indecision. Then the doorbell clanged again and one of the ladies ahead of her in the queue emerged, pushing a tartan shopping basket on wheels. 'Excuse me, dear, but I couldn't help overhearing you and Major Smythe-Brown. The Major is a newcomer to the village. He's retired from the Army, you know, used to live in Malta until his wife died. But I've lived in Kipwell all my married life, that's since before the war. My dear husband – God bless his soul – had quite a lot to do with Gawaine Devere, one way and another. If you

161

have a few minutes to spare, why don't you have a cup of coffee with me?'

'Well, thank you . . .'

With a satisfied little nod, the woman pushed her shopper across the road and Pippa followed her.

She lived in a cottage not unlike Kitty's, except that it was far tidier and the appliances were all modern. Once they were inside, she said, 'I'm Mrs Lowe. And you are?'

'My name's Pippa Devere.'

'Good heavens! So you're a relation?'

'No. I don't think so. But I am a photographer. That's why I'd like to meet Gawaine Devere – to talk to him about his pictures.'

'Well, what a coincidence! Now, you sit there, while I make the coffee.'

'Please don't go to any trouble.'

'No trouble at all. It's nice to have company. Wallace and I always used to have coffee together at this time of the morning.'

She took china from the dresser, arranged shortcake on a plate with a paper doily, and made coffee in a pot. When the coffee was finally served, she went on, 'Now then, Gawaine Devere. Let me see . . . Wallace and I were married in 1936 – it would have been our golden wedding anniversary this year. I came from Brighton, but Wallace was a Lewes man. He worked at County Hall. If it hadn't been for the railway, we couldn't have lived in Kipwell but, as it was, he could commute to work every day.'

Pippa sipped her coffee and nibbled on a piece of shortcake. She had the dreadful feeling that Mrs Lowe was going to prove a waste of time.

Her next words did little to dispel that impression. 'To tell the truth, we were scarcely aware of Mr Devere's existence until after the war. I believe he had another home in London.'

'He had a studio in Porter's Place in Chelsea.'

'Well, that would explain it. Certainly he didn't spend much time at Yondover. Sometimes he came down for the weekend, but that was all. And during the war, I think he must have been posted abroad. Yondover was taken over by the government. Not that we knew anything about what went on up there. It was all very hush-hush.'

This promised to be more an account of what Mrs Lowe didn't know about Gawaine Devere than what she did, Pippa decided resignedly. Even she was aware that he had been a war photographer.

'Of course, the first thing the government did was to install mains water and drainage and electricity. You see, nothing much had changed up at Yondover since the last century, still hasn't for that matter. Well, a power line was put in on telegraph poles. I must admit that the poles did look rather unsightly, but so many of the benefits of modern living are, don't you think? Yet one gets used to them – they become part of the scenery. In any case, the whole country looked different during the war, with anti-aircraft guns and radar and barbed wire everywhere.

'Now, as I said, Mr Devere wasn't around during the war. But once the war was over, he came back and took up residence at Yondover. And you'll never guess what he did then.'

Mrs Lowe looked expectantly at Pippa, who shook her head.

'He had the electricity supply and the telephone disconnected and all the telegraph poles taken down. Can you imagine such a thing?'

Pippa made what she hoped was the correct expression of incredulity.

'Then, in the early 1950s,' Mrs Lowe continued, 'the Central Electricity Authority began to put up a new high voltage grid line. Wallace was Deputy Borough Surveyor by then, so he was involved in the planning and negotiations with local councils. As you may have noticed, there is quite a lot of woodland around Kipwell – and most of it belongs to Yondover. After a number of meetings, it was decided to route the grid line through these woods, and Mr Devere was handed a compulsory purchase order. Despite all the bother with the telegraph poles, nobody anticipated any trouble. The pylons and cables weren't visible from Yondover and only a few trees had to be felled.'

'But Gawaine Devere didn't see it that way?' Pippa hazarded.

'You're quite right. Poor Wallace's life was made an absolute misery. Mr Devere took the matter to the High Court and even managed to get it raised in Parliament. He had been to Harrow and Oxford, you know, so he had a lot of influential friends. But the Electricity Authority wasn't to be overruled. So he took the law into his own hands. He and old Jethro Gurney . . .'

Jethro – that name was in the letter to Edith Spencer.

'. . . surrounded the area with barbed wire, laid landmines and chased the workmen who came to erect the pylons off his land at gunpoint. That was how he came to be known as Dynamite Devere.'

'He sounds an amazing character,' Pippa breathed.

Mrs Lowe considered this angle on the events. 'But a difficult man, and not very sensible when you think about it. Wallace always said he was cutting off his nose to spite his face. Personally, I think old Gurney led him on. Old Gurney's passed away now, but in my opinion he was never quite right in the head. You could say the same about Millie and Ted, for that matter – that's old Gurney's wife and son. He married late in life. Millie was much younger than him. She was a London girl who came down here during the war.'

Mrs Lowe sighed and poured more coffee. Then she continued, 'But that wasn't the end of it. Some years later – around 1964 it must have been because Wallace retired just afterwards, he simply couldn't take any more, he had a bad heart, you know – it was decided to build a bypass round Kipwell. Until then, the A27 trunk road used to come right through the village. I can't describe to you what it was like. Cars roaring through at all hours of the day and night. Charabancs – and articulated lorries. They were damaging the structure of our houses. The church tower had to have extensive repairs.'

Pippa sucked in her breath. 'And the bypass went across Gawaine Devere's land? And he laid more landmines and went after the workmen with guns?'

'Him and the Gurneys. It's a wonder to me they never killed anybody.'

Pippa frowned. 'Surely Gawaine Devere was paid compensation for the loss of his land?'

'Of course he was. But money can't mean anything to him. He inherited a fortune from his grandfather, you know. And what has he ever had to spend it on, shut up in Yondover like that?'

'So that's the reason for all the private property notices and why Major Wotsit warned me against going up to Yondover?'

'Major Smythe-Brown,' Mrs Lowe corrected. 'He was right. Any stranger venturing on Yondover property still takes their life in their hands. If you go up on Uffing Down and look across to Yondover – not that my poor old legs will get me up there any more – you can see Ted Gurney patrolling the grounds with a shotgun in his hands.'

'But why?' Pippa asked.

'I honestly don't know. It isn't even as if the land is well looked after. People tell me that what used to be lovely meadows are full of nettles and thistles. As for the gardens, they're just a mass of weeds. And the house – it used to be so picturesque . . .'

'How does Gawaine Devere live?' Pippa asked.

'I can't imagine. Padden's make up an.order every week, which Millie or Ted Gurney comes down to collect.'

Pippa frowned. The image Mrs Lowe had depicted of Gawaine Devere was at such total odds with the impression she had received from his photographs that she found it almost impossible to believe they were talking about the same man.

'Was he always so reclusive?' she asked.

'Now there's the strange thing!' Mrs Lowe replied triumphantly. 'No, he wasn't. When Wallace and I first came here, people in the village still used to talk about the wild parties that were held up at Yondover – I'm going back a long way, of course, to the late twenties. I remember hearing about all sorts of smart guests travelling down from London and getting up to all kinds of antics at Yondover. If Mr Devere was a photographer, that would probably account for it. Photographers seem to lead such glamorous lives. Take Lord Snowdon and Lord Lichfield . . .'

'You never heard mention of a Miss Edith Spencer, by any chance?'

'Edith Spencer? Now that name rings a vague bell. A rather severe-looking woman, a governessy type? But if you're looking for a romantic interest in his life, I'm afraid you're barking up the wrong tree, my dear.'

Pippa frowned. Mrs Lowe had used exactly the same words as Mr Kingsley. 'You see' – Mrs Lowe lowered her voice – 'rumour has it that he is what in my young day we used to call a pansy.' A faint flush coloured her cheeks. Then she added hastily, 'But there may be no truth at all in that. People do like to gossip, particularly in a small village like this – and if there isn't any scandal they'll create it.'

Unlike Mrs Lowe and her generation, Pippa found nothing embarrassing or shocking about homosexuality. 'So he was never married?'

'Not that I'm aware of. If he was, there'd be a record of it in the church.' From which Pippa had to assume that others before her had attempted to probe into Gawaine Devere's past.

'And he has no family, no brothers or sisters?'

'Again, if he has, we've never seen hide nor hair of them in Kipwell. Of course, the people who must have known all about those days were the Pughs from Kipwell Grange. But they had to sell the Grange because

165

of death duties and I've no idea where they're living now. The Grange belongs to an Arab, although we only see him during Glyndebourne.'

At that moment the clock struck twelve and Pippa exclaimed, 'I'm afraid I shall have to be leaving. My grandmother is in hospital in Arundel and I have to visit her this afternoon. Thank you so much. It's been so interesting . . .'

Needless to say, she then had to tell Mrs Lowe all about Kitty's fall and listen to an account of how Wallace had fallen and dislocated his shoulder, so it was a quarter past twelve before she reached the car, having promised to call in again if she returned to Kipwell.

At the forbidding five-barred gate and the track leading up over the Downs to Yondover, she stood for a moment, then fetched her Nikon from the boot of the car and took a series of quick pictures of the gate, the church and Uffing Down.

Midway through his life, something had happened to change Gawaine Devere from the brilliant photographer who threw wild parties to a hermit who shut himself away from the world in a disintegrating house behind barbed-wire fences – something, in short, which had changed his entire personality.

A series of images flitted swiftly through her mind. An emaciated man's face staring out from behind barbed wire. Women in front of a pile of corpses. Two little girls with unhealthily large, glittering eyes.

There could be only one explanation. It had to be Gawaine Devere's experiences during the war that had made him stop shooting pictures and start shooting at people.

Kitty was reading when the first visitors entered the ward that afternoon – or rather, she was looking at the words in *This Little World* but taking few of them in.

'Your granddaughter's a bit late today,' the woman in the next bed remarked. 'She's usually the first to arrive.'

'Oh, I expect she's been held up,' Kitty said brightly. 'Probably my neighbours have waylaid her. There's no stopping Colonel Wakehurst once he starts talking. Or maybe she can't find anywhere to park.'

But, deep in her heart, she knew that neither of these reasons was correct. As Pippa had gone to Worthing on her quest for Gawaine Devere, now she was following the trail to Kipwell . . .

'Kitty, I'm sorry I'm late!' Pippa materialized, breathless, at her side. 'How are you feeling today?'

'Much better,' Kitty assured her. 'My temperature has finally gone and I'm starting to feel quite with it again.'

'And all the bumps and bruises?'

'Don't hurt nearly so much.'

'Oh, that's good. I see you've been reading. Did my choice of books meet with your approval?'

'You matched my mood exactly.'

Pippa picked up *This Little World* and opened it to the dedication. '. . . *each of you cherishes in his heart the vision of some particular village . . . so here is an imaginary village . . .*' she read aloud, then flicked through the pages. 'No wonder you like this story, Kitty – one of the characters is called Catherine. And she plays the piano. And this is extraordinary! Uffley Mill!' Pippa's eyes lit up and she leaned forward eagerly. 'You remember I was telling you about a photographer called Gawaine Devere?'

So it was as she had feared. Forcing her voice to remain even, Kitty said, 'Of course I remember.'

'Well, I know you were very tired.'

'I think my fall shook me up more than I realized.' But she had to know. Whatever Pippa might have found out, however uncomfortable, she had to know. 'You'd been to Worthing,' she prompted.

'That's right. Well, in Worthing I was told Gawaine Devere lived near a place called Kipwell and as I was up early this morning I decided to drive over there. It's a little village, overlooked by a steep hill called Uffing Down. Isn't that a super name? I wondered whether it's called that because everyone is huffing and puffing by the time they reach the top.'

Kitty managed a weak smile.

'I found out quite a lot about Gawaine Devere, but I didn't see him. He's a recluse apparently. His house is miles from anywhere, right up on the Downs, and he's looked after by a housekeeper, Millie Gurney, and her son. There's a lot of land attached to the house which is fenced off with barbed wire and the housekeeper's son – Ted, his name is – apparently patrols the grounds with a gun.

'Gawaine Devere himself is known locally as Dynamite Devere. I met a woman called Mrs Lowe who has lived in Kipwell since 1936. She didn't know he was a photographer, but her husband was a surveyor with the Council and he . . .'

As Pippa repeated all she had learned about Dynamite Devere, Kitty felt herself gradually relaxing. Mrs Lowe had been after her time. Her knowledge of Giles was limited to high voltage cables and bypasses, matters which had been widely reported in the press at the time.

But she could not help but feel horrified at the thought of Jethro, for whom the mere sound of a gun being fired had been sufficient to plunge him back into a state of shock, laying landmines and shooting at workmen. And her heart cried out at the vision of her beloved Yondover fallen into such a terrible state of disrepair.

Then Pippa said, 'I've been wondering all the way back what could have happened to turn the person who took those brilliant photographs into a recluse. You see, he wasn't always a hermit. In fact, from what Mrs Lowe said, he must have been a rather outrageous character. Apparently he was homosexual and, according to her, he used to throw really wild parties, although the parties had stopped by the time she and her husband moved to Kipwell, so she's only talking from hearsay.

'I think that the war changed his life. His studio was destroyed during the war and his home was taken over by the government. And he retired from photography after the war. When I was at the Royal Photographic Society in Bath, I saw some of his war photographs in an exhibition. They made a tremendous impact on me – so heaven only knows how he must have felt, seeing those sights in person.'

Kitty did not trust herself to say anything.

Pippa sighed. 'Well, whatever the truth, I have a feeling I've reached the end of the line, although I could write to him, I suppose. He might be pleased to know that, all these years on, somebody appreciates his work.'

For the first time since Pippa had begun her account of her morning, Kitty felt a real frisson of fear. There were only three people still alive who knew the full story of her marriage to Giles – Adam and Eve and Giles himself. She knew her secret was safe with the first two. But how would Giles react? How would he respond to a letter from Pippa?

'From what you've told me, he wouldn't bother to reply,' she said, in what she hoped was a casual tone, but that sounded decidedly shaky to her own ears.

Pippa nodded. 'Yes, you're probably right. Oh, well, it's been interesting.'

Kitty slumped back against the pillows. By a hair's breadth, danger seemed to have been averted.

CHAPTER 13

Long after Pippa had left the hospital, her words continued to echo in Kitty's ear: 'I've been wondering all the way back what could have happened to turn the person who took those brilliant photographs into a recluse. You see, he wasn't always a hermit. Apparently he was homosexual and he used to throw really wild parties . . .'

From the deep recesses of Kitty's memory came lines from a poem:

> . . . the scent comes back
> Of an unhappy garden gone to wrack,
> The flower-beds trampled for an idiot's sport,
> A mass of vermin batt'ning there, a mort
> Of weeds a-fester, all the green turned black,
> And through the sodden glades of loss and lack
> The dead winds blow of hate and false report.

Despite herself, she could not help but feel a sudden surge of pity for an old man immured by his own mistakes.

For the mistake *had* been his, although she had been the one to be blamed. Their marriage might just have worked, had he not been so confused and complex a personality, floundering in the search for his personal and sexual identity. But he had brought his fear and guilt with him to their marriage bed, then, unable to overcome his inhibitions, widened the emotional distance between them by installing a physical divide in the form of twin beds. He had buried himself in his work and involved them both in a social programme which had made communication between them all but impossible and ultimately – decades later – led to the exposure of the secret he had most wanted to keep concealed.

But nobody, apart from Adam, was aware of what had happened within the privacy of their own four walls. So far as the rest of the world was concerned, she had been the guilty party. It was she who had been unfaithful. It was she who had left Giles.

But that was leaping ahead. First had come the wedding and then the honeymoon.

They had been married the April following their engagement, not at St Peter's in Kipwell but, by special dispensation, at the Berkshire cathedral of which her maternal grandfather was Dean. This was at her father's own request, for he saw in the occasion an opportunity to remind the ecclesiastical élite of his existence. The Bishop officiated at the ceremony and the guests were carefully selected, not for the affection in which they were held by bride or groom, but for their position in society. Sir Hector and Lady Maude Pugh were present, of course, but only at West's insistence were the Gurneys permitted to attend, while the likes of Cook, Polly Clark, Bob Ireland and other villagers had to content themselves with a private celebration.

Not that Catherine had been unduly upset. The only person she would have really liked to be present was Sonja and she understood that it was too far for her to come all the way from Berlin.

The rest of the pews had been filled with relations whom she knew only distantly and by friends of Giles from university and from London. Her bridesmaids were chosen by her father, two young cousins, granddaughters also of the Dean. Adam was Giles's best man.

'If G.G. were not my closest friend, I should be deeply envious of his good fortune today,' Adam had said, in his speech during the reception at the Deanery. 'As it is, I can only offer the two people dearest to my heart my sincerest best wishes for a long and happy life together.'

Later, Catherine and he had found themselves momentarily alone together in the crowded room and Adam clinked his glass against hers. 'I mean it,' he had said. 'I hope you will be happy.'

She had been surprised to see a troubled expression in his eyes, but could only assume that his feelings towards her were actually deeper than he had let on. Then Giles had joined them, placing his arm possessively round her waist, and Adam's face had resumed its usual good-natured smile.

They had caught a late afternoon train up to London and spent the first

171

night of their married life at an hotel. Giles had left her alone in their room to wash and change, then, after a discreet length of time, returned to ready himself, before they went downstairs to the restaurant for dinner. She was vaguely aware, during their meal, that his stammer had returned, but since she was herself feeling nervous about the night ahead, she had not paid any great heed to this symptom of nervousness on his part.

After dinner, they had danced for a while, then Giles had suggested that she must be feeling tired and she went back up to their room, where a maid had unpacked their overnight bags and turned down the sheets of their double bed.

Like most of her generation, she had come ill-prepared for the physical side of marriage, although, having lived in the country, she was not entirely ignorant of the reproduction process. She might have grown up in the liberated 1920s, but she was still essentially a product of the prudish Victorian age. Matron had seen the pupils of St Margaret's through puberty and Prudence Fellowes had taken advantage of the lingerie department in Harrods, while shopping for her trousseau, to warn her daughter, 'I'm afraid the reality of marriage won't live up to your romantic ideas. But there are some things women simply have to put up with.'

Now Catherine had undressed and put on the prim, high-necked, long-sleeved nightgown her mother had chosen and which the maid had laid out on her pillow. Then, turning off the light, so that the room was illuminated only by the glow of the street lamp outside, she slipped between the crisp white sheets.

It was so long before Giles came up that she had fallen asleep, but she awoke with a start as she became aware of him padding softly about the room. He slid into bed and lay beside her.

Breathlessly, she had waited for him to take her in his arms, but when he did not, she was unsure what to do. If he believed her still to be asleep, he might not like to waken her. But if she made the first advance, he might think her too forward. In the end, she whispered, 'Giles?'

'You're awake? I didn't r-realize . . . I d-didn't want to d-disturb you.' His hand had found hers. As on the first occasion he had kissed her, his hand was shaking. Realizing that he was more frightened than she was, she was seized with pity and moved towards him. He lifted his hand and brushed against her breast, causing a tingle of excitement to run through her. Releasing her hand, he tremulously allowed his own to fold around her breast and caress it.

His touch had released a flood of previously unknown sensations within her, above all a warm, melting, yearning feeling that made her want to press against him and wrap her limbs about him. But again, not knowing how she was supposed to respond, she remained where she was, inwardly quivering and outwardly motionless. Eventually, he reached out with his other arm, drew her to him and kissed her. Now that she was lying so close to him, she realized it was not just his hands which were shaking, but his entire body.

Gradually, as the night wore on, they had both gained in confidence. His fingers undid the ribbons of her nightdress and hers crept within his pyjama jacket. But although their abdomens were close against each other, so that she could feel the male part of him moving inside his pyjama trousers, he did not touch her below the waist until, suddenly, breathing heavily, he drew up the skirt of her nightgown and pushed her legs apart.

Her mother was right: the reality of love did not match up to Catherine's romantic expectations. When Giles took her, her body was crying out for him, but the act itself was an anti-climax, clumsy and painful, and his weight was almost intolerable upon her. After it was over, she felt messy and unclean, and the following morning, she was embarrassed to discover the bedsheets were stained with blood.

From London, they had taken the Pullman to Paris and thence travelled to Provence, where they stayed at a delightful pension in Arles recommended by West, who had spent many happy days there in the past. Catherine's and Giles's days were happy too – or at least, Catherine tried to convince herself that they were.

The surrounding countryside was beautiful, the weather was kind, the people they encountered on their travels were friendly and their hosts were most hospitable. Giles captured on his new Rolleiflex camera the ancient sights of Nîmes, Arles and Avignon, Alphonse Daudet's *moulin* at Fontvieille, the Pont du Gard and the Alpilles, the rocky foothills of the Alps, where Van Gogh had painted some of Catherine's favourite pictures, although Giles preferred the gentle subtleties of Cézanne to Van Gogh's brilliant colours.

Yes, their days passed in a blur of activity. But at the end of every sunlit day, night was waiting. As darkness fell, Giles's stutter would return and his hand would tremble as he lifted his wine glass at dinner. A brooding frown would settle on his brow and a veil fall over his eyes.

Twice more in the early stages of their honeymoon he made love to her and although her body was aroused each time she felt his tentative caress, when he took her it was as painful and unsatisfying as the first time.

After that, he remained in the bar long after she had retired to their room and drifted into an uneasy sleep in the vast double bed. Once, he was so drunk that he woke her as he blundered about the room, but she kept her eyes closed and regulated her breathing so that he should think she was asleep. Long after he had fallen into a stuporous slumber, she remained awake, hurt and unhappy, gazing into the darkness.

The only reason she could think of to explain his behaviour was that she disappointed him. By nature a warm and affectionate person, her every impulse made her want to cuddle up to him. Instinct also told her that if they were both unencumbered by nightclothes, their bodies would meld more easily together. But so long as Giles retained his pyjamas, modesty prevented her from shedding her nightdress.

Next morning, after the maid had brought their tray of coffee, she summoned up all her courage and asked Giles outright if he was disappointed in her. 'N-no,' he replied, looking away from her, 'it's n-not you.' Then he added, 'I c-can't sleep if I c-come to bed early. I always k-keep late hours.'

At his request, she breakfasted alone, but the proprietor's wife's solicitous enquiry as to her well-being was almost too much for her, and only by dint of great self-control did she appear composed while she picked at her meal. All the hotel staff knew they were on their honeymoon. Everyone must be wondering why Giles preferred the bar to his new wife's bed.

From then on, she asked for breakfast to be brought up to their room. Sometimes Giles ate with her, but usually he remained in bed, asleep or pretending to sleep, while she breakfasted on the small balcony, pretending to be engrossed in a book. Once they were away from the pension, however – or, more specifically, away from the bedroom – his spirits would gradually recover and Catherine would assume a forced gaiety, pushing the dark memories of the night to the back of her mind.

At the end of three weeks, they returned to London and, at Porter's Place, she found the problem of their future sleeping arrangements had already been resolved. Forsyth bowed them deferentially into the house and, as a maid hurried to help unload their luggage, Mrs Forsyth led Catherine upstairs. Here she saw that the master bedroom contained two matching single beds, separated by a bedside table. 'This is yours, madam, nearest the window,' the housekeeper said expressionlessly. Yet Catherine was sure she heard an undertone of matronly contempt for a wife whose husband did not even want to share a conjugal bed.

She had never really felt as though she belonged at Porter's Place. From noon onwards the house was filled with débutantes, elegantly coiffured and immaculately made up, wearing frothy evening dresses, chattering and laughing as they descended from the bedroom where they had been changing, on their way to the studio, ignoring her if they should pass her, as though she were merely an insignificant parlourmaid.

Used to the easy familiarity of Yondover, she had found it difficult to adjust to the superior correctness of the Forsyths, who called her 'madam' and expected her to give orders she did not know how to give. The kitchen was forbidden territory: if she simply wanted a biscuit to nibble, she had to ring a bell for a maid to bring it.

Giles's studio and darkroom were even more sacrosanct. Once and once only did she make the mistake of entering the studio while Giles was shooting. His sitter on that occasion was Daphne du Maurier, the granddaughter of George du Maurier, whose novels she greatly admired. Miss du Maurier was seated by the window, looking wistfully beautiful against a filmy muslin curtain. As Catherine came in, she turned her head and Giles said, 'Eyes to camera, please, Miss du Maurier.

'Whyte, move the boom to the right. No, too far, bring it back a bit. Yes, leave it there.

'Pickard, flood the spotlight more, it's too condensed.

'I still think that fill-in light is a little too strong. Move it back a foot.

'Miss Spencer, darkslide.'

Treading carefully over the cables snaking across the floor, Catherine went to stand behind him, laying her hand on the focusing cloth draped over his shoulders. Miss du Maurier again moved her head and Giles said, 'Miss du Maurier, look back into camera again, please.' The shutter clicked. Giles pulled out the slide and handed it to Miss Spencer, who placed it, with others, on the trolley beside her.

Several times more, the lights were moved, but Catherine could sense

Giles's dissatisfaction and, five minutes later, he thanked Miss du Maurier and the session was over. As the two assistants busied themselves with lights and backgrounds, Miss Spencer saw the sitter to her car.

Giles turned to Catherine and hissed, 'Don't you know better than to burst in like that?'

'I just wanted to see . . .'

'I don't give a damn what you wanted. You ruined my shot. You distracted her attention.'

'But I didn't say anything. I didn't even move. If anyone distracted her, it was your assistants moving those lights.'

'No, it was you, the curious onlooker. She's shy, but she was just starting to relax when – what happens? A strange young woman comes in and peers at her. Couldn't you see how tense she was?'

Mutely, Catherine shook her head.

'Never ever do that again,' Giles growled.

At that moment, Miss Spencer returned and cast her a pitying look. Catherine could not help but feel jealous of Miss Spencer. She made his appointments, ordered his film, paid his suppliers and acted as chaperone to his female sitters. She alone was trusted to load and unload his slides. She retouched his negatives and prints. She and Giles would spend hours together closeted in the darkroom, whereas Catherine had never even witnessed the mysterious process of a film being developed and prints made. She had never asked and never been invited.

No, Porter's Place was not Catherine's house and the people in it were not her people. Worst of all, Giles was no longer the man she had believed she had married. Not only did his personality seem to have changed, but he had changed his name as well. Giles, he had decided, was a rather common, peasant-sounding name, whereas Gawaine, his second Christian name – which he had found even more embarrassing when he was at school than his initials – now suddenly seemed to offer the advantages of being unusual, romantic and sufficiently refined for a society photographer of his standing.

Her only consolation, although this was short-lived, was that almost immediately upon their return from France, they were drawn into such a hectic whirl of luncheons, *thés dansants*, dinner parties, balls, concerts, theatre and night club visits, that by the time she fell into bed in the early hours of the morning, she was too exhausted to want anything but sleep.

176

To begin with, she threw herself into this new, glamorous existence, revelling in the excitement of cocktails, risqué exchanges, daring new dances and, best of all, jazz – music which aroused in her the same deep, primeval instincts as did thunderstorms. She loved being introduced to the smart set of which Giles had become a part as Mrs Gawaine Devere and finding herself the centre of attention. She was flattered by the compliments paid to her by the men and the apparently slant-eyed looks from their wives and girlfriends.

But it did not take her long to recognize her new-found acquaintances as vultures of society, preying on Giles's vanity and feeding on his ambition. What she had believed to be envious glances in her own direction had, in fact, been idle curiosity about a country parson's daughter, who had attended a rather obscure finishing school and not made her début. For a brief while she had been a novelty. Then, like the Ladies and Honourable Misses who flocked to Giles's studio, the wives and girlfriends treated her with disdain, while their equally fickle partners discovered other new-comers with whom to flirt.

If Giles was aware of her discomfort, he chose to ignore it. He was, she soon realized, possessed of a ruthless determination to succeed in his profession, which was why, she now saw, he had refurbished Porter's Place without taking her feelings into account. He was very jealous of other photographers, particularly those of his own age who seemed to be doing better than himself. The sight or even the mere mention of Tunbridge, Baron, Cecil Beaton or Dorothy Wilding – this last a woman, to make matters worse – would throw him into a deep depression.

Giles's dark moods were, in fact, the most difficult feature of his personality with which Catherine had to contend. He did not have a quick or violent temper: indeed, only once during their marriage was she ever to hear him raise his voice in anger. Nor did he sulk or become petulant if things did not go to his liking. Instead, his stutter would return and, as had occurred during their honeymoon, it would be as if a shutter closed over his eyes, so that his vision was turned inward upon himself and he fell into a brooding silence that could last for days on end.

Catherine continued to interpret his moods as a reflection upon herself, for he did not allow them to intrude upon his work, except for snapping at his assistants: with his clients he was always patient and charming.

Freed from the artificial constraints of the honeymoon, the bedroom had come to assume less importance in their lives and Catherine had discovered that separate beds were fashionable. Yet she could not help but be aware that something was lacking in their marriage and blamed this on herself, certain she was failing him.

Once, after he had emerged from such a depression, he admitted that he had suffered in this way ever since he was a small boy. 'It happens for no r-reason,' he explained: 'It's as if I-I-I have been plunged into a black tunnel. Then s-suddenly, I see l-light again and everything is all right – until the n-next occasion. There's nothing you can do, C-Catherine, except l-leave me to get out of it in my own t-time.'

The rest of the household seemed unaffected by his disposition. The Forsyths remained deferentially efficient, the parlourmaid still sang off-key as she cleaned out the grates in the early morning and, under Miss Spencer's direction, the studio continued to run like clockwork.

But Catherine could not remain so detached. She grew to dread his moods and, when they occurred, they cast a shadow over her, dragging her spirits down with his, so that she found her normal optimism deserting her. She felt listless and lost her appetite. Sometimes she would burst into tears, which – far from arousing Giles's sympathy or remorse – would plunge him into an even blacker mood.

There was nobody in whom she could confide. Sonja was far away in Berlin, preparing for her own marriage to Felix, and Catherine's feelings were far too complex to express on paper. In the past, she would probably have found the courage to talk the matter over with West, even though Porter's Place was his wedding gift and Giles his own grandson, but she had not seen him since her marriage.

She grew increasingly homesick for Yondover and missed West so badly that the pain was like a physical hurt. Giles, on the contrary, seldom mentioned them and when she suggested going down to Kipwell, would reply, 'There are too many bookings. I can't afford to let any of my clients down. Later on in the summer we'll go, but not now.'

This dismissal of the place he professed to hold so dear and the people who cared so much for him cut her to the quick.

Then something even more shattering occurred. Some three months after their marriage, they had gone in a group to a disappointing revue at the London Pavilion, a slightly better dinner at a new restaurant and then moved on to an overcrowded night club in Soho. They had eventually settled themselves at a table and Catherine had found that she was separated from Giles. Her own neighbours were the monocle-wearing youngest son of a baronet, called Archie, whose conversation seemed not to extend beyond 'I say,' and 'By Gad!' and the terrifyingly intellectual Hermione Chalcott, who also sported a monocle, had an Eton crop and was an embarrassingly vociferous advocate of contraception.

Waiters were just serving champagne, when the band stopped playing and the dancers returned to their tables. In this lull, a voice suddenly made itself heard. 'Why, hello, Cynthia dahling,' Catherine heard it say, a few tables away, 'left Henry at home tonight, have we? Oh, dear, I am sowwy. Do give him my love and tell him to get better soon.' It came nearer: 'Sawah, dear, what a divine dwess.' 'Gertwude! I haven't seen you since the Clermont-Blythe's little do. Yeth, of course I wemember. The champagne was like dog's piss and as for the caviar . . .'

Finally the voice's owner wafted into view, a tall young man with golden curls, wearing a dinner jacket and trousers so well-fitting they looked as if he had been poured into them, a pink dress shirt and a huge, floppy magenta bow-tie and matching cummerbund. He kissed his fingers extravagantly to various ladies as he made his way between the tables, causing the diamonds to glitter in the dress ring on his right hand.

At the top of their own table he paused, his eyes – a curious mauve-blue – sweeping assessingly over their company. Then his lips formed a smile, revealing perfectly formed, very white teeth, and he drawled, 'Why, Horsey, dahling, fancy finding you here! I've thought about you so often, dear boy, ever since I was sent down. What a long time ago that seems, doesn't it? But we had such fun, didn't we? Those lovely photographs you used to take. I must come wound to your studio, so you can do some more of me.'

'By Gad!' Archie exclaimed and his monocle popped out of his eye.

'Oh, Christ,' Hermione Chalcott muttered in her deep baritone. 'Boy Tate . . . That bloody pansy's all we need to complete a perfect evening!'

'But neither of us can hold the candle to Boy,' Catherine heard Adam saying, 'who is so aesthetic as to be almost effete . . . There's a topping photograph Giles took of him. If you didn't know, you'd never realize he wasn't a woman . . .'

Homosexuality had been an unknown concept while she was at school, but after three months in London she was considerably more enlightened.

She forced herself to look past the curiously staring face towards her husband. Giles's cheeks had flushed a deep red and he was gazing almost beseechingly at the flamboyant figure looming over the table, who was saying, 'A little bird told me you're mawwied now.' He fluttered his long eyelashes questioningly at the two pretty girls to either side of Giles. 'Aren't you going to intwoduce me to the lucky lady, Horsey?'

Giles finally found his voice. 'P-p-please, B-b-boy . . .'

Boy Tate tossed back his curls and laughed. 'Oh, don't worry, dahling, I pwomise I'm not jealous.'

Suddenly, sickeningly, everything fell into place. Comments Adam had let drop. Giles's reaction whenever Boy Tate was mentioned. She might have been the first girl Giles had ever kissed, but she was not the first person . . .

The band chose that moment to burst into life again. Anxious to avoid an embarrassing and potentially ugly scene, couples rose from around the table and took to the floor. Whether intentionally or not, Archie came into his own. Replacing his monocle, he turned to Catherine and said, 'I say, would you care to dance?'

She was trembling so much that she was not sure she could even stand and was grateful for Archie's outstretched hand. When she was on her feet, she looked again at Giles, but he was still staring at Boy. Shakily, she told Archie, 'I'd be grateful if you could see me to a cab.'

Once alone in the bedroom at Porter's Place, Catherine neither turned on the light nor undressed, but drew a chair up to the window. Although the evening was warm, she was shivering uncontrollably. Very slowly, she went across to her bed, wrapped herself in the counterpane and returned to her seat.

Some while later – how long, she had no idea – she heard the front door open and footsteps sounding on the staircase. The door opened and closed again. Giles came and stood at the window.

When the silence between them became unbearable, she said, 'I don't understand.'

To her dismay, he fell to his knees and, burying his face in her lap, began to cry, convulsive sobs racking his body, his tears soaking through the counterpane and the flimsy material of her dress.

For a long time, repugnance and pity raged within her. Finally, pity won. Her hand reached out and stroked his hair and, gradually, his weeping abated. 'P-p-please, K-K-Kitty,' he whispered, 'f-forgive me.'

'I don't understand,' she repeated.

He remained on his knees, his voice muffled in the counterpane, his stutter so bad that his words were at times almost incomprehensible, as he tried to explain the events which had led to that evening's confrontation. His had been a lonely childhood, he said. At school, the other boys had laughed at his name, at his stutter, at his lack of ability on the sports field, while he was always being caned by the masters for misdemeanours he wasn't aware of committing. Then he had been befriended by one of the prefects, who had invited him up to his study, comforted him and, in due course, initiated him in the art of male love.

'I-I-I knew it was wr-wrong,' he stammered, 'b-but I-I-I couldn't help myself. It was so w-w-wonderful to be w-w-wanted.'

After the prefect left, there had been nobody until he went up to Oxford and met Boy. Boy in those days, he claimed, had been quite different from the Boy Catherine had seen that evening. Being so pretty, he had suffered even more at school than Giles. 'H-he w-was a lost s-soul like myself,' Giles said. 'I-I-I loved him like a b-brother.' But the relationship had quickly passed beyond that of brothers.

She stared bleakly over his head. The first Christmas she had met Giles he had already had his first homosexual experience. The summer before she had gone to Vevey, when he and Adam had come to Yondover, he and Boy Tate had already been lovers . . .

Then, at the beginning of their final year, Boy was discovered in a seedy hotel room in bed with another man – and sent down. Giles had been so shocked at finding out that he was not the only one receiving Boy's favours that he had contemplated suicide. 'If it h-h-hadn't been for Adam, I-I-I would have k-killed myself,' he said. 'It w-was Adam who stopped me . . .

'And then, last s-summer, I-I-I met you again. Y-y-you seemed so n-natural, so sp-p-pontaneous. You had s-such a w-wonderful gift for l-life. I th-th-thought it w-would be p-p-possible for m-me to . . . W-w-when you saved my life in the th-thunderstorm and told me you l-loved me, I-I-I h-hoped . . .'

She wanted to block up her ears so that she did not have to listen. 'Do you still love him?' she forced herself to ask.

'I-I-I don't kn-n-now. H-h-he has changed. L-last night, he was s-s-so hard, so cruel.'

Outside, dawn was breaking over London. Birds began to sing in the square opposite. There came the clopping of a horse's hooves, the rumble of a cart, the roar of a car, the calling of men's voices, labourers on their way to work and, from downstairs, the sound of the parlourmaid singing off-key as she set about her morning chores. Another day, another life.

She could not bear to stay here. She could not bear to remain in the same room, in the same house, in the same town as Giles. She pushed him aside and, rising to her feet, said, 'I have to get away.'

He gazed at her imploringly, his eyes red and swollen, his face haggard. 'I-I-I l-love you, K-Kitty. P-p-please don't leave me ... I-I-I c-can't h-help the way I am.'

The anguish in his voice tore at her heart, but her heart was like a stone, grey and numb and mortally cold. She shook her head. 'I need time – to think – to come to terms – to sort all this out in my mind.'

'B-b-but where will you g-go?'

There was only one place she could go. Only one place where she could find peace. And only one person who could help her put together again the shattered remnants of her life. 'To Yondover,' she replied.

Never had a journey seemed so long as that one to Kipwell. Never had fellow passengers on a train seemed so determined to make conversation. Never had Frederick Gurney been so cheerful when she finally disembarked, so intent on asking after her and Giles's life in the big city and so slow to carry her bag across the footbridge to the solitary horse-drawn hackney. Never had the drive up to Yondover seemed so slow and never had she been more reluctant to see Lady Maude on her big, roan stallion or her father emerging through the churchyard lychgate. She pulled her hat down further on her head and shrank back against the seat, so that they should not recognize her. At some point she would have to admit her presence, but not today . . .

Yet only after the hackney had deposited her at Yondover and West had opened the front door, his smile of welcome changing to a frown of concern as he noticed the pallor of her cheeks and recognized the pain in her eyes, did her self-control break down. Only when she was in the arms of the one person in the world she trusted absolutely did she relax the mask she had been wearing ever since Giles's dreadful confession and give way to her grief.

For a while, West simply let her cry. Then he asked, 'Do you want to tell me about it?'

Suddenly, she did not want to talk about the night that was gone. Later, perhaps, but this was not the moment. She was too exhausted, too confused. Now, it was sufficient that she was at Yondover and West was near. She shook her head. 'I haven't slept,' she gulped.

'Ah, that might account for quite a lot . . .' He put his arm around her shoulder and slowly led her up the stairs to his old attic nursery, with the rocking horse and the toy theatre and the teddy bear sitting on the pillow. 'Get into bed,' he said tenderly. 'I'll be back in a few moments.'

When he returned, he was carrying a mug of hot milk. 'I've put some brandy in it,' he said. 'It will help you sleep.'

She drank the soothing milk, then slid down under the bedclothes. 'West, will you stay until I go to sleep?'

'Yes, I'll stay.'

She reached out her hand and he took it in hers. 'I feel like a child,' she whispered.

'You are a child, Kitty-Cat. My child.'

It was dusk when she awoke, opening her eyes to a strange room, with curtains blowing gently in the breeze and roses peeking in through the window. Then everything came flooding back to her – the night club, Boy Tate, Giles . . .

She got out of bed and saw that while she had slept her bag had been unpacked and a ewer of water and a bowl placed on the chest of drawers. She washed and dried herself on a towel smelling of lavender. Then she dressed, the floorboards creaking beneath her feet as she moved about the room. Just as she finished her toilette, there was a knock on the door and Fanny entered.

'I thought I heard you up and about,' she said. 'I looked in earlier a couple of times, but you were so sound asleep I didn't like to disturb you.'

Never had that round figure and those rosy cheeks seemed so dear. 'Oh, Fanny!' Kitty cried. She was about to throw her arms around her and kiss her, when something about her expression stopped her. 'Fanny, what's the matter?'

The housekeeper sat down on the edge of the bed. 'I don't know what's brought you back here so sudden like, Miss Kitty, but I think you ought to know that the Master's not been well. It's his heart. He had an attack . . .'

For a moment it felt as if Kitty's own heart stopped beating. 'A heart attack?' she echoed faintly.

Fanny nodded sombrely. 'He was taken bad a couple of days after the wedding. Luckily, it was in the early morning and Gurney was able to ride down and fetch Dr Jenkins. Mr Westrup was in the Lewes hospital for about a fortnight before he was allowed home.'

'But why didn't he tell us?'

'Well, Miss Kitty, you and Master Giles were on your honeymoon.'

'But when we came back?'

'Why then you was having such a gay time, he didn't want to spoil your happiness. Anyway, there was nothing you could do. You'd probably have done more harm than good, Miss Kitty, fussing him and getting him over-excited. And that's what I'm frightened of now. You see, Dr Jenkins warned him that another attack could happen any time. He's given him some pills to take if he feels queer, and put him on a diet. But most of all, he says that Mr Westrup must not over-tire himself or have any kind of worry.'

She allowed time for her words to sink in, then continued, 'If as how I'm right and those tears what I saw from the window this morning mean there's trouble between you and Master Giles, please keep it to yourself and don't worry Mr Westrup.'

Kitty gazed unseeingly past her. The trouble between herself and Giles, as Fanny called it, was nothing compared to the fact that West had nearly died – that he could die at any moment . . .

Fanny rose heavily to her feet. 'I hope you'll pardon me for speaking out of turn, Miss Kitty, but I thought you ought to know. And now I must be getting on. The Master's in the music room. He says to join him there when you're ready.'

West was playing Liszt when Kitty entered the music room. He turned his head and smiled at her, looking so like his old self that she found it almost impossible to believe that what Fanny had told her was true, until she realized that he was much thinner than he used to be and there were lines on his face which had never been there before.

She went past him and sat down on the step on the French windows, breathing in the scents of the garden and letting the notes of the music waft over her, calm and soothing. Rafe appeared and, after nuzzling at her hand, settled at her feet. A full moon was rising and, in the twilight, phantom-like bats were flitting in and out from the eaves.

When the final cadences of the étude had died away, West rose from the piano stool and came to sit beside her. 'Feeling better?'

'Much,' she assured him. 'West, I'm sorry about this morning. Giles and I had a bit of a tiff last night. It was our first argument.'

'Do you want to tell me what happened?'

'Oh, it was rather silly. We were at a night club . . .'

He gave a relieved laugh. 'And let me guess! Giles was jealous because you were dancing with another man?'

She seized upon the excuse and nodded.

'Well, that won't do him any harm. No man should take his wife for granted – well, certainly not one as pretty as you.'

She bit her lip, wondering how to phrase her next statement without causing him anxiety. In the end, she asked, 'Will it be all right if I stay here for a few days?' Hurriedly, she added, 'I've missed Yondover . . .'

'Kitty-Cat, I understand. I felt exactly the same when I lived in London. Does Giles know you're here?'

'Oh, yes. I told him.'

'In that case, of course you can stay. Though if I may interfere, perhaps you should telephone him from the village in the morning and patch up your quarrel – maybe suggest he comes down at the weekend. By the sound of it, you could both do with a change of scene and some fresh air.'

Kitty was saved from the need to respond immediately to this by the sound of Fanny's voice calling that supper was ready.

'We eat in the kitchen these days,' West said. 'I hope you're hungry. Fanny has prepared your favourite meal. Freshly caught plaice.'

Conscious of Fanny's gaze upon her, Kitty did her best to do justice to the supper. Surprisingly, it was Gurney who kept the conversation going, treating them first to a lugubrious account of his trip to the sea to buy the fish, including a description of every danged motorist he had encountered on the way, then going on to tell Kitty about the particularly bad attack of blight which was affecting his potatoes. 'What with blight and them danged thrips what 'ave got at the gladiolus, us've been 'avin' a rare bad time 'ere,' he informed her.

West laughed. 'Gurney wouldn't be happy if he didn't have something to moan about.' Kitty noticed that he was merely picking at his food, pushing it about his plate to make it look as if he was eating.

After the meal, he said, 'It's a lovely evening. Do you fancy a walk, Kitty-Cat?'

Fanny frowned warningly and Kitty replied, trying to sound casual, 'That would be nice. We could stroll over to the paddock and see Honey.'

But once they were outside, wandering arm in arm across the lawn with Rafe racing ahead of them, he said, 'You can see Honey tomorrow. Let's go up on Uffing Down.'

'West, no! It's too . . . I'm wearing the wrong shoes.'

He sighed. 'Fanny's told you, hasn't she?'

'Yes, and I'm glad she did.'

'Sshh, Kitty-Cat, don't say any more. Just take off your high heels and let's walk up on Uffing Down. I'll be all right, I promise.'

Very slowly, they went up the steep chalk path to the top of the hill, stopping frequently on the way for West to regain his breath. When they reached the top, he lowered himself to the ground and she sat down beside him.

Eventually he said, 'You were telling me the truth, weren't you? You and Giles have only had a lovers' tiff? Apart from this one little argument, you are happy together?'

At some point in the near future – unless she could find some miraculous way of avoiding it – the truth would have to emerge. But not now. Now, for the first time in her life, she must lie to West. 'Yes,' she replied quietly, 'we are very happy.'

The moon was hanging in the sky like a big, round, creamy cheese and, in its glow, she saw his features soften. 'That is all I need to know. If you are both happy, I can die in peace.'

'West, no!' The cry escaped involuntarily, disturbing the sheep grazing around them.

186

He gazed out over the Weald. 'Kitty-Cat, I'm seventy-six years old, six years past my allotted span of three score years and ten. Yet these last six years, since I have known you, have been more precious to me than all those which went before, for in you I have relived the visions of my youth and witnessed the culmination of my dreams.

'Until I met you, I considered my life a failure. My birth caused my mother's death. I was a disappointment to my father. My wife left me for another man and my daughter was taken from me before I ever really knew her. Even in Giles I could find no hope, for he seemed to have inherited all my weaknesses and I could see no way of correcting in him the faults I had been unable to cure in myself.

'Other men in a similar position know the satisfaction of a career to fill the emptiness in their personal lives, but even this was denied me.'

'You had Yondover,' Kitty interjected, a lump in her throat.

'Yes, I had Yondover . . . But until you came into it, there were times when it seemed little more than a shell, inhabited by four people who were weary of living. You invested Yondover with life, Kitty. You brought laughter and joy – and, most important of all, love.

'And now I have the satisfaction of knowing that you and Giles are happy and will go on being happy in the way which Marion and I were denied, I can face with equanimity the idea that my life is ending.'

Tears were streaming down Kitty's cheeks and she could not stop them. West turned and, with his finger, wiped them away. 'Please don't cry.'

'But I can't bear the thought of you not being here . . .'

'You have Giles now.' Then he smiled. 'And I shall never be far away.' He pointed up into the vaulted arches of the sky. 'That is where heaven is – all those stars you see are souls, keeping watch over us mortals. When you need me, Kitty-Cat, you have only to come up here to the top of Uffing Down and my spirit will be with you. At night it will be among the stars and, in the daytime, it will be flying with the gulls and singing with the skylark . . .'

Fanny was waiting when they returned to the house, glancing anxiously from one to the other of them, but Kitty had dried her tears and West said, 'It's all right, Fanny, you needn't fuss. I've confessed to Kitty that I've been unwell and she has taken good care of me. We've had a lovely walk. In fact, I feel better than I have for a long time.'

Fanny's expression relaxed. 'All the same, you know what the doctor said about going to bed early, Mr Westrup, and getting plenty of rest. It's gone ten o'clock now, well past your usual bedtime.'

'To hell with the doctor!' West exclaimed. Then he nodded, 'But you're right, Fanny, I am a little weary. I shall sleep well tonight.'

He put his head round the kitchen door and called, 'G'night, Gurney. G'night, Jethro.' At the foot of the stairs, he paused and patted Rafe. 'Good night, old chap. You can sleep with your mistress tonight.' Then he held out his arms to Kitty and folded her to him. As his lips brushed her hair, he murmured, so softly that only she could hear him, 'I love you, Kitty-Cat.'

The following morning, she was awoken very early by Rafe jumping off the bed and leaping on to the wide window sill, where he sat making a strange keening sound. She slipped out of bed and stood beside him, stroking his pelt reassuringly. The morning was calm, the sky a pinky-gold colour like the skin of a ripe apricot. Suddenly, a gust of wind rattled the open window, shook the roses, streaked across the lawn and set the leaves on the trees and bushes on the far side of the garden a-tremble. Rafe followed its progress with his eyes, then gazed up towards Uffing Down and howled.

When, a short while later, Fanny burst into the room, distraught, Kitty did not need her words to know that West was dead.

'Oh, West . . .' Kitty was awoken by her own strangled cry. Tears were pouring down her cheeks.

A cool hand brushed across her forehead. Nurse Willis's pretty little face loomed over her, breaking in upon her memories with such suddenness that she was again uncertain for a few moments as to where she was, confusing West's death with her own presence in hospital. 'Mrs Pilgrim, what's the matter? Do your bruises hurt?'

Her bruises? Oh, of course . . . But no, the pain in her body was nothing to the ache in her heart.

A hand took her wrist. 'You're very hot and your pulse is rather high. I wouldn't be surprised if your temperature is up again.' A thermometer was placed in her mouth, then taken out again. 'Well, I was wrong. You must be too hot under the bedclothes. I'll take off one of the blankets. Now, have a sip of water.'

Kitty drank the water, then turned over on to her side and was soon drifting again, across the years, back to Yondover – back to a Yondover without West . . .

She could not clearly remember the sequence of events following West's death, but she could recall the funeral quite vividly – black-clad figures standing in the churchyard as her father's voice intoned, with the detached piousness of one who has suffered no personal loss: '*Forasmuch as it hath pleased Almighty God of his great mercy to take unto himself the soul of our dear brother here departed, we therefore commit his body to the ground: earth to earth, ashes to ashes, dust to dust . . .*'

She herself had been too stunned to cry, but her mother had sniffled into her handkerchief throughout the ceremony, while Lady Maude had kept blowing her nose in great trumpet-blasts. Marion McDonnell had sent an orchid spray, which she had thrown in on top of West's coffin as it was lowered into the grave, and Gurney had placed a bunch of roses on top of the mound of earth after the coffin was covered.

Someone must have telephoned Giles, for she was aware of him being at Yondover before the funeral, but he must have slept in his own room, while she remained in West's attic nursery. Certainly she had no recollection of any conversation taking place between them until after the service, when they were back at Yondover and the lawyer from Lewes had read out West's will. This had been made several years earlier and contained no surprises. Apart from small legacies to the Gurneys, his entire estate went to Giles. Not that she had expected anything, but it would have been comforting to have been left some small, personal memento. But why should West have thought of that, when he had assumed that everything which was Giles's would be shared with her?

After the lawyer had departed, Giles had said, 'I-I-I have to g-go back to London, but if y-y-you want to stay here, I-I-I shall f-fully u. lerstand.'

So a new pattern had evolved in their lives. Giles had lived at Porter's Place and she at Yondover. For the sake of appearances, she had occasionally gone up to London and Giles had spent the weekends at Yondover, although they had remained in separate rooms.

What bad, sad years those had been, when the shadow of West's death and the dark cloud of her own deep unhappiness had hung over Yondover, when Rafe had wandered round with his tail mournfully between his legs and the Gurneys had seemed, overnight, to age.

Yes, those were seemingly endless, desolate days, spent trying to fill the emptiness left in West's wake. Thankfully, there had been a lot to do, for Fanny was no longer able to manage all the housework on her own and refused to have a girl in from the village to help, while the heart seemed to have gone out of Gurney, when it came to tending West's gardens, and she had taken over much of his work. Only Jethro seemed stoically to accept the finality of West's death, mutely changing his allegiance from grandfather to grandson, looking up to Giles as the master of the house.

And those equally interminable weekends, when she and Giles had found themselves alone, with nothing in common except their memories of the man who had brought them together. Worst of all had been the nights, when Giles, fortified with drink, had come to her room, begging her to forgive him, trying to take her in a fumbling embrace, telling her that he no longer cared for Boy and that he loved only her.

She had sensed he was speaking the truth. She felt that for a man to love another man was unnatural, abnormal. She could well believe that Giles, who had known so much instability and insecurity during his childhood, longed, desperately, to be normal, to be like other men, to have a wife and children . . .

Often she had wondered whether she might have been better able to accept their situation if he had made a clean breast of his relationship with Boy Tate earlier, before they were married or at least before Boy Tate's and his paths had crossed, as he must surely have been aware that they must. Yet how could he have done? To admit to being a homosexual in those days was to admit to committing a criminal offence. And if he had, her own reaction would have been just the same. Indeed, her shock and revulsion, coming so soon upon his rejection by Boy Tate, might well have been sufficient to tip him over the psychological edge upon which he was teetering and perhaps drive him to suicide.

Gradually, her own initial shock about his affair with Boy Tate had worn off and she had come to see it as something quite apart from her. At that time Giles had scarcely been aware of her existence, certainly not aware of her as anything more than a child. She had even understood how a lonely, vulnerable young man could find consolation in another young man's embrace. She could also understand how he must have felt when, after Tate had rejected him, fate had thrust him, on the rebound, into her own arms.

So far as she was aware, however, nobody else at the night club had recognized that encounter with Boy Tate for what it was. Tate already had a notorious reputation and few, if any, friends. Her own abrupt departure was put down to a sudden, probably female indisposition, and her subsequent absence from London to West's death. Neither did anyone, including her own parents, find anything unusual about her decision to remain at Yondover. Now West was dead, it was her husband's home. For a variety of reasons, many couples found it convenient for the wife to stay in the country, while the husband spent the weekdays in town.

But Giles's confession that last night at Porter's Place had killed all her love for him and the words she had once so longed to hear now seemed like a blasphemy. And in his heart Giles must have known, as she had, that he was trying to resurrect a love which had never really existed, for after a while he had stopped coming to her room and ceased to protest his love.

So they had lived privately apart, while in public presenting a united front, in order that appearances were saved. Divorce was something neither of them had ever mentioned. So far as Giles was concerned, marriage – even a loveless one – offered a vital shield of respectability. As for herself, she stood to lose even more than Giles did from a divorce, for it was unlikely that she would then be able to remain at Yondover.

No one, not even the Gurneys, had realized how badly their marriage was foundering. They had not known of the shutter which had closed over Giles's mind, cutting her off from him, so that when they met it was increasingly as strangers. Least of all had anyone suspected her own sense of isolation and the aching loneliness in her.

Oh, yes, there had been parties, although 'wild' – the adjective Pippa had used – would be too strong to describe them . . .

After the final breakdown of their marriage, Giles had immersed himself in his work to the total exclusion of everything else. During the week, her own and the Gurneys' lives had followed the same pattern as when West was alive, getting up at daybreak and going early to bed, eating dinner at midday and supper at six. In fact, her life had in many ways taken over where West's had left off. His garden had become her garden, his plants as carefully looked after as when he was alive and replaced with exactly the same variety if any of them perished. Rather than make shrines of his rooms, she had taken them for her own use. She did the household accounts in his study, read the books in his library, dabbled with painting in his studio, played his piano after supper and slept in the long, attic nursery. And, because of this, it sometimes felt as if he were not really dead, but had just gone away on a brief visit and would soon return . . .

But on Friday nights, the tranquillity had been destroyed by cars jolting up the drive, careering over flower beds, parking on the lawn. Voices would screech: 'Oh, what a quaint little cottage!' 'Dahling, just look at that divine view!' Once they were inside the house, she would hear them calling from room to room: 'Oh, I say, isn't it deliciously primitive? There isn't any running water!' 'But rainwater's terribly good for your complexion, dahling.' 'And no electric lights! You'd think Gawaine . . .' 'I'm simply dying for a cocktail.'

Then the gramophone would start up, blaring out across the garden, and, taking a deep breath, she would go down to meet her husband's guests, the society darlings who made up his clientèle, the lounge lizards, the fashionable actresses, the *mondain* actors, the literary lions. How she had hated those weekends, those people with their shallow talk and slick manners, who conversed across her as though she did not exist, who intruded upon her solitude and violated her privacy.

Sometimes she had overheard them discussing her. 'Isn't she such a country bumpkin?' 'I can't imagine what Gawaine sees in her.' 'Have you tried talking to her, dahling? She's such a bore! The only things she knows anything about are plants and horses.'

She was only nineteen, little more than a child still, yet there was nobody at all with whom she could share her anguish. Even had they known the circumstances, her parents would not have sympathized. Marion McDonnell, who would possibly have understood, had fallen ill and herself died not long after West. As for Adam, he had by then left Oxford to start work at a City legal practice in Fenchurch Street, and although he occasionally came down to Yondover at weekends, she never saw him alone.

Not even to Sonja could she open her heart, for Sonja's letters from Berlin spoke of troubles of her own – of the economic and political crises overtaking Germany, as businesses failed and banks collapsed in the wake of the Wall Street Crash.

Remembering West's last words, she had gone up on to Uffing Down, but instead of finding his comforting presence in the birds and the stars, she had been only more bitterly aware of his loss. Far from sensing him all around her, so blurred suddenly was his image in her memory that she could not even remember how he had looked . . .

CHAPTER 14

The following morning when Pippa came downstairs, she found two letters for Kitty lying on the mat. One was a large manila envelope, with a typewritten address and marked PRIVATE AND CONFIDENTIAL. The other was A5 size and handwritten. She picked them up and took them with her into the kitchen, putting them on the table while she boiled the kettle.

It was as she was drinking her coffee that the postage frank on the smaller envelope caught her eye. Something Publishing it read, becoming illegible as it met the edge of the envelope's enclosure. Then she was struck by the fact that whoever had sent the letter had spelled Kitty's Christian name wrong and addressed the envelope to Mrs Katherine Pilgrim. It was an easy enough mistake to make and probably she would have given the matter not a second thought had she not so recently re-read Katherine Fountain's *Enchanted* books.

Glancing across to the dresser, her eye fell on Kitty's sketchpad with its unfinished picture of roses. She went into the living room and took *The Enchanted Mountain* from the bookshelf. It was published by Astra Publishing and the publisher's logo matched that on the smudged postage frank.

Kitty was feeling much brighter when Pippa arrived at the hospital that afternoon. 'The doctor came round this morning,' she announced. 'He said that provided my temperature remains normal for another twenty-four hours, I can go home tomorrow. Sister says that you can pick me up at ten. I am looking forward to it so much! I feel as if I've been in here for weeks.'

'Oh, that is good news!' Pippa perched herself again on the edge of the bed. 'You must tell me what clothes you'd like me to bring in.'

They discussed the whereabouts of the necessary items of Kitty's wardrobe, then Pippa said, 'You had post this morning.' She reached in her bag and handed Kitty the two envelopes, the one from the publishing company on top.

Kitty glanced at them, then put them on her bedside table.

'Don't you want to read them?' Pippa asked.

Kitty wasn't falling into that trap. Pippa had already raised enough ghosts. 'No, they'll wait.'

But Pippa cocked her head on one side and looked at her with such an expression that Kitty knew her secret was already out. 'The other night,' she said, 'when I was looking for books for you to read, I found some of my favourite books from my childhood. The *Enchanted* books.'

Kitty let out a long sigh. It was quite extraordinary the way things were happening. 'How did you guess?'

'I recognized your style of painting, although at first I didn't know *why* I recognized it. Then, when this letter came this morning, spelling Catherine with a K, I suddenly put two and two together. It's incredible! I used to love those books. And they haven't lost any of their appeal now I'm older. In fact, if anything I think I enjoyed them more now than I did when I was a kid.'

'So you already knew them?'

'Of course! I used to have the whole set.'

Kitty felt deeply moved and also rather astonished. The last thing she would have expected was for Sebastian to allow her books in his house. However, the *Enchanted* books had reached the peak of their success about the time that Pippa was a little girl, so perhaps he had decided that to have forbidden her to read them would have been to make an issue of them and – as every parent knew – forbidden fruit always tasted sweetest.

'But why didn't Mum and Dad tell me you were the author?' Pippa went on.

There was a simple answer to that. 'Perhaps they didn't know,' Kitty replied. 'There was no reason for them to associate me with Katherine Fountain.'

'And in which country were they set?'

'In Austria.'

'You obviously knew those places very well. There are amazing little bits of detail that you couldn't have made up if you'd never been there – like the Old Man in the Mountain.'

Kitty gazed out of the window and, for an instant, seemed to glimpse the white peak of the Hohe Steinberg against the incomparable, hyacinth blue of an alpine sky. 'Yes, the Old Man is a real mountain,' she murmured, 'but I changed its name.'

'So did you live in Austria? Is that how you speak German?'

'Yes, I did, for – er, for a while.'

Her glance alighted on the envelope from her publisher and, confident that whoever had confused her names was not a harbinger of bad tidings, she said briskly, 'Well, now my secret's out, I may as well open this, I suppose.'

'Oh, yes, please do!' Pippa exclaimed.

Inside the envelope was a handwritten air letter with an Australian stamp and Sydney postmark, addressed to her c/o Astra Publishing, Covent Garden, London WC2, bearing the request, 'Please forward'. It read:

> *Dear Ms Fountain,*
>
> *I have just spent a few wonderful days recapturing some of the magic of my childhood, thanks to your books. How glad I am that the* Enchanted *series has been reprinted. I read them when they were first published in the 1950s, when I was a little girl in England, but when my family emigrated to Australia I had to leave many of my possessions behind, including my books, as we had so much luggage to take with us.*
>
> *After my marriage, I lived in the outback, where books were not easily available and I tried in vain to obtain copies of your stories for my own children. Now I'm back in civilization and, finally, my family understand what I was raving about. My daughter in particular, now in her early twenties, is captivated by the charming stories and delightful illustrations. We all want to know if you have ever thought of doing more books. If so, I assure you that here, at least, on the other side of the world, you have*

devotees who, if no longer in the first flush of youth, will
be among the first to buy them.

With renewed thanks for the immense pleasure you
have brought us and very kindest wishes,
Yours sincerely, Susan Davies (Mrs)

She handed the letter to Pippa. 'Isn't that nice? I am always surprised when people like Mrs Davies write to me.'

Pippa read the letter, then asked, 'And *have* you thought of doing any more books?'

She shook her head. 'Anything I wrote now would be considered very old-fashioned. I'm out of touch with the way children's minds work. Children nowadays want to read about robots and spacecraft and computers and other things I know nothing about. All I see are old fogeys.'

'I disagree,' Pippa said. 'So far as your books are concerned, Mrs Davies's letter is proof that grown-ups don't necessarily buy children's books for their children at all. They buy them for themselves. Like fathers and electric train sets. I think you should do some more.'

Oh, how simple everything appeared when you were Pippa's age. The wonderful thing about being young was that you were setting out on a journey of discovery: there was always something new and exciting to look forward to. You conceived an idea and assumed you could make it happen, taking no account of what was involved. Yes, enthusiasm and energy – those were the great advantages of youth. And a superb ignorance of the real world. But when you were old, all you could do was look back . . .

'No,' she said firmly. 'Quite apart from the fact that I don't have any ideas, I'm too old – and too tired.'

And, suddenly, she did feel tired again, desperately tired, as if the emotional pressures of the past few days had finally caught up with her, draining her of all strength. She flopped back against the pillows and closed her eyes.

'Oh, I'm sorry,' Pippa said. 'I keep forgetting you're not well.'

But it was more than that . . .

You do not know how dear it cost me to write the *Enchanted* books . . . Had I not needed so desperately to earn a living, I doubt that I would have finished them. It was not the stories themselves, but the fact that they

197

were never really my stories in the first place. They belonged to Leo. That was why I chose Fountain as my pseudonym: it was the English translation of Leo's surname . . .

You do not realize that you have resurrected memories which had been better left where they were in the dead annals of the past. But it is not your fault. You are not to know that I have spent over half a lifetime trying to forget.

To forget my dear memories of West and bitter ones of Giles and the indescribable anguish of losing Yondover. To forget what it was like to sit on the top of Uffing Down or clamber up the crags of the Greiskopf to the glacier which formed the Old Man's beard and gaze out across the heart-piercing beauty of mist-filled valleys and rose-capped alpine peaks. To forget laughter that trilled like a mountain stream. To forget music so pure that the soul's delight took fire. To forget kisses that burned on smouldering lips and sinuous bodies that melted each into each . . .

No, you do not know the unconscionable effort it has cost me to cut everything down to size, to live in a little house, with high walls surrounding me, so that I may not look out into the blue beyond and be tempted to remember all that I have so painstakingly forgotten. You are not to know the courage it has taken to plant sweet roses and a small patch of gentians in my garden, when once I knew roses in wild profusion and gentians like an azure sea; or to listen to recorded music on a tinny wireless set, where once I was present at its tumultuous creation . . .

She tore the stamp from the envelope. 'I'm saving stamps for the hospital scanner appeal. But I always wonder what happens to them. Surely every collector in the world must already possess British first and second class stamps? Still, Sydney's more unusual.'

After Pippa left, Kitty opened the other envelope. Buff and businesslike, it did not look as if it contained exciting tidings and, indeed, its contents appeared quite formidable. She put on her spectacles and glanced through William John's short letter.

Dear Kitty,

Please find attached your draft accounts for the year ended 30 April 1985. When you have had time to study them, maybe you would be good enough to telephone me,

so that we can discuss certain items arising from them,
including your investments and tax situation.

She looked down the tabulated columns of figures in the balance sheet and profit and loss account. Try as she might, book-keeping would always remain a mystery to her and, even had her brain been functioning better, she would not have understood what the figures meant.

That was why Adam had insisted upon her engaging an accountant after she had started writing the *Enchanted* books, and introduced her to William. Now, Astra sent her royalty statements and cheques straight to him and he arranged for all her bills to be paid by direct debit or standing order. In fact, her only real involvement with money was to pay in the occasional cheques she received from the local art gallery, which sold her watercolours. Those earnings went into a separate account, which she used to buy herself little treats – like her gas stove and the central heating.

Well, there would be time enough when she was home again to reply to William. In the meantime, if he wanted to discuss tax and investments, she had to assume that her finances were in a healthy state – which was more than could be said for herself!

After nearly thirty years, William should know her well enough to realize that she had absolute faith in his judgement. Yet still it remained a never-ending source of amazement to him that she took so little interest in her finances and it was completely beyond his comprehension that she might simply be glad to have enough income to pay tax on and a little left over to invest. 'You should care,' he had insisted on more than one occasion. 'You've worked hard for that money, and all those Treasury crooks are going to do is squander it.'

But William had not known her when she was on her beam ends. Neither had he had the Reverend Thurston Fellowes as a father nor witnessed the effect that Samuel Lambourne's money had had on West and Marion McDonnell.

All that had ever mattered to her was that she should have money enough to cover her everyday needs and a small reserve to insure against the proverbial rainy day. In the event that she was incapacitated – and this little accident proved how easily that could happen! – and couldn't look after herself, she had no intention of being dependent upon anyone.

199

What it all boiled down to in the end, in fact, was that money was only important when you didn't have any.

That night, Kitty took her farewell of Nurse Willis, who had been so kind to her during the night shifts – during which she lived through more experiences than anyone could possibly imagine – and next morning she was duly released from hospital. Although she still could not remember falling, her concussion seemed to have left no lasting ill effects, other than an annoying listlessness, which she was assured was quite usual under the circumstances. She had some tablets to take – her blood pressure was, apparently, a little high – but, fearing a fuss, she decided not to mention this to anyone. Apart from that, she was fine.

There was no need for Pippa to stay on. Indeed, Kitty needed more than anything to be alone again, in the comfort and security of her own home, with her old familiar things around her, so that, in her own time, she could come to terms with the traumas of the last few days – all of which Pippa, albeit unwittingly, had introduced.

The District Nurse was going to call in each day to change the dressing on her shoulder and to check that her bruised ribs were progressing satisfactorily, while Mrs Wakehurst had declared herself only too delighted to do her shopping and the Colonel to do any of the slightly heavy jobs around the house or garden.

Before Pippa left, Kitty nerved herself to take a look at Edith Spencer's album. She went through it early in the morning, before Pippa was awake, sitting at the kitchen table with Tabitha on her lap, as the sun rose over the top of the lilac tree in the Wakehursts' garden.

'*The exhibition currently being held at the Burlington Gallery establishes Gawaine Devere's position among this country's greatest living photographers*,' one review stated. She flicked ahead through the album, but was unsurprised not to find the print of Leo included. Giles had doubtlessly insisted upon those negatives being destroyed.

'*Society photographer Gawaine Devere has been commissioned to take a portrait of His Majesty King George V . . .*'

Yes, those prints, symbolic of Giles's prestige in the photographic world of the 1930s, were all there, as were others, more surreal but presumably equally famous at the time, although she was unfamiliar with them.

Kitty moved on to the snapshots, skipping over pictures of Porter's Place and lingering on views of Yondover, of the house and the gardens, of Fanny and Gurney standing in the courtyard – Fanny shrunk with age, Gurney stooped and leaning on a stick – of Jethro pruning apple trees, of Giles himself peering into a camera.

She shivered and, with a sense of relief, heard Pippa's footsteps moving about in the room above. She no longer felt jealous of Edith, as she had in the long-ago first months of her marriage. Instead she felt sorry for her. Poor, loyal Edith, husbandless, childless, doomed to spend the last years of her life in sheltered accommodation, with only her memories of past, reflected glory for company, and the occasional letter from Giles to lighten the dreariness of her days.

That afternoon, before Pippa returned to Dulwich, she and Kitty took photographs of each other sitting by the kitchen window. In Kitty's case, her head was turned slightly away from the camera so that the bruise on her forehead did not show. They were not intended as proper portraits, more as a memento of their meeting, and Pippa promised to send her grandmother copies of both when she had had them processed.

It was after this that they discussed Sebastian for the first time. Pippa introduced the subject. 'Do you mind if I tell Mum and Dad that we've met?' she asked.

Kitty studied her hands, aware that, however she replied, a more detailed explanation was going to be required of her. And she didn't mind giving it – but not now. She needed time to think things through and, at the moment, her mind simply wasn't up to it. Her brain still did not seem to be working properly. Everything was slightly out of focus, a little bit the wrong way, almost as though she had had too much to drink. In the end, she said, 'I can't make that decision for you. You must do whatever you think fit.'

'You're still not feeling quite right, are you?' Pippa said, looking at her with concern.

'I just feel very tired.'

'You'd prefer me not to say anything, wouldn't you?'

'I suppose so. But I don't want you telling lies on my behalf.'

'There's no need for me to lie. They don't know that I was coming to see you. But will you tell me one thing? Does it upset you that you and Dad have lost contact with each other? Or did you want it this way?'

Kitty shook her head. 'No, it's something I bitterly regret. But in case you think you can work a miracle, I'm afraid you can't, Pippa. The rift between your father and me is too wide for you to bridge.'

'Will you tell me, one day, what happened?'

'Maybe, but not today.'

Pippa got out of her chair and knelt beside her, taking Kitty's hands in hers. 'Thank you,' she said.

'For what?'

'For being my grandmother. For being a new friend. For being here.'

Tears stung behind Kitty's eyes, a sure sign that she was not her usual self. 'You're a very sweet girl,' she said. 'Thank you for coming to see me in the first place and for staying while I was in hospital. I do appreciate it. Now you must be getting back to London. I don't want you driving all that way in the dark.'

'I can come and see you again, can't I?'

'Of course. And I'll try not to fall down any steps next time.'

Pippa had a quiet, pleasant weekend all to herself. On Saturday morning, she duly paid the milkman then did a bit of shopping, as well as taking the roll of film she had shot in Sussex to the chemist to be processed. In the evening she went out for an Italian meal with a couple of friends, both of whom were also – coincidentally – manless. It was, they all agreed, one of the best Saturday evenings they'd had for a long time.

Next afternoon, she rang Kitty and was glad to hear her sounding chirpy. Her bruises didn't hurt nearly so much and she could hardly feel the cut on her shoulder. It was such a lovely day, she had been for a walk in the Castle park.

If only, Pippa thought, as she put down the phone, she could effect a reconciliation between her grandmother and her parents. When she hadn't known that Kitty was alive, her absence hadn't mattered. But now she knew she existed, it seemed such a shame that she shouldn't be part of the family.

She did wonder whether to ring Eve and tell her that she had been to see Kitty but instinct told her that Eve would be no more forthcoming than she had been before. Eve had given her Kitty's address on condition that she said nothing to anybody else until she'd heard what Kitty had to say. And, as yet, Kitty hadn't really said anything.

So, difficult though she found it to curb her impatience, she decided there was nothing for it but to wait until her next visit to Arundel, when she hoped Kitty would be well enough for her to ask her to fill in the vital missing background.

On Monday, Pippa started her new job. She and Tim arrived simultaneously at nine o'clock. 'First of all, coffee,' he announced, when they were inside the studio. 'You know where the kettle is. I take mine black, strong and no sugar.'

First of all, however, it was washing up a sink full of dirty mugs.

'Thanks,' Tim said, taking the mug she handed him. 'Now, let's get set up. We've got two shots today. At twelve o'clock, Derek Dwyer. You know him? Labour MP. That should be pretty straightforward. We'll need a white background for him. Then at three we've got the novelist Vanessa Armitage. She's going to be more tricky. Simon should have organized a car to pick her up, but maybe you'd better check with the taxi company. You'll find their telephone number on the job sheet, which should be hanging on a hook in my office. Yes, we'll need a different background for Vanessa Armitage and much softer lighting . . .'

At that moment, the phone rang. Tim left her to find it buried under some newspapers and then to answer it. 'Hello. Tim Collins's studio.'

A fraught-sounding female voice asked, 'Is he there?'

'Yes, who's calling please?'

'Sandra.'

She held the phone towards Tim. 'It's someone called Sandra.'

'Oh, Gawd,' he groaned. 'I wonder what the problem is now.'

While he was dealing with Sandra, Pippa went in search of the job sheet. In Tim's office, too, confusion seemed to reign. Having rung the cab company, discovered that Simon had not booked a car and rectified that, she decided the best thing she could do was try to bring a little fundamental order to the studio. She emptied the ashtrays, found a broom and started to sweep.

Tim came off the phone and nodded approvingly. 'Good girl! That was Dwyer's agent. There's been a change of plan. Dwyer's coming at eleven. And he can only spare half an hour. When you've finished sweeping, can you put the background up? You'll find bo-poles and clamps in that cupboard over there. I've got a few calls I must make. I'll be in the office if you need me.'

When she had done all that, she went to his office door to ask what lights he wanted.

'A couple of striplights on the background and a soft box in front. A polyboard, white side out, to his left . . .'

She set these up as best she could, then went back to the office to ask, 'Where do I find your cameras?'

'Ah! Come with me to the toy cupboard.'

To her amazement, the 'toy cupboard' – as Tim referred to the strong-room where he kept his cameras – was meticulously tidy. 'The rest of the place is a tip,' he admitted, 'but I'm neurotic about my gear. It's my one discipline.' Pointing to a large case, he said, 'There's the Sinar. Set it up with a 210 lens.'

After that, it was taking meter readings, doing a couple of Polaroids – with herself pretending to be Derek Dwyer – moving the lights a bit, loading film and then the politician arrived.

Talk about being thrust in at the deep end, Pippa thought, as she made coffees. But he hardly changed my lights. So I got that right. Now I must be sure I don't make any boobs while he's actually shooting.

Derek Dwyer was hardly a film star in looks and made it obvious that he considered the session a necessary evil. Tim, however, knew his subject. He questioned Dwyer about a bill being discussed in parliament, to which Dwyer was strongly opposed, then shot him in pugnacious stance, his fist clenched, brow furrowed and chin thrust forward. So, although they had very little time, Pippa was rightly confident that every frame would be brilliant.

Vanessa Armitage, for all that she was a best-selling novelist and would therefore, Pippa had assumed, be used to being photographed, proved a nervous sitter. It took all Tim's charm to get her to relax and, even so, the first ten sheets of film seemed unlikely to yield any good results. He finally did a number of different shots of her, including some wearing a hat, which made her look absolutely captivating.

After she had left, Tim said, 'Thank God she brought that hat with her. I don't know what I'd have done otherwise. Mind you, I hate being in front of the camera myself.'

At the end of the day, Nick came in. 'Just returning Tim's flashmeter,' he explained. 'So, how's the first day been, Pippa?'

'Great.'

He glanced round the studio. 'Place looks different somehow.'

'Pippa's been tidying up,' Tim said through his open office door.

'You can come round to my studio any time you like.'

'Hands off! She's mine.'

'Ah, well. I'm going to the pub. Anyone else fancy a drink?'

'No thanks. I'm going home to see the kids.'

'You family men are so boring . . . Pippa?'

'Thanks, but no. Another time, maybe.'

For all that she had enjoyed her day, it had been tiring finding out where everything was and adapting to Tim's way of working. She also recognized Nick's type and had no intention of letting him think that she was easy game. In any case, she had made the mistake once of getting too involved at work. From now on, her professional and social lives were going to be carried out on two separate planes.

As her first week progressed, Pippa began to feel totally at home with Tim and in his studio. He was an excellent photographer but the complete opposite of Richard in almost every other respect, taking life absolutely as it came and never getting in a panic. If anything, he was too easy-going, which was doubtless why – remembering what he had said at her interview about keeping no assistant for more than two years – his past assistants had grown complacent. With his complete approval, she was starting to impose order on the chaos Simon had left in his wake, without detracting from the studio's comfortable, informal atmosphere.

It made a nice change, too, having other photographers in the vicinity. Nick was constantly popping in to borrow something or ask for advice, to have a coffee or a drink – and to chat her up. Dominic, too, was a frequent visitor, also usually on the scrounge. And there were others she met in the course of the week, all of whom had worked for Tim at one time or another.

'One day they'll get their own gear,' Tim grumbled good-temperedly. 'Simon's going to find it a bit more difficult, though. It's a bit far to come all the way from New York to borrow a sync lead.' But it was clear that he was as fond of them as they were of him.

The most inspiring thing, so far as Pippa was concerned, was that they were all embarked upon potentially successful careers of their own.

'Tim's a bloody good teacher,' Dominic informed her. 'I learned more from him in my first month than I did in three years at college.'

'I think I already have,' Pippa confessed. 'It's funny, he appears so laid-back.'

'I know. But he's really on the ball. He's a kind of guru to us all. Anything you need to know, he has the answer – or he knows how to find it.'

On Friday evening, their last shoot for the day finished early. After Pippa had cleared away and set everything up ready for Monday, Tim asked, 'So, how do you feel at the end of your first week?'

'I've really enjoyed it.'

'Good, and I must admit that it's a pleasure having you here. I've no reservations at all any more. Well, got anything planned for the weekend?'

'I'm not sure at the moment. If the weather's OK, I may go out and take some pictures.'

'That's what I like. A sucker for punishment. Incidentally, if you want to use the studio or darkroom at any time, you've only got to ask.'

'Thank you, that's really kind.' She hesitated. 'Since you seem to know everything about photography, have you ever heard of a photographer called Gawaine Devere?'

'Funny you should say that. I've kept meaning to ask you the same question. Some of his war photographs are on exhibition in Bath.'

'Yes, I've seen them.'

'And *is* he a relation of yours?'

She told him the entire story.

'I'd like to see that album,' he said, when she had finished.

'It's in the car. Shall I get it?'

'Yes, do that.'

She fetched it and he went through it very slowly. 'Well, I can understand why you were so impressed,' he said. 'Amazing stuff. He makes me feel as though I'm a rank amateur. So, have you written to him?'

'I don't think there's a lot of point really.'

'No, I expect you're right, not if he is a recluse. All the same, it is intriguing.'

On Monday, Sebastian and Valerie returned from holiday, both considerably more relaxed than when they had left and tanned the colour of mahogany. The cruise had been better than her father had anticipated: their cabin extremely comfortable, the service and the food excellent, and his fellow passengers more congenial than he had feared.

Although she was unable to collect them from the airport, Pippa had prepared a meal for them and put a bottle of champagne in the fridge. What was more, she was home in time to join them in it, for Tim – unlike Richard – did not stay any later at the studio than he needed.

'It sounds much better than your last job in every respect,' Sebastian said, when she had finished telling them about Tim and the various jobs they had had in during the week. 'I must say I'm rather relieved. You didn't seem to be heading in quite the right direction before.'

Pippa did not react to this comment. Instead, she decided to risk telling him, not about her visit to Kitty but about her abortive attempt to see Gawaine Devere.

'While you were away,' she said, 'I tried to find out a bit more about that photographer – you remember, Gawaine Devere . . .'

Her father grunted. 'The crackpot who had women half drowning in lakes or popping out of tree trunks.'

'Well, I discovered that he lives in Sussex. I didn't actually manage to see him, but I found out quite a lot about him.'

When she had finished describing Dynamite Devere's campaigns to preserve his land, her father erupted, 'The fellow's clearly a nutcase! Thank God you didn't get to see him. Sometimes I think you haven't got the sense you were born with, Philippa!'

She bit back an angry retort. But her father's reaction decided her that she would, after all, write to Gawaine Devere. Just a little note, telling him about her discovery of his pictures. Despite what Mrs Lowe and Kitty had said, he might be pleased to know that, all these years on, somebody still appreciated his work.

Ever since Pippa's visit and Eve's extraordinary outburst, Adam's thoughts had kept returning to Kitty, wondering whether she and Pippa had met and, if so, how they had got on. Whenever the phone rang, he half expected it to be Kitty, half hoping it would be – yet at the same time half hoping it wouldn't. Each morning, when the postman called, he hurried to the door to see if there was a letter from her, disappointed when there was none – yet at the same time rather relieved, in case Eve should see the letter.

So, he imagined, must a married man feel, who is having an affair. But, in his case, he had no cause to feel guilty. He had never been unfaithful to Eve and he was not about to be unfaithful to her now. Would he were even capable of it at the age of eighty!

Not that Eve had referred again to Kitty or Pippa since that memorable afternoon. To all outward appearances, their life had resumed its usual, even tenor, as though nothing had disturbed it. Yet something in Eve's manner told him that she felt she was holding the upper hand. He could feel her waiting for him to make some little slip and thus inadvertently prove her point.

So, because he was above all a peace-loving man, who had always disliked emotional scenes, he succeeded in convincing himself that no news from Kitty was good news, as had always been the case in the past.

Because Kitty did not ring or write – and nor did Pippa for that matter – the whole thing had undoubtedly been a storm in a teacup. Young people had these sudden enthusiasms – and then dropped them, when something more exciting came along. Pippa had been about to start a new job. Probably she had become immersed in that and forgotten all about Kitty.

At Rose Cottage, Kitty kept debating with herself whether to ring Adam and tell him about Pippa's visit. Had it not been for her fall, she probably would have done. But her fall added an extra complication. If he thought she was unwell, he would worry about her and probably feel he ought to come and visit her. And, fond though she was of him, she wasn't in the mood for seeing him. She wasn't really in the mood for seeing anyone – well, not at the moment, not until she was fully recovered. No, better to let things ride and hope the storm would blow itself away . . .

CHAPTER 15

Spring – fairest of all the seasons – had come to Yondover. Although there was still an early morning sharpness to the air, the daytime sun had warmth in it. All was gold and green and blue. Daffodils, narcissi and jonquils formed a carpet of yellow, against yellow banks of forsythia. Clumps of wild primroses peeped out from beneath hedgerows. In West's wood, the trees were bursting into tiny leaf and between them ran a river of scyllas, chionodoxa and grape hyacinths, interspersed with shy wood anemones. Catkins danced in the breeze and pussy willow shone silver. The first, giant bumble bees emerged from winter hibernation, together with the first butterflies from their chrysalises: yellow brimstone and green-veined white.

So I felt I must write and tell you that I think your photographs are brilliant . . .

Day after day, that line from Pippa's letter continued to haunt Giles Gawaine Devere, as he went about his daily chores, pumping water, sawing logs, working with Ted in the vegetable garden and inspecting his domain to ensure that no fences had been damaged, no vandals entered the woods, no poachers tried to snare foxes or badgers, and no hunter shot at rabbit, pigeon, magpie, pheasant or woodcock.

When Ted had brought Pippa's letter up from the post office, Giles had looked at the unfamiliar writing on the envelope, slit it open, read its contents, then ripped it in two, as an unbidden and unwanted reminder of a past he had long put behind him. But although his immediate reaction was to throw the pieces on the fire, something had prevented him.

He had known who Pippa was as soon as he saw her name and address, for Adam insisted upon keeping him informed of the bare facts of Kitty's and Sebastian's lives, although he was well aware that Giles was uninterested in anything or anyone outside Yondover. His was the simplest of existences:

his life was devoted to nature, to its preservation and the contemplation of its beauty. As it had been for West, Yondover was his world: as the Gurneys had sufficed West for company, so Jethro's widow, Millie, and her son, Ted, were the only people he needed.

His most forceful feeling had, in fact, been one of anger towards Edith. What the devil had possessed her to keep his pictures in a photograph album for Sebastian – of all people – to stumble across after her death?

Yet, upon more sober reflection, he realized that it was to have been expected of her that she would retain some souvenir of his work. It had been Edith who, at the outbreak of war, had insisted upon moving his negatives, together with the most valuable of his cameras and lenses, from Porter's Place to Yondover, where, even though the government had taken over the house, they had indeed been safer than if they had stayed in London to go up in flames when 10 Porter's Place was blitzed to the ground.

During the war she, too, had worked for the Ministry of Information, in her case in London as a retoucher, removing details which could have been useful to the enemy before pictures taken by war photographers like himself were released for publication. Recognizing the style of his work, she had collected editions of the *Illustrated London News* and *Picture Post* in which his photographs had appeared and, after the war, had given them to him – not realizing that the very last thing of which he wanted to be reminded were his wartime experiences.

Yes, even when he had retired to Yondover, Edith had clung to her conviction that, because photography had been all-important to him, it would prove impossible for him to give it up. After the war, following the deaths of her widowed mother and aunt, she had even moved to the south coast in order to be near him when he started to work again. Not until Boy Tate's posthumous autobiography was published in 1968 had she finally stopped trying to persuade him to resume his career.

But, for all that, Edith had been a good sort, like a sister in many ways. After Kitty had gone off to Austria, Edith had always accompanied him on his visits to Yondover and he had come increasingly to value her undemanding companionship, while at the same time feeling secure in the knowledge that nobody was likely to misinterpret their relationship. He had been well aware that one hint of scandal could have destroyed all he had achieved in as many seconds as it had taken him years to build his reputation. The mere fact that Edith was a woman had helped counteract the scurrilous rumours Boy Tate had delighted in spreading about him.

And later, after Porter's Place was bombed, Edith had taken Millie back to her own home and looked after her, until the Land Army was formed, when she had arranged for her to be sent to Kipwell.

He would never forget that evening. He had been dining with friends in Mayfair and, instead of going down to the shelter when the alert sounded, he had gone up on the roof. Throughout the war, he had found it less unnerving to be out of doors, where he could see what was happening, than in a shelter, where all he could hear was the noise. Nothing, he had realized, played quite so much havoc with the nerves as imagination. So he had watched the extraordinary and terrifying spectacle of German bombs dropping along the line of the river all the way from the docks to Chelsea – and must, unwittingly, have seen the one that fell on Porter's Place.

Upon returning home, it had been to find the house razed to the ground. The Forsyths and Cook had been killed outright, but the new housemaid, Millie, who had run for shelter in the cellar, had survived. It had taken the rescue men five hours to get her free from the rubble and, understandably, the girl had been a gibbering wreck.

By the time Millie came to Kipwell, Fanny and Gurney were both dead: they had died within weeks of each other, shortly after being forced to leave Yondover, when it was requisitioned by the government for whatever hush-hush work had been carried out here during the war. Millie had taken over their room in the station master's house and worked for the Pughs on the Home Farm, along with Jethro, both of them digging for victory. After the war ended, they had married and, a couple of years later, Ted had come into the world.

But now, forty-seven years after Porter's Place had been bombed and Edith had ceased to be his employee, her blind and irrational devotion was rebounding upon him in a manner which she would have been the first to deplore.

How furious she would be if she knew that her album and books had fallen into the hands of Kitty's son . . .

She had hated Kitty: not while they were living together as husband and wife, but after Kitty had left him. Then, so intense had been Edith's fury on his behalf that she had destroyed every negative and every print

211

from the portrait session with Leopold Brunnen and, had she dared, would have destroyed every picture he had ever taken of Kitty too.

Her bitterness and anger had been far more intense than his own. But she had not been aware of all the circumstances: she had not realized that he was as much if not more to blame. Even had Edith been the sort of woman to whom one could confide one's inner feelings, he could not have brought himself to confess to having had a homosexual affair. Even when Boy's memoirs were published, so loyal and trusting had Edith been that she had still refused to acknowledge the truth.

When Kitty had left him, he had thrown himself into his work, until he had reached what would probably be regarded now as the pinnacle of his career, with his portrait of King George V. He had never been a particularly sexual man: in his few close relationships, he had sought affection and emotional release more than the gratification of his carnal instincts. He had indulged in the occasional, discreet affair, but none had lasted long. After one young woman had taunted him with being a boring companion and an unsatisfactory partner in bed, he had decided upon absolute celibacy.

Yes, Boy Tate had exacted full revenge for that one transgression.

Tate's Gallery, his book had been called. Edited by his last boyfriend, whose name was as unforgettable as the book's title – Crispin Laye – it was as nasty and vituperative a set of memoirs as had ever been published: a masterpiece of smutty inference and character assassination.

Giles had, in fact, been let off relatively lightly compared to some of the other men with whom Boy claimed to have had affairs, including Members of Parliament, of the Church and the aristocracy. According to Boy, Giles had been the degenerate influence upon a shy, innocent undergraduate: he had been the one to seduce Boy and then callously desert him for another.

The book had sparked off so many law suits that it had been quickly withdrawn from the shops. But the damage was done. Even if nobody in Kipwell had actually read it, Giles was sure they must have read about it in the papers. The villagers already disliked him because he had opposed the construction of the bypass and dubbed him Dynamite Devere. He had imagined them changing that to Horsey and warning young boys not to go near Yondover.

So he had erected even higher fences around himself and withdrawn completely from the world. Not once since 1968 had he set foot outside the boundaries of his estate. Not once had he spoken to anyone other than the Gurneys. His only sources of information as to what was happening in the outside world were the *Daily Telegraph*, which he occasionally asked Ted to purchase, and a spasmodic correspondence with Adam.

Now Pippa's letter had come, a bolt from the blue.

Were that letter from a complete stranger, he would have ignored it. But Pippa, although it would appear that she knew nothing of his marriage to Kitty, was not a total stranger: she was Kitty's granddaughter – perhaps his own granddaughter, too . . .

Yet what would meeting her achieve? What purpose would be served by hearing her praise images which he had long ago dismissed in his own mind as being a self-indulgence, contrived and over-complex, distortions of the visual truth to suit his own abstract fancy? Or was he exaggerating? Was it possible that he had not, as he believed, sacrificed his integrity for fame and fortune and that there had been value and virtue in those early pictures of his?

Perhaps it was merely vanity, but there was in him a longing to leave some part of himself behind when he was gone, some proof of his having existed. If the influence of his pictures and the knowledge he had acquired were to live on through somebody else after his death, then maybe his life would not have been entirely in vain.

Evening was approaching. His day's work was done. He stood at the back door, gazing across the courtyard towards the old dairy which housed the darkroom West and old Gurney had built for him when he was a schoolboy. It was nearly sixty years since he had last been in there, for after moving to Porter's Place with its purpose-built darkroom he had had no need of it, and since the war he had taken no more photographs.

Viewed down the long avenue of the years, he had made many mistakes during his lifetime. Had giving up photography been one of them? The decision had been deliberate: yet not totally without regret.

The war. Everything came back to the war. His entire life had changed the day war had broken out . . .

The weekend before Chamberlain had made his unforgettable announcement on 3 September 1939 that 'this country is at war with Germany', he had been to Puddles. He had returned in a dark mood and his depression had deepened during the week.

213

After Chamberlain's broadcast, unable to bear the thought of staying indoors, he had walked along the Embankment, where he had come across a young woman leaning against the railings, tears pouring down her cheeks. Her appearance had been foreign and she might well have been a Jewish refugee. But perhaps she had been crying only because of a lovers' tiff. Or maybe her husband had been conscripted and she had feared she would never see him again.

Whatever the truth, that girl's face had expressed what he had felt in his heart. Despair. Despair for himself and his wasted years, despair at what man could do to man, despair for the future of the world.

His Rolleiflex had been round his neck and he had seized a picture of her before she had time to realize what he was doing. It had been the first unposed portrait he had ever taken, yet more telling in its simplicity than any of the studio shots for which he was celebrated.

That portrait had convinced him that he possessed the objectivity necessary to shoot pictures under any circumstances. When he was behind the camera, it had always been as if part of his brain became disengaged and he was conscious only of the mechanics of taking a photograph. He felt no personal emotion. Even his stutter went.

On the spur of the moment, he had volunteered to the Ministry of Information as a photographer, in the hope that his images would make people aware of the horrors of war and he could thus make his contribution towards bringing the war to an early end.

To begin with, he had been sure he had made the right decision. Not until after the Battle of Britain had he been posted abroad and, while he remained in London, there had existed that much vaunted spirit of comradeship and above all that quirky, humorous, English stubbornness, which, despite the odds stacked against them, had convinced all but the most pessimistic that victory must be theirs.

The objectivity upon which he had prided himself had seemed well founded then. However great the scene of destruction at which he was present, however abject the suffering of the people he was photographing, he had been able to stand apart. Even when Porter's Place was hit, though his heart had grieved, his eyes had not blinked nor his fingers trembled as they held the camera and clicked the shutter.

After the Battle of Britain, the Ministry of Information had sent him on a photographic tour of RAF bases, travelling the length and breadth of the British Isles, visiting the fighter stations from which the Battle of Britain had been fought, meeting some of the pilots who had survived and the unsung heroes of Coastal Command, Fleet Air Arm and Bomber Command.

It was at that point that he had first become conscious of the sense of separateness which would accompany him through to the end of the war. In London, he had been part of a community which was both civilian and military, and where everyone had been exposed to equal dangers. Now, in a uniquely military environment, despite his rank of Squadron Leader, he was the outsider: he could not share the lives of those brave airmen – he was merely a voyeur.

After that, they had sent him abroad. There had been few countries that he had not visited at some time or other. He had taken thousands, if not tens of thousands of pictures, but although the Ministry of Information had been pleased with them and many which had not constituted a security risk had been published, few had made him feel proud. Technically they were good, but the moral aspects of his job had tormented him. Often he had felt that all he was doing was producing propaganda pictures, which glorified war instead of depicting its horrors.

As for the suffering he had recorded – in hospitals and on the battlefield – he had grown increasingly convinced that those pictures should not have been taken at all, but the subjects left alone to die in dignity. But that was the dilemma which had confronted him daily and to which he had to try to shut his mind. His ability to remain objective had been the reason for his volunteering. The intellect, he had believed, would take over from the emotions. But he had found it impossible to remain dispassionate. A man would have had to be made of stone to remain unmoved by some of the harrowing scenes he had witnessed.

In the final years of the war, he had gone to Normandy with the Allied Expeditionary Force. That was the closest he had come to being killed. He had been holding his Rolleiflex to his eye – the same Rolleiflex he had used to take the portrait of that girl, so long ago, on the Embankment – when a German sniper had shot at him. The camera had absorbed the bullet and saved his life.

Many were the occasions afterwards when he wished it had not. He had been in Germany when the concentration camps were liberated and in Japan after Hiroshima. He should have been jubilant when the war

215

ended. Instead, he had felt an even darker and more overwhelming sense of despair than on the day it had broken out. Then, he had believed his images might help bring the war to an early end. But some of the sights he had witnessed and photographed – sights which defied description and comprehension – had made him finally abandon all hope for mankind.

No picture could convey the depths of degradation to which the human mind was capable of descending. His images had proved futile. They had changed nothing and they never would.

At that moment, Ted appeared, a tall, spare figure, dressed in dark green overalls, mud-caked boots, a flat cap pulled forward over his gingery hair, his usual morose expression on his face. Giles nodded to him and he changed direction, following him across to the old dairy, where he looked at the large and extremely rusty padlock securing the door, sucked in his breath, went away and returned with a hacksaw.

Neither of them said a word, but there was nothing out of the ordinary in that. Sometimes, whole days passed when not a word of conversation was exchanged at Yondover. Ted was by nature taciturn, as Jethro had been before him, and old Gurney before that. As for Millie, though doubtless she enjoyed a good chinwag when she went down to the village, she had learned over the years to save her breath in the company of her employer and her son.

Having cut through the metal, Ted pushed at the darkroom door and, when it failed to move, put his full weight against it. With a complaining creak of the hinges, it fell open.

The air inside smelled musty. Walls, windows and surfaces were festooned with cobwebs. But once Giles's eyes had acclimatized themselves to the dim, eerie light coming through the doorway and the red, safelight panel in a corner of the blacked-out window, he could see that otherwise everything in the small room was almost exactly how he had left it. The lead-lined sinks on their heavy wooden frames, the neatly stacked enamelled dishes and the high tank into which Jethro would pump water from the well. The horizontal Abbeydale enlarger, with its acetylene light source, a corroded brass lens still in place. The bookform print frame. Safelights dotted around, some containing candles, others spirit lamps. Rows of brown Winchesters with peeling labels. Kilner jars of dry chemicals. Shelves of dusty books of formulae. Enamelled buckets, jugs and dishes. Glass measures. Thermometers. The nickelled clock, for timing development, fixing, washing and exposures. The line, complete with clothes pegs, where they had hung prints to dry after blotting them. The paraffin stove, complete with kettle and teapot. Two cups and saucers. A couple of chemical-stained, brown overalls hanging from hooks. Some disintegrating towels.

Having opened the door, Ted had departed. He was alone. Or was he? He had an uncanny sense of some other presence in the darkroom with him. And then he seemed to hear West's voice. 'Anyone can be taught to use a camera and take a photograph,' he was saying. 'But not everyone can make a picture. That is a gift which cannot be taught. You are blessed with that gift, Giles.'

Since receiving Pippa's letter, he had often found himself thinking about West, but this was the first time he had seemed so close. How old had he been when West had uttered those words? Seventeen or eighteen, he supposed. And West must have been about the same age he was now. It was strange: as a young man, he had never thought of West as being old; he had always seemed ageless, immortal. His death had come as a terrible shock, all the more so because it had coincided with Kitty leaving Porter's Place. For a long time, he had plagued himself with the fear that he might have been the inadvertent cause of West's sudden, final heart attack, even though Kitty had sworn that she had lied about her true reason for coming to Yondover. West had been so sensitive to other people's feelings, he had known things without being told: it had been virtually impossible to pull the wool over his eyes.

Like West, he was not overtly religious, but he did believe in God – in an omnipotent power, beyond man's comprehension – who was responsible for the creation of the universe and for that spark – call it life or the soul – which differentiated living organisms from inanimate matter. Regardless of what theories of evolution scientists might have developed over the centuries, they had yet satisfactorily to explain the origin of life.

Whether, upon death, that spark was extinguished or whether it moved on into another form, he had no idea. But, if there was a life after death and the dead were aware of what continued to take place on earth, he was sure that West was the kind of man who would long ago have forgiven him for what he could not forgive himself.

Or had West not only forgiven, but was now also offering him the chance to make reparation for all his past wrongs? He could not believe

217

that God, with whatever characteristics one chose to endow him, had time or inclination to attend to the everyday doings of his subjects. But why should the spirit dead lose interest in those for whom they had cared during their mortal existence?

It was perhaps a whimsical notion, but could it be that West had guided Pippa to Edith's photograph album and sent her on the path to Yondover? It was not himself as a person but his images which had inspired her to write. Was this West's way of telling him that there still remained to him one last opportunity for redemption, that although he had failed as a man, he still had a chance to prove that he had not, after all, failed as a photographer?

CHAPTER 16

Pippa looked in puzzlement at the unfamiliar, crabbed writing on the envelope, then she noticed the Lewes postmark and her heart gave a lurch of excitement.

Inside was a single sheet of cheap notepaper.

> *30 April 1987*
>
> *Dear Miss Devere,*
>   *Thank you for your letter. I have decided that I would like to meet you. You will find the entrance to Yondover beside the church. My manservant, Gurney, will be waiting at the gate at 11 o'clock on Saturday, 9th May, to conduct you to the house. I should be grateful if you would keep your appointment strictly confidential, as my personal privacy is very important to me and I rarely receive visitors.*
>   *Sincerely yours,*
>   *G.G.D.*

Her life seemed suddenly to be taking giant strides forward, almost as if fate were applauding her for having taken the step of leaving Richard and granting her all kinds of bonuses. First there had been the lucky break in getting the job with Tim Collins and then finding her grandmother. Now, in the very same week, she was having two more strokes of good fortune.

The first of these had occurred on Monday when one of Tim's earliest clients, from when he had started out fifteen years ago – a firm of architects called Lightfoot Godfrey – had asked him to recommend a photographer to do a job for them. If it had been a one-off job, he would probably have done it himself, even though the fee was low, for one of the partners, Rickie Lightfoot, had become a friend as well as a client, and he didn't like to let him down.

However, it was an ongoing project. A photographic record was needed of a house on Streatham Common that was being taken over by the Julian Powell Trust and completely refurbished for use as a drug rehabilitation centre.

'You had some rather nice architectural shots among your college work,' Tim had said to her. 'You could do this.'

Her first reaction was that she couldn't be in two places at once. Much as she would love to do a proper, commissioned job – which, if badly paid by Tim's standards, was a lot of money so far as she was concerned – she didn't want to leave Tim's studio and stop doing the portraiture which she was enjoying every bit as much as she had anticipated. Even more, in fact. For every day brought something new. It would be crazy to sacrifice her long-term future for short-term gain.

'Don't worry, I don't want to lose you either,' Tim said, when she explained her reservations. 'But this is a pick-up put-down sort of job, something you can do at weekends or in the evening – if you don't mind sacrificing your free time.'

On that basis, she, Tim and Rickie Lightfoot had had a meeting, at which it had been agreed that she should have a go. She and the architect responsible for the Updike House project, Chris Markowski, were going to meet on-site in a couple of weeks' time.

And now, as if that were not excitement enough, there was this letter from Gawaine Devere . . .

In view of her father's reaction when she had told him about her first trip to Kipwell, she said nothing about this new development, although she could not help but hear Mrs Lowe's voice saying, 'You can see Ted Gurney patrolling the grounds with a shotgun in his hands.'

However, to be on the safe side, she did tell Tim. That way, if she didn't return, someone would know where to start looking for her.

The clock showed exactly eleven o'clock when Pippa parked in the same place as before, beside the five-barred gate with its notice of PRIVATE PROPERTY – TRESPASSERS WILL BE PROSECUTED.

From the other side, a man appeared.

Pippa got out of the car. 'Mr Gurney?'

He nodded, unsmiling, then unlocked the massive padlock, unwound the heavy chain and dragged the gate open a couple of feet. Once she was through, he re-secured it, then led the way without another word along a rutted tractor path.

After a short while, the track began to climb steeply. Gurney loped steadily ahead, without so much as a backward glance in her direction.

They reached the top of a ridge and there, in a hollow, surrounded by tall trees so that only the roof and chimneys were visible, stood a solitary house, the smooth mound of Uffing Down rising behind it. Gurney strode on and she hurried to catch up with him, down the slope, through a gate in a crumbling wall overgrown with brambles, and across what must once have been a magnificent lawn but was now only roughly mown.

The gnarled and knotty trunks of climbing roses barricaded the front door. Gurney continued past some French windows, also clearly long unopened, into a courtyard, flanked on two sides by the house and on the other by tumbledown stables, where chickens pecked amid grass and groundsel. In the centre was a covered well.

'Wait here,' he commanded and disappeared through a door, from which the paint was peeling, as everywhere else on the exterior of the house.

Eventually, he re-emerged and in his wake came another man, dressed in a tweed jacket and twill slacks. He was of medium height and had a mass of thick silvery hair, bushy grey eyebrows and piercing brown eyes, which regarded her across half-spectacles perched on a forceful nose.

She smiled and stepped forward, holding out her hand. 'Hello.'

He ignored her outstretched hand. 'I-I-I am G-g-gawaine Devere.'

His pronounced stutter took her aback. To cover her surprise, she said, 'Thank you so much for agreeing to see me.'

Gurney nodded curtly and left them together.

'Y-y-you haven't told anyone else y-you're h-here?'

'Nobody else at all,' she assured him.

'S-s-so why did you want to s-s-see me?'

Pippa embarked, once again, on her explanation. 'As I wrote and told you, my father bought some old books at an auction earlier this year and among them was a photograph album and some *British Journal of Photography Almanacs* containing some of your pictures. In one of them there was an envelope addressed to Miss Edith Spencer. I got your address from her solicitor.'

His eyes bored expressionlessly into hers.

'I've never seen anything like your pictures before,' she floundered on, hoping she did not sound too gushing. 'They're just so – perfect. Then there's the coincidence of our names . . .'

'I-I don't take photographs any more,' he said. 'I-I haven't taken any for many years.'

'Can I show you the album?'

He shrugged.

She delved into her bag and pulled out Edith Spencer's album, laying it on the cover of the well. Silently, he went through it, his features quite impassive, so that it was impossible to guess what he was thinking. When he came to the end, he closed it and handed it back to her without any comment.

An awkward silence ensued. Then he asked, 'H-haven't you brought any of y-your own w-work? I-I-I am familiar with my own p-pictures. Yours are w-what interest me.'

After considerable deliberation, she had brought her portfolio with her, although it had not only seemed presumptuous to expect Gawaine Devere to ask to see her work but she was not at all sure that she wanted him to see it. 'Well, yes, I have actually, but I left my portfolio in the car.'

'Gurney can fetch it.' He went to the edge of the courtyard and shouted, 'Ted!'

A few moments later, Gurney reappeared and Pippa handed over her car keys.

There followed another long silence, broken only by the song of a blackbird perched on the stable roof, the twittering of sparrows and the clucking of the chickens at their feet.

Pippa searched desperately for something to say to keep a conversation going. Normally, under such circumstances, one would expect to compliment someone on their house or garden, but Yondover was so dilapidated and overgrown that it was difficult to find any aspect of it to praise without drawing disparaging attention to the rest.

'Was this originally a farmhouse?' she asked, eventually.

'I-I-I b-believe so.'

'Has your family always lived here?'

'My g-great-g-grandfather bought it in the mid-1800s. I-I-I inherited it from m-m-my grandfather on his d-d-death.'

'Do you have a lot of land?'

'A fair bit. I don't cultivate it, as you've probably noticed. I d-d-deplore what's happening to our countryside. Hedgerows and t-trees being chopped down. Animal habitats, plants, insects, b-b-butterflies, birds, they're all being sys-sys-systematically destroyed. No pesticides or chemical weedkillers are ever used here. I-I-I won't have them.'

After this exceptionally long speech, during which his stutter seemed slightly to abate, he looked impatiently towards the front of the house, clearly hoping for Gurney's speedy return.

Pippa wondered whether to mention his wars over electricity pylons and the bypass, but decided against it in case he should suspect that she had been prying into his past and take offence.

'As I also told you in my letter, I'm working as a photographer's assistant now,' she said in the end.

'Oh. Who are you w-w-working for?'

'A portrait photographer called Tim Collins.'

'Never h-h-heard of him.'

They lapsed again into silence.

Finally, Gurney returned and handed Pippa her portfolio.

With considerable trepidation, she unzipped the case, explaining – as she had to Tim at her interview – that the pictures had all been college projects.

'W-what c-cameras do you use?' he asked.

'Most of these were shot on thirty-five mil – on a Nikon F3.'

He grunted disparagingly. 'The only thirty-five m-millimetre c-c-camera I've ever used was a L-L-Leica III. D-d-didn't think much of it.'

'What camera did you prefer?'

'The Gandolfis made all my st-studio cameras to my own s-sp-specification. Away from the st-studio I-I-I used a R-r-rolleiflex.'

He returned to her portfolio. 'What d-did you do to this?'

It was a picture from the series she had done with Deborah and Caryn. Although she was far from proud of them, she had included some so that Gawaine Devere could see why his own montages and surrealist pictures had made such an impression upon her. Now, she rather wished that she had left them out. 'I used a Cokin number three diffuser filter to get the soft focus effect.'

'Hmm. And this?'

'That was taken on E6 film processed C41.'

'What the d-d-deuce is that?'

'They're colour processes.'

He grunted. 'In my day we used Dufaycolour. And w-w-what on earth did you do here?'

'I only partially bleached the image in the first stage, then I used a selenium toner.' He frowned and she asked hesitantly, 'Are you familiar with that process?'

'N-nothing new about s-s-selenium t-toning. But in m-my day . . .'

He reached Battersea Power Station on a misty morning. 'Aaah, this is m-m-more like it.'

Then he went through the rest very slowly, asking no more questions, his expression inscrutable.

When he came to the end, he reached into the pocket of her case, taking out contact sheets and prints which she had either never got round to enlarging or had been uncertain whether they warranted inclusion.

The last picture of all was an enlargement of the portrait she had taken of Kitty at Rose Cottage. Pippa had put it in at the last moment, not so much because it was a lovely image, capturing the very essence of Kitty's personality, but in the hope that it might trigger a spark of recognition in Gawaine Devere and she would discover that they were after all – however distantly – related.

'That's my grandmother,' she explained.

But all he said was, 'Y-y-ou are v-v-very alike.' Then he demanded, 'Why isn't it in with th-th-the others?'

'I only took it a few weeks ago. It wasn't posed or properly lit.'

'That's why it works,' he snapped. 'I-I-I don't know what they t-taught you at that c-college of yours, but I suspect that it w-wasn't ph-ph-photography. Ph-photography is recording l-l-life as you see it through the c-camera lens. M-manipulative techniques are all v-v-very well, but they should b-be an adjunct to the c-c-compositional properties of the image, n-n-not an end in themselves. The t-trouble with those f-first pictures you showed me was that there was s-so much c-c-clutter in the way, I couldn't s-s-see if you had a ph-ph-photographic eye.'

He closed the case and stared at her over his spectacles. Then he said abruptly, 'But now I-I-I believe that you have. You c-can come here again if you want to.'

It was not yet half-past twelve when Pippa found herself standing again beside the church, with Gurney padlocking the gate behind her. Well, at least she had met Gawaine Devere, even though the visit could hardly be described as a great success. However, he had said she could come again.

Outside Padden's she found a telephone booth and dialled her grandmother's number. The phone rang and rang and she was just about to give up when Kitty answered rather breathlessly.

'Kitty, it's Pippa. Can I pop in and see you?'

'Pippa, darling! Of course. What a lovely surprise. Where are you?'

'I'll tell you when I see you.'

'How long will you be?'

'About an hour, I should think.'

'Drive carefully . . .'

'Don't worry, I always do. Bye for now. See you soon.'

On this occasion, upon reaching Arundel she knew exactly where to go and where to park. Furthermore, Kitty was waiting for her, opening the door almost before the knocker had a chance to fall. 'How lovely to see you, darling,' she said, lifting her face to be kissed. 'Come in and tell me to what I owe this unexpected pleasure.'

Pippa followed her down the hall and into the kitchen. 'First of all, are you well and truly better now?'

'Oh, yes, thank you. I'm right back on form. I've been out in the garden all morning, planting gladioli.'

'Good. You look very well, I must say. Hello, Tabitha, you dear old puss. I've missed you.'

'I assume you haven't had anything to eat, so I've made us a snack.'

'You shouldn't have done that.'

'Why ever not? One of the worst aspects of living alone is eating alone. That's why I'm so pleased to have Tabitha for company.'

Kitty put various appetizingly garnished dishes of quiche, cheese, hard-boiled eggs and salad on the table.

'Mmm,' Pippa murmured appreciatively, 'bits and pieces – my favourite sort of meal.'

'Mine, too.'

'Have you made all this since I rang?'

'It didn't take a moment. I nipped up the road to the delicatessen for the quiche and I had the rest in the fridge. Now, tell me about your job. Is it turning out as you hoped? Are you enjoying it?'

It was quite extraordinary, Pippa thought, how they were meeting again as though they had known each other all their lives, picking up the threads almost where they had left off.

'The job's great,' she said. 'And Tim's a really good photographer. I'm so glad I made the change. And we've photographed some fascinating people . . .'

She reeled off some of the famous names who had been in the studio and her grandmother looked suitably impressed.

'What's more, I may be getting a proper commission all of my own.' She told her about Updike House.

'How very exciting! What a wonderful opportunity.'

'Yes, I'm really thrilled.'

They finished eating and her grandmother put her plate with a few choice morsels on the floor for Tabitha and cleared the rest into the sink. 'Now, how about a coffee?'

'Not for the moment, thank you. First I'd like to look round your garden. It looks an absolute picture.'

'Yes, it really comes into its own in the spring. Well, if you're sure you're interested . . .'

She pulled on a pair of Wellington boots and an oversized labourer's jacket inscribed 'Mowlem'. 'This jacket is a godsend,' she remarked. 'I bought it years ago from a charity shop and I don't think it will ever wear out. But whenever I wear it into town I always expect to be hauled on to a building site and told to get to work.'

Pippa chuckled.

They went out of the back door. 'Isn't the aubrietia lovely?' Kitty said, pointing to a mauve plant cascading over a low wall which separated the small terrace from the rest of the garden. 'And just look at these scyllas and grape hyacinths! Don't they remind you of a waterfall? Oh, and I must show you – the bluetit eggs in the nesting box have just hatched – five babies. I do hope Tabitha doesn't get them.

'Now this is my new rose arch. I'm rather proud of it, I must say. I built it myself. And these roses – I know they don't look much at the moment, but they'll be fine in the summer – are called High Hopes. Now I must show you where I've put my gladioli. Not that there's much to see. At the back I've planted "Sweet Song" and "Dream Castle" and at the front "Foxfire" and "Smidgen". Aren't they delicious names?'

'What's that?' Pippa asked, pointing to a brilliant blue trumpet-like flower growing in a little rockery.

'Oh,' Kitty murmured, getting down on her knees to gaze at it more closely. 'Oh, it's the first gentian . . .'

When they were indoors again, drinking their coffee, Pippa said, 'Now I must tell you where I've been this morning. Do you remember, when I was here before, I showed you a photograph album? Well, I decided in the end that I would write to Gawaine Devere after all. And he actually replied.'

The cup in Kitty's hand shook as she placed it carefully on the saucer. 'And . . . ?' she asked.

'Well, that's where I was before I came here. It was a weird experience. He was very – taciturn, I suppose would be the right word – but that could be because he has a bad stutter. Basically, I showed him the album, then he wanted to see my portfolio. He didn't think much of that, which isn't altogether surprising. However, there was one picture that he did seem to like – and you'll never guess which one that was.'

'If you remember, I have never seen any of your work,' Kitty murmured.

'But you've seen this particular picture,' Pippa said, 'because I sent you a print. It was the one I took of you, here, by the kitchen window.'

'You showed him that?' Kitty asked faintly.

'I had an enlargement made. It just happened to be in there.'

'And what did he say about it?'

'He said you and I are very alike. And that it worked as a picture.'

'And that was all?'

'Well, yes and no. He said that it showed that I had a photographic eye and I could go back and see him again.'

'And will you?'

'Yes, I think so. But not until I have something new to show him.'

Kitty took her courage in both hands. 'What was the house like?'

'I don't really know. He didn't invite me in. We stood outside and

227

talked – as far as we did talk. But everything was overgrown and the house looked very dilapidated. I found it rather sad . . .'

Somehow Kitty struggled through the rest of the afternoon without arousing Pippa's suspicions. But, after Pippa had left, she felt in the same state of emotional exhaustion as she had when she was in hospital and fate had first set her off along her unwitting trail into the past.

Pippa thought she hadn't seen through that little ruse with the photograph. Like all young people, she forgot that the old were capable of practising their own deceptions . . .

At Yondover, Pippa's visit left a curious aftermath. There was nothing overt to signify that it would make any deep or lasting impression upon the lives of the inhabitants. Ted did not so much as mention the episode. Yet there was something in his stance and his expression, as he went about his work, which revealed an inner perturbation: though whether this was annoyance at Giles's unexpected weakness in allowing such a violation of their privacy or whether he had welcomed the idea of an outside influence possibly changing the monotony of their routine, it was impossible to tell.

As for Millie, she gave sharp, verbal expression to her disapproval at the way Giles had treated his guest, not even inviting the young lady into the house, when tea had been laid ready for her and she had baked one of her special seed cakes for the occasion. To underscore her annoyance, she pointedly fed the cake to the birds.

Giles himself was well aware that his reception of Pippa had been churlish. For a while, he toyed with the idea of writing to apologize to her, but did not do so: a bare apology would not suffice and the truth was impossible to express.

He had not meant to be impolite or so harsh in his criticism of her work. But, when he had come out of the back door and seen her standing there – looking so unnervingly like Kitty at the same age – he had wanted only to get rid of her as quickly as possible. Above all, it was her smile that had disturbed him – so warm and spontaneous, it seemed to set those extraordinary gold flecks dancing in her eyes, like splashes of sunshine dappling through trees.

That was what Pippa had captured in her portrait of Kitty – that was the indefinable quality which gave it the edge of excellence.

Yes, that portrait of Kitty had come as an even greater shock than seeing

Pippa. It had simply not occurred to him that her portfolio might include pictures of her family. Kitty had been quite recognizable: if anything, she had grown more attractive with age, for experience had added character to her face. Yet, in retrospect, being confronted by her picture had also had a positive effect, for it had made him realize that Kitty no longer possessed the power to move him, either to remorse or anger: he could view her image dispassionately, as he might that of a stranger.

Considering they had been taken on a thirty-five millimetre camera, Pippa's portraits had been quite competent. Her architectural shots had not been bad either. Not that he approved of her choice of subject matter. Monstrous-looking buildings.

Edith's snapshots of Yondover had been the other shock he had received that afternoon. So accustomed had he become to the Yondover of today, he had forgotten how it used to look when he had first known it, when West was alive. Edith's pictures, depicting Yondover in all its former glory, still lovingly cared for by Fanny and Gurney even though West was dead and Kitty had gone, had filled him with a sudden sense of remorse, far greater than any regret he felt at his reception of Pippa. The Yondover of Edith's album was the Yondover West had bequeathed to him upon his death. It was far more than a legacy: it was his heritage. And he had betrayed it.

His feelings towards Yondover had always been ambivalent: he had loved it, but never really felt as though he belonged in it. When he was a boy, it had been West's home; and later, after he and Kitty were married, emotionally it had been more hers than his. In fact, the most surprising thing was not that Kitty had left him, but that she had left the Yondover she had loved so deeply.

He had come to live here almost by default: because, at the end of the war, with Porter's Place a bomb crater, he had possessed no other home. Not that he had wanted to live in London: the ruins and the rubble had been too distressing. Except for the two Rolleiflexes he had used throughout the war and the Gandolfis he and Edith had brought here at the same time as they had moved his negatives, all his equipment had been destroyed. Apart from those negatives, all his pre-war work had gone up in flames. As for his clients and friends, far too many of those had died. In any case, human contact had become distasteful to him. Yondover had offered the solitude he had craved, the refuge he had needed from the world of men.

Five years of occupation by whatever government department had been stationed here had already changed Yondover's character. As well as electricity, water and drainage services had been installed and the old Sussex barn turned into a wash-house, with baths, showers and urinals. The cart track leading up to the house had been surfaced and the stables turned into garages. Had the electricity cables been underground like the water services, he would have let them stay, but the poles and wires had formed a jarring line across the rolling hillside, as had the ugly concrete of the road.

The mains current had been disconnected and the poles taken down. The barn had been returned to its proper use. But the concrete road would have cost a fortune to dig up, so he had left it and gradually a coating of soil had formed over it, as nature reclaimed her own.

Elsewhere, too, he had done nothing to stop the gradual encroachment of weeds, the trees crowding ever nearer to the house or the buildings themselves growing ever more dilapidated, for the decay had reflected the darkness of his mood and the wilderness increased his sense of personal security. In a way, Yondover had been his scapegoat. Whether consciously or not, he had made it suffer for the wrongs the world had inflicted upon him.

Yet whilst he had neglected Yondover's more domestic aspects, the surrounding land had been another matter. He had found himself, like West before him, identifying with the hapless creatures of the wild. Hunting, shooting and angling became an abhorrence to him. In the early years, before the publication of *Tate's Gallery*, he had written endless letters to Members of Parliament and the press, protesting against these so-called sports.

But he was pitting himself against the influential land-owning class and other wealthy people to whom being a member of the Hunt and invited to shooting parties represented social cachet. Furthermore, an end to such activities would have robbed them not only of their entertainment but a valuable source of income from letting out the rights. So all he could do was to prevent them from intruding upon his property and encourage their prey to take sanctuary in his meadows and among his trees.

He had also discovered in himself a passion for trees and wild plants. Much of his money over the years had been spent on saplings and seeds, on increasing the size of West's wood and reintroducing varieties of wild flowers which modern methods of agriculture had rendered almost extinct. As they had flourished, so they had attracted rare species of birds and butterflies.

This was the Yondover which he had vigorously defended against the world. Not by nature a belligerent man – far from it – he had refused to suffer the slings and arrows of outrageous fortune, and literally taken arms against a sea of troubles. When words had not persuaded the authorities to change their minds over that high voltage grid line and the bypass, and the Courts had judged against him, he and Jethro had overcome their hatred of the weapons of war to fight for the rights not of themselves but of defenceless nature.

Though he personally lived without electricity, he did not refute its benefits. Neither did he deny the necessity for the bypass. His objection had been that, in order to cater for society's needs, trees and plants must be slaughtered, animals and birds evicted from their habitat.

It would have been feasible to place both pylons and bypass along a different route: alongside the railway, for instance. But that would have involved greedy farmers, who would have demanded extortionate prices for their land. The authorities had believed they had found a soft touch in him. Well, they had been mistaken. And, even though he had lost, his defeats had in fact been disguised moral victories. Although unsuccessful in themselves, his struggles had eventually helped lead to the founding of the Ombudsman, giving individuals the means to protect their own rights against powerful government institutions.

In the meantime, however, venerable beeches and oaks had been felled to make space for monstrous metal towers, linked by cables carrying lethal loads of electricity, and a tarmac road, along which thundered cars and lorries, belching their noisome effluents into the atmosphere and causing the deaths of countless insects, rabbits, hedgehogs, foxes and birds, not to mention human beings.

Of Samuel Lambourne's original estate, little was left. West had spent vast sums on Yondover and, later, after Giles and Kitty were married, on Porter's Place, so that when Giles had come into his inheritance, it was to discover that many of the stocks and shares had been sold and the capital was much diminished.

He had still been more than comfortably off. As well as Yondover, there had been the house in Porter's Place. His own career was in the ascendant, his earnings more than enough to maintain the lifestyle he desired. Even when the Wall Street Crash and its reverberations across Europe had led to the Depression of the 1930s and a decline in the value of the remaining shares and the income deriving from them, it had not affected him unduly.

Even when, after the war, the Labour government had nationalized the railways and all private shareholders were bought out at a fixed rate, he had not been particularly concerned. The proceeds from the sale of those shares, together with the money realized from the Porter's Place site, would have been sufficient to yield interest enough to provide him with an adequate income for the rest of his life, had it not been for that cruel stroke of fate which had led the Central Electricity Generating Board to locate their pylons on his land and the Ministry of Transport to route its bypass through his woods.

The litigation costs of waging those two battles had made massive inroads into his already much diminished capital. Adam had given his advice for free, but his colleagues in the legal profession had, understandably, been less generous. Both cases had gone to the High Court and in both cases he had had to pay all costs.

It was then he had hit upon a brainwave. The solution to his problems could be to give Yondover to the National Trust, with himself remaining as a life tenant. His pride would not allow him to tell even Adam how dire his circumstances were but, giving conservation as his excuse, he had asked Adam if he would investigate the possibility.

In the summer of 1965, a representative from the National Trust's regional committee had looked over the house and walked round the grounds. Because the property was not of national importance, he had said, and would therefore not attract sufficient visitors to be self-supporting, he thought it unlikely that the Trust's Properties Committee would consider its acquisition.

The land, however, was an entirely different matter and the Trust might well be interested in acquiring such an area of unimproved grassland, woods and river bank. But selling the land would have meant forfeiting his privacy. The price for financial peace of mind was simply too high.

In the end, he had merely changed his will, so that upon his death his entire estate went to the National Trust. If they refused the bequest, he had stipulated that Adam, as his executor, should approach other charities.

Since then, he had continued to struggle by. But, in the process, Yondover had continued to deteriorate into its present state.

Was it too late to make amends for years of wanton neglect? Did he have enough time left to rebuild crumbling walls, to repair and to redecorate; to hack back undergrowth, redig and resow lawns, reinstate flower beds and borders – and maybe even clear and resurface the drive, so that, should Pippa ever come again, she need not park by the church?

Now, less than ever, did he possess the money required to carry out the repairs which were so badly needed, for it was as much as he could manage to pay the basic household expenses and Millie and Ted's modest wages. Yet something could be done by dint of sheer hard work and elbow grease . . .

CHAPTER 17

Ever since she had come out of hospital, Kitty had been fighting temptation. Several times she had peered at the little attaché case under her bed, then firmly walked away. What purpose was to be served by disturbing the dust on its lid and opening locks stiff with age? Yet it seemed to exert an almost physical influence over her. You are stronger than you believed, it seemed to reproach her. You have walked again with West. You have listened to the lark on Uffing Down. You have confronted the spectre of Giles. You have leafed through Edith Spencer's album.

Now, Pippa's account of her meeting with Giles forced her finally to bring the little case down to the kitchen. Look at what else has been, it seemed to say. Maybe it will not hurt as much as you believe. Amid the souvenirs I contain of the past, you may even find solace and reassurance of a kind you did not expect . . .

How strange to open the catches and see again the bundle of letters she had received from Sebastian during the war, her own notebook journals meticulously dated, the small volume of her poems, the original sketches for the *Enchanted* books, a few handwritten sheets of music and dried flowers preserved in slivers of tissue paper itself so fragile that she feared it would disintegrate at a touch of the fingers.

For a long time she looked, almost overwhelmed by the memories the mere sight of these objects aroused in her. Then she took the diary labelled 'August 1927, Berlin' and flicked through the pages. How immaculate her handwriting had been and how detailed her observations:

> Tonight we attended a concert given by an Austrian pianist and
> composer called Leopold Brunnen. It consisted of two works – one
> by Alban Berg and the second a piano concerto by Brunnen himself.

The reaction of the audience to the Berg was hardly enthusiastic, but when Brunnen's own composition began, people could not contain their derision. Brunnen conducted from the piano and presented a most unconventional figure, with shaggy dark hair flopping into his rather wild eyes, and clothes that seemed in constant danger of parting company with each other. His concerto was scarcely under way before people were hissing, booing and shouting at the unmelodious cacophony of sounds being produced by the orchestra, whilst others were laughing at the antics of the composer, as he leaped up and down from his piano stool, sometimes even standing on it to gesticulate frenziedly at the orchestra, then bending over to pound out a few more strident discords, with the result that his shirt became totally disengaged from his trousers, hanging out like a rumpled frill from behind his tail-coat.

When the concerto came to its final, inharmonious, crashing crescendo, he turned to the audience, gave a triumphant bow, then flung his arms wide and grinned broadly, whereupon the mood of the audience just as incomprehensibly changed and everyone burst into applause.

'He can't write music!' the man next to me exclaimed, clapping his hands above his head. 'But what an act!'

This morning several newspapers contained reviews of the Brunnen concert. None was complimentary. The music critic in the *Berliner Zeitung* quoted from Shakespeare's *Richard II*: 'How sour sweet music is, When time is broke, and no proportion kept!' Then he went on to say: 'Last night our intelligence was insulted by a performance of Leopold Brunnen's first and, it is hoped, last piano concerto. If he heeds my advice, he will leave composing to composers and comedy acting to comedians and concentrate on playing the works of the masters. For underneath that ridiculous exterior there may just lurk a gifted pianist.'

I am not sufficiently knowledgeable about music to know if this latter statement is true, but I wholeheartedly concur with the first.

Kitty had to smile. Judging by her style of writing, she had been badly affected by Pepys. And what a prig, taking her own opinions so seriously.

Yet for a girl whose musical tastes had been dictated by West's romanticism, Leopold Brunnen's music must have come as a severe shock.

She replaced the diary and took up the one for 1932, the third year of her marriage to Giles. The entries for the first months were brief and sporadic, often little more than a comment about the weather or mention of a plant coming into flower. The sort of diary, in fact, one would expect to be kept by an old lady, not a young woman of twenty-two.

But then came the summer . . .

Adam's wedding at St Margaret's, Westminster. After much persuasion by self and Edith, Giles took the photographs. Eve is one of those calm, classically beautiful blondes who is unaware of her own beauty. I overheard several men wondering why she had fallen for Adam when she could have taken her pick of them. I pray she will make Adam happy.

I have stayed on at Porter's Place for a few days after Adam's wedding and thank heavens I did, for this morning I received a telephone call from Sonja. We met for lunch at the Savoy, where she is staying, and, confronted by the problems facing her, my own faded into insignificance, so that I did not tell her about myself and Giles, but allowed her to assume that all is well with us.

I had absolutely no idea of the hatred being stirred up against Jewish people and, for that matter, intellectuals and communists in Germany by the National Socialist Democratic Workers' Party, which is led by a man called Adolf Hitler. To start with, I thought Sonja must be exaggerating, but when she described the insults to which people are subjected, the rallies and street battles, I had to believe her.

So fearful is Felix's father of the future that he has sold his bank and moved to London. Sonja, Felix and their year-old daughter, Hanna, are here for a week before travelling on to New York. Sonja is distraught, understandably heartbroken at having to leave her home and parents, and full of trepidation about the new life awaiting her.

This afternoon Giles took family portraits of Sonja, Felix and Hanna. I shall ask for an extra print to be made and have it framed, so that I shall feel Sonja's presence even though she will be the other side of the Atlantic. It is wonderful to be with her again, even under such distressing circumstances.

Yesterday evening I was in too great a state of inner turmoil to write up my diary. It was the Arendts' last evening. We went to a concert and then had a farewell drink at the Savoy. Oh, Sonja, dear, dear friend, when shall I see you again?

But although I scarcely dare to confess it even to myself, our parting was almost eclipsed by an occurrence so fantastic that even now I find it difficult to believe it happened and I am going to describe it word for word, so that in later years I can look back on yesterday and know that it was not a dream.

The concert featured the pianist Sonja and I saw in Berlin five years ago, Leopold Brunnen. He has apparently given up composing and the programme consisted of works by Chopin, Beethoven and a composer called Geza Kovacs.

Brunnen has changed almost beyond recognition. His suit was immaculate, if somewhat old-fashioned in cut, giving him a Byronesque appearance. His hair contains many silver strands, and he has grown thinner, so that his high cheekbones seem very pronounced. But it was his eyes which most caught my attention – eyes so dark as to appear almost black, with little, dancing highlights. For a few moments before the performance began they scanned the audience and I seemed to feel them alight on me.

In complete contrast to the Berlin concert, he immersed himself so completely in his music that he became apparently oblivious to his surroundings. Never have I experienced anything like his passionate rendering of Chopin's études nor the tempestuousness he brought to Beethoven's *Appassionata* sonata. But the high point of the evening was the Kovacs piano concerto – not a work with which I was familiar – but one of such powerful intensity that it held me spellbound and, when it ended, had many, including myself, unashamedly in tears.

After the last movement, there was absolute silence for a few seconds, then the lights came on and, as one, we all rose to our feet in ecstatic applause. Brunnen remained motionless at his keyboard, then stood up and bowed. His hair clung damply to his forehead, his arms hung limply by his side, as if every last dreg of energy had been drained out of him, but, as the applause continued, he eventually lifted his head and gazed into the auditorium.

For an instant, I felt his eyes again alight on me and I sent back a fervent message with my own. You have moved me to the very depths of my being, I told him. I believed my soul was dead within me, but you have brought it to life again. Thank you, oh, thank you . . .

At my side, I heard Giles mutter, 'I have to photograph him. That face, those fingers . . .' As we made our way out of the foyer, he repeated, 'I have to photograph him.' He grasped Sonja's arm. 'I'm going round to the stage door. You must come with me, in case he doesn't speak English.' Recognizing Giles, the doorman let us through, but when we arrived at Brunnen's dressing room, a man bearing a strong resemblance to him answered Giles's knock, coming out into the corridor to speak to us.

Sonja explained our mission, but the man said, 'My cousin is exhausted after his performance and has to rest. In any case, he will not be photographed. He is a musician, not a film star.'

Sonja translated this to Giles, who said, 'Explain that I'm not a press photographer. If Brunnen insists, I'll ensure that the pictures are never published, but are used solely in my portfolio and in the exhibition I'm holding in a fortnight's time.'

After this assurance, the man relented sufficiently to allow Sonja to introduce us and introduced himself as Konstantin von Strelow. For a few moments, they discussed the concert and von Strelow accepted the others' congratulations on his cousin's performance. Hesitantly, for it is a long while since I have spoken German, I said, 'The Kovacs concerto was wonderful. I have never before heard anything so moving.'

The door flew wide open and Brunnen appeared.

His glance wandered from Sonja to Giles to Felix and finally rested on me. Again our eyes met and under his gaze I felt the blood rush to my cheeks. Then he bowed in a manner to include us all and said, '*Leopold Brunnen, zu Ihrer Verfügung, meine Damen und Herren.*'

'Does that mean he'll let me photograph him?' Giles demanded.

Again, Brunnen glanced at me, as if I influenced his reply. Finally, he replied, '*Ja, ausnahmsweise lasse ich mich fotografieren.*'

Sonja translated, 'Yes, he will make an exception and allow you to photograph him.'

And then Brunnen added, '*Unter der Bedingung, dass Frau Devere dabei ist um zu übersetzen.*' On condition that Mrs Devere is there to translate. Of course, Sonja may have mentioned that she and Felix are sailing today and I did not notice, and it may mean nothing, but . . .

Brunnen was an hour late. By the time he arrived, one of Giles's dark moods was threatening to settle on him and, while he paced up and down the hall, I retreated to the sitting room, scanning the newspapers for reviews of last night's concert. But there was nothing. I assume that the concert hall was too small and Brunnen too little known to attract the attention of the critics.

Then the doorbell rang and Brunnen was standing there. He bowed towards Giles, then raised my hand to his lips and murmured that it was a great pleasure to see me again.

It was the first time since Miss du Maurier was here that I have been in Giles's studio while he is working. Beforehand, he had given me explicit orders of what I must and must not do, especially that I must not speak except to translate his instructions to Brunnen. Brunnen, however, insisted upon being introduced to Miss Spencer and the assistants and wanted to examine all the equipment in the studio before the session began, and I was hard put to it to translate all his questions and Giles's answers, for they involved many unfamiliar, technical terms. He continued to talk throughout the sitting, which took over two hours, with Brunnen changing from one position to another at the grand piano Giles's assistants had moved into the studio.

He began by asking where I had learned German and I told him about meeting Sonja at Vevey, which led on to my visit to Berlin. 'I, too, was in Berlin that summer,' he said. 'The occasion remains in my memory because it was the last time I performed any of my own work in public. I was so badly received that I decided to heed the advice of one critic, who suggested that I stick to playing other composers' music in future.'

239

I did not like to admit that I had been present at that concert and murmured something to the effect that that must have been a rather upsetting experience. Yet he did not seem unduly upset. 'It did rather injure my self-pride,' he smiled. 'But as I grow older I realize that the music of Kovacs reflects my inner feelings better than the atonality of Schönberg. At heart I am a romantic.'

When I expressed my surprise that Kovacs is not better known, he seemed amused. Then he explained that he had come across the manuscript of the piano concerto in a second-hand bookshop in Budapest, where he had been earlier in the year, and that there could be more of the composer's works of which nobody is aware. Then he asked me if I played.

'Not very well,' I confessed. 'But my husband's grandfather used to play beautifully. From him I learned the love of music – and art – and many other things . . .'

'Tell me about this old man,' Brunnen asked and, under his prompting, the words came pouring out of me, although I was speaking in German – or maybe because of that, because I knew Giles could not understand what I was saying. 'So even in England, there are bohemians!' Brunnen exclaimed. 'Ah, I should have liked to meet your West. I think we would have found a lot in common.' He made me describe Yondover and I found myself telling him about the garden and Uffing Down and Rafe and Honey and things I never speak about to anyone any more and because he did not seem at all bored, I went on longer than I should.

After the last plate was shot, he said, 'I hope you and your husband will take dinner with me and my cousin this evening.' Giles declined, explaining that he had a lot of work to do now in the darkroom. 'Then perhaps Frau Devere . . .' Brunnen said.

Brunnen came at eight in a taxi to take me to the restaurant, the Mad Magyar in Charlotte Street. It is the most wonderfully romantic place. We dined by candlelight and a gipsy violinist played hauntingly beautiful Hungarian folk tunes.

Giles was still locked in the darkroom when Brunnen arrived, so he did not know that von Strelow was not there. 'My cousin,' Brunnen said as we drove off, 'sends his apologies and hopes you will excuse him. He found he had another appointment.' Distractedly, instinctively convinced that he had never intended his cousin to be present, I asked if Brunnen lived in Vienna.

'Not if I can help it,' he replied. 'I hate to be restricted or contained. I am like you. I do not feel at home in cities.'

Astounded, I asked, 'How did you know?'

He laughed. 'A musician's ears pick up not only every note of music but every nuance of the human voice. When you spoke this afternoon of London and Berlin, your tone was flat. When you talked about Sussex and Vevey, the words rippled lightly from your tongue.'

He chose our menu, placing our order in fluent Hungarian. When I expressed my surprise, he explained that he had been born in Budapest and brought up to speak both German and Hungarian. Then he stated, 'And soon I shall speak English.'

I asked if he were planning to stay in England for some time and he told me that he had three concerts elsewhere in the country, after which he would return to Austria. Then he added, 'And you will return with me.'

It is two o'clock in the morning now. Giles is still in the darkroom. If he comes up, I must hide my diary and pretend to be asleep, for if he speaks to me I fear that I shall be unable to control my feelings and say things I may later regret.

'We shall live,' Brunnen went on, 'in a little house surrounded by flower-filled meadows, with towering mountain peaks all around and a brook splashing past us to the valley below. For weeks on end, we shall see nobody but the occasional cow-herd. You will teach me English – and I shall teach you love . . .'

Perhaps I should have reacted in indignation at his audacity or treated his words as a jest. Instead, I felt the blood rush to my cheeks and stared down mutely at my plate. He reached across the table and tipped my chin up with his hand, so that I was forced to look at him. 'This image does not appeal to you? Why not? You love mountains. And I believe you like me. So where does the problem lie?'

I felt like a swimmer, totally out of control and about to drown. 'For one thing, I'm married,' I stammered.

He shrugged. 'And so? You are not in love with your husband.'

241

The baldness of his words took me completely aback and I realized that not once since I was married have I actually acknowledged aloud to myself or anybody else that I do not love Giles.

'There is nothing to be ashamed of in making a mistake,' Brunnen said. 'I, too, am married. But my wife and I lead separate lives. I do not love her, nor she me. All that binds us is a piece of paper.' Before I could respond, he went on, 'Your husband may be a gifted photographer, but he lacks humanity. This was apparent to me, a stranger, in the way he treated his assistants – and certainly in the way he treated you. He places his work above all else in his life.'

Then he continued, 'But I am not interested in your husband. It is because of you that I allowed myself to be photographed. From the moment I walked onstage at that concert hall yesterday, I was aware of only one person in the audience. There were others all around you – and yet it was as if you were quite alone. I played for you. It was the best I have ever played. And afterwards, your eyes, which had been dull and clouded, were sparkling with light. I was filled with a great longing to take you away from the crowd and have you all to myself.

'Back in my dressing room, I was wondering how I could meet you, when I heard voices outside. Suddenly I heard your voice praising the Kovacs concerto. I knew instinctively that it was your voice, although it had never occurred to me that you might speak German. I was filled by a happiness so overwhelming that I wanted to sing and shout aloud. To be near to you I would do anything . . .

'Today, I was late because I was suddenly assailed by doubt. Perhaps I had been mistaken in the impression I had received of you. Maybe your sadness was merely temporary, due to your friends going to America. In the familiar surroundings of your own house, you might assume a different personality. Yet, this afternoon, as I listened to you speak and watched the changing shadows of your face – as I observed the relationship between you and your husband – I knew my first impression had been right. You try to conceal your unhappiness, but it is there. You are married, but you spend little time with your husband . . .'

At that moment, the waiter came to see if we were ready for our next course and was dismayed to find we had scarcely touched our food. Brunnen said something and the waiter laughed. 'I told him that we had appetite only for love,' Brunnen explained. 'As a Hungarian, he understands.'

When the waiter returned, he smiled conspiratorially and I noticed him glance at my wedding ring and realized he must have thought we were having an affair. A gipsy flower-seller came to our table and Brunnen bought from her a red rose corsage, which he raised to his lips, before handing it to me. Then he said, 'So tell me why you should not come back with me to Austria.'

'Oh, this is quite ridiculous!' I exclaimed, to which he replied, 'Most things in life are ridiculous. And love is probably the most ridiculous of all. Consider. What I should most like to do at this minute is to kiss you. Yet isn't the pressing together of two pairs of lips a bizarre expression of emotion? As for the physical act of love, that must surely be the most inelegant and absurd of all human functions. Yet the experience is among the most sublime . . .'

Then, before I could react, he insisted, 'Please try some carp. It's delicious.' After which he began to talk about his cousin and his impressions of London and it was as if our preceding conversation had never taken place.

And now here I am, back at Porter's Place, already wondering if it was all a dream, except that in the little vase beside my bed there is a single red rose. He said he would be back in London in two weeks' time, when he would view his portrait at Giles's exhibition. I shall not be there. First thing tomorrow I shall return to Yondover. It would be sheer folly to see him again. And yet . . .

I have been clearing a part of the garden which has become badly infested by ground elder. Each morning when I start work, a pair of ring doves settle on a branch above me and coo, 'Brunnen. Brunnen.' At sundown, a thrust perches on the highest branch of the oak tree in the paddock and sings the haunting melody of the Kovacs concerto. When I go to bed, I hear Brunnen's voice: 'You will come back with me. You will teach me English and I shall teach you love.' And when sleep comes, I dream of lying in a flower-filled mountain pasture and being gathered into his embrace. I awake in a mood of drowsy, warm contentment, only to discover that Rafe has crept into the bed beside me, snuggling his head on to the pillow next to mine, and my arm is around him, as I had been dreaming of it around Brunnen . . .

This is madness! If I force myself to think rationally, I know he was only flirting with me. He could not have picked me out in that crowded auditorium. He could not have recognized my voice through his dressing-room door. My fantasies and dreams prove one thing only – not that I am in love with him or he with me – but that my life is empty.

Oh, what a fool I am.

I went to the preview of Giles's exhibition. His portrait of Brunnen is superb. I do not know how it was done, but several images seem to have been put together to make one picture. The highly polished lid of the grand piano acts as a background, reflecting an inverted image of his hands and the piano keys. To the bottom left Brunnen is seated on a piano stool, his head thrown back and his hands raised prior to striking a chord. At the centre is a close-up of his hands, with their long, tapering fingers, poised over the keyboard.

According to Adam and Eve, who were also there, Howard Redmayne has already booked an appointment to have his portrait taken in a similar style.

We had been at the exhibition about an hour when Boy Tate arrived. He was wearing a black, wide-brimmed hat over his long, fair curls, a black cape swirling round his shoulders and carrying a gold-tipped ebony cane. With him was a shortish, tubby man with grey hair, shining, baby-pink cheeks and a cherubic smile. Beside me, presumably unaware of the past relationship between Giles and Boy, Eve giggled. 'Oh, look! There's Tate and Lyle!' She went on to tell me that Tate had given up on acting and has now embarked upon a literary career, writing a weekly column for *New Society Arts*, in which he presents his own inimitable views on cultural events. The magazine's editor, Gilbert Lyle, commonly known in society circles as Sugar Plump Fairy, which under different circumstances I should have found most amusing, is apparently his current lover.

Tate's voice came nearer, his lisp more pronounced than ever, until he reached the picture of Brunnen, where he stopped, his acolytes gathered fawningly around him. 'So this is the masterpiece we are all thupposed to admire.' He fixed the photograph with a limpid gaze. Then he tittered. 'It's clever, but is it art? What do you think, Gilbert, dahling? Don't you agree that it's wather over-contwived? Technically, I'm sure it's perfect, but aesthetically it leaves me cold. It's so scientific. If the pianist were not so deliciously handsome I could underthtand why Horsey should feel the need to manipulate his images, but as it is . . .'

I don't know quite what prompted me to act as I did: whether it was Tate's distasteful comment about Brunnen or his quite unjustified criticism of Giles's work; for however confused my feelings towards Giles, I do still care about him and I loathe Tate from the very depths of my being. Whatever the reason, I stepped forward and said, 'If you were to concentrate less on the techniques employed and simply enjoy the picture as a whole – for its overall effect – I think you will find it aesthetically extremely good.'

Tate stared down at me. 'I don't think I've had the pleasure . . . ?'

'No, we have never been introduced. I am Mrs Gawaine Devere.'

His glance swept over me, blatantly contemptuous. 'In that case, you are understandably pwejudiced in your husband's favour.'

'Not so far as his work is concerned,' I replied. 'Not being a photographer myself, I can only look at his pictures from an outsider's point of view. And this particular photograph pleases me immensely – as it does a lot of other people.'

'However, since you are not a photographer, one could contend that you are not qualified to comment upon the subject.'

'And one could, I would contend, say the same thing about you!' I retorted. And with that, I walked away, hoping nobody would notice the way my hands were trembling and my knees shaking, to where a waiter was standing with a much needed glass of champagne.

Seconds later, Adam appeared at my side, anxiously asking what on earth had got into me. 'Whatever it was, it's rid us of the presence of that poisonous pervert,' a familiar voice snorted and I turned to find Lady Maude beside me. 'Look at him! Can't wait to make his escape. Couldn't stand being upstaged. Good for you, gal!'

Although I knew Giles had, as a matter of neighbourly courtesy, sent the Pughs an invitation, I had not expected them to attend. 'Had to come to Town some time,' Lady Maude explained. 'Thought we might as well see what Giles's exhibition was about. Introduced him to the Duchess of Quantock. Hector and Quantock were at school together, y'know. She's a Lady-in-Waiting to Queen Mary. A bit of royal patronage never does anyone any harm. Now, who was that odious toad?'

Adam was just explaining Tate's position on *New Society Arts* when Giles appeared. His fists were clenched, his face white and his mouth formed a tight, hard line. 'How dare you create such a scene?' he demanded of me.

'He was being so unfair . . .' I found myself stammering.

'I am perfectly capable of standing up for myself,' Giles retorted. 'There was no need for you to interfere.'

Adam said something like, 'Hey, steady on, old chap,' to which Giles replied icily, 'If I need your advice, I'll ask for it.' Turning to me again, he said, 'You have made me look a fool.'

I came back to Yondover with the Pughs, who were leaving immediately. On the journey I was unexpectedly grateful for the diversion of Sir Hector's most erratic driving. He has had his car only a few weeks and insists upon driving himself. Lady Maude carried on an almost non-stop diatribe, voicing her almost equal disapproval of Giles and Boy Tate, until we were out of the traffic and the car picked up speed, the wind rendering it impossible for even Lady Maude to make herself heard.

Well, what is done is done. Yet now, if Brunnen does come back to London, I shall not see him. If he goes to Porter's Place and maybe to Bond Street and does not find me there, he will simply return to Austria. Maybe that is for the best . . .

We were having our midday meal when the telegram arrived. Tom brought it up on his bicycle, his face pouring with perspiration and flushed with importance. 'It be in a foreign language,' he panted. 'I cycled all the way up the hill.'

Ten little words and the whole world has changed hue. *ZUG KOMMT UM FÜNF UHR HEUTE ABEND IN KIPWELL AN.* In four hours' time, he will be here.

Fanny is scurrying round with broom and duster, Jethro is mowing

the lawn and Gurney polishing the trap and grooming Captain. I
gave them to understand that Giles invited Brunnen to Yondover.

I have never felt more nervous in my life. My stomach is churning
and my legs are like jelly. What have I done? What am I doing?
What am I going to do?

There is a full moon over Uffing Down and all the stars are very,
very bright. I am too happy and too aware of the impermanence of
my happiness to sleep. I want to savour each precious moment to the
full, before it is taken from me.

Apparently Brunnen arrived at the gallery just as I was letting fly
at Boy Tate. 'You were splendid,' he said. 'So proud, so dignified,
so English. But your husband − pfff − he does not deserve your
loyalty.'

In my excitement I apparently walked straight past him, as I left
the gallery. After that, he too left, without even bothering to look at
Giles's photograph. 'If I want to see myself, I can look in a mirror,'
he said. 'It was you I wanted to see.'

Fanny insisted that we ate in the dining room, which added to my
sense of unreality, for we live very informally when Giles is not here,
yet Brunnen made no attempt to flirt with me, but talked most
amusingly about his concert tour, which lifted my spirits so much
that I almost forgot Giles. Brunnen has a way of making even the
most commonplace events seem droll.

After dinner, we went to the music room and I sat by the French
windows with Rafe at my feet as I used to do with West, while
Brunnen played. I wanted the evening to go on for ever. When
bedtime came, I was worried in case Brunnen should try to presume
upon me, but he just lifted my hand to his lips and kissed it as I left
the room. And now I am sitting here and he is asleep downstairs . . .

Today was one of the most wonderful days of my life. I had been
afraid that Brunnen might be contemptuous of my unsophisticated
lifestyle and simple pleasures, disparaging of Yondover and
supercilious to the Gurneys. I need not have worried. After breakfast,
upon which he took great pains to compliment Fanny in broken
English, he insisted that I showed him round every room in the
house and there was no doubting the sincerity of his admiration. The

garden is at its most lovely, the roses laden with blossom, like that first summer I met West.

Rafe took to him like an old friend and he is an excellent horseman, which endeared him instantly to Gurney, who even allowed him to ride Conker. In the afternoon, we galloped across the Downs and I felt young again and full of the joy of living as I have not felt since West died.

This evening, he told me about his family background. His father's people were farmers from a remote mountain village in the Vorarlberg region of Austria. His great-uncle recently died, leaving the place to Brunnen, for he was a bachelor and had no children of his own. Presumably it was with this in mind that Brunnen asked me to return with him to Austria. But this evening he made no reference to that wild proposition.

His grandmother married a soldier, who was posted to Budapest after the Austrian Empire became part of the Dual Monarchy of Austria-Hungary, which is how Brunnen came to be born in Budapest. He was born in 1892, which means he is forty. Although the silver in his hair makes him look his age, he does not behave as though he were old. In many ways, he makes me feel much older than he is.

He was brought up with music. His mother was a gifted pianist and his father a keen violinist. Both are now dead. Brunnen's own studies at the University of Vienna were interrupted with the outbreak of war in 1914.

Perhaps because he was conscious that our two countries were on opposing sides – although he was engaged in the Italian campaign and did not fight the British – Brunnen skimmed over his military service. 'Mine was the task of training mules, loaded with ammunition, to climb mountains,' he said laughingly. Yet then he told me that he had been wounded in the leg, so I think the lightness of his words conceals a great bravery.

After the war, he struggled to earn a living as a pianist, playing in cafés and at dancing classes in Vienna, whilst starting to compose his own works. It was at a dancing class that he met his wife, the daughter of a rich industrialist. (Her name was – is – Hermine.) For a brief while, he believed he was heading towards success, until his hopes were dashed by his reception in Berlin. At that point, his marriage started to go wrong. Hermine, he said, did not want a failure as a husband. (I have the impression of her being like the débutantes Giles photographs – spoiled, beautiful and shallow.)

Herr von Strelow, he told me laughingly, comes from the wealthy side of the family. He owns a vineyard outside Vienna. An extremely cultured man, he has friends throughout Europe, and when his wife died a year or two ago, he interested himself in helping Brunnen start his career again, as a concert pianist, as a means of overcoming his own grief.

This afternoon we rode alongside the Kip to the estuary and then along the beach, for the tide was out and we could ride on the sand. The sea fascinated Brunnen. While I held Conker's reins, he took off his shoes and socks and rolled up his trouser legs and danced about in the waves, kicking up sprays of water, as though he were a child. I cannot remember laughing so much as at his antics. I do so wish that West could have met him. They would already be friends.
Tomorrow we shall go earlier, when the tide is high, taking bathing costumes and a picnic with us.

'If ever a composer was misnamed, it was Bach,' Brunnen said today. 'You know that the word *Bach*, in German, means brook? I have always felt that a composer of Bach's stature should have been called sea or ocean.'

Because the sea is such a novelty to him, I had assumed Brunnen could not swim, but I had ignored the mountain lakes of Austria. Above all, he loved the breakers, launching himself into them and letting them carry him back to the shore, apparently insensitive to the pebbles.

He can go for such long periods under water that on one occasion I (who can swim like a fish) feared he had drowned. I was starting to panic, when he burst out of the water beside me like a porpoise, grinned broadly, and dived back underneath me. He seized my ankles and I, too, was submerged. But the water was not deep and, almost immediately, he grasped my hands and pulled me to my feet. I was not wearing a cap and so my hair was soaked. With his fingers, he combed my hair out of my eyes, then he tipped my face up towards him. For a moment, I believed he was going to kiss me. Instead, he said, 'When I first saw you, I thought you were pretty. But I was wrong. You are beautiful.'

Nobody has ever told me before that I am beautiful.

After dinner, I found Debussy's *La Mer* among West's gramophone records. 'In the future, whenever I hear that music I shall think of today,' he said. Oh, so shall I.

Brunnen has such a different attitude to life from that to which I am used. If he feels lazy, he stays in bed all morning. If he is hungry, he eats. When he is happy, he laughs. He cares not a whit for convention, but lives according to his natural instincts – like an animal. It is an ability I envy. My own upbringing was so puritanical and guilt-ridden.

In our picnic today, Fanny included a bottle of her elderflower champagne. We were having our lunch on Greatling Head, overlooking the sea, when Brunnen suddenly asked, 'Do you know what it means – *Brüderschaft trinken*?' He entwined his arm through mine. 'First we link arms, and then we drink.' He took a sip from his glass and I did the same. 'Now we are allowed to call each other by our first names and we can do what I have been wanting to do ever since I first saw you.' And he kissed me . . .

It was only a brief kiss, little more than a brushing of the lips, but the mere touch of his mouth on mine set my body afire. When he drew away I felt an indescribable sense of disappointment.

'It is said that the eyes are the windows of the soul,' Leo said, 'and, in your case, this is particularly true. Never have I seen eyes so expressive. They are blue like the sky, and dappled with sunshine. When you are happy they shine, and when you are unhappy they cloud over. Like your voice, they betray your every thought.'

I did not dare to put his words to the test. Instead, I started tidying up our picnic things and he laughed. 'You are right, my little Kitty-Cat, my *Kätzchen*. We should continue our walk.'

It was early evening when we returned along the Kip and climbed up the hill beside the wood. At the top, Leo stopped, putting his finger to his lips, and from deep in West's wood I heard a nightingale singing, the first I have heard since West died.

Then it happened. He took me in his arms and kissed me again, only this time there was nothing fleeting about it. His lips pressed down on mine and his body was hard and strong against me. Then he lifted me up and carried me in among the trees, where the bracken grows high. And there among the bracken, while the nightingale continued to sing, we . . .

But no, there are no words to describe the piercing beauty of our love-making. It is enough to say that even in my wildest imaginings I did not dream that love could be like this. Never did I think to experience such exquisite joy, to feel so utterly free and uninhibited. I know I should feel guilty, but I can't. All I feel is a supreme happiness.

There are footsteps on the stairs. Is it Fanny or . . . ?

I feel wanton and abandoned and drunk with love. Leo plays my body as he does the piano, creating a music in me so sublime that it is above the pitch of sound, beyond the power of feeling. When dawn broke, he returned to his own room. Before he left, he said, 'I love you, *Kätzchen*.' I keep repeating his words to myself.

I was in a deep sleep when Fanny brought my morning tea and she asked anxiously if I was feeling all right. At breakfast she asked if I was not going to show Leo some of the sights of Sussex, if we were not to visit the Royal Pavilion at Brighton or the castle at Lewes. I translated for Leo, but he is rapidly learning English! (And I am learning love . . .) 'I like better your beautiful landscape than the towns,' he told Fanny. But we must be careful not to alert the Gurneys' suspicions.

My desire for Leo is like a madness, an addiction, and the more he sates my appetite, the more I need of him. Merely his touch sends the blood pounding through my veins. How did I live before I knew him?

For a while I sat with Leo in the music room, but as he kept repeating phrases of the music he was playing, stopping to jot down notes, I realized that, although it was quite unlike his early piano concerto (it was much more in the style of Kovacs), he was in the throes of composition and slipped away. After dinner, he played me his composition and, in the bass, I heard the roar of the sea on the shingle, and in the treble, the songs of the nightingale and the lark, a melody so sweet, so ecstatic, that I felt my heart must break with the sheer, aching beauty of it. 'That is how I feel when we make love,' Leo said.

My father came here today. He had heard that I was entertaining a male guest in Giles's absence. He asked me to remember my position and told me, 'People are swift to jump to the wrong conclusion.' For a moment I feared that Fanny must have found out that Leo had been spending the nights with me, but then he added, 'I understand the chap is a foreigner. I hope you have locked away the silver, Catherine.'

Leo was elsewhere at the time, but he must have seen my father depart, for over dinner he asked who my visitor had been. I shrugged with attempted nonchalance and said that it had merely been my father. I did not want to talk about my father, for I knew it must inevitably lead to discussion of Giles. I do not want to think or talk of either of them — or of Hermine either. I cannot bear that they should contaminate our dream. To my relief, Leo asked no further questions and we talked of other things.

The second visitor in two days. Lady Maude, this time. 'People are talking about you. Now don't misunderstand me, gal. After seeing the way Giles treated you the other week, I wouldn't blame you whatever you did. But when your little summer love affair is over and your paramour has returned to his own home, you still have to live here. Think of the long-term consequences, Catherine.'

Little summer love affair. How surprised she would have been to know that that expression shocked me more than the fact that she had guessed my secret. Her words suddenly brought home to me that I cannot have Yondover and Leo. Leo could never fit into life in Sussex. His character is too tempestuous, too un-English for our quiet, muted ways. In any case, Yondover is mine only in spirit. It is Giles's inheritance. If I want to stay with Leo, I shall have to leave Yondover.

252

Yet not once since he has been here has Leo referred again to his suggestion that I might go back with him to Austria. Perhaps upon closer knowledge of me he has regretted that impulsive statement. Perhaps he still loves Hermine. But why then does he say he loves me?

After Leo left my bed this morning, I could not sleep, so I took Rafe and went up on to Uffing Down. There was a thick sea mist and it was not until I reached the top that I realized Leo was already there. He was sitting on the wet grass, his knees hunched in his arms, an unusually serious expression on his face. He took off his jacket and motioned me to sit on it beside him. 'Your father and the Milady came to warn you about your reputation, didn't they?' he asked. My silence spoke for me. 'I am truly sorry,' he said. 'I have made an unforgivable mistake. And now I should leave, before I do you further harm.'

I could not help myself. I burst into tears. He drew me to him, holding my head against his shoulder. 'Please don't cry, *Kätzchen*. You will soon forget me again.'

'I shall never forget you,' I cried. 'I love you, Leo.'

'And I love you, too,' he said. 'And because I love you, I must leave you, for to stay will be to destroy your life.'

I was so distraught at the idea of losing him, I threw caution and decorum to the winds. 'But without you, I am nothing. Without you, I cannot live.'

He shook his head. 'No, your life is here. This is your place, your home. I am only a struggling musician. I have nothing to offer you in comparison to all this. Before I came here, I had thought maybe my farmhouse . . . But now I have seen Yondover . . . No, I cannot ask you to leave this. You belong here.'

'I belong with you,' I cried.

For a long time then he was silent. Then he said, 'That is what I would like. But I know it cannot be. So, my *Kätzchen*, we must part.'

The rest of the day has been very strange. In the morning, we worked in the garden, scarcely speaking to each other. In the afternoon, he suddenly disappeared and I was terrified that he had gone without saying goodbye. I could scarcely contain my relief when I saw him return over the ridge of the hill from the direction of Kipwell. Then he told me he had been to the station to enquire about trains.

I know he will not come to me tonight.

Giles arrived just as we were finishing dinner. Leo reacted with great calm, addressing Giles in quite good English, explaining that he had been so impressed by my description of Yondover that he had felt compelled to see the house before returning to Austria and, having seen it, found it so entrancing that he had stayed longer than he intended. It was impossible to tell from Giles's expression whether he accepted this explanation. Shortly afterwards, Leo politely withdrew, whereupon Giles, too, left me. For a moment, I feared that Giles had gone to stage a confrontation with him, but when I left the dining room, I could hear the murmur of his and Jethro's voices in the study.

I can scarcely bear to write of what happened last night. Giles came to my room. His figure swayed above me and I could smell the whisky on his breath. He placed his candle on the bedside table and threw back my bedclothes. I wrapped my arms about myself but he wrenched them apart and ripped my nightdress from top to toe, then, getting on to the bed above me, pinioned me to the mattress.

'You whore,' he muttered thickly, 'you slut, you whore.' I made to scream but he clamped his hand over my mouth. 'You don't scream when he comes to you, do you?' he hissed. 'With him, you whimper with joy. With him . . .' I cannot repeat his obscene descriptions of our love-making, but they were so detailed it was obvious that someone – I can only assume Jethro – has been spying on us. But worse still, he was using his words to whip himself up into a frenzy . . .

It is morning now and he is gone again. From my window, I saw Jethro driving him in the trap towards Kipwell.

I hurt, physically, mentally, emotionally. I must wash my sheets before Fanny sees them. I cannot bear that anyone should even suspect the depravities that have taken place in this room tonight. Not even – no, least of all, shall I say anything to Leo . . .

*   *   *

I am going to Austria. After last night, I want never to set eyes on Giles again. His behaviour has forced my decision. I no longer have any choice.

I did not tell Leo what happened, but merely said that, having been together in the same house with him and Giles, I had finally realized that my marriage was over and that my future lay with him. For a few moments, Leo's expression was so sombre that I was afraid he had changed his mind. Then his face lit up with joy and I knew that, once we are in Austria, everything will be all right. And I am sure it will be, for my love for Leo surpasses everything else, even my love for Yondover.

There was a sudden, loud bang on the door and Kitty jumped, letting fall the diary. So real had Leo become, so close his presence, that she had felt she need only turn to find him beside her. But Leo was not here. She would never again speak to Leo or Leo to her. Leo was dead.

Her heart was still pounding as she reached the front door.

It was Colonel Wakehurst. 'Hah! And how are we feeling today, Mrs Pilgrim? Looking a bit pale, I must say. The Memsahib wondered if you're feeling up to having a spot of tea with us?'

If she did not feel like having tea with the Wakehursts, she could refuse and no offence would be taken. But some human company would probably do her good. Mrs Wakehurst's home-baked Dundee cake, in which the fruit would inevitably have sunk, and Colonel Wakehurst's oft-heard Indian reminiscences would be better than being alone, brooding over the past.

'Thank you,' she said, 'I'd enjoy that.'

'Jolly good! Then we'll see you in – what? – half an hour?'

'That will suit me perfectly.'

It occurred to her suddenly that what she and most of her contemporaries led were not lives, but existences, pretending to ignore the fact that they had passed their allotted span of three score years and ten, yet terribly aware that death might come at any minute and claim them for its own. Yes, eventful though their past lives might have been and undying their memories, death was the only milestone awaiting most of them now. And so they created little rituals and routines to give a sense of purpose to their remaining days . . .

Colonel Wakehurst marched briskly back to his house, but Kitty remained for a moment, looking at the view across the rooftops. At that instant, there was overhead a honking and loud beating of wings. Shielding her eyes with her hand against the silver brilliance of the sun, she watched a skein of geese, coming from the direction of the Wildfowl Trust beyond the castle, fly past the towering bulk of the cathedral and out to sea.

The sight of them, together with her memories of Leo, aroused in her an almost uncontrollable longing. She was made aware of the immensity of the world — a world of which she had once been part and was no longer . . .

Tennyson's immortal — or should they more properly be described as mortal? — lines came unbidden to her mind:

> Deep as first love, and wild with all regret;
> O Death in Life, the days that are no more.

Slowly, she made her way back to the kitchen, where the diary lay shut on the table.

She did not need to refer to it to remember her father's words when she had told him that she was going to Austria with Leo. 'You're doing what?' he had raged. 'You're going off with some Hun, some unscrupulous scoundrel, some vagabond musician? Have you no sense of virtue, of duty, of honour? What about the Commandment that says thou shalt not commit adultery? What about your marriage vows, when you promised to forsake all others and keep yourself only unto your wedded husband, obeying, serving, loving and honouring him as long as you both should live?'

When she had tried to explain that she no longer loved Giles, but that she did love Leo, he had thundered, 'I have never heard such arrant nonsense. We are talking about your role as a wife and the mistress of Yondover, about your duty to your husband and your parents.'

Her mother, weeping, had pleaded with her not to act so rashly but her father had ordered her to be quiet. 'The trollop doesn't deserve your tears. She needs to be horse-whipped. I give you one last chance, Catherine. Repent your sins and I will forgive you. If not, I shall no longer recognize you as my daughter. Your name will be struck from the family Bible and never again mentioned in this house. It will be as if you have never existed and it would be better for you had you never been born.'

She put her diary back in the attaché case. One of the oddest aspects of being old was the way the present became fused with the past. Or perhaps it was part of a natural cycle. After all, was one not oneself about to become tomorrow's past?

CHAPTER 18

The Saturday following her visits to Yondover and Rose Cottage, Pippa had her first site meeting with Chris Markowski at Updike House. She arrived early and, parking in the small crescent outside the house, got out of the car and leaned over the iron railings, looking at its exterior. It was an attractive old building, set back from the main road.

That peace was suddenly destroyed by the deep roar of a motor bike, which drew to a halt behind her Metro. It was a very big, black bike and the rider, clad in black leathers, was a very big man, as he got off and pulled the bike up on its stand. Then he took off his gauntlets and removed his crash helmet and the slightly menacing image he had projected on arrival was instantly dispersed.

He had one of those faces which, although not conventionally handsome, was immediately attractive, with a shock of tousled, black hair, dark brown eyes and a wide, appealing grin. He could have been anywhere between twenty-five and thirty-five – it was one of those ageless, boyish yet lived-in sort of faces.

'Would I be right in assuming you're Pippa? I'm Chris Markowski.' He took her little hand in a bearlike clasp, towering over her. She noticed that he did not stoop as so many very tall men tend to. 'Have you been here long?'

'No, I've only just arrived.'

'Thank God, for that. I'm usually late. Well, I believe Rickie's briefed you on the background to this job?'

'Sort of.'

'It should be pretty straightforward. We need three sets of pictures – before, during and after. It's a protected building, so we have to ensure that we don't alter the appearance or original fabric. Though that's easier said than done, as you'll see when we get inside.'

'Do you want me to take any pictures now?' she asked. She had decided to err on the safe side and put her camera case, tripod and some film in the boot of her car. The last thing she wanted was to appear unprofessional.

'Lord, no. Today's purely a recce, so that you can gain an idea of what your job entails.' He reached into the inside pocket of his jacket and extracted some rather crumpled sheets of paper. 'I've brought you some floor plans. They're copies. You can write over them.'

'Is anyone living here?'

'The last tenants finally moved out a month ago. Incidentally, this ornamental stonework round the doorway is called Coade stone. It used to be made by a Mrs Coade, whose works were on the present site of County Hall. Well, having added to your sum of useless knowledge, shall we go in?'

They went inside, the floorboards in the empty entrance hall echoing to their footsteps. 'Where on earth do you start?' she asked, looking around her in dismay at the dilapidated interior.

'Crudely, by taking down a few walls,' he said, opening a door. 'These two rooms, for instance, were originally one, as you can see from the wainscots and the coving.'

'Do you know anything about the history of the house?'

'Indeed I do. Off the top of my head, it was built in 1790 and the first owner was a merchant called Charles Updike.

'Streatham, incidentally, was just a village then. It wasn't until well into the nineteenth century, mainly due to the railway, that it began to develop into a London suburb. When Updike died, the house went to a builder, who added several reception rooms and one of the servants' wings. After that, it belonged to an art collector – Rowland Horatio Ruff Dickinson his name was, would you believe – who needed masses of space to hang all his paintings.

'When he moved on or died – I can't remember which – it went to another builder. Nothing's changed much over the centuries. He was a Mr Webster. It was lucky to survive his ownership. Most of the big mansions in Streatham were demolished around the turn of the century to make room for lots of smaller houses. But he must have decided he'd made enough money from the development he'd built in his back garden.'

While he was speaking they had completed a tour of the ground-floor flat and were standing at a lovely, large bow-window overlooking a small garden, beyond which the roofs of neighbouring houses could be seen.

'It used to have several acres of grounds,' Chris continued. 'There were lawns, rose gardens, a rhododendron walk, greenhouses and even a vinery. Difficult to imagine, isn't it?

'Well, upon his death, it went to his daughter, Miss Rose Webster, who died a couple of years ago at the age of ninety-five. For a while, she ran a Seminary for Young Ladies here, but during the war it was requisitioned by the government and used as a billet for civil servants. After that, it was converted – if one can really use that word – into flats.'

'How do you know all this?'

'It's part of my job. I go through council records, library books and papers and talk to archivists. It can be quite interesting. Well, come on, let me show you the rest of the place.'

An hour and a half later, they had been through every room from the attic to the cellars and Pippa's floor plans were covered with copious notes.

'Now for a drink,' he announced. 'Got time for a quick one?'

'Sure.'

They left the building and walked up to a pub on the common.

'Updike House is the sort of job that really appeals to me,' he said, when they were settled with their drinks – beer for him and a glass of white wine for her. 'It combines my aesthetic ideals with my social creed.'

'What do you mean exactly?'

'I believe that environment influences people's behaviour more than is generally acknowledged, at least by politicians. There is absolutely no doubt in my mind that sixties' housing estates and tower blocks are responsible for the rise of hooliganism, vandalism, drugs-related and most other crimes. They are literally soul-destroying. The same applies to modern office build- ings and factories, for that matter. They may be practical, hygienic and worker-friendly, but they lack character and individuality. It's impossible to be creative in a concrete carbuncle.'

'I'm sure you're right.'

'I know damn well I am. And Prince Charles would agree with me.'

'But it would be very expensive to knock all those buildings down and rebuild.'

'Keeping people in prison is expensive, too. And no guarantee that they won't re-offend when they come out. At least Updike House, when we've finished with it, will offer a positive environment.' Then he gave a self-deprecating smile. 'Well, that's disposed of my little hobby-horse.'

'You really are a most extraordinary mixture, aren't you?' The words escaped before she could reconsider them.

He let out a guffaw of laughter. 'So you've discovered that already, without knowing any more about me!'

'I didn't mean to be rude.'

'And I didn't take it that way. But I think you owe me an explanation.'

'Well, riding a motor bike doesn't seem to fit in with your opinions on architecture.'

'Ah! I understand. You think that someone with my social and aesthetic views should ride a bicycle, wear open sandals and put a colander on his head?'

She grinned, remembering her old boyfriend, Matt.

'Well, I'm sorry to disappoint you, but I haven't believed in exercise since the man who invented jogging died young of a heart attack. No, I love my trusty steed – even in the most inclement of weathers.'

'What kind of bike is it?'

'A BMW – and I can tell from the look on your face that you are not the slightest bit interested in knowing any more.'

'Well . . .'

'However, if you take some good photographs of Updike House, I may offer you a ride as a reward. On the other hand, I may take you out in the MG that is my other, equally antique and impractical mode of transport.'

'Open-top?'

'Naturally.' He pulled out a packet of cigarettes and offered it towards her. 'Furthermore, I smoke.'

'No thanks.'

'You're not one of these reformed types, are you?'

'No, I've just never smoked. I tried once, when I was about fourteen, and it made me feel so sick I never bothered again.'

'I smoked my first cigarette when I was fourteen as well and decided it was the most delicious experience I'd had apart from drinking beer and kissing a girl. Since then I've been addicted to all three.'

'And how does that fit in with your views on drugs?'

'I don't go round mugging old ladies and stealing pension books in order to indulge my vices.'

'No, of course not.'

'Don't look so serious. It doesn't suit you. You get little frown lines on your forehead. Yes, that's better. Has anyone ever told you that you have the most extraordinary eyes? It's like they have gold dust in them.'

She smiled but did not otherwise react to the compliment. 'My grandmother has the same eyes.'

'They say like mother like daughter, but a grandmother should be an even surer guide.'

'To what?'

'To what a girl's going to turn into.'

'They say like father like son, for that matter.'

'In that case, there's no hope for me.'

'Why?'

'My father's a mad Polak. And my mother is Greek on her father's side and Spanish on her mother's.'

'Goodness! Where on earth did they meet?'

'In London. Where else? My father was a diplomat. He was fortunate enough to find himself in London before the war and managed to stay here. My mother, believe it or not, was the product of two Jehovah's Witnesses, who escaped persecution by coming to England. And to that I should add that I have an open mind regarding religion.'

'Do you have any brothers and sisters?'

'Two sisters. Melissa, she's the younger one, works for a big PR consultancy in Los Angeles. And Angela is in Vancouver. She's the stable one in the family – married, with two kids. She's a children's nurse and used to work at Great Ormond Street. But we're very close, even though we're so far-flung, and we have fantastic reunions when we all manage to get together, which happens about once every couple of years.'

'Have you travelled much?'

'Not as much as I'd like. Before I went to college I did a stint on a Kibbutz and while I was at college I back-packed round Turkey and India – but since then I've been too busy earning a living.'

'Did you ever consider working abroad?'

'I've toyed with the idea from time to time, but basically I like England. In any case, after I got married, I got bogged down with the usual house

262

and mortgage, which rather puts paid to any ideas of gallivanting round the world.'

For some reason, it had not occurred to her that he might be married.

'But that's all over now. Lizzie and I are in the throes of getting a divorce.'

'Oh, I'm sorry.'

'I'm not. She was a bitch – a beautiful bitch. Tall, blonde, with a superb figure – and completely faithless. I came back from a business trip to France and found a pregnancy testing kit in the bottom of the wardrobe. Since relations between us had been, well, cool, prior to my departure, I knew there had to be another man involved. So I took my belongings and went, leaving her a packet of condoms as a parting gift.'

It was difficult to know how to respond to that.

'Anyway,' he said, 'all's well that ends well. I had a few weeks sleeping on the sofa in a friend's flat, then Lizzie moved out and in with her yuppie lover, who apparently drives a Porsche and has a penthouse in the Barbican, as well as a yacht in Monte Carlo. And good luck to him, that's all I can say.'

He drained his glass. 'Well, that's enough of me. Let's talk about you now.'

'There's not much to tell. My parents are both English. I have no brothers or sisters. I've never been married. In fact, I still live with my parents. In other words, I've very ordinary.'

'That I do not believe. For one thing, you're the first female photographer I've ever met who takes architectural pictures. I somehow assumed architecture to be a strictly masculine domain.'

Pippa explained how Tim had passed the job on to her.

'That was decent of him. I've met him a couple of times. Seems a nice guy.'

'Yes, he's great. I'm really lucky to be working for him.'

'So portraiture's your main interest?'

'It's what I hope to end up doing. But I like buildings, too. My second-year project at college was on architecture.'

'Let me guess. The Lloyds building . . .'

She laughed. 'You've guessed right.'

'Ah, well, somebody said that in order to arrive at where you are, you have to go by the way of ignorance – well, something like that, anyway.'

'T. S. Eliot, in *Four Quartets*,' she told him.

'I should have guessed you like poetry.'

'Why?'

'There's a dreamy air about you.'

'Well, that certainly isn't the impression I mean to give.'

'Oh, I meant it in the nicest possible way. You were impressively efficient with all your note-taking while we were going round Updike House.'

'But I do have one little mystery in my life,' she said.

'Tell me.'

Yet again, she related the story of Edith Spencer's album and Gawaine Devere.

As Tim had done, Chris listened attentively and, when she had finished, asked if he could see the album. But, not anticipating that the site meeting might turn into a social occasion, she had left it at home.

'Bring it with you some time,' he requested. 'I'd like to have a look at it. And now, I suppose, we ought to discuss work. How long do you think it will take you to complete the first stage of the photography?'

'To be perfectly honest, never having done anything like this before, I don't know. I'll have a better idea once I get started.'

'You don't need to be too fussy. In many ways, the worse you make the place look, the better it will suit our purposes. The middle stage is more for record purposes. But when we've finished doing it up, it would be useful to have some quality pictures to show future clients.'

'So far as I am concerned,' Pippa replied firmly, 'there's going to be nothing slapdash about any of the photography. It will all be done to the very best of my ability.'

He smiled. 'I understand. And, to tell the truth, I'd have been disappointed if you were intending to do anything else.'

They met again the following Saturday morning for the first photographic session. This time, Pippa was feeling decidedly nervous, even though she had discussed the job in detail with Tim and he had given her a number of hints about the problems she was likely to encounter, as well as lending her a couple of lights. She had prepared a shot list.

'Let's go over it together,' Chris said.

Swiftly, he went down her list. 'Yes, we need that, and that. But there's no need for that, or that ... Pfff, it's still a lot of work. Well, I'll leave you to get on with it on your own. Here's a key, if you want to get out and take a breather. And I'll come back at the end of the day. Shall we say about five?'

It took her well into the afternoon to photograph just the first room and by the time Chris returned, she was still far from completing a whole flat.

'At this rate, you'll have finished the refurbishment before I've finished my photography,' she said ruefully.

'Don't worry. Everything always takes longer at the beginning. And we've got plenty of time. We're still arguing with the council and negotiating with contractors. Now pack up your equipment and come and have a drink.'

They went to the same pub again, but she could not relax. To add to the agony, it would be two days before the prints came back from the laboratory. 'The light kept changing. I was metering it and I've bracketed my exposures, but what if I've still got them all wrong?' she anguished. 'And I'm not sure I chose the right camera positions. The wide angle lens makes a room look bigger, but it also distorts the verticals.'

'Stop worrying,' he laughed, after she had been going on like that for quite a while. 'If the worst comes to the worst, you can reshoot. Now let's forget about work and talk about something else. You haven't brought that photograph album with you by any chance?'

'No, I'm afraid not.'

'Tell you what, why don't you bring it along when we have dinner this evening?'

'I wasn't aware that we were having dinner this evening . . .'

'You are free, aren't you?'

'I don't have time for a social life,' she laughed. That was even more true now than when she had been with Richard.

'That's what I hoped. So, half-past eight at Alonso's in Queenstown Road?'

'Well, thank you . . .'

She decided to wear her black velvet dress: short-sleeved, V-necked and calf-length, worn with black tights and shoes, it was smart without being too sexy. Instead of tying her hair back, she left it loose to her shoulders. She was fortunate that curly hair was in fashion: other girls had to have theirs permed, but she didn't need to. Finally, she applied some foundation, eye shadow and mascara. Normally, for work, she didn't bother with make-up, but it made a pleasant change to dress up.

Getting ready took longer than she intended and it was already quarter-past eight when she came downstairs. Then she remembered Edith Spencer's album and had to dash back to her room to fetch it.

She had just regained the hall as her father emerged from the lounge. 'You're looking very smart,' he said. 'Where are you off to then?'

'I'm going out to dinner with Chris.'

'Chris — which one's he?'

'The architect.'

'Yes, of course. Philippa, I don't want to interfere in your life, but don't you think you're overdoing it a bit? You work very long days during the week and now you're working weekends as well. You know what they say about all work and no play.'

'But I enjoy my work. In any case, this evening's social . . .'

'I still think you're burning the candle at both ends.'

She glanced at her watch. 'Dad, it's very sweet of you to be concerned, but I'm afraid I have to go. I'm already late.'

'Yes, of course. Well, drive carefully and have a nice evening.'

Fortunately, the roads were clear and she and Chris arrived simultaneously outside the restaurant in Queenstown Road. He was on foot. 'I live just round the corner,' he explained.

Then he cast her an appraising glance. 'You look extremely nice. I wouldn't have thought that black would suit you, but it does.'

He held the door open for her to enter the restaurant and a waiter led them to their table.

They ordered their meal, discovering tastes in common. For their main course they both decided upon flambéed pepper steak, agreeing that they loved the spectacle as much as the taste.

'Did you bring the album with you?' Chris asked.

He went through it very slowly, reading the press cuttings, studying Gawaine Devere's prints and gazing particularly long and hard at the snapshots of Yondover. 'What a dream place,' he murmured. 'Can't you imagine it back in the twenties — people playing croquet on the lawn and throwing open the French windows to dance in the evening?'

'It looks very different now,' Pippa told him.

The waiter brought their first course and Chris put the album aside.

'You see what I mean about Gawaine Devere's pictures, don't you?' she said. 'I'll never be as good as him, if I live to be a hundred.'

'Nonsense! Anyone can do anything they set their mind to provided they really want to do it enough.'

'My father's worried that I'm overworking.'

'Fathers always worry about their daughters. What does he do for a living?'

'He's an antiques dealer.'

'Of course. That's how you found the album. Have you confessed that you've met his mother and been to see Gawaine Devere?'

'No, I don't think there's any point in stirring up trouble until I hear what Kitty has to say.'

'Mmm, I'm a great believer in letting sleeping dogs lie. Well, you will keep me informed, won't you? And I wouldn't mind having the opportunity to see Yondover . . .'

For the rest of the evening, they talked about other things, enjoying each other's company so much that, when the head waiter handed Chris the bill, they were the only people remaining in the restaurant.

As they left, she wondered if he was going to invite her back to his place, but instead he stopped beside her car and asked, 'Will you be all right driving home?'

'Yes, I'm fine.'

Taking her chin in his hand, he turned her face towards him. 'Do you know what I like most about you, Pippa Devere?'

She shook her head.

'You're such a very natural and open person. Don't ever change.' He kissed her, hard and strong, then abruptly pulled away. 'Now off with you,' he said.

Sure enough, when the processed film came back, it was fine. Tim cast a quick assessing eye over the prints and said, 'Congratulations. Rickie should be happy enough with these. Are you going to deliver them in person or do you want to send them over on a bike?'

They were, as always, very busy in the studio, doing a sportswear shoot for a women's magazine. The art editor was being particularly difficult and her coterie of so-called assistants, all identically tall, slim and dressed in black, especially trying. Pippa had already decided she did not like fashion photography. There were too many hangers-on, none of whom seemed actually to do anything. In this case, one girl was arranging her divorce on one of Tim's phones and another organizing her house move on the other line. They all treated her as if she was something the cat had dragged in.

There was simply no possibility of delivering the Updike House pictures herself to Lightfoot Godfrey before their office shut for the day. She could, of course, always ring Chris and arrange to take them to his house, but she did not want to give the impression of being forward.

Professionalism won. The pictures were sent by motor-cycle courier, with a hastily scrawled note, saying she hoped they were OK.

An hour or so later, there was a ring at the studio door. She opened it, expecting it to be yet another consignment of clothes, to find a van driver carrying a big bunch of silver, heart-shaped, helium balloons on long, multi-coloured ribbons. 'Delivery for Pippa Devere,' he said in the tone of one who was surprised by nothing in life.

She signed for them and carried them into the studio. The magazine clones all turned expectantly, then looked puzzled. 'They're for me,' Pippa said with a feeling of triumph. Had any of them, she wondered, ever received such a wonderfully silly gift?

Each balloon bore a letter of the alphabet. The letters read: CONGRATU-LATIONS.

Next Saturday, Chris again let her into Updike House, then left her to work on her own. Apart from congratulating her once more on the previous weekend's shots and laughing about the reaction of the fashion women to the balloons, all he said before he went was, 'I'll be back about five. See you in time for tea.'

Following the boost to her confidence, she made much quicker progress that day and by the time Chris returned, she had shot most of the ground floor, including one or two detail shots which had caught her fancy.

It was a lovely, mild, early summer evening. Upon leaving Updike House, she put her cameras in the car boot, then, noticing that Chris was carrying two supermarket bags, asked if he would like to leave them in her car as well.

'No,' he said, 'my own car's just round the corner. But I may as well bring them with me.' Which seemed to indicate, Pippa thought disappointedly, that he was not intending to stay long.

They headed towards the pub and were just passing a small row of shops, when he suddenly exclaimed, 'Damn! I forgot the sugar! Won't be a sec.' He rushed into a shop.

When they came to the pub, however, he went straight on past it. 'It's too crowded in there,' he said.

Lots of people were sitting outside, drinking. 'We could sit on the grass,' Pippa suggested.

Chris did not respond, but took her hand and led her on until they reached a relatively uncrowded spot. Then he put down the bags and, with a mischievous smile, opened one of them to produce a red paper tablecloth, which he spread on the grass. This was followed by a packet of serviettes, two dishes, spoons, wine glasses and a bottle of sparkling wine. Out of the other bag – his smile broadening – he took the sugar he had just bought, a carton of clotted cream, several baguettes, then punnet after punnet of plump, red, juicy strawberries.

Pippa sat down on the grass, hugging her knees in her arms, watching him as he spread his feast, laughter rising inside her.

He turned to her with a mock indignant expression. 'We all have our little foibles. One of mine is a weakness for eating bread with strawberries.'

'But there are *thirteen* punnets!'

'I have an uncle who is a baker.'

The laughter burst out of her. 'Is he Polish or Greek or Spanish?'

'Oh, this uncle is from Hungary.'

'Hungary? You didn't mention any Hungarians last week.'

'Well, maybe I misunderstood, and he was always hungry.'

'Chris, you're crazy!'

In response, he merely grinned and opened the bottle of wine.

CHAPTER 19

Kitty was at the kitchen table, pricking out seedlings – pansies, clarkia, delphiniums, hollyhocks, love-in-a-mist and love-lies-bleeding – a foretaste of summer and summers yet to come. The radio, as always, was tuned in to the classical music programme. Suddenly she heard the announcer's voice say, 'Our next piece is by a composer who created his own legend. Its first public performance was in 1933, when it was used as the theme music for a German film called *Der Alptraum* and attributed to an early nineteenth-century Hungarian composer named Geza Kovacs. In fact, it was written by the Austrian Leopold Brunnen.'

She stood motionless, a seedling in one hand, dibber in the other. Every now and again, something like this happened and, when it did, it seemed like a miracle.

'Not until after the real composer's death did the truth emerge, when the film's director, Max Zydowitz, published his autobiography. Because it is such an unusual story, I'll recount it briefly.

'Leopold Brunnen was born in Budapest in 1892. He came from a musical family and his overriding ambition was to be recognized as a composer. He studied musicology and composition at the University of Vienna under Adler and Schönberg and was greatly influenced by them, with the result that his earliest compositions were jarring on the contemporary ear. When he played his own first piano concerto in Berlin in the mid-1920s, his performance was torn to shreds by the critics. His career had apparently reached a dead end.

'For some five years, he struggled to make a living, playing in cafés and for dancing classes. Then he had a burst of inspiration. He decided to borrow another man's identity. He claimed to have discovered some of Geza Kovacs's piano scores in Budapest and passed off his own works as being those of Kovacs. It was plagiarism reversed and he took a perverse delight in fooling the critics who had sought to destroy him.

'When Max Zydowitz's autobiography was published in 1962, some musical experts contended that it was impossible for a composer to write in two such very different styles and that Leopold Brunnen had not only adopted Geza Kovacs's name but stolen his music. However, since Leopold Brunnen had died by then and Zydowitz himself had nothing to gain by fabricating such a story, it has since been generally accepted that his account is based on truth.

'We are now going to listen to Leopold Brunnen's *Alpine Symphony*. The poor sound quality is due to the fact that this is an original recording.'

Kitty turned up the volume, then sank down on a chair. She closed her eyes and the music swelled out, filling the room: music as natural and sublime as birdsong; music as tumultuous and passionate, unpredictable and unconfined, as the auditorium of sky and mountains in which it had been composed and first performed; music that spoke to the ear and to the eye, to the senses and to the heart.

And it seemed to her that she was no longer at Rose Cottage, but high in the Austrian Alps, and the sunset sky was indigo and purple and gold, and the snow on the peak of the Hohe Steinberg above Bergsee was tinged with crimson.

And Leo was not dead at all, but alive, like his music. For death, though it might have robbed the world of the man, could not take away the music he had created. That lived on and would live on for ever. It was here all around her, that supreme expression of Leo's inner self, his soul, his spirit – vibrant and vital, free and uninhibited, unfettered and untamed, immortal and eternal.

When Leo's music finished, she turned off the radio, for no other work – by however a great a composer – could match it.

The afternoon was close, the air very still. From the distance came a bang. It could have been a far-off clap of thunder or a car back-firing or a door slamming. But, for an instant, it sounded like the shot from a gun. Then came a rumble. It could have been a train pulling out of the station or a lorry grinding up a hill or the rolling of thunderclouds over the sea. But, for an instant, her mind back in Bergsee, she mistook the sound for the rumble of snow falling in an avalanche.

No, memory, for all that she would like it to delude her, refused to gainsay the reality . . .

She had not returned the little attaché case to its proper place under the bed, but left it beside the dresser, as though aware that it was not yet finished with. Now, pushing aside the seed trays, she lifted it on to the table, opened it again and took out the volume of her diaries which started in summer 1932.

The first entries were rhapsodic descriptions in German of her new surroundings and her happiness at being with Leo.

We arrived today in Bergsee and I have fallen hostage again to the beauty of mountains. The last part of our journey was completed by horse-drawn cart along a trail that led through a sun-speckled forest, fragrant with resin, until it emerged into meadows, where peasants were scything hay. After reaching the hamlet of Waldhaus, the track began to rise steeply. Here, no attempt had been made to cultivate the land, but gentle-eyed, beige and white cows grazed. Like the peasants, they raised their heads impassively to watch us as we went by.

After another mile or so, we breasted a ridge and it was as if theatre curtains had been drawn back to reveal a stage set. Beneath us, the track zigzagged down the mountainside towards a small lake of so brilliant a turquoise blue as to make the sky look pale in comparison. Trees, through which cascaded iridescent waterfalls, reached right down to its shores.

The track skirted the shoreline beneath sheer cliffs until it reached a small village on the opposite shore, a cluster of dwellings huddled round an onion-spired church, tucked into the mountainside. That was Bergsee. Beyond that, a path snaked up the mountainside, mauve with heather, between pasturelands interspersed with woods of pine and spruce, dappled by the shade of scudding clouds and dotted with occasional little wooden huts. Our driver pointed. Over there is where our farmhouse is situated.

Dominating the horizon is the majestic buttress of the Hohe Steinberg, higher by far than any of the neighbouring peaks, pockets of snow lying in gullies on its sheer northern face and a light dusting of newly fallen snow covering its slightly rounded summit.

The only access to Bergsee is by a covered footbridge over a rushing stream, its planked floor strong and wide enough for a horse and cart to traverse but not a car. We are spending our first night in the Berghof Himmelblick, which I prefer to think of as 'glimpse of heaven', instead of the more prosaic 'view of the sky' which is its literal translation. This is an earthly paradise, although the Himmelblick itself is a primitive inn, little changed, I imagine, since it was first built as a staging post, two or three hundred years ago.

The village possesses no modern amenities or facilities. There is no electricity, no telephone, no transport except for the weekly Postbus.

There is a timeless, other-worldly quality about Bergsee. The hands of the church clock have stopped at five to twelve, so that it seems as if morning never ends and midnight never arrives. Thus it is as if time itself has stopped in the little cobbled square, with the church on one side and the Himmelblick on the other and the cattle trough in the centre fed by a gurgling fountain, the water from which flows away down a gully to meet the Steinbach river by the lake.

Because the village is so remote, the people are extremely insular. Apart from the priest, they have received only a very basic education and possess little or no knowledge of the world outside their valley. Many of them have never even been as far as Lech or over the Flexenpass, let alone to Innsbruck, Salzburg or Vienna. Needless to say, they have a correspondingly deep suspicion of foreigners.

We must seem to them like creatures from another planet, particularly as we speak in virtually a foreign language. Every Austrian province – every valley, for that matter – has developed its own dialect over the centuries. Leo's Viennese is scarcely comprehensible to them, or their patois to him. I don't think they even realize that I am English. Because it is such a pious, Catholic community, Leo is telling people that I am his housekeeper.

Today we visited our new home. We climbed up the path from Bergsee, until we reached a rocky outcrop and there the path branches into two, one track leading on up the Hohe Steinberg, the other to the Alpele. Some way along this path, nestling in a natural hollow in the mountainside, out of sight from the village below, is our farmhouse.

It has a steep roof and very small, shuttered windows. As in most farmhouses, the cowshed forms an integral part of the house. Leo explained that, in winter, the warmth from the cattle helps heat the rest of the house. When I remarked that it must get rather smelly, he laughed and asked, 'What's the smell of a little wholesome manure compared to freezing to death?' Not that Leo intends to keep cows, thank heavens.

At the back is an area which I plan to make into a garden. There is some grass, beyond which an invisible stream courses away over rocks and between pine trees into a deep-sided valley that allows a view to the furthermost end of the Bergsee lake and the mountains beyond.

It is a panorama unscarred by any sign of human occupation, so beautiful that it hurts, as if the rest of the world does not exist, as if our house with its garden-to-be is a world of its own – a world within the world.

Protruding from the end of the house is a raised balcony with carved railings, supported by sturdy wooden pillars, under which piles of logs are stacked and in front of which stands a weatherbeaten garden bench. Leo and I sat there in silent contemplation of the enchanted landscape, until evening began to draw in and the sun, a huge, golden orb, prepared to dip behind the black ridge of the mountains. The sky was indigo, streaked with gold, splashed with purple and carmine, its colours reflected in the deep waters of the distant lake.

We have moved in. The house itself makes Yondover seem modern in comparison. There is no running water except for the stream outside the door and our privy is a little hut up among the trees. For lights, we use tallow candles made in the village, and the house is heated by wood-fuelled stoves. Leo finds it all a tremendous adventure, chopping firewood and shooting game. Each time he comes back from the village it is with a new hint from the locals as to how to survive the winter.

I am on the balcony, looking across the valley towards the black silhouettes of the mountains and up into the vaulted arches of the heavens. A huge, creamy moon is rising, the contours of its own valleys and mountains so clearly defined that I feel I must almost be seeing it through a telescope, and each star in the galaxy is so bright and so near that it seems I need only reach out a hand to pluck one from the sky.

This is a moment that I must remember for the rest of my life. I must impress every detail of it upon my mind, so that I can call it back, whenever I feel out of tune with the world.

Konstantin has sent Leo a piano from Vienna. It came by train to St Anton, from where it was brought on a cart to Bergsee. The last part of the journey, up the Alpele, was the most difficult, but Leo was in his element. He used men as he used mules during the war, when he served in the mountain troops. The piano was tied around with ropes and two teams of men were harnessed to the front of it. Other men were deployed to lift it at the sides and the rear. And thus, as Leo shouted directions, it was conveyed up to the farmhouse.

When it reached here, however, it would not go through the front door. So, to the great astonishment of the villagers – most of whom have never even seen a piano before – Leo announced that it should be put in the cowshed.

This caused much excited argument, for the climate up here is too harsh for arable crops and so cattle and dairy products are the lifeblood of the village. The peasants need to gather three harvests every summer to ensure their cattle have fodder enough to see them through the winter. They simply cannot believe that Leo has no intention of farming.

Yet, at the same time, I think they look up to him and admire him, because he is so different from anyone they have ever encountered before, and Leo revels in his nonconformity, playing up to his bohemian image.

The carpenter is going to put in a proper floor and panel the walls of the cowshed, to make it into a proper room. It will be the best room in the house.

Today, we climbed the Hohe Steinberg. After the forest, we came to the high pastures and then to a wild, rugged, rock-strewn country, where no cattle grazed and no trees grew, where blueberries and whortleberries seized tenuous hold among the stones, interspersed by clumps of heather and fragile rock-roses, and where the footpath quite disappeared in the loose scree and could be followed only by means of red marks painted on boulders. Birds, which could have been eagles or hawks, wheeled blackly through the sky.

Then we saw the marmots. First, a brown, weasel-like face poking out of a burrow, then the rest of the animal emerged, sitting up on its hind legs, scenting the air. Then another appeared, then another and another, screeching excitedly, as they scampered busily over the rocks.

After that, our surroundings grew more bleak, more spartan, more primeval. What had been mere patches of white became clearly defined beds of snow. We cornered a bluff and were confronted by a river of glacial ice, ridged, as though the water had frozen while it was still moving.

When we looked back the way we had come, it was to see beneath us wave after wave of mountains, riven by dark, secret valleys, ebbing away into the blue, misty yonder. It was as if Leo and I were alone at the top of the world.

In mid-October, she had written: 'It snowed a little in the night and we awoke to a fairytale world. All day we walked, drinking in the beauty. This must be the nearest one can get to heaven on earth.' And a few days later:

Leo is composing a new piece called the 'Snowflake Sonata'. It is lovely. The piano notes are just like the flakes of snow outside, swirling in the wind, then, as the wind abates, falling more gently, gradually blanketing the ground and silencing even the stream, until everything around is reduced to a hushed whisper.

This evening, Leo made an astonishing admission. The piano concerto which he attributed to Geza Kovacs he had, in fact, written himself. Nobody other than me and Konstantin von Strelow is aware of this. 'Have you heard the joke about the Hungarian recipe for an omelette which begins, "First steal six eggs"?' Leo asked me. He enjoys his own joke even more. It is his way of cocking a snook at the musical establishment which so derided his efforts at composition.

Chamois and red deer have come down from the mountains. They are becoming so tame they eat from my hand.

Then, in December, came a sudden switch to English and with it a change of mood:

I can no longer ignore the secret which I have been trying to conceal from myself. Since arriving in Austria, I have not had a single 'monthly'. To begin with, I assumed it was due to the change of climate and diet, but now I must consider the other alternative, although I feel well in myself and have not put on any weight, or at least all my clothes still fit me. I don't know whether to tell Leo or wait a little longer until I am certain. I suppose my hesitation is due to one thing. If only I could be really sure that, if I am going to have a baby, it is Leo's and not Giles's. But it must be Leo's. It must.

Christmas Day 1932. I am so stupidly childish. I had expected so much of our first Christmas together. I had decorated the house and prepared as near a traditional Christmas meal as I was able to under the circumstances. Then, as my gift to Leo, I had decided to tell him my news and give him his own personal Christkind! But it all went wrong. In a voice cold as the snow outside, he said, 'I wanted you, not a family.' I burst into tears and this made it all worse.

She looked up from her diary and gazed sightlessly out of the window. Now, of course, Leo's reaction was understandable. But, at the time, she had been totally unaware that he already had a son.

Why had he not told her about Franz at the same time as he had admitted to being married? Was it because of guilt, because he was ashamed of running away from his responsibilities? Yes, that had to be the reason. Leo might have been almost childlike in his emotions, governed by his instincts and impulses, but there had been no dark or evil side to him. He had never been wantonly cruel or unkind. He had never intentionally inflicted a hurt upon anyone.

25 January 1933. I have never imagined snow like this. It keeps on falling, heavy, silent, unremittingly monotonous, veiling the sky, concealing the mountains, burying everything under its suffocating shroud. It is over the window sills and every day Leo has to dig out the path from the door. Apart from Leo, the only human being I have seen for weeks is Gebhard Nussbaum, the inn-keeper's young son.

Gebhard had been the only real friend she had made in Bergsee. He must have been about ten at the time but he was big and strong for his age, with one of those honest, open, peasant faces, fair-haired, ruddy-cheeked and blue-eyed.

How Leo had teased her about him, taking for granted the boy's kindnesses: the path he would dig through the snow, when Leo had grown bored with the task; the logs he brought when their own stocks were depleted; the haunch of venison, the urn of fresh milk, the cheese, the bread, the pickled cabbage, which would appear when their larder was empty; the bottle of Schnapps, when the temperature sank far below zero. 'Here comes St Bernard,' Leo would laugh, recognizing no reflection upon his own inability to provide properly for her and the child growing within her.

Oh, the wild desolation of that icy, snow-bound farmhouse. She had forgotten – or wanted to forget? – the misery of that first winter in Bergsee: the slanting blizzards and the claustrophobic sense of being shut off from the rest of the world, so that it seemed as if there was only Bergsee at the end of its dark valley.

Forgotten how homesick she had felt and how she had used to gaze out on the mountains, trying to convince herself that the rest of the world did still exist: trying to imagine life continuing at Yondover; Sonja in New York, Adam in London, even Giles . . .

Forgotten the biting cold and gnawing hunger, when there was no milk or bread and Leo's hunting trips failed to yield a catch. Forgotten having to melt snow to obtain water to drink, to wash, to cook. Forgotten the problems of preserving food and eking out meagre supplies to last until the spring and cooking on a stove fuelled by timber often too damp to burn.

Forgotten how she had missed books and letters and strange, little, unforeseen things, like the thrush's song and the wind blowing across the

Downs, bringing with it the tang of ozone. Forgotten how much she had missed the companionship of Rafe and Honey and the Gurneys. Forgotten how she had gazed down upon the cottages by the lakeside, yearning for the hand of friendship to be extended to her as it was to Leo. Forgotten how the villagers in that close, prejudiced community had ostracized her once her pregnancy had become obvious, recognizing her for the adulteress she was . . .

22 March 1933. Leo has been away for three days, skiing up in the mountains. There is nothing about me to make him want to stay with me. I am so huge and ugly and tire so quickly. Yet I love him so much. When I am with him, I am complete. Without him, I am nothing. To be with Leo is to be with life itself.

3 April 1933. It's all over. The pains started very early in the morning and Leo rushed down to the village to fetch Gebhard's mother. Then he went out and I did not see him again until the evening, by which time our son was born. It was very bad. I have never known such pain. At one point, I thought I must be going to die and I think Frau Nussbaum did too, for I saw her making the sign of the cross over me. But already that has ceased to matter. I am alive and so is our son. Leo was very tender, very gentle and I am convinced now that everything will be all right.

7 April 1933. Today I got up for the first time. I am still very weak, but I suppose that is natural. Leo is very funny in his attitude towards the baby. He keeps coming to look at him, but as soon as the baby cries, he goes away. He wants to name him Johann Sebastian after Bach. Until now, I had not even thought about what he should be called. I suppose I did not want to tempt providence. But now his birth must be registered, it has become a matter of urgency. Since we are not married, he will have to bear my or rather Giles's surname. I am worried as to the effect this will have on Johann Sebastian when he grows older, for the whole village is aware that he is illegitimate, but Leo is unconcerned and says it will strengthen his character. Well, that is a problem I must face when I come to it.

10 May 1933. Leo has gone to Berlin, where Konstantin has

arranged a concert for him. 'If I stay here, my inspiration will die,' he told me before he left. 'I need change. I have to see other places, other faces.' But I know that it is I who have driven him away.

20 May 1933. Today Leo returned in the best of spirits and it was as if the sun had come out again. Unlike the last time, he was well received in Berlin. Among the people to whom Konstantin introduced him there was a film producer called Max Zydowitz, who works for the big UFA film company and was so impressed by Leo's description of Bergsee that he may make a movie here. Herr Zydowitz is coming to see us during the summer.

8 June 1933. The miracle of spring in the mountains. The valley echoes to the calls of countless cuckoos and swallows are building their nests under the overhang of the roof as they used to at Yondover. The snow melts and suddenly the meadows are full of flowers – crocuses, celandines, vetch, clover, daisies, wild narcissi and gentians.

Leo took us to a meadow which was a cerulean sea of gentians, reaching as far as the eye could see, until it merged into the dark of the forest. He laughed. 'They look like water, don't they?' And he ran into them, carelessly crushing the blossoms, calling, 'See, I am Christ! I can walk on the waves!'

During the rest of that summer of 1933, she had made few entries in her diary, which indicated that she must have been happy, for she had tended to use her diary as a confidante, to describe the bad times in her life but seldom to record her joys. And this was reassuring, for it meant that she had shared her happiness with others, but not inflicted her troubles upon them.

There was one entry to mark the arrival of Max Zydowitz:

Herr Zydowitz is a strange man. He's not much taller than I and not at all handsome, but I cannot help but like him. We have talked quite a lot about Berlin. He did not know Sonja's family, but he knew the Arendts. In his opinion, they exaggerated the dangers of Hitler and the National Socialists and did not need to leave Berlin. He says Germany requires a strong leader.

He is slightly older than Leo, and in love with the film star, Hildegard Schroeder, whom he hopes will play the leading role in his film. I simply cannot imagine an actress as beautiful as Hildegard Schroeder reciprocating his feelings.

12 December 1933. The film crew arrived today. They are staying at the Himmelblick and Gebhard has been promised a part as an extra, while Leo's (or rather, Geza Kovacs's!) *Alpine Symphony* is to be used as the theme music. It is difficult to know who is the more excited of the two.

Max Zydowitz and Hildegard Schroeder arrive in a few days, but one of the actors is already here. He is Rudi Walch and Gebhard talks incessantly about him. He is from St Anton in the Tirol and, as well as being an actor, he is a European skiing champion.

31 December 1933. This evening, Leo was down in the village – I have scarcely seen him since the film people arrived and, when he is here, all he talks about is the film. Suddenly, there was a knock on the door and Max Zydowitz came in. 'I've come to keep Leo's pretty little kitten company,' he announced, his voice slurred, taking a bottle of champagne from the inside pocket of his greatcoat. 'Poor little *Kätzchen* . . .'

He opened the champagne and filled two glasses, then sank down beside me on the settle by the kitchen stove. 'Poor little *Kätzchen*,' he repeated, gazing at me from those mournful brown eyes of his. 'What a terrible, wicked world it is. Fancy treating his little *Kätzchen* like that . . .' For a while, he lapsed into silence, then suddenly he demanded, 'Why does fate curse us? Why do we both love those who do not love us in return?' The church bells pealed in the new year, and he stood up. Clumsily taking me in his arms, he kissed me, then left me alone to my demented fears of losing Leo and with only Johann Sebastian, asleep in his cot, for company.

It is gone two o'clock now and still Leo has not returned.

Hildegard Schroeder – the one great love in Max Zydowitz's life. In his autobiography he had admitted that she was the reason he didn't marry until so late. He had kept on hoping that she would give him a chance –

despite the fact that she had three husbands after the athlete she had married in order to get to America in 1936.

Der Alptraum had been Hildegard Schroeder's first big break. Later, she had openly admitted to having pretended to be in love with Max in order to obtain the starring role, even though she could not ski.

Der Alptraum . . . Such a portentous title. Instead of meaning alpine dream, as might be assumed, it literally meant nightmare . . .

Had Leo slept with Hildegard Schroeder? And with those other women he had met on his travels and invited to Bergsee – the Italian Contessa, the German industrialist's daughter, the rich American widow . . . ? Kitty could not remember their names: she merely retained a hazy image of them, gazing adoringly at him as he played, rhapsodizing over the music and their idyllic surroundings, and Leo basking in their adulation.

It seemed almost certain. To Leo, sex had been as natural a physical impulse as eating and drinking. Once he had even said to her, 'I was married when I met you. Surely you didn't expect me to be faithful to you?'

But, if so, he had not loved them. With no one else had he experienced the ecstasy – that complete harmony, that absolute union and communion of body and mind – which had been unique to their own love-making and as essential to their survival as the very air they breathed. And Leo had known that, which was why he had always returned to her. The others had been mere passing fancies. She alone had been the one true love of his heart.

Yes, Leo had needed her as the solid foundation to his life. She had been his foil, his buffer, the bedrock of his existence. Left to his own devices, he would not have cooked or cleaned or, often, even slept. He had needed her, too, for moral reassurance. Although he had laughed off the hostile reviews of those Berlin critics, their words had continued to haunt him. She alone had known of the endless hours he had spent at the piano, agonizing over a note, a chord, a phrase, a passage, a harmony. She alone had been constant in her worship at the fount of his genius.

Oh, Leo – such a complex personality. In many ways he was so confident, in others so insecure, so unsure of his own abilities, so constantly in need of reassurance – of his virility, his musical virtuosity and the potency of his personality.

13 January 1934. Hildegard Schroeder seems determined to break Max's heart. Having tried to steal Leo from me, she then set her sights on Fritz Hedemann, a little known actor, who plays the villain in the film. And now it is the turn of Rudi Walch, whom she has enticed into giving her skiing lessons. According to Gebhard, who avidly absorbs all the gossip, Max caught her red-handed in Walch's bed.

There was, apparently, a terrible row. Max wanted to sack Walch, but the others finally prevailed upon him not to, for without Walch the film cannot be completed. At the end of *Alptraum*, there is a scene where Walch has to ski down the mountainside in the path of an avalanche, which is started by Hedemann, who intends to destroy his enemy. Apparently, there is nobody in Austria apart from Walch who is expert enough as a skier to do such a stunt.

30 January 1934. We nearly had a tragedy today. Rudi Walch could have been killed. They were filming the avalanche scene, which was supposed to be faked. But somebody started a real avalanche. Hildegard Schroeder had hysterics, accusing Max of bribing one of the locals to kill Walch.

31 December 1934. Leo is in Berlin for the premiere of *Alptraum*. I would have loved to go with him, but it would be ridiculous to expect Johann Sebastian to make such a long journey. Happy new year, world . . .

It was not until long after the war that she had seen *Alptraum*, when it was shown, late at night, on BBC2 television. It was a romantic thriller, typical of the period when Hitler had just come to power and was trying to promote his image of a new Germany, portraying fit, healthy, sporting young Aryans revelling in the outdoor life – in other words, the sort of *Schmalz* guaranteed to attract large German audiences at the time. Good had triumphed over evil and the hero had won his girl.

Yet it had been a masterpiece of its type. Few other films could ever have depicted skiing so excitingly or portrayed the mountains in such glory. There had been incredible views of virgin, snow-covered mountains against peerlessly clear skies; breathtaking shots of skiers making vertiginous leaps from sheer cliff edges or hurtling down precipitous slopes; long icicles

283

curtaining candle-lit windows; startled deer amid trees weighted down by snow; children building a giant snowman and youths staging a snowball fight (Gebhard somewhere among them); Hildegard Schroeder, beautiful even by modern standards, wrapped in a hooded, fur-trimmed cape, riding in a horse-drawn sleigh across the frozen lake; a crowd of people gathered in a snowstorm beside the church; and one sequence, more spectacularly dramatic than any of the others, of Rudi Walch, crouched low on his skis, racing against death, as the avalanche threatened to engulf him.

Almost overnight, Bergsee had been transformed from an impoverished, isolated, farming community, a remote hinterland into which only the most intrepid cross-country skier ventured, into Austria's latest, most fashionable winter resort.

After the success of *Der Alptraum*, the villagers' respect for Leo had known no bounds: even the priest had given him a hearty *Grüssgott* and allowed him to play the church organ. Leo had, she supposed, been like one of the pop stars of today, with his fans and celebrity acquaintances. He had drawn Bergsee to the attention of the world. He had brought to them that vital – and until then missing – quality of Romance. Above all, he had been responsible for their burgeoning prosperity. And because of Leo, the people of Bergsee had taken Johann Sebastian to their hearts, accepting Leo's son as one of them.

She flicked forward a few pages in the diary.

9 July 1935. Konstantin is here. He brought with him lavish presents for all of us: food and wine, dress material for me and clothes and toys for Johann Sebastian. 'You have only to let me know if there is anything you need and I will send it,' he told me. 'You inspire Leo to write great music. For you, nothing is too much.'

13 July 1935. Today, for the first time since I arrived in Bergsee, I have been out of the valley. Konstantin said it was time I came out of the wilderness and reminded myself of what the real world looks like! Leo did not come with us, but stayed behind with Johann Sebastian. We drove to Lech and over the Flexenpass to Innsbruck. It was indeed very strange to walk on pavements again, to go into shops and be among crowds of people. Konstantin insisted upon buying me some new shoes and a hat which I cannot imagine having an opportunity to wear again. We lunched at a wonderful old inn facing the Goldnes Dachl, from the balcony of which Mozart once gave a concert.

Konstantin is such a kind, generous man and so easy to be with. I felt quite sorry when our day ended.

14 June 1936. Today the cows went up again to the Alm and Johann Sebastian announced seriously, '*Wenn i gross bin, da werd' i Hirt sein, wie d' Hannes.*' Leo roared with laughter and informed him that, if he had any say in the matter, Johann Sebastian was not going to spend the rest of his life looking after cows.

How strange, now, to imagine Sebastian chattering away in a mixture of Leo's Viennese and words of the local dialect picked up from his friends in the village. For, little imagining the disadvantage it would later prove when he went to England – never imagining that he would ever go to England – she had insisted upon him growing up to speak only German.

13 November 1936. Now Johann Sebastian has passed babyhood, now he can walk and talk, Leo has become besotted with him. The two of them do everything together. Every night, before Johann Sebastian goes to sleep, Leo tells him a story about a little boy called Roman. But when Leo is away, I have to make up the next episode. My difficulty is that Roman has become so real to Johann Sebastian that he thinks of him as a true person and when I introduce events which he doesn't think could really happen, he gets very annoyed. Tonight, for instance, I introduced a Sunflower Fairy and Johann Sebastian told me in no uncertain terms that Roman did not believe in fairies. When, he demanded, was Vati coming back?

30 June 1937. We have staying with us an Italian violinist, whom Leo met last year in Florence. Tonight, they staged an impromptu performance of Geza Kovacs's latest composition – a Romance for piano and violin – and a most extraordinarily moving thing happened. The evening was fine and the doors to the music room stood open. Slowly, people started to come up from the village and gather in the yard.

They cannot have been aware that they were the very first to hear the piece. Indeed, it is unlikely that they had any inkling what they were listening to. Composers' names mean nothing to them: I doubt if anyone in Bergsee, other than the priest, has heard of Bach, Beethoven, Schubert or Mozart. Yet to them, as to me and to Johann Sebastian, has been vouchsafed the incomparable blessing of witnessing music in the creation and being present at its premiere performance.

They listened, rapt in silent attention, and when the music was finished, they burst into applause. And I could see from the expression on Leo's face that their applause meant more to him than that of the most cultured audience in any European capital, more than the ingratiating praise of any musical pundit, and much, much more than the admiration of those women who make their summer pilgrimages here, to fawn and flirt and hear the maestro play.

14 September 1937. I have taken up drawing again and often, when Leo is away, Johann Sebastian and I spend our days up on the high pastures. While he keeps Hannes company, watching the cows, I sketch. Today, Gebhard found us and sat watching me in fascination as I tried to recreate the landscape before me and suddenly I was reminded of myself as a young girl, meeting West for the first time.

5 December 1937. Leo decided Johann Sebastian is old enough for the Krampus – ogres dragging chains and uttering blood-curdling yells, who visit the homes of all the children in the village, to ascertain whether they have been good during the past year and deserve to receive presents from St Nicholas. Johann Sebastian was terrified as the Krampus performed their ritual interrogation, and in the end I made them stop. But when Leo removed his hood and mask, Johann Sebastian ceased to be frightened and hooted with laughter. He is such a brave little man. I am so proud of him.

6 December 1937. St Nicholas brought Johann Sebastian a pair of little, hand-carved skis and we took him skiing for the first time. I wrapped my arms round him and Leo held his arms round both of us. Then, with a triumphant whoop, Leo started us off down the mountainside, and the three of us hurtled through the snow, faster and ever faster, until the slope levelled out and we glided to a halt. It was hilarious. Johann Sebastian loved it. Each time we reached the bottom, he pleaded to have another go. And Leo laughingly called him a little snowbunny, as we plodded back up the slope.

28 April 1938. A letter from Adam this morning, suggesting that we return to England. Reading between the lines, it is clear that he is worried about the effects on us of what is called the 'Anschluss'. However, Konstantin, who was here last week, is very much in favour of a union between Germany and Austria, although he does not like Hitler or the National Socialists. As Leo says, so far as Bergsee is concerned, the Germans are our friends: the village owes its rising prosperity to a German film company.

Skipping a few more pages, she reached the entry for 9 August 1939.

Today must surely count as one of the worst days of my life. Yesterday, Adam turned up. The first I knew of his arrival was Gebhard rushing up from the village to say that we had an English visitor. For a dreadful moment, I thought it must be Giles, then I saw Adam toiling up the mountainside.

We sat in the garden. For the rest of my life, whenever I remember our conversation, the fragrance of the pinks growing almost wild in the border by the log store will come back to haunt me – that scent and the notes of Leo's music, the slow unfolding of a melody, harmonies hanging on the air, interweaving themselves, and then, suddenly, replaced by a new melody in a major key.

'I've come to take you back to England,' Adam said.

Grimly, he went on to spell out the facts. He believes that, having annexed Austria, forced Czechoslovakia into submission and signed a non-aggression pact with Italy, Hitler has set his sights on Poland. And if Germany invades Poland, whose safety Britain and France have guaranteed, it could mean war between Germany and England, which would mean we would find ourselves behind enemy lines and might be interned.

I refused, point-blank, to leave, finding it quite impossible to believe that we are in any danger and certainly not that we stand so close to war. In any case, if war did break out, this must surely be one of the safest places in the world.

Adam grew very angry, accusing me of blind stupidity and arrant irresponsibility. He burst in upon Leo. If we would not consider our own safety, he insisted, we should think of Johann Sebastian. To my surprise, having heard him through, Leo agreed. If Adam really believed war was imminent, Johann Sebastian's safety was paramount and Adam should take him back to England without delay. And it would be sensible if I went with them. But his own departure could not take place at such short notice, for he would need exit and travel permits. However, next month he has a concert booked in Paris, for which he will be granted the necessary visas.

I scarcely slept last night, trying to decide where my priorities lie. In the end – rightly or wrongly – I decided to let Adam take Johann Sebastian to England and to follow with Leo in a month's time.

This morning, we went to St Anton to see them off. Johann Sebastian was so excited about going on a train for the first time that he did not realize the seriousness of the occasion. With great difficulty, I held back my tears until the train had disappeared from sight. Please God that Adam is wrong and war does not break out.

Sunday 3 September, 1939. Leo has just returned from the village. Polish soldiers apparently attacked German troops the night before last. This morning England declared war on Germany. We have left it too late.

At that moment, Tabitha leaped on to the table and sat herself on the open diary. Shakily, Kitty laughed. 'You're right,' she said, 'I don't need to read any more.'

She placed Tabitha on the floor, closed the diary and replaced it in the little attaché case. No, if you remember Leo, do not remember the pain, but the joy. Not the tears, but the laughter. Not Leo's death, but his life. Not the agony, but the ecstasy. Not the nightmare, but the dreams . . .

CHAPTER 20

But her memories of Leo, so vividly revived by his music, would not go away. His presence seemed to haunt Rose Cottage, as it had the farmhouse after his death, a disturbing, restive spirit, demanding attention, refusing to depart. It was like an unfinished melody, in which the notes drifted off, inconclusively, into the ether, instead of ending in the grand finale one had anticipated . . .

Der Alptraum – the nightmare.

It was six years after the actors had left that the film's ultimate act had been played out.

They had scarcely been aware of the war during its first few months. *Sitzkrieg* they had called that period after the invasion of Poland – the sedentary war. Half a dozen men of conscription age had been called up from the village – Gebhard, to his chagrin, was still a year too young. In the surrounding mountains, soldiers from alpine commandos could occasionally be seen, dressed in white camouflage. Apart from that, it had not felt as though they were at war and they had continued to hope for an early peace.

That winter of 1939/40, the weather had been a far more implacable enemy than any military foe. Only the very oldest inhabitants could remember so severe a winter, as temperatures plummeted far below zero and the road to Bergsee was completely blocked by snow several metres deep. Never had Kitty felt so cold, as though the very marrow of her bones was frozen within her. For weeks on end, she and Leo had survived on the barest of rations, unable even to leave the farmhouse, because of the snow piled up higher than the doors. Both their tempers had grown frayed and they had become irritable with each other.

Then, in March, as the sun had increased in warmth, the slow thaw had begun. Finally, the road to Lech and over the Flexenpass had been cleared and urgently needed provisions brought in from the outside world.

It was towards the end of March that Franz had arrived . . .

Leo, desperate to get out after his enforced incarceration, was skiing, so she had been alone in the house, glad to have a little time and space to herself. There had been a knock at the door and she had opened it to find a young man on skis in the white uniform of the alpine troops. He had raised his arm in the Hitler salute and said, 'I wish to see Herr Brunnen.'

She had been cut off for so long that she had become unused to strangers and that unexpected vision of military officialdom had caught her completely off her guard. She had stammered, 'He is skiing on the mountain.'

'Who are you?'

'His housekeeper.'

His upper lip had curled in a sneer. 'So you are his English whore.'

She had flinched and he had given a derisive laugh. 'I am his son, Franz Brunnen.'

'His son?' she had repeated, uncomprehendingly.

She remembered thinking, for a brief moment, that it must be some cruel jest. Then she had looked at him more closely and recognized the facial similarity to Leo, despite the hood drawn down over his forehead and up round his chin. But his eyes contained none of the dancing vitality that sparkled in Leo's. Franz's eyes were cold and hard as stone.

Weakly, she had asked, 'Please, will you come in?'

And he had replied, 'I would rather go to hell.'

Then he had launched into a flood of bitter invective. 'My mother gave that *Schweinhund* everything,' he had said. 'Without her, he would have been nothing. She supported him all the time he was struggling to establish himself as a composer. Without her, he would still be playing in cafés and at dancing classes. My mother lifted him out of the gutter. He owes all his success to her.

'Then you came along and seduced him. You stole him from us and bred him a little bastard. Since then we haven't seen him. No, now he's rich and famous, he pretends we don't exist. We could be starving for all he cares. He never sends us any money. But you have your furs and jewels. You gallivant round Europe, staying in the best hotels, dining in fancy restaurants . . .

'You control him. Under your influence, he has become a coward. He is a mouse not a man. He won't even fight to defend his country. He won't fight for the cause of the greater Germany. He's a traitor – a traitor to his family – a traitor to his country.

'You English scum are all the same. You think you rule the world. But you wait, we will wipe you from the face of the earth. As for him . . .'

And then he had spat.

If the spittle was aimed at her face, he miscalculated, for it did not hit her but landed at her feet. Yet that did nothing to detract from the utter contempt behind the gesture.

By the time she had recovered from her shock, he had thrust his poles into the snow and swooped away. She had pulled on her outdoor clothes and ski boots, found her skis and buckled them on. But Leo had made too many trails during the last few days for her to know which to follow. She had gone up as far as the Wiesele, scanning the high slopes. She had shouted his name and her words had echoed round the mountains: 'Leo, Leo, Leo, Leo, Leo . . .'

In the end, she had returned to the house to wait. How many hours she had sat there, her stomach knotted with fear, she did not know. Then, from way above, had come the sharp report of a gun, its echo bouncing round the valley.

She had rushed into the yard and there she had heard, in the stillness of the afternoon, the ominous creak of an over-heavy load of snow, detaching itself from its icy hold, and a sonorous rumble as it commenced its journey down the mountainside, gathering more and more snow to it as it fell, sweeping away everything in its path, gaining all the time in momentum.

For a week, search parties risked their own lives scouring the mountain in the hope of finding Leo alive, then the search was abandoned, to be resumed in the summer. In the absence of a body, the cause of death could not be established. But the entire village had heard that incriminating crack of gunfire.

It was in none of their interests that the authorities should become involved. They wanted no police investigations, potential murder charges and trials. Not when Gebhard Nussbaum admitted to having fired the gun which had set off the avalanche.

Gebhard had told her the true story of what had happened, sobbing like a child in his distress. He had been tracking deer in the forest above the farmhouse when Franz had arrived, and he had witnessed, from a distance, their confrontation. He had seen Franz set off up the mountain and stalked him, sensing he was up to no good.

Then Leo's distinctive figure had come gliding down from the peak of the Hohe Steinberg. Gebhard had watched Franz conceal himself, the white of his uniform merging into the snow. He had seen Franz reach in his pocket and pull out a length of wire, flexing it between his hands.

'And then I knew that he was going to kill Herr Brunnen,' Gebhard had told her. 'I was too far away to stop him. So I fired my gun. I fired into the air. It was the only way I could think of to warn Herr Brunnen. I knew the risk I was taking of setting off an avalanche, but I had no alternative. Then the avalanche started. And now I have killed Herr Brunnen. I know I have killed him . . .'

Nobody else, apart from Gebhard and herself, had seen that figure in white, who had appeared from nowhere and disappeared again into nowhere. Nobody else, except Gebhard and herself, had known that Leo's son had come in search of his father with the intention of murdering him.

Frightened of being disbelieved if he told the truth, Gebhard had concocted a story about a chamois which had appeared so suddenly within his range, presenting such an irresistible target, that he had simply pulled the trigger without thinking.

The village had combined to form a conspiracy to protect him. His gunshot had clearly been the indirect, not the direct cause of Leo's death, they agreed. The foolish boy should have known better, they said. He should have been aware that, in this most treacherous of seasons, the slightest disturbance in the atmosphere could start an avalanche. But he had not known that Leo Brunnen was skiing up by the Todesloch-Joch.

Remembering *Der Alptraum*, they had used the film as a cover-up. The fate which had nearly overtaken Rudi Walch had happened to Leo Brunnen. And Leo had been foolishly reckless. He should have known better than to ski alone at such an altitude during the avalanche season. But what else would you expect? He was a musician and all artists were mad. It was an accident – a tragic one, indeed – but an accident.

After that, no more alpine troops were seen in the vicinity of Bergsee and when, a couple of days later, the Norwegian campaign was announced, it was assumed that they were part of the force sent – as the Nazis explained the invasion at the time – to protect Norway's freedom and independence.

Not that Kitty had been in a fit state to pay any attention to the progress of the war. Leo's death had left her devastated in a way that not even West's had done. West had died from old age, but Leo's life had been cut short in his prime. West had been given a proper funeral – Leo lay in an unmarked grave, buried under feet of snow. She had been at Yondover when West died and had at least had the solace of the Gurneys' companionship. Now, the only person to break in upon her solitude was Gebhard, though his presence gave her scant comfort. She remembered him sitting with her, for hour after hour, gazing at her in mute appeal, hoping for words of absolution for a crime he had tried to avert and ended up by committing.

Yet, although he could not know it, her sense of guilt had been stronger even than his. She had been the cause of Franz's hatred. She had been the woman who had kept Leo away from his wife and son. To add to everything else, the last words she and Leo had exchanged had been in anger. If anyone was in the wrong, it was her . . .

Hardest of all to bear had been the silence of the farmhouse when Leo was no longer there: a silence which was absolute, surrounding her like a tomb. She had moved around the building like a ghost herself. It had been as if she had become incapable of all emotion except guilt, as if the heart within her had frozen colder than any glacier. She could not eat. She could not sleep. She could not even weep. Perhaps, if she had been able to give expression to her grief, it might have found release and gradually ebbed. But it had lain too deep for tears and so it could not arise and go.

Neither could she. She felt bound to Bergsee as strongly as though she were tethered by invisible ropes, bound by the quite unrealizable hope that Leo might still be alive, bound by the conviction that if she left Bergsee she would be leaving him.

Then, something had occurred to force her out of her dazed state. It happened on her thirtieth birthday. Gebhard had climbed up from the village. The mayor had received a memorandum from Feldkirch, ordering her immediate arrest as an enemy alien, belatedly bearing out Adam's fears. The mayor, Gebhard had assured her, bore no malice towards her, but he had no other choice than to obey orders.

To Gebhard, saving her must have seemed a heaven-sent chance to atone for Leo's death. He had told her to pack a rucksack, then, after allowing her a few brief moments to say farewell to the house which had been her home and Leo's for nearly eight years, he had made her put on her skis and hurried her up to one of the huts high on the Alm, where hay was stored and cowherds took shelter during stormy weather and mountaineers could take refuge should they find themselves stranded.

That night, they had commenced their journey, travelling west towards Bregenz on the shore of Lake Constance, where the village priest – one of the few villagers with any knowledge of the world outside their valley – had a cousin who was also a priest, and who would be able, the *Pfarrer* had assured Gebhard, to help Kitty get into Switzerland.

Never would she forget that nightmare trek, although how many days and nights they had travelled she could not recall. She simply knew that it had been the longest, most strenuous and most dangerous journey she had ever made on skis, even though the *Firn* snow had made it possible for them to follow the priest's instructions and keep away from the road and thus avoid the risk of being stopped by a police patrol. Yes, apart from the risk of avalanches, the conditions had been ideal for cross-country skiing, for during the daytime the top few inches of snow had melted, leaving the surface smooth above the hard-packed frozen snow beneath.

Gebhard had been strong, agile and fearless, as well as being sustained by a sense of purpose. No slope was too steep or icy for him to descend, no gully too formidable for him to shoulder his skis and scramble up, no ravine too perilous for him to attempt its crossing. But, as well as being emotionally exhausted, she had been weak from lack of food and sleep. Time after time, she had lost her balance and fallen. Time after time, Gebhard had rescued her from snowdrifts, helped her over boulders, even carried her on occasions when the terrain had become so hostile that she had felt incapable of continuing and, had she been on her own, would have sunk into the comforting softness of the snow and waited for death to take her away and reunite her with Leo.

At night-time, the temperatures had dropped again to well below freezing. They had slept in more of those little huts, lying huddled together, fully dressed, on a makeshift mattress of last summer's hay. Gebhard had brought food with him, bread and cured meat, and to quench their thirst they had eaten snow.

Finally, they had begun their last descent. As they had skied down from the high mountains towards the lake, the climate had changed, the snow had become soft and eventually grass had shown through. They had taken off their skis, which Gebhard had hidden in a cleft in some rocks, ready for his return journey.

Down in Bregenz, it had been summer. The gardens were full of flowers and people were sunning themselves by the lakeside. Curious glances had been cast at them in their winter clothes. They had easily found the *Pfarrer*'s cousin's house beside the church and the priest, after taking a swift look at the letter of introduction Gebhard had brought with him, had ushered them quickly indoors.

Gebhard had remained only long enough to drink a cup of coffee, then he had set off back to Bergsee. She had wanted to thank him, but been unable to find adequate words. Instead, she had kissed him on the cheek and told him simply, '*Leb' wohl.*' Fare well . . .

How she had spent the rest of that day was a blank. Presumably she had taken a bath, for she must have been filthy. And maybe she had slept, for she could not recall holding any conversation with the *Pfarrer*'s cousin.

After nightfall, he had driven her up into the foothills, where he had drawn off the road and parked in the shelter of some trees. For a while, they had sat in silence, looking over the apparently deserted landscape, illuminated occasionally by the thin light of a half-moon appearing and disappearing behind the clouds. Then a motor-cycle patrol had passed. 'Now it's safe,' he had said. 'God go with you, my child.'

She had run in the direction he had pointed, stumbling over tussocks of grass and protruding tree roots. Suddenly a torch had flashed and a voice shouted, '*Halt! Wer da?*' Convinced it was an Austrian sentry, she had thrown herself to the ground. Footsteps had approached. She had heard the clicking of a rifle, sensed someone standing over her and prepared herself to be shot. Yes, that moment she remembered. She remembered how she had felt no fear, that death had held no terror for her. Indeed, she had thought that it would be better to die: for what use was freedom if one had nothing to live for?

A boot had prodded her in the ribs and she had looked up. At that instant, the moon had come out and she had recognized the distinctive Swiss cross glinting on the button of his uniform.

'I am English,' she had whispered.

*　　*　　*

The Swiss border guards and the Swiss police had all assumed she was a spy. And who could blame them? So long was it since she had used her native tongue, she had spoken English awkwardly. She could have been an Austrian travelling on a forged British passport. Yet something about her must have decided them to give her the benefit of the doubt. And she had been so obviously exhausted that they must have realized she was incapable of attempting to escape their custody.

Her timing could hardly have been worse. It was June 1940. The Germans had just invaded France, having already overrun Norway, Denmark, Holland, Belgium and Luxemburg. The Italians, too, had just come into the war on the side of Germany. Switzerland was virtually an island in the midst of enemy-held territory and its neutrality no guarantee of safety.

She had been taken, under police escort, to the British Embassy in Bern. Several times during the journey, she had felt faint.

Outside the Embassy, a queue of people had been waiting, with suitcases, bags and bundles, past whom she had been marched almost as though she were a criminal.

How alien and stiflingly formal the atmosphere in the British Embassy had seemed, how antagonistic her interrogators. But again, who could blame them? Her story must have seemed to transcend all bounds of credibility. She had told them about Leo, about Adam and Sebastian – even about Giles – yet still they had regarded her with patent disbelief.

Eventually, they had left her alone in a barren, windowless office. How long she had remained there she had no idea, for time had become suspended and all sense of reality had forsaken her.

Then the door had opened and a man had entered.

His face had been lined, crinkled round his grey eyes, with deep clefts to either side of his mouth and furrows on his forehead, belying the fact that he was only thirty-five. He had sat across the table from her, studying her with one eyebrow raised in that typically quizzical manner to which she was to grow so accustomed. And he had asked, 'How do you feel about surprised penguins?'

The room had spun round. When she had come to, she was lying on a couch in the Embassy sick room and a plump matronly figure was holding a cold compress to her forehead. 'That's good,' she said. 'Now you have a nice cup of tea and I'll let Mr Pilgrim know you're all right.'

Her first question, as he came through the door, was, 'How did you know?'

His eyebrow had shot up and he had given her a half-smile. 'Oh, over the years I've heard quite a bit about you, one way and another. My name is Pilgrim, by the way. Piers Pilgrim. Curly and I were at school together. You broke his heart when you married Devere. Then when you skedaddled off to Austria . . .'

It had felt utterly unreal to be sitting there, sipping tea and nibbling digestive biscuits, listening to Piers, with his public school accent, referring to Adam by his old nickname and talking about Giles.

'Are you able to contact Adam?' she had asked. 'Since the war started, I haven't heard anything from him. Sebastian . . .'

'I'm sure your son is fine. But communications are a bit difficult at present. However, I'll do my best to get in touch with them for you.'

'Thank you,' she had said. 'You're very kind.'

'Not at all. Purely selfishly, I'm delighted our paths have crossed.'

Piers had been more than kind. He had taken her home with him, overcoming protocol and red tape by telling his colleagues at the Embassy that her husband was one of his best friends. The fact that he was prepared to lie on her behalf had moved her to the very core of her being.

His flat was in a newish block not far from the Embassy and she remembered how strange she had found it to wash in a modern bathroom, to use a flush lavatory and hear traffic in the road outside. Over dinner that evening he had brought her up to date with the events of the war.

'The French government will surrender,' he had prophesied darkly. 'England will be the next target. The Luftwaffe is poised all along the Pas de Calais and the North Sea. Churchill is evacuating all remaining troops from mainland Europe and many of the ships taking them back to England are being bombed.'

She had thought of Franz's last threat: 'You wait, we will wipe you from the face of the earth.'

'Do you really believe the Germans will attack England?' she had asked.

'Yes, I'm afraid so.'

This final disappointment had been too much and the last of her self-control had deserted her. The tears which she had held back for so long had flooded out and she had wept as she had never wept before, nor ever wept since.

Piers had held her in his arms, until she had no more tears left to cry, then he had led her into a bedroom and laid her on the bed.

They had made love. Yes, it had been love, even though they had known each other for only a matter of hours. It had been love, even though she was not in love with him, nor he with her. It had been love: love born of desperation and loneliness and fear, of gratitude and a longing to belong to somebody, even if it was the wrong person in the wrong place. It had been love, even though, as she opened herself to him, she had known that the body could give only what the body gave and that, once the moment of union was over, the heart's desolation would be all the greater. Yet still it had been love . . .

Afterwards, he had fetched them both a glass of wine and lit them both cigarettes and said, 'Tell me.'

She had told him everything – about Leo and Sebastian, about Franz, about Gebhard, about Giles and West . . . The words had simply spilled out of her, all her pent-up grief and guilt, all her confused and convoluted feelings.

Dawn had broken and the golden giant on the Zytglogge clock tower had hammered six times on his bell. Piers had got out of bed, wrapped the eiderdown tenderly around her and kissed her. 'Sleep,' he had said.

That evening, he had brought her news from Puddles. A telegram from the Foreign Office in London stated that 'Curly' had been contacted. 'Bach' was in excellent health and doing well at school.

She had slept for the best part of a week. Piers had already left for work when she woke in the mornings, so she saw him only in the evenings when he returned. Gradually, she had recovered her strength, both physical and emotional. But, in the meantime, the Battle of Britain commenced and it was impossible for her to leave Switzerland. So she had remained with Piers.

Their affair had been a phenomenon of the war. If they had met under different circumstances, at a different time, in a different place, it would not have happened, for they were neither of them promiscuous by nature. She had still been – always would be – in love with Leo, while Piers was happily married, with two children. His family were in England, living in Hampstead, not far from where she had lived before her father was transferred to Kipwell.

He had been so gentle and understanding towards her, never intrusive, never demanding. He had never forced his attentions upon her, never pushed her into a situation where she might have to do what she did not want to do. Above all, he had accepted her as she was. Once, she had asked him if he thought her foolish and irresponsible for the way she had behaved in the past, and he had quoted, *'The heart has its reasons which reason does not know.'*

Throughout the war, she had been racked with guilt and ridden with fear on Sebastian's behalf. By thinking to send him to safety with Adam, she seemed to have consigned him to even greater danger. From listening to the BBC and from the English newspapers she saw, very out of date by the time they arrived in Switzerland, she knew of the horrendous punishment the Luftwaffe was meting out on England. At any moment, Puddles could be the target of German bombs, Hill House might no longer be standing and everyone in it dead.

With a wife and children of his own, Piers had understood what she was going through. Because of Piers, she had been able to write to Sebastian and Adam, her letters going in the diplomatic bag, although, because all correspondence was censored, everything she wrote tended to be stilted and rather superficial, often little more than proof that she was still alive.

It had often been several months before she received a reply. Yet when a letter came from Sebastian, she had read and re-read it so many times that the notepaper was starting to disintegrate when she put it away with the others.

Not that his letters were much more informative than hers, but they had given her precious insights into his life. 'The Professor took me and Elliott on a treasure hunt today.' 'I swam six lengths crawl today and am in the house relay team. I prefer swimming to cricket.' 'I came top in history and arithmetic.' 'Aunt Eve let me have a party for my birthday but it rained, so we had to stay indoors.' 'Elliott and I are going camping with the Cubs.'

Adam's letters were longer and more detailed so far as Sebastian's progress at school was concerned and contained a certain amount of other news. But he could not tell her about the effects of the war on their everyday lives, any more than she could tell him what life was like in Switzerland.

Night after night, she had prayed. Please, God, let Sebastian live. He is only young. He has a whole lifetime ahead of him. If either of us must die, let it be me. I will do anything you demand of me, God – anything – if you will let Sebastian stay alive . . .

Yet for all that she had prayed, it had been to a God in whose existence she did not really believe – or, if God did exist, it was as a god of wrath, not of goodness and mercy. For why else should He allow man, whom the Bible said He had created in His own image, to commit the evils which were taking place in the world beyond the snowy ridge of the mountains?

As soon as she was well enough, she had telephoned Madame Valentin, who, to her surprise, had remembered exactly who she was. 'Of course, Mademoiselle Catherine, the little friend of Sonja!' she had exclaimed. 'How are you and what are you doing in Switzerland? But, of course, come and see me . . .'

Going to Vevey and meeting Madame Valentin again had marked a vital turning point in her life. Less tolerant than Piers of her personal problems, Madame Valentin had opened her eyes to the immensity of what was happening in the world beyond Switzerland.

They had sat in the garden of the *Internat*, sipping iced coffee, looking out across the lake towards Mont Blanc. Madame Valentin had changed little in the twelve years since Kitty had last seen her. Although she was approaching sixty, she still possessed the slim, svelte figure of a woman half her age. Her hair was immaculately groomed and her clothes, if a little dated – and whose weren't? – still had style.

They had conversed in French, which Kitty had found, to her surprise, she could still speak fluently. 'And what are you proposing to do next?' Madame Valentin had asked, after she had described, less emotionally than she had to Piers, her marriage to Giles, her flight to Austria, Leo's death and her escape to Switzerland.

She had shrugged. Piers had offered to try to obtain her a clerical job at the Embassy, but her typing was rusty after years of non-use and, apart from her linguistic skills, she possessed no qualifications.

'Then you had better stay and help me,' Madame Valentin had announced.

It was not, however, a teaching post which she had offered. The war had necessarily curtailed her intake of pupils. Fewer teachers now looked after far fewer girls, mainly the daughters of diplomats and the staff of the international organizations in Geneva. There were no German girls among them.

'You see,' Madame Valentin had stated grimly, 'although my husband was of the Lutheran faith, I am Jewish.'

That afternoon in Vevey, Kitty had learned the reason for the long queues of refugees waiting, every day, outside the British Embassy and American Legation in Bern. Madame Valentin had described the legislation passed by the Nazis, since they had come to power, to deprive the Jews of Germany of their citizenship and all their other rights.

In Bergsee, there had been no Jews. So far as Kitty had been aware of the laws and measures Madame Valentin detailed, she had related them only to Sonja and her family, and to Max Zydowitz, all of whom she knew were safely in America. Now she realized they had been among the fortunate ones, who had possessed the foresight and financial means to get away early.

Neither were Jews the only ones seeking refuge, Madame Valentin had continued. People of all races, religions and political persuasions were under threat of their lives from the New Order the Nazis were imposing upon each country they conquered.

Switzerland was a small country, she had explained, lacking in basic resources: most of its fuel and food was imported; and the Germans and Italians were making it increasingly difficult for supplies to get through. It was a sheer impracticality for Switzerland to give permanent sanctuary to all who needed it. Kitty had been fortunate. Others were less so.

There were times in one's life, Kitty had since realized, when the apparently disconnected events which had constituted one's life's path suddenly acquired a purpose, like pieces of a jigsaw puzzle slotting together to form a picture. In her own case, her two years at finishing school in Vevey, her old friendship with Sonja, her fluency in French and German, the country and mountain lore she had learned in Sussex and at Bergsee, together with her recent experience of escaping from Austria, had all combined to assume a sudden importance and usefulness.

Many of the refugees arriving in Switzerland were sick, injured and often near starvation. All were suffering psychological trauma. They needed medical attention and time to regain their strength. Then, they had to move on. Since Britain had come under siege, only one country remained in a position to take them in – the United States.

301

There was one route only for them to travel from Switzerland: through southern France to Spain and thence to Lisbon in neutral Portugal, the one remaining port in Europe from where it was possible to get a boat to New York.

It was a journey fraught with danger, which, as the war progressed and the German hold over Europe grew stronger, would become increasingly treacherous.

Soon, the *Internat* ceased altogether to be a school and became a last stop before the refugees embarked upon the next stage of their flight. Because they would be continuing their journeys under false identities, they had to learn some basic French. Above all, they needed to be fit, so that they could walk long distances and, when they reached the Pyrenees, climb those rugged slopes.

In this, she and Madame Valentin had done their best to help them, as well as listening with heartfelt sympathy to the ordeals they had suffered and trying to infuse them with courage for those trials which still lay ahead.

The funds to support the *Internat* in its new role had come mainly from the Jewish communities in Switzerland, Britain and America. Sonja and Felix, in particular, had been unsparingly generous with their own money, as well as organizing fund-raising activities and doing everything in their power to help those refugees who succeeded, despite impossible odds, in reaching America. Max, meanwhile, had produced films to make the American population aware of what was happening on the other side of the Atlantic and galvanize support for the war effort.

After America entered the war at the end of 1941, however, there was nowhere for the refugees to go. So they remained in Switzerland and the *Internat* became a long-term hostel. So far as was possible, their small community had been self-sufficient. The lawns were dug up and planted with vegetables. They had kept chickens, ducks and rabbits. That was when Kitty had become a vegetarian. She simply could not bring herself to wring the neck of a poor helpless animal in order that she should not starve.

The reports of intimidation and persecution which the Jews brought with them had worsened as the war progressed. Yet, at the same time as the Greater German Reich had extended throughout Europe and into the Soviet Union, the number of Jews reaching Switzerland, instead of increasing, had dwindled. Those who did miraculously escape told of ghettos, massacres and death camps, in which the Nazis were systematically exterminating the Jewish race . . .

Few people, beyond the International Red Cross and Jewish organizations in Geneva, had wanted to believe those stories. Piers, in fact, had ruined his career prospects by insisting upon bringing them to the notice of his superiors, who had demanded proof which was not available and shut their minds to a truth so horrific as to seem beyond credibility.

As the war had drawn towards its close and the Russians had liberated Majdanek and Auschwitz, and then the British had entered Bergen-Belsen, the world had received its first inkling of the atrocities and the genocide which had been carried out. But they had known about it in Switzerland long before then. That was why she had remained in Vevey, even when it might have been possible for Piers to arrange her passage to England. She wanted to do something worthwhile – something important – with her life.

After the war, many accounts had been published and films made of people's heroic escapes from Germany and German-occupied territories, as well as those who helped them on their way. So courageous had those people been and so nightmarish their experiences that she had hesitated even to talk about – let alone to boast – of her own, particularly since, by acting as she had, she was guilty of a gross dereliction of duty towards her own son.

It was not as if she could lay claim to any outstanding acts of bravery. She had not faced torture or death at the hands of the Gestapo. But in her small way, she liked to think that she had helped some of the victims of war and Nazi brutality along the road to freedom.

Tabitha scratched at the rug by her food bowl, miaowing plaintively. With a jolt, Kitty returned to the present. While she had been lost in her memories, evening had drawn in. The light in the kitchen was failing.

She fed Tabitha, then took the little attaché case upstairs and put it back under her bed, where it belonged.

How amazing, in retrospect, that, in her distraught state and in the few moments Gebhard had allowed her to pack her belongings, her first instinct should have been to save such items of immense personal value as that case contained. Or maybe it was not so surprising. Clothes, jewels and other worldly possessions had never meant much to her.

But her old diaries, her poems and the sketches she had later used in the *Enchanted* books, the fragile dried flowers picked long ago on the Alpele and the unfinished symphony Leo had been working on before his death – they could never be replaced.

CHAPTER 21

When Giles announced that they were going to try to restore Yondover to some vestige of its former glory, Ted's reaction was predictably antipathetic. Millie, on the other hand, made no attempt to conceal her delight.

Dust covers were removed from furniture in rooms long uninhabited. Grumbling mightily, Ted was made to carry chairs and settees out into the garden, where Millie attacked them with wicker beaters to get rid of the dust. Then he was told to take the carpets out and hang them over the clothes line, where they too were beaten until the grass beneath was covered with a grey film, after which he had to stagger round to the front lawn with them and drag them across the grass to raise the pile.

Curtains were washed and windows cleaned, then down on her knees Millie went to polish the floorboards, at which point Ted muttered, 'It ud seem a shame to spoil the ship for an 'a'porth of tar. Ol' John 'as bin doin' a bit of decoratin' on 'Ome Farm. Oi'll see if 'e doan't 'ave a pot or two of paint to spare.'

Old John had. And the lath and plaster walls, which had yellowed over the years, became white again, with the result that rooms which had been dim and dull seemed suddenly full of light. At least two stops brighter, Giles estimated.

Witnessing the transformation thus far effected, Ted's enthusiasm increased and he took to the garden to indulge in a savage attack of pruning, lopping back and thinning out, the results of which, he assured Giles, would show next year – 'Or mebbe year after.' Trees were denuded of ivy and Russian vine. Overhanging branches were sawn off and the roses which had grown across doors and windows were cut back to the main trunk. Self-seeded buddleia and rosebay willow herb were uprooted, along

305

with nettles, thistles and brambles, while the more tenacious bindweed and ground elder were fiercely attacked.

Giles was not idle either during those summer months. For the first time in decades, he found himself waking in the morning with a sense of anticipation.

His first task was the darkroom, a job he trusted to neither Millie nor Ted. He started by getting rid of the festooning cobwebs, then threw out – albeit with a feeling of compunction – the chemical-stained overalls and disintegrating towels. After that, he took down all the books from the shelves, dusted them off and leafed through them, to rid them of their musty smell. He cleaned the sinks, washed out the enamelled dishes and emptied the aged contents of the brown Winchesters and Kilner jars.

The floor swept and mopped, he turned his attention to the apparatus, removing ancient candlewax from the safelights, polishing the wood of the Abbeydale enlarger and cleaning the green corrosion from the brass mount of its lens. To his amazement, all except one of the thermometers still worked and so, too, did the nickel clock.

Finally, there was the water supply to see to. That took almost as long as the rest of the work put together, for the tank had to be thoroughly cleaned out and mended where, in a couple of places, it had rusted through. Yet for all that the work was arduous, there was pleasure in it.

When he had finished in the darkroom, he turned his attention to the attic. Like the darkroom, he had scarcely set foot in it since the war, for it was a room he had shunned, because of its association with Kitty. Although it had originally been West's nursery, more than anywhere else in the house it bore Kitty's imprint. This was where he had photographed her and Sonja when they were girls. This was where she had slept while they were leading separate lives. This was the scene of their last encounter . . .

He had to stoop as he went through the doorway and only in the very centre, under the apex of the roof, could he stand upright. Here, too, the atmosphere was musty and he levered open the window to allow in some air.

Beneath the window was a single bed, the once bright colours of the patchwork quilt covering it bleached by the sun to light pastel shades. In one alcove stood a washstand, with ewer and basin, and in another a wardrobe.

Evidence remained still of West's childhood days, a shelf of boys' books, a mouth organ, a rocking horse, a threadbare teddy, a cardboard theatre with faded, plush curtains.

There were boxes, crates and items of furniture which the Gurneys must have put up here at the beginning of the war and Ted and Millie had probably added to since. Opening one of the boxes at random, he found it to contain tarnished silver candlesticks, flower vases and fruit bowls, all wrapped in yellowed newspaper.

Mirrors were stacked against the wall – and pictures. Moving one, he was confronted by an oil painting of a girl and a dog running through a field of poppies. Until this moment, he had completely forgotten that picture of Kitty and Rafe, which used to hang in West's bedroom. He turned it back, so that it again faced the wall.

He had a far more specific purpose in the attic than to voyage down memory lane. It was up here that he and Edith had stored the filing cabinets containing his negatives and his studio cameras when they had moved them from Porter's Place.

He undid the strap on the big leather case containing his full-plate Gandolfi and lifted the clasps. This had been his favourite camera, the one on which he had shot his portrait of King George V. Not surprisingly, nearly fifty years of being shut away, unused, had taken their toll: the bellows were covered in mildew, the brass was corroded, the trackwork had seized and the rubber of the Thornton Pickard roller-blind shutters had perished.

It was August now. Three months had passed since Pippa's visit. Every day, he had awaited with impatience Ted's return from the village and, each time there was no letter from her waiting at the post office, he had experienced a sharp stab of disappointment.

Was he building his hopes on sand? Why should she want to see him again, a bad-tempered old man, whose last reception of her had been discourteous to the point of rudeness? Yet to deny the hope would have been to lose all remaining purpose in life.

He carried the camera case downstairs. Best that Pippa did not come just yet. He wanted the Gandolfi to be in full working order before she arrived and that – like everything else – would take time . . .

*   *   *

307

Then the miracle happened: Ted came back from the village with a letter. She had been very busy, Pippa wrote. Weekdays she had been assisting Tim Collins at his studio, and at the weekends she had been working on an assignment of her own, photographing a house in Streatham for a firm of architects. Now, however, the first stage of this project was completed and she had a bit of time to herself. Since he had said that she could come and see him again, she would like to take him up on his invitation and show him some of the pictures she had taken during the summer.

He replied by return, suggesting that she arrived at eleven the following Saturday and that, on this occasion, he hoped she would take luncheon with him.

This time he was prepared for her: she could not deal him any shocks. The worst that could happen would be that her new pictures were a disappointment. And since life had taught him to nurse no extravagant hopes, he had little there to fear.

Millie prepared for the event as though for a royal visit, changing her mind a dozen times a day about what food to serve, what tablecloth to lay and which china to use.

Finally, the day of Pippa's visit arrived and, auspicious omen, it was one of those all too rare, clear, bright August days. Before he went down to meet Pippa at the gate, Ted arranged a couple of deckchairs and a small table in the shade of a tree.

Glimpsing them from the sitting-room window, Giles had a sudden memory of returning with Adam, long ago, from Oxford and finding Kitty and Sonja sitting in just that spot with West . . .

He went into the kitchen, where Millie was setting a tray with cups and plates. Everything in the kitchen remained just as it had been when he was a boy: the dresser stacked with crockery; the deep, stoneware sink; the copper and the mangle; herbs hanging in bunches from the low, dark oak beams; bowls of apples and eggs; Fanny's old rocker – now Millie's – beside the black, open range, in which a fire glowed brightly. On the rack, tea towels were drying and on the mantelshelf stood a jar of spills, a clock and some china ornaments.

Under a bibbed pinafore, Millie was wearing her Sunday best – a brown tweed skirt and a rust-coloured blouse. Her grey hair was drawn back in a bun with a little ribbon tied round it. Strange how, in old age, she was starting to resemble Fanny, as though she had taken over the character of the woman whose kitchen she had inherited.

'And what be you a-wanting in my kitchen, Mr Giles?' she demanded. 'I haven't got time to be wasting in idle chat.'

He wandered out into the courtyard and scattered a few handfuls of corn to the chickens, whereupon some sparrows descended to join in the feast, together with the tame robins that nested every year in one of the stables. Swallows and house martins darted, twittering, through the air, plucking at insects. And, overhead, in the cloudless blue sky, a skylark was pouring out its silver melody.

He went round to the front of the house and there Pippa was, with Ted, entering the garden. She was wearing blue denim shorts and a white T-shirt, which showed up the tan on her legs and arms. Sunglasses concealed her eyes. She was carrying her portfolio case.

Shyness assailed him, as he approached her. 'S-s-so you g-g-got here all right,' he said in a gruffer tone than he intended. Neither were they the words he meant to say.

'Yes, thank you. I had a very good journey. Amazingly there wasn't a lot of traffic on the road. On such a super day I expected everyone to be going to the coast.'

'C-c-come and sit d-down.'

Millie appeared, drying her hands on her pinafore.

'Millie, this is M-M-Miss Devere.'

Millie bobbed her head. 'Pleased to meet you, miss.'

'Millie is m-m-my h-h-housekeeper.'

'I'm pleased to meet *you*, Millie. Oh, and can I ask you both, right away, to please call me Pippa. I'm not used to being called Miss Devere.'

Millie nodded dubiously, then said, 'Shall I bring some coffee, Mr Giles?'

He looked questioningly at Pippa, who nodded. 'Yes, please. That would be nice.'

As Millie left, Pippa asked, 'Excuse my curiosity, but why "Mr Giles"? I thought . . .'

'G-G-Gawaine is my second name. I-I-I used to use it professionally.'

'Oh, I see.' She glanced around her. 'It looks different from when I was last here. Have you been doing a lot of work in the garden?'

'Yes, Ted's been b-b-busy.'

'It looks very nice. And the lawn looks lovely.'

'Ted m-m-mowed it this morning.'

Millie returned carrying a large tray, which she placed on the table. As well as a coffee pot, a jug of cream, sugar, cups and saucers, it contained a plate of scones, another of biscuits and a slab of fruit cake. 'All homemade,' she announced proudly.

'It's a real feast,' Pippa exclaimed.

When Millie, beaming with satisfaction, had finished fussing around the table and left them alone, Giles said, 'So, P-P-Pippa, t-tell me what y-y-you've been doing since we last met.'

'Well, I've been busy, too . . .' She proceeded to tell him about some of the shots they had done at the studio, naming sitters, a few of whom he had heard of and most of whom he hadn't. Then she went on to describe her project at Updike House, telling him about an architect called Chris, with whom she had apparently become great friends, and the problems the builders were encountering now they had commenced work.

After a while he found himself only half listening, not because he wasn't interested, but because it was so much more fascinating to watch the changing expressions on her mobile face.

Then she was suddenly saying, 'I've brought some pictures to show you, if you would like to see them.'

'Y-y-yes, of course.'

She opened her portfolio case and took out a sheaf of 10 × 8 black and white prints. 'These first ones were taken at Updike House.'

He took them from her and leafed through them slowly. They were all detail shots: some ornamental stonework over a doorway; a fireplace; a spider's web in a top corner of a room; a bow-window; a wrought-iron balcony; a beam of light falling across broken floorboards. Others incorporated evidence of builders at work: debris following the demolition of an internal wall; a shattered pane of glass in a window frame; a ladder leading up to a loft; a carpenter's trestle; a sideview of a labourer wheeling a barrow of cement.

What an improvement over the pictures she had shown him last time. The prints themselves were excellent, testifying to her ability in the darkroom. And each shot was composed and lit in such a way that it enhanced the subject, giving a tangible sense of texture, confirming his initial impression: the girl had an eye for a picture.

310

'What do you think?' she asked.

'W-w-what do you think?' he retorted. 'They're your photographs.'

'I've given a lot of thought to what you said and I know you're right. Filters and special lenses and unconventional printing techniques should only be used to enhance the properties of an image. What I was doing was being clever for the sake of it, though that wasn't my intention. But those prints you've just looked at have nothing about them to make them stand out. They're ordinary.'

'Only because they are e-e-everyday objects. Imagine if you had never seen a l-l-ladder or w-w-wheelbarrow before. You understand? Your photographs f-f-focus the eye on the subject and make it appear interesting.'

Pippa nodded doubtfully. 'Maybe. But there's something I still don't understand. Please don't get me wrong. Don't think I'm trying to compare my work with yours. But in your surrealist pictures you weren't recording life as you saw it through the lens. Those pictures weren't representational. They were expressing ideas – they were a product of your imagination. So why are you so insistent that I shouldn't try and do the same thing?'

'Pah! My pictures were t-t-typical of the period. We wanted to do what p-p-painters had been doing for centuries. Ph-ph-photography was still a relatively new m-m-medium then. We wanted to u-u-use it to impose our own interpretation on the s-s-subjects we were photographing.' He paused and looked unseeingly across the garden. In his mind, the various stages in his career coincided with milestones in his personal life. How to explain to her without having recourse to experiences he would prefer not to share? Or were the two really not interconnected?

'In other words, they were experimental?' she asked.

'Every new s-s-style is experimental. Impressionism, Expressionism, Cubism, S-S-Surrealism – they were all n-new in their time.'

Pippa frowned. 'So why shouldn't I experiment?'

'No reason at all.' Then, suddenly, everything fell into place. He did not need to use examples from his own life. 'Before an artist – a good artist – can produce abstract p-pictures, he has to be able to draw. He has to know the basic rules of form and c-c-composition. Then he can break the rules.' He could hear his own voice growing stronger, the stutter less pronounced. 'The same applies to photography. First you must possess a full grasp of all the basics. Then you can experiment. Then you can apply

311

your own s-s-style. And I mean that – your own style. Not s-s-somebody else's.'

The obstinate little frown vanished from her forehead. 'Oh, yes, I agree with that. Well, in that case . . . Do you want to see the rest? These are all people shots. This is Chris on his motor bike. This is a builder at Updike House.'

He nodded curtly. If a picture needed explaining it did not work.

'This is a chauffeur who brought someone or other to the studio. I liked his reflection in the car. And this is my mother at a wedding we went to a couple of weeks ago. That hat! And this is my father in typical pose.'

Suddenly he was grateful, after all, for the explanatory commentary. So this was how Sebastian looked now . . . A handsome if rather serious-looking man, peering over the top of the *Financial Times* through half-rimmed spectacles. Very different from the schoolboy he had met long ago at Puddles . . .

During lunch – Millie had eventually decided upon roast beef, with all the trimmings, washed down by her own elderflower champagne – Pippa suddenly posed the question which, he realized, he should have been expecting all along. But so wrapped up had he been in his own introversive thoughts that it had not occurred to him that she might be seeking a further explanation for what she had originally described – and, he had therefore assumed, accepted – as the coincidence of their names.

'Do you think there is any possibility that we could be related?' she asked.

'I-I-I-I-I . . .' He could get no further.

But his stutter unexpectedly stood him in good stead. She jumped to his rescue, not recognizing the panic that assailed him. 'No, I expect it's just wishful thinking on my part. I asked Dad, of course, when he gave me the album. But I'm afraid he had never heard of you.' She smiled gently to show that he should not take umbrage at this remark.

Whose son was Sebastian, Giles wondered again, as he had when Adam first told him that Kitty had had a baby. Was Sebastian his own son, conceived in a moment of jealous passion – or Leopold Brunnen's, conceived in illicit love? He was as unsure now as he had ever been.

Back in 1933, when Adam had passed on to him the news of Sebastian's birth, they had argued: he had said that one or other of them should go

312

to Austria and force Kitty to return, while Adam had insisted that Kitty had the right to lead her own life.

Not that he had really wanted Kitty back. By then, he had realized their marriage could not be repaired. But a son would have proved him to be a real man in his own eyes, as well as those of the outside world, putting paid to any slurs and squalid innuendoes Boy Tate might spread about him.

Then war had loomed on the horizon and Adam had gone to Austria and brought Sebastian back with him to Puddles. The very first weekend, he had hurried down to Dorset to see him. The moment he had set eyes on the boy – ignoring the fact that Brunnen, too, was dark-haired and brown-eyed – Giles had convinced himself that Sebastian was his own flesh and blood.

That was when he had decided to divorce Kitty on grounds of desertion and apply for legal custody of Sebastian. He had instructed Adam to commence proceedings and stated his intention of taking Sebastian with him to Porter's Place. But, although Adam had agreed to act for him in respect of the divorce, he had refused to part with Sebastian. Kitty, Adam had insisted, had entrusted the boy to his guardianship and while there was a chance that she might return to England, Sebastian should remain in Puddles.

It was the closest he and Adam had ever come to falling out. Giles had wanted Sebastian at least to be aware that he was his real father, but Adam had persuaded him that for the boy suddenly to acquire a new father, having so recently been parted from the man he knew as his father, could have an extremely disturbing effect upon him. In the end, they had agreed that Sebastian should call him 'Uncle Giles', as Elliott did.

The very fact that he and Sebastian seemed to share circumstances in common had sharpened his belief that they were father and son. His own parents had died when he was five. Sebastian had been separated from his at the age of six. He had had a friend and mentor in West: Sebastian should have 'Uncle Giles' . . .

'And your name didn't seem to ring any bells with my grandmother either,' Pippa was saying. 'Although, if we are related, it would presumably be through her first husband. And, after he died, I assume she lost touch with his family.'

Giles grunted, trying to fathom out the reasoning behind this statement.

Then he realized that Pippa must think Leo was Kitty's first husband and that Devere had been his surname.

'I didn't tell you about my grandmother, did I?' Pippa went on. 'It all happened because of Edith Spencer's album and your photographs. I'm not boring you, am I?'

It was best to leave her to do the talking, even if she was going to tell him things he did not want to hear. 'N-n-not at all.'

'Well, I wanted to find out about you, so I went to the Royal Photographic Society in Bath. They were showing an exhibition of war photographs. Some of your pictures were among them. Did you know about it?'

He took his head, bemused and befuddled by the swiftness with which she darted from topic to topic and place to place. He kept his thoughts with Sebastian.

'Then I went on to see Uncle Adam and Aunt Eve in Dorset. They aren't really my uncle and aunt. My father was evacuated to them during the war and they brought him up with their own son.'

With hindsight, of course, Adam had been right to put Sebastian's interests first. Sebastian had naturally been upset at being separated so suddenly from his mother and Brunnen. He had been confused by his new surroundings and, to make matters worse, had spoken no English. Yes, that had been an extraordinary experience: to meet the boy he believed to be his son, only to discover they could not communicate.

And then the war had intervened. Not that he would have volunteered for service if Sebastian had been living with him. On the contrary, the main reason for him volunteering had been because Adam had refused to let him take the boy to London.

Thwarted on every other count by Adam, he had, however, won his way in one matter. Albeit reluctantly, Adam had agreed to let him undertake all financial responsibility for Sebastian's education.

'Then, just before I left, Aunt Eve told me that some paintings I had admired had been done by my grandmother. Can you imagine? I didn't even know, until then, that I had a grandmother. My father once told me she had disappeared during the war. I had thought she was dead.'

'W-w-why sh-sh-should he t-t-tell you th-th-that?'

'I honestly don't know. Adam says Dad felt his parents had abandoned

314

him and he could never forgive them. But my grandmother is such a sweet person, I don't believe she would deliberately hurt a fly.'

There was only one word to describe his own feelings during the war towards Kitty – hatred. Until then, his bitterness had been tempered by his low opinion of himself, by a sense of shame and disgrace. But once he had taken his place in the world of men, he had been free to acknowledge his own anger.

Yet while England was being blitzed, while gallant servicemen were sacrificing their lives, while millions were dying in concentration camps – Kitty had been living in the safest place in all of Europe, in neutral Switzerland. Small wonder Sebastian could not forgive her . . .

Fortunately, Millie entered the dining room at that moment and Pippa stopped to tell her how much she was enjoying her meal and to ask her about the elderflower champagne.

'Why, that's an old recipe of my mother-in-law's,' Millie replied. 'But you be careful, miss, not to drink too much of it, for it's a rare strong potion, for all it tastes so innocent.'

'That's probably why I'm talking so much,' Pippa laughed. And, following Millie's welcome interruption, she was quiet during their dessert, allowing Giles slowly to regain some of his equilibrium.

But something had gone out of the day. He could no longer bring himself to proceed with the afternoon he had planned, in the darkroom among his old cameras. At the end of the meal, he said, 'I-I-I usually take a w-w-walk in the afternoon. W-w-will you j-join me?'

He felt more himself once he was out in the open air again, crossing the courtyard and passing through the open gateway, overgrown by a crimson-leaved vine, with white and pink valerian clutching tenuously to crevices in the wall.

They went past Millie's herb garden and Ted's vegetable garden, with its neat, marshalled rows of plants, overseen by a scarecrow which could have been Ted himself, tall and spare with sparse straw hair sticking out from beneath a flat cap, a morose expression on its sacking face, its trousers secured round its waist with a length of string.

They entered the orchard, where the grass was long and mingled with dandelions, clover, vetch and buttercups, the air sweet with the cider smell of ripe apples, and drifted through it into the paddock with its ancient

315

oak. With each step, Giles seemed to leave further and further behind him the shadows of the past that Pippa had resurrected.

Then they were on the edge of West's wood and wandering into its calm, shady depths, between beech and hornbeam, oak and birch, over a sun-dappled carpet of last autumn's leaves, beechmast and bracken, between the tall, brown cusps of early summer's foxgloves.

'It's so quiet,' Pippa murmured. 'And the way the trees arch overhead – it's like being in a cathedral.'

'I-I-I-love t-t-trees,' he said. 'M-m-my grandfather planted most of this w-w-wood. The original wood, down by the road, is very old, but he extended it u-u-up the hillside. I-I-I've added to it over the years.'

They came out of the wood on a ridge overlooking the little River Kip, as it wound its meandering way towards the sea, then climbed up, past the dewpond, and there was Yondover beneath them, in its sheltered hollow, and beyond it, the great hump of Uffing Down, its lower slopes seeming to embrace Yondover like the arms of a mother around an infant on her lap, reassuring, protective and benign.

Back at the house again, he felt composed enough to take her into the darkroom, at which she marvelled, although for none of the reasons he had hoped. To her, everything in it was a curiosity. It was the first time she had seen an Abbeydale enlarger, safelights with candles in them or a red window in a darkroom.

However, listening to her replies to the questions he posed about modern darkroom techniques, he realized that film sensitivity had increased so much since the war that far more precision was needed at the developing stage than in his young day. As for the resin-coated, bromide printing paper which Pippa apparently favoured, with its quick washing and drying times, it sounded quite miraculous. But his own darkroom, without an electricity supply, would simply not be up to the task of processing it.

So much for his dreams of taking pictures with her and sharing with her that unique sensation of watching the image develop. But that became of minor importance once he showed her his Gandolfi in its big leather case, which he had left purposely in the darkroom. She gazed at it in awe. 'And that is the very camera you used to take your portrait of King George the Fifth? That's amazing. Can you still get film for it?'

'I d-d-don't know.' Not wanting to tempt providence too far, he had stopped short of taking this final step.

'If I bought some, would you let me take a picture on it?'

'What sort of p-p-picture do you want to t-t-take?'

'Why, a portrait of you, of course.'

He shook his head. 'No. I-I-I hate to be on the wrong side of the c-c-camera.'

'Oh, please.'

The expression on her face was so appealing, he found himself beginning to relent. 'Well, w-w-we'll see,' he said.

Chapter 22

When dusk fell and Pippa had still not arrived, Kitty started to worry about road accidents and think about calling the police and hospitals. Then the telephone rang. 'Kitty, it's me. I'm in a phone box in Kipwell. I thought I'd better let you know that I've only just left Yondover. I'll get to you as quickly as I can.'

Her initial reaction was relief. 'As long as you're all right, that's all that matters.'

'I'm fine. I've had a wonderful day. He was so different this time. I'll tell you all about it when I see you. See you soon.'

Kitty went back to the painting she was currently doing of her garden. She had sketched the outline during the day and was now filling in, from memory, some of the details. The low stone wall was scarcely visible for trailing lobelia and alyssum, massed with vivid tubs of geraniums, fuchsias and petunias. Between the cobbles grew clumps of thyme, interspersed with tufts of thrift, pinks and bellflowers, thronged with butterflies and humming bees. Her new rose arch was heavy with honeysuckle and coral pink roses and, beyond that, her flower beds were a riot of colour.

Then a reaction set in. What had kept Pippa so long at Yondover? What had she and Giles been talking about? What had Giles said to her? Had he told her about their marriage? If so, then he must have told her about Leo and Sebastian . . .

Her picture suddenly seemed to lack form and substance. The flowers became featureless blobs of colour and all sense of perspective seemed to have disappeared. It was time to stop. She packed up her paints, washed out her brushes and made herself a pot of tea. Tabitha woke up, stretched, had a last snack, then pointedly made her way upstairs to bed.

Finally, the door knocker banged. She hurried down the hall, opened the door and there was Pippa, an excited smile on her face, kissing her and apologizing for being so late. And Kitty was filled with the strange certainty that everything was all right in the world — or, if it wasn't quite right yet, it would be.

'Do you want anything to eat?' she asked, as they went into the kitchen.

'No, thanks!' Pippa exclaimed, sinking down on to a chair. 'I couldn't eat another bite. I had *the* most enormous lunch. Roast beef, Yorkshire pudding, roast potatoes, runner beans. And, before that, I had scones and fruit cake. *And* we had afternoon tea as well. But I didn't have the heart to refuse anything. Millie had gone to so much effort.'

'Then something to drink?'

'I tell you what! Millie gave me a bottle of her home-made elderflower champagne. Apparently she inherited the recipe from her mother-in-law. Kitty, you just *have* to try it. It's as I imagine nectar to taste.'

Fanny's elderflower champagne . . . A picnic on Greatling Head . . . A nightingale singing in West's wood . . . Then he carried me in among the trees, where the bracken grows high . . .

Pippa, meanwhile, had taken a bottle from her bag, fetched two glasses from the dresser and was pouring the wine. 'I'll put the rest of the bottle in the fridge to cool down. Oh! Is that a picture of your garden? Doesn't it look great! I wish I could paint as well as that.'

Viewed from a distance, the painting looked better. Maybe it would turn out all right after all.

Pippa took a sip. 'Do you see what I mean about nectar?'

Kitty did not need to taste it to know. 'Yes, it's like dewdrops.'

'You're right!' Pippa exclaimed. 'That's exactly what it's like. Now, I must tell you about today. It's been absolutely amazing! I still can't get over it! He was just so different from last time! He was still shy and had the stutter, of course, but he was so friendly.

'We walked through the grounds. I do hope you'll come there with me one day. I know you'd love it. They've done quite a bit of work on the garden since I was last there, so it didn't appear quite so derelict. And he has the most beautiful woods, so well cared for, so peaceful . . .

'Then I saw his darkroom. *That* was incredible! The water has to be pumped from the well. And there's no electricity. But everything was there. It's all workable. And he showed me the camera he used to take his portrait of King George the Fifth. I'm going to get some film, and next time I go he says he'll let me take some pictures with it. Oh, and I showed him *my* latest pictures – I've been working really hard since I saw you last – and he was really nice about them. Do you know, I think I value his opinion more than anyone else's. Isn't that strange? Though I suppose it isn't really . . .'

'So you've been talking about photography all day?'

'Most of the time.'

'Did you tell – er, Gawaine Devere – that you were coming to see me?' The question was out before she could stop it. But it had to be asked.

'Yes, I did actually. Why?'

Hastily, Kitty said, 'Oh, I just wondered. I thought he might be worried about you having to drive all the way back to London.'

'I don't think such an idea would occur to him. His is quite an unreal existence. I don't believe he's aware of the world beyond Yondover.'

Kitty felt the tension starting to go out of her. He, too, had had the opportunity to tell Pippa that they were once married and, for whatever reason, he, too, had decided not to. From now on, it would be as difficult for Giles as it would be for her to go back on the impression he had given.

In fact, in many ways, she and Giles were not all that dissimilar – they had both put their past lives behind them and created their own little worlds.

'But I didn't tell Mum and Dad that I was coming to see you,' Pippa went on. 'Or that I was seeing Gawaine Devere. I just said I was spending the weekend with a friend.' She studied the little bubbles in her glass. Then she lifted her head. 'Please, Kitty, will you tell me what happened between you and Dad? Why did he cut you out of his life?'

The question was inevitable. The surprising thing was that it had taken Pippa so long to ask it.

Suddenly, Kitty seemed to hear herself asking Marion McDonnell, all those years ago, 'Please, would you mind telling me – what went wrong in your marriage? Why did you leave West?' And Marion McDonnell murmuring, 'Yes, perhaps you, of all people, should know the whole story . . .'

Now she was the same age as Marion McDonnell must have been and Pippa was a grown woman, capable of forming her own judgements, older than she had been when she had become engaged to Giles – the same age, in fact, as she had been when she had gone to Austria with Leo . . .

320

Pippa, too, was entitled to know the whole story. Well, not the whole story, but as much of it as concerned her.

'It's difficult to know quite where to start,' she said hesitantly. 'But I want you to realize, before I say anything more, that I loved your father and tried always to do what was best for him.'

She paused and was silent for a few moments, collecting her thoughts, then she went on, 'I don't know if you are aware of it, but your father was born in Austria.'

'In Austria? No, I had no idea . . . So is Dad Austrian by nationality?'

'No, he was entitled to dual nationality.'

'But his father – your husband – was Austrian?'

She did not want to lie, but neither did she want to tell the entire truth.

'Yes,' she said hesitantly, 'Leo was Austrian.'

'So was that why the *Enchanted* books . . . ?'

'The *Enchanted* books started life as bedtime stories for your father, when he was a little boy. In fact, Roman was based on him. That was one of the reasons I wrote under a pseudonym. I didn't want him to be laughed at in the way that Christopher Robin suffered when A. A. Milne wrote about him. Not that I was expecting the *Enchanted* books to become as famous as *Winnie the Pooh*, I hasten to add.'

Pippa opened her mouth to ask another question, then closed it again, and Kitty was glad she did, for she needed to tell this story in her own way and at her own pace.

'We lived in a remote village,' she went on, 'so we were virtually unaware of what was going on in the outside world. We had no idea that war was imminent, until Adam suddenly turned up. That was in the summer of 1939. Your father was six. Adam wanted us to come back to England immediately, but that was impossible . . .

'Austria had become part of Germany by then and the Nazis had introduced strict regulations. In order to leave the country, Austrian citizens had to obtain special exit permits, which Leo did not have. I had every confidence in Adam. I knew your father would be in safe hands with him. Rightly or wrongly, I chose to stay with Leo. So, Adam brought your father back to England and we intended to follow as soon as we could. But, within days, Germany had invaded Poland and the war had started. We were caught behind enemy lines. The winter that followed was severe

321

and we could not get out of the village. Then the thaw came. Leo was out skiing when he was caught in an avalanche and killed.'

She hurried on, before Pippa could interrupt. 'I managed to escape to Switzerland, but having reached there, I could get no further. Travel was restricted to high-up diplomatic and military personnel. As a civilian I had absolutely no priority. I was stuck there for the duration of the war. Then, in May 1945, when Germany capitulated, I was finally able to return to England. I went straight to Puddles. I remember how tranquil it seemed after the ruined cities and battlefields I had passed through on my journey, a sleepy little English village apparently quite untouched by the war, and how relieved I was.

'Eve was the only person in when I arrived at Hill House. She took me up to the guest room, sitting on the bed, chattering nervously, while I tidied myself after my journey. Then we heard the front door open and the sound of boys' voices. She told me to follow her in a few moments. It was six years since I had last seen your father. As you can imagine, I was very excited and very nervous . . .

'I went downstairs and into the sitting room. Your father was standing by the French windows. He was twelve by then and taller than me. Eve said, "Sebastian, your mummy's here."

'He stared at me from eyes which bore no glint of recognition, then said, in a voice which froze the blood within me, "I don't have a mother." '

'Oh, what an *awful* thing to happen!' Pippa exclaimed.

'But understandable. From six to twelve was half a lifetime for him.'

'Yes, but surely, once he recovered from the shock . . . ? I mean, lots of other families were separated during the war. When I was at Puddles, Adam told me that something like one and a half million children were evacuated. Then there must have been others whose parents were in the services, for instance?'

'You're quite right. And I wasn't the only parent, by any means, to be treated by my child as a stranger on my return. Nor am I the only one not to have succeeded in healing the rift. I have since met several others who have suffered the same experience.'

'Have you ever tried to explain to Dad what happened to you?'

'Of course. But it was very difficult. At the time, he was too young to understand. And later . . . well, then he didn't want to listen. He had closed his mind to me. And the simple truth is that I should not have stayed in Austria in the first place. I should have come back to England with him and Adam. I was given a choice – and I did not choose Sebastian. Your father knows this and that is why he – quite justifiably – hates me.'

'So what did you do after that?'

'Well, I had no money and, naturally, I couldn't expect Adam and Eve to look after me as well as your father.' There was no need to mention Eve's jealousy and the way she had continued to poison Sebastian's mind against her. 'Quite apart from the financial aspects, Eve had her hands more than full with the two boys – and Adam's father was still alive then, dear old Professor Berkeley. It seemed best for me to go to London, where I stood most chance of getting a job. I wanted to take your father with me, but Eve insisted that it wasn't fair to uproot him again – certainly not until I was settled, with a home of my own.

'Getting a job in post-war London wasn't easy – nor was finding somewhere to live, for that matter. My first job was as a waitress, which paid enough for me to rent a basement flat in Bayswater. It was damp and dingy. The house next door had been hit by a doodlebug, its end wall blasted away, so that its rooms were laid bare to the public gaze and its roof open to the elements. However, it was better than nothing and the rent was cheap.

'After a short while, I managed to get a clerical job in the head office of an engineering company. There was a grammar school near where I lived and I decided that it would be possible for me to work and be home in time to look after your father when he came out of school. Adam and Eve brought him and Elliott up to see me, but your father didn't like Bayswater and didn't want to change schools either. I can't blame him. In his position I think I, too, would have preferred Puddles. So he stayed at Hill House and I remained in London.

'Then, in 1950, a sort of miracle occurred. It was my fortieth birthday and I was walking through Russell Square, deep in my thoughts, taking stock of my life – as one does on such occasions . . .'

She stopped, remembering.

Five years had passed since she had come to London. The five longest, most utterly miserable years of her life. Five years of living in that dreadful basement flat in Bayswater. Five years of doing that tedious job at the engineering firm.

Sebastian was in the sixth form. Next year, he would be taking his matric, leaving school and going out fully fledged into the world. His attitude towards her had remained as coldly indifferent as at their first meeting and she no longer tried to fool herself that it would ever change.

Her parents were both dead. She had learned from an aunt that they had moved to Kent, where they had been killed during the Battle of Britain. Right to the end, her father had remained unrepentant, leaving her nothing in his will. All his estate had gone to a Church charity.

She was forty. Apart from Sebastian, she had no family. She had no real home and no money. Money, that was the root of her current problem. She needed to earn more, not just to get herself out of Bayswater but so that she could take over at least the financial responsibility for Sebastian, for although Adam had never mentioned it, she was greatly aware of her indebtedness to him.

At that instant, in her abstraction, she had collided with a man walking towards her. She had apologized. And he had exclaimed, 'Good God! Kitty!' It had been Piers . . .

'While I was in Switzerland,' she explained to Pippa, 'I had become friendly with a man at the British Embassy in Bern called Piers Pilgrim. Then, one day, when I tried to contact him, I was told he was no longer working there. I assumed he had been posted elsewhere, as happened all the time.

'Then I bumped into him – literally – in Russell Square! We went to the bar of a nearby hotel and caught up with each other's lives. It turned out that he had left Bern so suddenly because his wife had been killed in a bombing raid. After a period of compassionate leave, he had left the Foreign Office and gone to work in the family firm, a publishing company founded by his great-grandfather.

'Well, the result of that chance meeting was that he offered me a job which, needless to say, I accepted. In those days, Pilgrim Publishing was a small firm, occupying one floor of a house in Bedford Place. Piers's father was still in charge when I joined. He was one of the old school, who looked after his employees and his authors as though they were part of the family.

'I began as a typist, but as soon as the opportunity arose, I was allowed to try my hand at proof-reading, then at copy-editing. Having always been an avid reader, it seemed quite incredible to be paid to do the thing I enjoyed most.'

'Was that when you started writing the *Enchanted* books?' Pippa interjected.

'No, they came later.'

Reading manuscripts and dealing with authors had, in fact, inspired her with the idea that perhaps she, too, could write a book. Yet virtually as soon as she had commenced writing, she had known she would never finish it. She had needed nobody to tell her it was not right, that something was badly lacking in it. She had known exactly what that was. So long as she was describing things and places and action, she wrote well, but the moment she tried to describe people's inner feelings – her mind froze. It was like baring her own soul naked to the world. She could not do it. It was simply too personal, too near the knuckle. It hurt too much.

'. . . Anyway, to cut a long story short, Piers asked me to marry him. We had a very quiet wedding in a register office. For one reason or another, none of the people we would have most liked to attend could be there. Your father and Elliott were doing their National Service, and couldn't obtain leave. Eve was ill, so Adam had to stay and look after her. Piers's father was also ill – in fact, he died a couple of months later. Piers had already taken over the running of the company by then. As for Piers's children, Margaret was just about to have a baby and I can't remember where Jeremy was . . .'

Pippa pulled a sympathetic face. 'It sounds a bit of a disaster.'

'These things happen.'

There was no need for Pippa to know about the hostility which she and Piers had encountered from their respective children: no need for her to know that Sebastian had refused, point-blank, to attend the wedding; nor that Margaret and Jeremy had done everything in their power to try to stop Piers from marrying her, accusing her of being a scheming fortune hunter, only after his money.

How that had hurt, to the extent that she had told Piers she had changed her mind and wanted to call off the wedding. But he had seen through her excuses and married her in defiance of his children. 'There are certain occasions in life when one is entitled to be selfish,' he had said. 'And this is one of them.'

'. . . But Piers and I were very happy for as long as it lasted. I stopped working after our marriage. Piers had a lovely house in Hampstead and we did a lot of entertaining. We also went to the theatre a lot and to concerts. And, every summer, we took long holidays, in the South of France or Italy.'

Yes, that brief holiday in life – so utterly different from her experiences with Giles at Porter's Place . . .

'What I did not realize at the time was that the company was in dire financial straits. I think it had never recovered from the war, when publishing had suffered like other non-essential trades. Piers, unfortunately, was not a good businessman. He had no real commercial sense. He was a gentleman publisher. He published books he liked and they were not necessarily the kind of books that were popular and sold well.

'I assume that he wanted to protect me, which was why he didn't tell me. Or perhaps he couldn't bear to acknowledge the truth even to himself. Then, suddenly, things came to a head. A printer who was owed a lot of money forced the company into receivership. The bank withdrew its support and, in order to meet the demands of all the creditors, Piers was faced with having to sell everything – including the house. Being bankrupted was simply too much for him. He had a massive heart attack . . .'

The anguish of Piers's death came back to revisit her. His grey, drawn face on the pillows, his last, gasping, strangled words: 'This was not what I intended, Kitty. I wanted to make up for everything all those other bastards did to you . . .'

'How terrible,' Pippa murmured. 'How long had you been married?'

'Four years. That happened in 1956.'

Margaret and Jeremy had blamed her. In an acrimonious scene after Piers's funeral, they had accused her of having forced their father to lead an extravagant lifestyle beyond his means and of having done them out of their rightful inheritance.

After Piers, there had been no more men in her life. Occasionally, some well-meaning soul had tried to match-make and she had found herself seated next to an available bachelor at a dinner party. But she had learned that it was as easy, if not easier, to repulse men's attentions as it was to attract them.

Of course, she would have liked to grow old knowing the affectionate companionship shared by couples like Adam and Eve. Deep down, that was why she had married Piers. She had never been in love with him, not in the way she had been in love with Leo. But she had cared for him deeply – as he had for her. Having said that though, Leo remained the only man with whom she would really have wanted to grow old . . .

'So what did you do then?' Pippa asked.

'After that I came to Arundel. Have you ever heard of Eleanor Bagshaw? No? I have all her books in the other room. You should take a look at them some time. She was a remarkable woman, a botanist, who travelled the world collecting plants. As well as being published by Pilgrim, she was a great personal friend of Piers and his father.

'Well, she took pity on me and asked if I would like to come and work for her, as her secretary and companion. She lived in a big house on the outskirts of Arundel. Rose Cottage belonged to her and she let me live here, rent-free. When she died, I had saved up just enough money to be able to put down a deposit on it – so I was able to remain.

'When I came to work for her she was already very old – well into her eighties – and writing her autobiography, which I completed from her notes after her death. The fact that I had been able to do that made me think again of trying to write a book of my own.

'Eleanor's autobiography was published by Astra, who had acquired Pilgrim's backlist. Astra is part of a huge, international media company now. Staff come and go all the time, so you are never sure who you are dealing with. But in those days, it was much smaller and much more personal, very like Pilgrim had been in fact. I talked to an editor I knew there about doing some children's stories and showed him some sketches I had done while I was in Austria. He was very enthusiastic.

'So, basically, that is how the *Enchanted* books came into being. I never set out to be a writer or an artist. Like most other things in my life, it happened by chance. It's strange how things work out, isn't it?'

She drained her glass and stood up. 'And now, Pippa dear, I really am very tired. I must go to bed.'

Sleep, however, came easily to neither of them. Pippa lay awake, going over in her mind the incredible story Kitty had told her. Before she eventually drifted off, she had reached two conclusions. The first was that if Kitty's first husband was Austrian, there could be no relationship between him and Gawaine Devere.

And the other was that it would not be possible to work a miracle and change her father's heart overnight. A plan of campaign was needed, something rather devious, possibly with the collaboration of Adam and

327

Eve. But, in order to do that, she would need to go to Puddles again, for this was not a matter to be discussed over the phone . . .

For her part, Kitty tried to read for a while, but whether it was due to Fanny's – no, Millie's – elderflower champagne or because she was simply over-excited, the words on the page kept swimming before her eyes. Yet when she turned off the light, although she felt absolutely exhausted and emotionally drained, her brain refused to switch off.

She had still told Pippa only half the story, with the result that Pippa now believed Leo had been her husband and Sebastian his son. And by doing that, she was perpetuating the lie.

Why should it all be so complicated? Could there not be an end to the lies and prevarications? If only Sebastian would give her the opportunity to explain . . .

Yet that seemed unlikely now. The truth of the matter was that he did not need her. The need was entirely on her side.

The weather was so lovely the following morning that they had breakfast in the garden. While Kitty made tea, toast and boiled eggs, Pippa put up deckchairs and laid a small table.

Tabitha lay stretched out on the lawn, basking in the sun.

'See how her coat has bleached in the sun,' Kitty said, bringing out a laden tray. 'My hair used to do the same when I was young.'

'I'm glad I don't have to wear a fur coat in the summer,' Pippa said, pushing up the sleeves of her T-shirt and rolling her shorts further up her slim thighs. 'This is a real sun-trap. And the garden looks beautiful. Which reminds me, I meant to say last night how super that picture is you're doing. You've really captured the feeling of your garden.'

'Do you think so?'

'Why? Aren't you happy with it?'

'It looks better this morning than it did yesterday evening.'

'You'd probably been spending too much time on it. You can get too close to something and then you can't see it in perspective any more.'

'Mmm, I know what you mean.'

'I find the same thing with my photographs. But if I take a break and then go back to them, I can usually see where I've gone wrong.'

'I was so busy talking about myself last night there wasn't time to ask you about your job. You are still working for the same photographer?'

'For Tim? Oh, yes! And I'm enjoying every minute of it. For the past few weeks, we've been doing a fabulous job for a whisky company. They've been producing a series of ads all featuring well-known people who drink their brand – pop musicians, sportsmen, businessmen, TV personalities, writers, politicians . . . It's been very hectic and pretty fraught on occasions, like when one of them has decided they can't make their appointment after all. But it's much more fun than fashion. I don't like fashion – or put it this way, I don't the people in fashion.'

It was strange, Kitty thought, how things had come round almost full circle. There was Pippa, whom she had met only because of Edith Spencer's album, doing the job Edith herself had done all those years ago.

'And how is your other project going – the building in Streatham?'

'Updike House? Well, as I told you on the phone, I think I've finished the first stage of the photography. Now Chris has a record of how the place looked in its original state, the builders have moved in. I'll be taking progress shots as they go along. Then, eventually, when the refurbishment is completed, every room will need to be photographed again.'

'What a lot of work.'

'Yes, it is, but I don't mind. Especially since I'm working with Chris.'

Pippa paused and Kitty sensed that she was expected to pick up on this name. 'Chris?' she asked.

'He's the architect in charge of the project. And, well, to be honest, he's become a bit more than that. We're going out together.'

'Oh, do tell me more about him.'

'Well, he's rather difficult to describe. He was born in England, but his father is Polish and his mother is half-Greek and half-Spanish. I haven't met them yet, because they spend the summer in the South of France. They have an apartment near St Tropez. But when they come back to London, Chris will introduce me.'

'Goodness, Polish, Greek and Spanish – what a mixture.'

'He's quite mad! When I sent him over the first pictures I'd shot of Updike House, he sent me a bunch of heart-shaped balloons. We were doing a fashion shoot at the time and all these women from the magazine . . .'

Pippa went on to describe the strawberry picnic, her first outing on Chris's motor bike, a hilarious visit to a fairground where they had spent most of the evening on the dodgems because neither of them liked heights, a punting trip up the Thames from Henley when Chris had got his pole stuck in the mud and almost fallen into the river, and various outings in his sports car.

'But I don't want to give you the wrong impression. He can be serious, too. He has really strong opinions about architecture. The plans he's drawn up for Updike House are absolutely brilliant, keeping all the original features at the same time as allowing for modern plumbing, heating, lighting and so on.'

'He sounds very interesting. I'd like to meet him.'

'Oh, he's heard all about you and wants to meet you, too.'

'You must bring him with you next time you come.'

'Thank you, I'd like to. I've got to take him home some time. I don't quite know how Dad is going to react to him. You see, apart from being quite, quite mad, Chris is married – well, he's getting a divorce – and Dad has very old-fashioned, moralistic views about sex and marriage. It's strange, considering how close he and Elliott are. So I keep putting off the evil moment . . .'

Fleetingly, Kitty thought of the Reverend Thurston Fellowes and Samuel Lambourne.

Pippa picked a daisy and started stripping off the petals. 'I do like daisies. They remind me of childhood – of making daisy chains and *Alice in Wonderland*.'

'Colonel Wakehurst keeps telling me I should get rid of them but I simply can't bring myself to.'

'Oh, do leave them! I think it would be lovely to have a whole lawn of daisies. Now, wait! He loves me. He loves me not.' She was left with one satisfying petal. 'He loves me!'

How could he fail to? Kitty wondered, looking at the animation in Pippa's face and the warm light sparkling in those eyes which were, oh, so like her own. And all I pray, she thought, is that he will make her happy . . .

CHAPTER 23

By the time Pippa arrived home that evening, she had made up her mind not to say anything at all to her parents about either Gawaine Devere or her grandmother. Her resolution went by the board, however, when she entered the lounge and her father confronted her with, 'And where exactly have you been, Philippa? I know you haven't been working, because we've had Chris on the phone. And I know you haven't been staying with any of your friends, because your mother has rung them all.'

Pippa's immediate and natural thought was that an emergency must have arisen. 'Why, what's happened?'

'Your boss was trying to get hold of you.'

'My boss? Oh, you mean Tim. Why? What did he want?'

'Something about your job tomorrow. Your mother has the details.'

'I'd better give him a bell.'

'You're not doing anything until you've told me where you have been.'

It would have to be tonight of all nights that her father decided to play the heavy-handed parent, wouldn't it? 'I've been staying with a friend.'

'What friend?'

Pippa shrugged with attempted nonchalance. 'I don't see that it's your business, Dad, how I spend my weekends. I'm not a child any more.'

'So long as you continue to live in my house, how you conduct your life remains my business. I asked you a straightforward question and I expect an honest answer.'

Pippa clenched her teeth and said nothing.

'In that case, I must assume the worst. Presumably, you have been spending the weekend with a man – a man, moreover, who is not your present boyfriend. Am I right?'

Briefly, it occurred to her to lie. But why the hell should she? 'Actually,'

331

she said, trying to keep her voice calm, 'I've been to see Gawaine Devere.'

'Gawaine Devere? That lunatic? Didn't I tell you to stay away from him?'

'I'm sorry, Dad, but I really don't think it's up to you to tell me who I see or don't see.'

'And if you had been murdered?'

'There was no likelihood of that.'

'How did you know? You told me yourself that he has been known to take pot shots at intruders.'

'Because I had already visited him once.'

'You had already done what?'

'I went in the spring and he asked me to come back again, so I did.'

'And may I ask why you went to see him?'

'Because I wanted to find out if we were related.'

'And what was the outcome?' Sebastian imparted a scathing emphasis to his question, which was not wasted on Pippa.

'It would appear that we aren't.'

'So having discovered that he is not a cousin or uncle five times removed, you nevertheless spent a night at his house?'

Pippa retreated again into silence.

'Philippa, I remember the pictures in that photograph album. Naked women in extraordinary poses among trees and waterlilies. I'm not a fool, I wasn't born yesterday. I understand the way men's minds work and since you're a very attractive girl . . .'

She was not easily roused to anger, but when she was pushed too far her temper flared out. 'How dare you! Those pictures were art, not pornography! It's *you* who have the perverted mind, not him.'

'Don't you dare talk to me like that!'

They confronted each other across the room. Sebastian's face was pale with rage, while Pippa's cheeks were burning in her fury.

All her good intentions flew to the wall. To hell with being wary of resurrecting old ghosts. To hell with any pledges of secrecy. The impulse to shock and to hurt was stronger than any other consideration. He had asked for the truth and he could bloody well have it, slap-bang on a plate, with no fancy trimmings. To reveal where she had been might not do Kitty any good, but it couldn't possibly make things any worse.

'Right, well, I will tell you where I spent last night,' she said, enunciating each word with icy deliberation. 'I was with your mother.'

If she had not been so angry, she might almost have found his expression comic. Then he exploded, 'What the fucking hell were you doing at my mother's?'

'Just because you refuse to have anything to do with her, doesn't mean that I shouldn't. I like her. I think she's one of the nicest people I have ever met.'

'And exactly how did you come to make her acquaintance?'

Pippa cast all vestiges of caution to the wind. 'Eve told me about her when I was down at Puddles in the winter.'

'Eve? What the fuck—'

At that moment, Valerie entered the room. 'What on earth is going on in here?'

Sebastian glared at her, then with one last irate glance in Pippa's direction stormed out of the room, slamming the door behind him.

'Pippa, what's happened?' her mother demanded.

But Pippa was too upset to say anything beyond muttering, 'Ask Dad.' Then she, too, rushed out of the door.

Upstairs, in her bedroom, she locked the door, flung herself on the bed and burst into tears.

Valerie had no idea what words had passed between her husband and her daughter, although it was not difficult to guess the reason behind the argument, for she had sensed Sebastian working up towards a fight ever since the first phone call had come for Pippa. She had been in the kitchen, putting the dinner plates in the dishwasher, and suddenly heard raised voices, at which point she had hurried to intervene.

Sebastian and Pippa were more similar in temperament than either of them realized. When they met head on, each of them believing themselves to have right on their side – which fortunately did not occur very often – they were equally intractable.

After over twenty-five years of marriage, she knew her husband well enough to allow him time by himself to calm down a little before she began the process of mediation. Then, armed with a propitiatory tumbler of whisky, she went to his study, taking care to knock before she entered.

Sebastian was still seething under the surface, she could see that, despite the apparent calmness of his expression as he looked up from the papers he was shuffling about on his desk. Wordlessly, she put the whisky on a coaster and laid an arm lightly round his shoulder.

Eventually, he asked, 'Did you hear where she has been?'

She shook her head.

'She's been to see that screwball photographer, Gawaine Devere – and she's been staying with my mother.'

Valerie let out a long, slow breath. No wonder he had flown off the handle. Yet, simultaneously, she could not help feeling a sense of relief. Ever since she had met Sebastian, his feud with his mother had perturbed her. She understood why he felt hurt by his mother's treatment of him, but once he was older, surely he could find it in him to forgive and forget?

When Pippa was born, she had suggested that this might be the occasion to settle their differences. Then, when the *Enchanted* books were published and she had discovered from Adam and Eve that his mother was the author, what better opportunity could have arisen to bury the hatchet? Pippa had loved those books. Her childish admiration would have overcome any awkwardness in the reunion between mother and son. But Sebastian had steadfastly refused. Now, however, Pippa had broken the deadlock . . .

'How did she find out?' Valerie asked.

'Apparently Eve told her.'

'Eve?'

Sebastian drew himself together. 'Listen, Valerie, what's done is done and can't be undone. I'll talk to Philippa when I'm feeling calmer. But in case you are harbouring any notion of a fond reconciliation between me and my mother, forget it.'

Rarely had Sebastian been so glad to hear the distinctively loud exhaust note of Elliott's Jaguar in the mews as the following morning. It was remarkably early for Elliott, not yet ten o'clock. Usually he didn't turn up until at least eleven and more often than not it was noon before he put in an appearance. According to him, none of their clients did any business before lunch, to which Sebastian's standard retort was that since Elliott was seldom there before lunch, he wouldn't know.

Today, however, he was in no mood for arguing with Elliott. Although in business matters he was prepared to stand his ground and drive a fair bargain, he was not by nature a confrontational person. Emotional scenes upset him and he was still badly shaken from his contretemps with Philippa.

Elliott came into the office looking unusually sartorial, in a dark pin-striped suit, black tie and black shoes. 'It's poor old Archie's funeral today,' he explained.

'Of course. I'd forgotten.' Archibald, twelfth Earl of Tebworth, had been a friend of the Professor and Elliott was attending the funeral on behalf of the Berkeley family.

Elliott poured himself a cup of coffee. 'Sad when an old family comes to the end of the line . . .' Then he studied Sebastian quizzically. 'Something up? You don't look your usual self.'

'Oh, it's nothing. I'll get over it.'

'Come on, spit it out. I've got a few minutes in hand. It should only take me a couple of hours to get up to Tebworth and the funeral isn't until twelve.'

'Well, I may as well tell you, I suppose, since you're undoubtedly going to hear all about it anyway.'

Elliott lit a cigarette and waited expectantly.

'I don't know the exact circumstances,' Sebastian said, forcing his voice to sound even, 'but it would appear that your mother took it upon herself to tell Philippa about my mother, with the result that Philippa spent this weekend – guess where?'

If he was expecting shock, horror and sympathetic surprise, he was disappointed.

'About time too,' Elliott said. 'I've always felt that it was ridiculous to go on nursing a grudge for as long as you have.'

'I'm not nursing a grudge.'

'Oh, come off it. Of course you are. Now I fully accept that what your mother did to you when you were a kid was wrong. But you're a grown man and she's an old lady. Let bygones be bygones.'

'You don't understand, do you?'

'I understand that you've been making a mountain out of a molehill for years. OK, I admit that the circumstances were slightly more complicated, but basically your mother did the same thing as many other parents had to do during the war. She wanted you to be safe, so she sent you away to where you would be safe. And, let's face it, you could hardly have landed in a better billet.'

'Elliott . . .'

'Hear me out, please. You must admit that the parents were absolutely scrupulous about treating us equally. I can't remember a single occasion when I was given any favourable treatment over you. Quite the opposite, in fact.'

'I agree. Your parents could not have treated me better if I had been their own son and I shall always be grateful to them.'

'Then why do you persist in carrying that bloody great chip on your shoulder?'

'It's not a chip.'

Elliott shook his head. 'You remember what is written up in the temple at Delphi? *Know thyself*. Ponder on't.'

The grandfather clock in the corner of the office struck ten. 'And at this point, I am afraid,' Elliott said, 'I must be making a move, otherwise poor old Archie will go to his grave without me.'

Know thyself . . . Long after Elliott had gone his words continued to echo in Sebastian's ears.

Introspection, like retrospection, was not in his character. There was, he had always felt, something weak and essentially selfish about people who were always analysing their own motivation. He was a practical man who, if he had to sum up his philosophy in life, would probably use the words, *'Let us then, be up and doing . . . Still achieving, still pursuing . . .'*

But Elliott's accusations had come uncomfortably close to the mark. Was he nursing a grudge? Was he making a mountain out of a molehill? Did he have a bloody great chip on his shoulder?

Basically your mother did the same thing as many other parents had to do during the war. She wanted you to be safe, so she sent you away to where you would be safe.

Certainly, that had been tough but, as Elliott said, he had landed in a soft billet. No, there was more to it than that. Come on, think, sort it out in your own mind, then put the whole bloody matter behind you.

Except that he couldn't put it behind him. That was the problem. Eve and Philippa between them had made an issue of it. All the more reason, then, to have a satisfactory answer to put an end to this nonsense. And where had it started in the first place? Yes, of course. That damned photograph album.

So, back to the beginning. Back to Austria . . .

His memories of the first six years of his life in Austria were indistinct, but he had, he assumed, been happy. He had a hazy impression of a house on a mountainside and his own loft bedroom with a view up to the peak of a mountain which had looked like an old man's face. Before he went to sleep, his father had used to tell stories woven round that mountain, the central character of which had been a little boy called Roman, who had adventures with a wizard in the wood and a magic snowman.

Those were the stories which his mother had used in the *Enchanted* books. His father's stories . . . Not that he had read the books himself but he had gathered the gist of their contents from Philippa. He had not wanted the books in the house. However, they were so popular that Valerie had insisted it would be wrong if Philippa missed out on them.

He could not remember what his father looked like or even what his name had been. All he could really remember about him, apart from the stories about Roman, was his music. He had always been playing the piano – a grand piano in a room that opened out on to a courtyard. He, too, had been allowed to play that piano sometimes, as a special treat . . .

His father had been playing the piano on the day that Adam had arrived. Now that day he did remember. Every moment of it was etched on his memory as clearly as if it had been yesterday . . .

He could see the strange man, whom his mother had introduced as 'Uncle Adam', toiling up the mountainside. The two of them had sat in the garden talking in English, which he couldn't understand.

At the time, of course, he had been totally unaware of what was going on in the outside world. Only later, when he was older and understood the complex events which had led Europe down the road to the Second World War, had he been able to place the milestones in his personal life within an historical context.

All he had known then was that the serious expressions on his mother's and Uncle Adam's faces and the grim tone in their voices betokened ill.

Suddenly, Uncle Adam had stood up and burst angrily into the house. In mid-bar, his father's piano had stopped. Sebastian had sidled along the wall to eavesdrop. The conversation had switched to German, so he could understand. 'Adam is right,' his father had been saying, 'we must think of Johann Sebastian.' And his mother had agreed.

Next morning, they had all gone to a railway station. His parents had seemed in such a gay mood that he had forgotten his premonitions of the previous day. Until the moment when the train had arrived and only he and Uncle Adam had embarked, it had not occurred to him that they might not all be travelling together. Then his father had told him to behave himself in England and his mother had promised that they would soon see him again. They had both kissed him. Judas kisses. The kisses of betrayal.

To begin with, he had forgotten his forebodings and enjoyed the novelty of being on a train, rushing excitedly from window to window to watch the countryside speed by. Uncle Adam had spoken a little German, even though it bore scant resemblance to whatever bastard dialect had, until then, been his own mother tongue. Night had fallen and, when he had awoken, there had been the thrill of seeing the sea for the first time and going on a ship. But after they had landed in England, tiredness and the dull pang of homesickness had set in. Everything had seemed so grey and totally alien . . .

Eventually, they had arrived at Puddles. The house, he remembered, had appeared awesomely big and oppressive at first sight. Aunt Eve, too, had seemed intimidating to begin with, so different was she from his own mother. As for Elliott, his reception of the newcomer had been unmistakably hostile.

The Professor, Adam's father, had been the only person in the Berkeley household with whom Sebastian had felt any immediate affinity. The Professor had acquired a smattering of some dozen languages in the course of his work, including Greek, Latin, Mandarin, French and German. With the help of a dictionary, he and Sebastian had made themselves understood – they had made a game of seeing who could find the correct word or expression quickest in the other's language. It was not a game in which Elliott had joined . . .

In those early days, most of his problems were caused by Elliott, who had understandably resented the intrusion of another child into the household and was jealous of the way Sebastian had deflected attention from himself. But Elliott was by nature a gregarious creature and had found it impossible to remain aloof for long, especially once he had recognized in Sebastian's disadvantages an opportunity to lord his own superiority.

Later, Elliott had refused to admit feeling any animosity towards him, just as he denied that they had ever had any difficulty in making themselves understood. But Elliott had probably genuinely forgotten. After all, he hadn't been the one to suffer the taunting of cruel schoolboys and the callousness of equally brutal schoolmasters. No, Elliott had not been the one to be mercilessly teased because he was assumed to be a German . . .

In his mind's eye, Sebastian saw himself walking across the quad to the tuck shop, followed by some half-dozen goose-stepping boys with one arm raised in the Nazi salute and one finger across their upper lip in a pretend Hitler moustache. 'Rabbit' they had nicknamed him, after the Flanagan and Allen song, *Run rabbit, run rabbit, run, run, run*, which they parodied to 'Run Hitler, run Hitler . . .' And to make matters worse, the only sport at which he was any good was cross-country running.

The teachers had been no better. He remembered Mr Pilkington, a sour little man who had lost a leg and all compassion in the first war, snarling, 'Devere, say that sentence again after me. "We must learn to walk before we can run." ' And himself repeating, 'Ve must learn to valk bevor ve can run.' And Pilkington going, 'We, boy, we', and the other boys in the class sniggering. 'Class, be quiet!' Pilkington had growled. Then, 'Devere, come out here.' He had been handed a piece of chalk and made to write the proverb on the blackboard and say it aloud, again and again, and still he could not contort his tongue round that wretched letter 'w'.

How he had longed to conform, to be the same as everyone else, to be accepted as a member of a clique, to belong to a team. But the activities at which he was any good tended to be solitary pursuits. The only group that wanted him was the choir and, once he started senior school, that was responsible for his life being made a misery in quite another way, for choirboys were accused of dressing up like girls and smutty innuendoes were made about them being queer. He had been thankful when his voice broke and he had an excuse to leave.

The only gift he had possessed which might have aroused the admiration of his fellow pupils was a natural ability to play the piano. But once the music master – he could remember his name, too: the Reverend Hatfield – had discovered he was playing a Chopin étude without looking at the music, the cane had cracked across his knuckles. Playing by ear was an aberration, he had been informed, and after that he had lost all interest in music.

But, thanks to Adam, at least he hadn't suffered the additional handicap of having a name that was obviously Germanic, like Heinrich Rosenberg. He wondered fleetingly what had become of Heinrich Rosenberg. He was probably a millionaire now. Rosenberg, too, had arrived in England without his parents and, sensing a common ground, had tried to make friends with him. But Sebastian hadn't wanted to be best friends with a German, let alone a Jew. He wanted to be accepted – and that meant being more English than the English.

It wasn't until he had come to apply for his first passport that he had learned that Devere was not his father's but his mother's surname. Adam had explained that his mother had lost his birth certificate but, because she was English, her son had been entitled to take her nationality. In view of the wartime prejudices he was sure to encounter, Adam had deemed it sensible to drop the Johann from his name and register him on his arrival in England as Sebastian Devere.

He had been at Puddles for about a year when Aunt Eve had taken him up to his room and told him that his father was dead. He could still recall his feeling of blankness at hearing her words. She must have been expecting him to cry, but – quite apart from having learned the hard way, at school, that big boys didn't cry – he couldn't produce any tears. By then, his father and mother had become shadowy figures. He had possessed no photographs to remind him of what they looked like; already Uncle Adam and Aunt Eve had begun to seem like his own parents, Elliott his brother, Professor Berkeley his grandfather.

Indeed, once Aunt Eve's message had sunk in, he had felt almost a sense of relief: the protracted agony of uncertainty was over. In his mind, separation and death became synonymous and, with a child's logic, he decided that both his parents were dead and he would never see them again.

After that, he had put his Austrian past behind him and adapted more easily to his new way of life. Lacking Elliott's lively personality and, above all, his prowess at sports, he had never achieved his popularity, but he had possessed a degree of physical strength and developed a moral stoicism which had deterred the other boys from bullying him.

Upon going up to senior school, he had passed the cruel initiation ceremonies – acts which were, with hindsight, worthy of the Gestapo. He had run the gauntlet of some thirty boys lined up on either side of the corridor after the mandatory cold shower, all chanting 'Run, rabbit, run,' and each beating him with their folded wet towels as his naked body sped between their ranks. When a dozen of them had swooped on him, debagged him and painted his genitals with gentian violet, he had not cried, but struggled and kicked so strenuously that he had cracked the collar-bone of one of his persecutors. After that, they had turned their attentions to more vulnerable targets and he had felt himself rise in Elliott's estimation.

Or had he? Suddenly he remembered the Wimshurst machine. It had been a kind of dynamo that generated electricity and Elliott had hit upon the idea of wiring it to the inside door of the physics lab and to the floor outside the door, which was duly soaked in water. When the science master had stepped on to the patch of water and taken hold of the door handle, he had received an electric shock. The class had dissolved into fits of laughter – all except Sebastian, the unwitting scapegoat, who had still been furiously turning the handle of the Wimshurst machine as 'sir' burst apoplectically through the door.

Then there was the time in the scouts, when they had made a rope bridge and slung it between two trees across a stagnant river. Sebastian had been the last to cross. Elliott had undone the rope on the far side and he had fallen into the water. It had not been deep: he had been in no danger of drowning. But he had emerged, coughing, spluttering and covered in duckweed, to the undisguised glee of his fellow scouts. He had been the only one not to be awarded a bridge-building badge.

But it was not his schooldays and his relationship with Elliott that he was exploring – it was his relationship with his mother . . .

During the course of the war, his mother had written to him, but her letters had been so meaningless – with no point of commonality – that they could well have come from another world. Aunt Eve had made him reply, a task he had come to dread, so arduous and pointless had it seemed.

Then, without any warning, his mother had turned up in Puddles. He and Elliott had returned from school and Eve had hurried down the stairs to meet them, looking unusually tense and nervous. She had sent Elliott away on some pretext, put her arm round him and led him into the sitting room. 'There's a surprise for you,' she had said, 'your mummy's here.'

She had gone away and returned with another woman, whom he had not recognized. If Eve had not told him who she was, he would not have known. So far as he was concerned, she was a stranger.

She had stayed only a few days, then gone to London. He had been relieved to see her go and hoped never to see her again.

Then Adam and Eve had taken him and Elliott to visit her in Bayswater. He could still visualize the slum in which she had been living. Elliott had been fascinated by the novelty of their surroundings, but he had squirmed in his chair, refusing to eat anything, wondering all the time when they would be going home.

She had asked if he would like to stay on with her, but the last thing he had wanted to do was live in such squalor with this woman who called herself his mother. Neither, much though he had disliked his public school, had he wanted to start all over again at a Bayswater grammar school, rubbing shoulders with the snotty-nosed, ragged-clothed urchins who were playing outside amid the rubble and bomb craters.

He shuddered still to think what would have become of him had he done so. But that half-hearted offer had been worth little more than the breath it had taken her to utter the words.

Then she had married Piers Pilgrim. The date of the wedding must have been deliberately chosen to ensure that he could not attend, even had he wanted to. He had just started his National Service. After a week at an RAF induction camp in Lancashire, he had been sent to a training centre on the top of Cannock Chase – a former POW camp where the trainee airmen were given as little freedom as the previous inmates. Nobody was allowed a forty-eight hour pass until they had completed their first four weeks of square-bashing. In any case, an airman's service pay of 28/6d a week just about kept you in beer and cigarettes (not that he had smoked or drunk in those days), got you through the NAAFI or saw you to Birmingham and back.

His National Service had been the most tediously boring period in his entire life. Both he and Elliott had been offered Short Service Commissions, which they refused, since that would have entailed remaining in the RAF for three years instead of two as non-commissioned airmen. From Cannock Chase, he had been posted to an even more desolate, godforsaken spot in the north of Scotland, to work in Accounts. His only consolation for those two wasted years was that he learned book-keeping, which had proved extremely useful after he and Elliott had set up in business.

In contrast to himself, Elliott – lucky as always – had been transferred to Adastral House in London, where he had worked in public relations and worn civvies most of the time.

Their National Service over and done with, they had gone up to Oxford and then, of course, he had met Valerie. His mother had become an increasingly distant figure again, until, suddenly, she had published *The*

Enchanted Mountain. She had sent him a copy, together with a note explaining that she had written under a pseudonym so that he should not be exposed to any ridicule. He had read the book and glanced at the illustrations, then sent it back to her, intending to insult her as she had insulted him.

It was not that he was afraid of being laughed at. By the time the *Enchanted* books were published, he had grown a thick enough hide to be inured to any amount of teasing and taunting. No, what had hurt him about them was the way in which his mother had stolen his childhood memories, memories which he had treasured as being intensely precious and deeply personal. In fact, she had stolen his childhood not once, but twice over: first, when she had packed him off to England; and the second time, when she had taken experiences which he had believed to be unique to him and published them for all the world to read.

But all that had happened thirty years ago. Those scars had long since healed. And, looking at things from a purely mercenary angle, thank heavens, with hindsight, that she had written those books, otherwise – in view of the fact that Pilgrim had died leaving her penniless – she would probably have been after him for money by now. Not that she could have made a fortune from them – children's authors in those days didn't earn the kind of royalties blockbuster writers were paid now – but presumably they served to supplement her pension and keep her independent.

No, the simple fact of the matter was that his mother had been a stranger when she came to Puddles at the end of the war and she had remained a stranger ever since. He felt no emotion towards her whatsoever. Not anger. Not resentment. And certainly nothing as extreme as hatred. Indifference, he supposed, would be the best word to sum up his feelings in her respect.

It was ridiculous, therefore, for Elliott to accuse him of nursing a grudge against her – as ridiculous as if he were to be accused of bearing malice towards Elliott himself because of those childhood humiliations.

Adam and Eve had had the responsibility and hard work, not to mention the worry and expense, of bringing him up. They were his parents. His loyalty was to them – not to that woman who called herself his mother.

What, then, had provoked his most uncharacteristically vehement outburst yesterday evening?

Then, in a flash, it came to him. It was not the fact that Philippa had been consorting with his mother that had angered him. What had actually upset him was that Eve had meddled in a matter which did not concern her and that Philippa had gone behind his back.

By the time Elliott returned, Sebastian was feeling almost his normal self. The best way to deal with Eve and Philippa, he had decided, was to ignore what they had done. He could make allowances for Eve. She was an old lady, probably growing forgetful and not realizing what she was saying.

As for Philippa, well, she had emerged unscathed from two meetings with Gawaine Devere, so presumably she would not come to any harm if she visited him again. So far as his mother was concerned, to forbid Philippa to see her would be to make even more of an issue of the matter than he had already, distorting it out of all proportion. Philippa, although she was so young, was not lacking in common sense. He hoped she would soon see through his mother's façade and recognize her for what she really was.

Yes, that was undoubtedly the most sensible way to handle the whole affair. Least said was always soonest mended . . .

His mood was further improved by the fact that, after the usual slow start to the day, business turned out to be brisk. He even sold a Biedermeyer cabinet, bought in a moment of aberration, for a far higher sum than he had ever dared hope.

Elliott returned from Tebworth in ebullient mood. 'What a wake! We discovered some hundred-year-old port in poor old Archie's cellars. Though, mind you, like poor old Archie himself, it was rather past its prime. Nevertheless, it served to give him a good send-off. Dear old boy – I was always very fond of him. He was my godfather. Did you know that? I'd forgotten it myself, I must confess, but I was reminded in a rather pleasant fashion. He left me a picture that apparently caught my fancy when I was a kid. It's a Turner . . .'

'Congratulations,' Sebastian said drily.

Elliott grinned. 'Don't overdo the enthusiasm.'

'You obviously started coffin-polishing at an early age.'

'Now that was quite uncalled for.'

'Sorry. But you do sometimes seem to have all the luck.'

'Well, you know what they say. It's not *what* you know but *who* you know . . .'

And the family into which you were fortunate enough to be born, Sebastian thought grimly, returning to his reflections of earlier in the day. Being brought up by the Berkeleys was not the same as being a Berkeley.

'He's one of nature's gentlemen,' a mutual friend had once said of Elliott. But nature had little to do with it. Elliott possessed the innate self-confidence of those born into the English upper middle class, which even a public school education could not fully impart. Elliott did not give a damn for other people's opinions of himself or for keeping up appearances. He had never craved security and respectability. It had never occurred to him that he might not dress as the mood took him, always do exactly what he pleased or say whatever came into his head.

Elliott had been born with a silver spoon in his mouth, whereas Sebastian had been born with no advantages whatsoever. He had always had to work at everything – even at being liked . . .

CHAPTER 24

The clouds were so low that Uffing Down could not be seen from Yond-over. The rain was blowing in diagonal sheets, swept across the Downs in great gusts by the wind. 'Best get darn there early. Doan't want 'er waitin' about. Though I doubt as 'er will be comin' in this 'ere weather,' Ted muttered gloomily, as he set off, his cap pulled down low over his forehead and his collar up around his ears.

Giles tried to prepare himself, as he stood at the window watching for Ted's return. She would not come. Ted would return alone, his cheerless prognostications confirmed. And who could blame her if she decided to abandon her visit? In her letter, she had said that she was working again at Updike House, which was why she could only come on a Sunday. And, on this occasion, because she was so busy, she would not be able to go on to see her grandmother afterwards. But she had some film for his camera and was looking forward so much to taking some pictures with it.

His eyes scanned the horizon, but no living soul was to be seen. Nothing moved, except a lone seagull against the scudding clouds and a stunted tree bending in the wind. It was the sort of day on which neither man nor beast would venture forth without very good reason.

Behind him, the damp wood spat and spluttered on the fire Millie had lit in the inglenook fireplace in anticipation of Pippa's arrival. The wind howled down the chimney, sending a cloud of smoke into the room. The rain beat remorselessly against the window. Ted's vicious onslaught on the garden, although it might pay dividends in years to come, had the effect, on this dismal late September morning, of making the prospect all the more bleak and uninviting.

The climbing roses still bore a few sodden blossoms. Old man's beard trailed hoar over crumbling walls. To purple-leaved brambles clung the

346

last browning blackberries. The trees in West's wood were gold and amber, scarlet and crimson, when he had walked there earlier that morning, their fallen leaves forming a rich, mulchy carpet of russet and copper.

Winter was being held in abeyance, yet there was a limit to how long its arrival would be delayed. The swallows had already departed on their long journey south. Soon, wind would strip the trees. Frost's icy fingers would yellow the moss in the lawn, blacken the nettles and shrivel the bracken. Snow might come to blanket the earth in a stultifying shroud.

As in nature, so it was in the seasons of a man's life. This year had seen his eightieth birthday. The December of his life was already upon him . . .

Then they hove into sight. Not one but two figures: not just Ted but Pippa as well! And, suddenly, the day no longer appeared desolate and even the fire seemed invigorated, giving out a new heat.

He strode out of the room and into the kitchen. 'They're just coming over the hill!' he told Millie.

'Well, I never did.' She put the kettle on the range. 'Now I hope you've not let that fire go out in the sitting room, Mr Giles.'

'No, Millie, the wood was a bit damp, but now it's burning well.'

He went to the back door and there was Pippa coming across the courtyard, her hair plastered flat against her head, her face streaming with water, her anorak and jeans soaking wet. Fleetingly, he was transported back in time to another downpour and another girl, standing on the edge of West's wood. He heard his voice saying, 'You are so spontaneous – so natural. You have such a wonderful gift of life.'

'We didn't think as you'd be coming in such a weather,' Millie clucked.

'Why, I wouldn't dream of letting a little bit of rain put me off.'

'Little bit of rain. Stair rods would be more like it. And just look at you. Drenched to the skin.'

'Oh, it's nothing. I'll soon dry off.' Then Pippa glanced at the pool of water forming around her feet on the kitchen flagstones. 'I'm sorry, Millie, I'm dripping all over the floor!'

'Don't you worry about that, dearie. It's only good clean water. I'll soon mop that up. But I don't want you catching a chill. You come along with me.' Without any more ado, she marched Pippa out of the kitchen.

Ted came in and planted himself down on a chair beside the range. 'So 'er be come after all,' he stated. Lugubriously, he stuffed his pipe with

347

tobacco, tamped it down, lit it and puffed a cloud of smoke into the room. 'Thought 'er probably would.'

Some ten minutes later, Millie and Pippa returned. Pippa had a towel wrapped turban-like round her hair and was dressed in one of Millie's skirts, bunched at her waist with a belt and reaching almost to her ankles. Millie arranged her wet jeans and anorak on a clothes horse and stood it in front of the range, then busied herself making tea.

'Now, Mr Giles, you and Miss Pippa go on into the sitting room,' she said. 'I'll bring your coffee along in a moment.'

'Oh, what a lovely room,' Pippa exclaimed. Then she unwound the towel from her head and, kneeling on the hearthrug in front of the grate, threw her hair forwards to dry in the warmth of the fire. Half turning her head, she said, 'I've brought the film with me. We are going to take some pictures today, aren't we?'

'Y-y-yes, if you want to.'

'Of course. And you are going to let me take a portrait of you?'

'If you i-i-insist.'

'It's such a pity the weather's so bad.'

Judging by the speed at which the clouds were racing across the sky, the wind was as strong as ever, but the rain was already lessening and the light growing stronger.

'There's l-l-light enough through the w-w-window.'

'Can we start now?'

Her enthusiasm was endearing, reminding him suddenly of himself when he was young. He nodded. 'I-I-I'll go and fetch the tripod and camera.'

He went up to the attic and returned first with the tripod and then with the camera case. She was already setting up the tripod near the window. 'I've never seen a tripod like this before,' she told him.

'What's d-d-different about it?'

'Well, it's incredibly heavy for a start. And the ball and socket head. And this big platform.'

He grunted, taking the Gandolfi from its case and laying it on the living-room table. 'You're the ph-ph-photographer. You c-c-can set it up.'

It became immediately obvious to him that she did not know how to begin. Hesitantly, she undid several of the brass knobs, then shook her head ruefully. 'I'm sorry, it's quite different from the monorail cameras I'm used to.'

He undid the base catch under the carrying handle and the camera opened up.

'Now what do I do?'

What were modern cameras like? he wondered. But, for some reason, her lack of familiarity with the camera increased his own confidence.

'First, lock the b-b-back lightly,' he instructed. 'N-n-now, lock the f-f-front in the forward position and secure the c-c-catches. Now, the front will locate in the upright p-p-position. That's it. Lock the knobs. Now, undo the r-r-rear knobs and align the index with the bottom of the b-b-brass plate. Right. Now the camera is upright, lock all the knobs. Is the b-b-back movement square?'

He watched her fingers carefully. She had good, sensible, practical hands, the nails just long enough to load film but not so long as to get in the way. She handled the camera firmly but did not overtighten the knobs.

'I wouldn't like to do this in a hurry,' she commented. 'But I suppose it's habit, like everything else.'

Habit? That camera had once been an extension of himself – his eyes on the world.

'Now, lift up the front, until the b-b-bellows are parallel. The only knob which should m-m-move now is the f-f-front focus.'

She nodded. 'Yes. So why doesn't the back focus move?'

'There's a lock knob opposite the focusing knob. Move that slightly.'

'Oh, I see.'

He took a lens from a chamois leather bag and dropped it into position. Then he lifted the camera and screwed it on to the tripod for her.

She went to the front of the camera. 'I hate to say this, but I've never seen a lens like this before either. What is it?'

'A Goerz Dagor 360mm f6.8. One of the f-f-finest lenses ever made.'

She studied it, then tried to cock the shutter, to no avail.

He showed her the German shutter settings. 'You c-c-can't cock it on the Z setting,' he explained. He moved the setting to M, cocked the lever and pressed the release arm to fire the shutter. 'I-I-I assume you d-d-do know how to load slides?'

She gave a relieved laugh. 'Yes, at least I can do that. Though I've never worked with full plate before. But where shall I load them?'

'In the d-d-darkroom. G-G-Gurney can take you over under an

umbrella to keep the s-s-slides dry.' He went into the hall and called, 'Ted!'

Ted emerged from the kitchen.

'Take Miss Pippa to the d-d-darkroom.'

While she was gone, he positioned a chair by the window, so that the light would fall on the left side of his face. Strange how the years fell away and how easily everything came back, as though he had never stopped taking pictures.

In due course, she returned and placed the slides on the table, then looked into the ground glass screen. 'Do you have a focusing cloth?'

'In the case.'

The moths had been at it, but it was still serviceable.

'Would you mind sitting on the chair?' she asked.

It was only as he took up position that he realized fully what he had agreed to. Even now, although she was nowhere near ready to take a picture yet, he could feel himself starting to grow tense.

She draped the focusing cloth round her shoulders and rummaged in her bag. 'Oh, how stupid of me! I seem to have forgotten my Minolta. I know I put it on the table to bring with me.'

'Your w-w-what?'

'My exposure meter. I knew I'd need it, particularly since I wouldn't be able to use Polaroid.'

'Polaroid? What's th-th-that?'

She stared at him in astonishment. 'Instant film.'

'What do you n-n-need that for?'

'To check the exposure and lighting. But large format Polaroid needs a special processor, which requires electricity, so, of course, I couldn't use it here.'

He shook his head in perplexity. 'What film are you using?'

'Tri-X 400 ASA.'

He was not acquainted with Tri-X but 400 ASA was what he had been used to think of as 320 Weston. He looked up at the sky, held the palm of his hand up to the light and said, 'One tenth at f16.'

'Are you sure?'

'Of course I'm sure,' he snapped. He had been reading the light ever since he had first started taking photographs with West.

She did not argue, but closed the aperture to f16, set the shutter speed control to 10, cocked the shutter and put the first darkslide in the back of the camera.

Finally, they were ready. Or rather, the camera was ready, but the photographer was nervous and the sitter even more so. She looked at him from above the camera and said, 'Smile, please.'

Every muscle in his face was stiff, his jaw tight, his teeth clenched. This session was going to turn out a disaster. He should have heeded his instincts and not agreed to be the subject . . .

'Move your head slightly to the right,' Pippa said. 'Now down a bit. Look into the camera. Yes, that's nice.'

But, as she pressed the cable release and the shutter clicked, he knew damn well that it wasn't. And he could see from her expression that she knew it too.

Six sheets of film she shot and he knew, with certainty, that each was worse than the one before. It was his fault, not Pippa's. They should have started with the Rolleiflex, where all she would have had to do was wind the film on between frames, and progressed, at a later date, to the Gandolfi. And they should certainly have started with a better sitter, someone like Millie, for instance, who would not have been worrying about the camera and the photographer. Millie, after a glass of elderflower champagne, would have smiled quite naturally into the camera. Then Pippa, too, would have been more relaxed and able to concentrate better on the unfamiliar camera, instead of having to work so hard at trying to put him at his ease. On the other hand, if she was going to be a good photographer, she had to learn to direct and get her subject to do and look as she wanted . . .

She decided to change his chair and alter his position, but still it did not help.

One precious sheet of film remained. Not that she told him this. But he knew. He had been counting.

She cocked the shutter, left the camera and came over to him. He assumed she was going to adjust his jacket or move a lock of his hair.

Instead, she kissed him.

It was only a little kiss, not even on the mouth, just a brush of her lips against his cheek.

Then she was gone again.

One little kiss, but it contained more warmth than all the heat given off by the fire. One little kiss, but it rekindled a flame within him that had been so long suppressed it was almost extinguished. One little kiss, but it made him feel young again and full of hope and as if the December of his life were not approaching . . .

The shutter clicked.

It was dark when Pippa left and Ted took the storm lantern to light their way down the windy, rainswept hillside.

Giles himself went to the music room. For a long time he sat at the piano, without raising the lid. The perfume of night-scented stocks seemed to hang on the air. There was a melody in his head and the whisper of words spoken a long time ago. Schubert and Shelley . . .

He searched among the scores in the piano stool and found the sonata. His fingers were clumsy as they touched the ivory keys and the piano needed tuning.

> Music, when soft voices die,
> Vibrates in the memory . . .
> And so thy thoughts, when thou art gone,
> Love itself shall slumber on.

Pippa kissed me. And the love that was slumbering within me quickened and became alive again.

Giles's letter plopped innocently through the letterbox at Hill House and on to the mat, lying there until Adam and Bertie returned, muddy and bedraggled, from their early morning walk. Even when Adam recognized the distinctive handwriting on the envelope, he felt no sense of foreboding. He had not forgotten Pippa's visit in the winter, but he had all but forgotten its original purpose – the photograph album and her quest for Gawaine Devere.

Throughout the summer there had been no news from either Pippa or Kitty. And Elliott, during his brief visits – for his parents' respective birthdays – had not mentioned Sebastian other than in passing, mainly in connection with business.

In the meantime, there had been other matters to occupy Adam's mind. Eve, having made an excellent recovery from her hip replacement operation, had caught a bad summer cold, which she had been unable to shake off for weeks, although she now seemed finally to have got over it. They had also decided to have the outside of the house redecorated before the onset of winter and, in the process, it had been discovered that the asbestos guttering needed replacing. As a result, the herbaceous borders near the house had been trodden underfoot and virtually ruined by careless builders. Since Adam had never really been an enthusiastic gardener and Eve was no longer as agile as before, they had decided to do away with the flower beds and have them laid with turf.

All these things, though apparently minor, had required a lot of organization and created major disruptions in their everyday lives, so that events in the world outside Hill House and Puddles had taken on a distant perspective.

Having divested himself of Wellington boots and raincoat and towelled Bertie down, Adam took Giles's letter and, hearing Gladys's vacuum cleaner in the sitting room, retreated to the library, traditionally his private sanctum ever since Elliott and Sebastian were boys and he had needed a quiet room in which to concentrate his thoughts and deal with his personal paperwork. Out of habit, he sat down at the desk by the window and lit a cigar. Then he slit open Giles's envelope with a paper knife.

Giles had never been a good correspondent. His letters had always been short and to the point. And this one was no exception:

> Dear Adam,
>   I need to see you as a matter of urgency and would be grateful if you were able to come to Yondover as soon as possible. I recognize this is a bit of an imposition and if you are unable to come then let me know. You are, of course, welcome to stay the night here, although the comforts we offer are somewhat limited. Please let me know what day and time to expect you and I will make sure Gurney is waiting at the gate.
>   Trusting you and Eve are both well,
>   Yours, as ever,
>   G.G.D.

Adam's immediate and quite natural assumption was that, as on the last occasion Giles had summoned him to Yondover, the matter of urgency

would be financial. Then, on reflection, it occurred to him that Giles –
like the rest of them – was no longer as young as he had been. Perhaps
he was suffering from ill health and finding himself confronted by the
impossibility of remaining in his old home. To whom else could an old
hermit turn for advice?

The last time Adam had visited Yondover, he had made the journey
there and back in a day, the thought never crossing his mind that he might
need to stay the night. However, that had been some twenty years ago . . .

He went across to the bookshelf containing road maps and atlases and
took out the latest *AA Handbook*. No, it was no great distance to Kipwell,
especially now the new M28 motorway bypassed Southampton. It should
take him three, maybe four hours at the most. If he set off early, he could
be at Yondover by eleven and, even allowing for Giles's business taking
them into the afternoon, still be back home not long after dark.

On the other hand, in order to reach Kipwell, he had to drive right
past Arundel. He would be within a stone's throw of Kitty's house. If he
took up Giles's offer and spent the night at Yondover, he could stop off
and see her on his way back. Eve need never know . . .

When he showed Eve Giles's letter, she pursed her lips and said, 'I can't
see what on earth he can possibly want that requires you to go all that
way in person. Why can't he be more precise? A matter of urgency. Huh!
So you're expected to drop everything for him.'

'He is my oldest friend,' Adam pointed out mildly but firmly. 'And I
am probably his only friend. In any case, I would like to see him again.
It's been a very long time. However, if you need me here, I won't go.'

'Don't be ridiculous! Of course I shall be perfectly all right on my own
for a day. I'm much more concerned about you. It's such a long way to
drive.'

'No, not really.'

'Well, I suppose you could always stay the night, as he suggests.'

Adam knew that if he showed too much enthusiasm for Eve's suggestion,
his wife was quite capable of putting two and two together. 'I'd prefer
not to,' he said.

'When were you thinking of going?'

'Oh, as soon as possible, I think. Let's see. It's Tuesday today. If I reply
by first-class post, he should get my letter tomorrow. Yes, I'll go on
Thursday.'

In the end, at Eve's insistence, he took an overnight bag with him, just in case his meeting with Giles dragged on and he did not feel up to making the return journey the same day. Although neither of them had mentioned Kitty, he could not help but be aware that she was at the back of both their minds. In view of the fact that he was going to see Kitty's former husband, it was inevitable.

As things turned out, he did not stop off to see Kitty. When he passed Arundel on his outward journey, he gave a little wave in her direction. And when he returned from Kipwell, later that same day, as dusk was falling, he drove straight on along the A27 without even considering breaking his journey at Rose Cottage.

His brain was reeling from everything Giles had told him and before he talked to anyone he needed to get things absolutely clear in his own mind.

The week that followed Pippa's visit to Yondover was so busy in the studio that it was not until the weekend that she had the opportunity to develop her pictures of Gawaine Devere. She could have stayed after work, but because Tim's darkroom was small – which meant she was going to have to process the sheets one at a time in three dishes to avoid scratching them – she would probably have ended up working all night and, being tired, also ended up making an irreversible mistake.

So, because Saturday was Updike House day and the evening was, as always now, spent with Chris, it was Sunday before she was able to start. Just processing the ten sheets of film took her most of the day and at the end of it, when she hung them up to dry naturally overnight, the only thing which was absolutely certain was that each sheet bore an image and was sharp.

Naturally, she had told both Tim and Chris what she had been doing and Tim cast a practised eye over the negatives on Monday morning before she put them safely into envelopes until she could print them up. 'I can see I shall soon be out of a job,' he grinned. Then, more seriously, he added, 'Large format portraiture is difficult at the best of times and doing it on an unfamiliar camera makes it infinitely harder. But, having seen Gawaine Devere's own pictures, I can only congratulate you on your courage in choosing him for your first victim.'

The next week, too, was infuriatingly hectic, so it was again Sunday before she could get back into the darkroom. With mounting excitement, she studied the negatives on the lightbox, then selected the last sheet she had shot. After switching on the safelights, she set up the contact printer, placed the negative on it and put a sheet of bromide paper behind the negative. From experience, she guessed the exposure to be five seconds. Removing the bromide paper from the contact printer, she put it into the developer and rocked the dish.

Had her daring, impulsive action achieved the effect she had hoped? Had she captured the expression she was looking for?

After thirty seemingly interminable seconds, the image began to appear. She was holding her breath and her heart was pounding so furiously that she could hear its every beat. Slowly, oh, so incredibly slowly, the details emerged, the strands of his hair, the lines on his forehead and cheeks, the texture of his skin . . .

She'd got it! No doubt it would be hours before she managed to get the ultimate print – but she'd got the shot she'd been after!

His mouth was not drawn in a straight, tight line, but tilted slightly at the corners, which changed the contours of his cheeks and the thrust of his chin. But it was Gawaine Devere's eyes which were the focal point of the picture. It was to his eyes that one's attention was irresistibly drawn.

Those eyes beneath their bushy brows were soft and shone with a luminosity that had nothing to do with the daylight coming through the window, but seemed to reflect a light that came from deep inside him, from the depths of his innermost soul.

Almost, one would have said, as if they were the eyes of a man in love.

CHAPTER 25

In her dream, Kitty was in West's wood, only it wasn't as she remembered West's wood, but more like the kind of forest described in Grimms' *Fairy Tales*, the trees dense and threatening, hung with creepers and populated by evil creatures of the night. The sky was black and the wind was howling in a manic frenzy. She was frightened, but not on her own account. She had come to the wood with somebody, but had lost her companion. She was looking for them, but she did not know who she was searching for or where to find them, only that it was a matter of life and death that she find whoever it might be as quickly as possible. She tried to call out, but her voice would produce no sound that was audible above the wind. She tried to run, but her feet remained rooted to the ground. The trees crowded in around her, swaying in the gale. Fear turned to panic. She began to cry, wild tears of desperation and desolation.

Her tears woke her up and she discovered the storm was real. Outside, the wind she had heard in her nightmare was screaming and howling in a night that was still pitch black. It was a terrible wind. A wind which had blown the window wide open and threatened to wrench it from its hinges. A wind which was slamming doors and seemed to shake the entire building upon its foundations, so that it rattled and creaked and groaned. A wind which was creating chaos in the outside world, judging by the sounds of smashing glass, the crashing of dustbins, the shrill of burglar alarms and a host of other indefinable, deafening noises.

When she switched on her bedside light, it was dead. She got out of bed, made her way to the window and, with considerable difficulty, shut it, peering out into the night. If there was a moon it was concealed, but towards the east the sky was just beginning to lighten, silhouetting the roofs of neighbouring houses. Dimly, she could see objects scudding through the air.

Yet still her dream was more real to her than reality. Who had she been looking for? Someone was in danger. But who? Suddenly she thought of Tabitha. But her probing hand found the cat curled up at the foot of the bed, oblivious to the tumult raging outside.

She tried the main light switch by the door, to no avail. Either a fuse had blown or the storm had affected the mains supply. She felt for her dressing gown on the back of the door, put it on and made her way cautiously downstairs. There was no power in the hall either and when she peered out of the living room not a single light in the whole road.

The noise was terrifying. She had never heard wind like this before. Perhaps someone had let off a nuclear bomb and the third world war was about to break out. Or was this the end of the world?

'Now, get a grip on yourself and stop being so ridiculous,' she muttered aloud, finding comfort in the sound of her own voice. 'Calm down. Go to the kitchen and make yourself some tea. It will get light soon. Then you'll be able to see what's happening out there.'

She found the matches and lit a gas ring, which cast a dim glow over the immediate vicinity, only to be almost obliterated when she stood the kettle on it. Where was the torch? Somewhere on the dresser. She groped among familiar objects suddenly strange in the darkness, as the gale continued outside. 'Keep calm. It's only the wind . . .'

But her dream continued to haunt her. Who had she been looking for in West's wood?

'Oh, I really must have a tidy up. I can never find anything. Ah, here it is. That's better. How terrible to be blind and live in perpetual darkness . . . Teapot. Tea caddy. Water. Careful now. Don't scald yourself. Mug. Milk. What time is it? Good gracious, half-past four!'

No wonder there were no lights anywhere. Nobody else was up. But of course they were. Nobody could sleep through all this commotion.

Gradually it grew lighter but, as dawn came, the wind seemed to increase in force, shrieking dementedly in its savage fury. Black clouds buffeted across the sky. Never had clouds moved so fast. Drinking one mug of tea after another to steady her nerves, she stood at the kitchen window, watching the wind wreak its havoc, attempting to destroy whatever stood in its path, bearing with it slates, tiles, television aerials, flower pots, dustbins and lids, chimney-pots, fencing panels, tree branches, leaves and litter – her rose arch, her trellis. The wind tossed its trophies high into the sky, whirling them round in a vortex, smiting them to the ground, lifting them up again and bearing them on into neighbouring gardens.

A gust more powerful than any so far, an almighty crash and a shattering of glass. For a moment, she thought the whole of the back of the house was being blasted away. Something hurtled past the window. It looked like a door. Then a frame. She hurried to the back door and there, where her porch had stood, was merely the brick base and her Dorothy Perkins rose writhing in contortions.

Then, incredibly, the telephone rang. 'Mrs Pilgrim? Wakehurst here. Just touching base. Now, keep all the hatches battened down and no going out of doors. This is no mere storm, but a hurricane. Fortunately, I had the battery radio on standby and am in tune with the Met Office. Gusts of up to a hundred and twenty miles an hour are blowing out there. As soon as it's over, I'll be round.'

Grateful for the reassuring sound of another human voice, she returned to the window. Sometimes the wind abated and there was almost a lull, as if the hurricane had exhausted itself. Then, with a scream of triumphant frenzy and a blast which threatened to lift the very roof off the house, it would pick up strength again, with renewed violence.

Finally, at about eight o'clock in the morning, the hurricane started to move away, leaving in its wake a fearsome detritus, Colonel Wakehurst's lilac tree uprooted and her own precious garden apparently laid waste and littered with debris.

The front door bell rang. Very jittery, she went to answer it and found Colonel Wakehurst on the doorstep, an extraordinary apparition in great-coat, boots and a wartime tin helmet. 'That came as a bit of a surprise, what? No warning of a hurricane on the weather forecast last night. You don't seem to have suffered any damage at the front. What about the back?'

'I've lost my porch and my rose arch . . .'

He strode masterfully down the hall and into the kitchen. 'Hah! That seems all right. Nothing structural. Now, let's have a look from outside. You stay here. Wind's still buffeting. We're not through yet.'

It was only then that she realized she was still in her dressing gown.

He returned from the garden. 'Nothing to worry about there, although your television aerial seems to have disappeared.'

'I've never had an outside aerial. My television has its own little wire one attached.'

'Hah! Useful under the circumstances. Well now, if you'd care to join us when you're dressed, the Memsahib is preparing some breakfast. First feed the inner man, what! Then clear up the mess. Like in the Blitz, what!'

That was a phrase she was to hear many times that Friday 17 October, 1987, as the inhabitants of Pannet's Row gathered to discuss the hurricane, survey the damage and then repair it. There was a great spirit of camaraderie, as neighbour gave neighbour a helping hand, volunteered advice, lent tools, ladders, wheelbarrows and rakes, and, most reminiscent of the legendary wartime spirit, supplied each other with mugs of tea.

During the morning, Pippa phoned. 'I'm sorry I didn't ring earlier, but I have been thinking of you. Are you all right? And Tabitha? Oh, thank heavens. I was really worried. Yes, we're fine. A tree fell on Mum's Volvo, which meant Dad couldn't get the Range Rover out of the garage, which didn't please him, as you can imagine, but apart from that we were very lucky. It was incredible coming to work though. Some of the huge trees which have been uprooted – it's absolutely heartbreaking. And Tim says there's hardly a tree standing on Clapham Common.'

Later, when the electricity was restored and she could watch the television, Kitty recognized how lightly she had come off. Her garden had looked far worse than it was. A day spent tidying it up had restored it virtually to its former pristine order. Apart from the loss of her porch, rose arch and trellises, she was already back to normal.

Elsewhere, people had fared far, far worse. The news showed how huge trees had been uprooted, vast areas of woodland flattened, buildings collapsed, houses and cars crushed by fallen trees, church spires toppled, pylons, cranes and lorries overturned, piers wrecked, light aircraft upended, caravans blown away, ships blown aground. Six of Sevenoaks' famous oak trees had fallen. Countless ancient and rare trees had perished at Kew Gardens and Wisley. Two thirds of the trees comprising Chanctonbury Ring were gone. Views of London showed the parks littered with fallen trees. Many people had been injured, several killed. The full death toll was not yet known.

Over the weekend, the news continued to be dominated by the hurricane, with more horrifying pictures of the devastation and stories of great individual courage in the face of tragedy.

It was on Sunday evening that the newsreader announced: 'One of the casualties of the hurricane was eighty-year-old Gawaine Devere, who was struck by a falling tree in the grounds of his Sussex home.'

An aerial picture showed the escarpment of the South Downs at Kipwell and the trees in West's wood collapsed like fallen skittles.

The newscaster continued, 'A leading portrait photographer during the 1930s, Gawaine Devere saw war service as a photographer, after which he retired to his country estate in Sussex, where he lived as a recluse, fiercely resenting any intrusion upon his property. His battles to protect his woodland against the erection of a high voltage grid line and the construction of a bypass around the local village of Kipwell hit the headlines during the 1950s and '60s. Nothing, however, could protect Mr Devere and his beloved trees from the power of the elements.'

Kitty switched off the television and sat very still and silent. The memory of her dream on the night of the hurricane returned with sudden clarity. Then another memory came, from far longer ago, of two young people on horseback in West's wood as a storm was gathering. There had been a deafening clap of thunder and Pegasus had reared up in fright. She had calmed the horse and Giles had said, 'You saved my life.'

Now, West's wood was flattened and Giles was dead . . .

Their marriage might have ended over half a century ago, but he had been an integral part of her life. While he had not made her happy, she bore him no malice.

Moments later, the phone rang. 'Kitty, it's Pippa. Have you been watching the news? Have you heard about Gawaine Devere?'

'Yes, I've just seen it.'

'It's so horrid. He was such a lovely person. I know I didn't know him very well or for very long, but I'm going to miss him. I do hope he didn't suffer too much. I suppose he was the sort of person who would find it difficult to remain inside under such circumstances. He loved his trees.'

'Think of it this way, darling,' Kitty said. 'He was very old. If he had survived the hurricane, the shock of all the damage might have proved too much for him. If he had to die, this is probably the most fitting end.'

'Yes, that's one way of looking at it . . . I hope Millie and Ted are all right. The trouble is there's no way of contacting them.'

361

'People from the village will have been up to see them.'

'Yes, I'm sure you're right . . .' Pippa paused. 'I took a wonderful picture of him last time I was at Yondover. I was so looking forward to showing it to him. And now it's too late.'

At Hill House, Adam pressed the remote control to switch off the television and turned to Eve. 'Extraordinary how things turn out. If I were superstitious I'd say he'd had a premonition.'

'I'm glad you went to see him when you did.'

'Yes, so am I.'

They lapsed into silence, both thinking about Giles and, in particular, Adam's last meeting with him, the details of which Adam had recounted to Eve after his return.

It was Eve who broke the silence. 'Would you mind getting me a drink? A brandy, I think. I don't know if I've got another cold coming on or if it's just, well . . . shock is too strong a word, I suppose. But I do feel sad. After all, Giles had quite an influence on my life one way and another.'

'Yes, of course.' Adam hurried across to the sideboard and poured them both brandies.

Eve cradled the glass in her hands before taking a sip. Then she said, 'I've been doing a lot of thinking in recent months. About us. About Kitty. And about Sebastian. I suppose Pippa's visit sparked it all off. I know it's a bit late, but I would like to apologize for the scene I made after she went. I'm not sorry for having told Pippa about Kitty – but I am sorry about the accusations I threw at you.'

Adam reached across and touched her hand. 'There's no need to apologize . . .'

'But I behaved quite ridiculously. I shocked myself.'

'If I'm honest, I think it probably did me a lot of good, shook me up, stopped me taking you for granted.'

'Maybe, but I'm still ashamed of myself.'

'For goodness' sake. It doesn't matter. Forget it.' Then, remembering the words he still, all too often, neglected to say, he added, 'I love you, Eve. That's all that matters.'

She shook her head and looked away from him into the fire. Then she said, 'I want to ask you a question. And I would like you to give me an

362

honest answer. When you went to see Giles the other week, did you go and see Kitty as well?'

Without hesitating, he replied, 'No. I would have told you if I had.'

Eve gave a rueful little smile. 'I know that really. I just had to be sure.'

'Eve, I'm . . .'

She held up her hand to stop him saying any more. 'As I said earlier, I've been doing a lot of thinking. Not just about us. Or even Kitty. But about Sebastian, too. And I've come to the conclusion that I have been wrong about him in many respects, allowing myself to become blinded to his faults, always taking his side against Kitty's, because I was prejudiced against her. But now I'm not so sure that it was all her fault. When did Sebastian last give us a call? How long is it since he last came to see us?'

'He's made his own life . . .'

'You don't need to make excuses for him.'

Adam frowned, trying to fathom the direction in which she was heading.

Eve took another sip of brandy. 'I think you ought to phone Kitty now and make sure she's all right, that she survived the hurricane. I had been going to suggest it anyway, but in view of Giles's death . . .'

'Listen, Eve, you are more important to me than Kitty or Giles. The last thing I want to do is upset you.'

'No, it may sound illogical to you, but it would actually upset me more if you didn't get in touch with her. Let's face it, you're going to have to see her some time anyway, either at Giles's funeral or later . . .'

'Not necessarily.'

'Don't be silly, Adam. Of course you will. You'll have to.'

'Well, I must admit . . .'

'Then go and phone her now.'

'I don't understand . . .'

'Women.' Eve finished his sentence for him. 'You don't understand women.'

'That's certainly true,' he agreed with alacrity.

'You see . . .' Then Eve changed her mind and decided not to explain her thoughts. She stood up. 'I'm feeling rather shivery. I think I'll get an early night. I'll go and put the kettle on for a hot water bottle and while I'm doing that, you ring Kitty.'

No, there was no need to spell things out any more than she had. Let him work it out for himself, as she had done.

He might have loved Kitty, but Kitty had never loved him. Kitty had never really been a threat to their personal happiness, except in Eve's own mind. It had taken her enough years to realize it, but she had got there in the end.

So allow Adam his dream for a little longer. It could hurt nobody and it was just possible – more than possible in fact – that some good might come of it.

Scarcely had Kitty put down the receiver after speaking to Pippa than the phone rang again. This time, it was Adam.

'Kitty, how are you? It sounds as if things have been rather grim your way. Are you all right?'

'Thank you, yes, I'm fine. It was rather frightening, but I was fortunate. The worst thing to happen to me was the loss of my porch and my new rose arch.'

'Thank God for that. We had a strong gale, but obviously nothing anywhere near as severe as you did in Sussex.' He paused. 'I don't suppose you've been watching the news?'

'Yes, I've just heard – about Giles.'

'Ah, so you know. A bit of a shock, eh?'

'Yes, it was a shock.'

'Are you all right?'

'Well, naturally I'm upset.'

'Of course. I don't expect you have a drink in the house, do you?'

'There's some sherry, I think.'

'As soon as I ring off, go and pour yourself a large glass.'

Funny how the masculine mind always seemed to think that alcohol was the panacea for all ills. 'Maybe I'll do that.'

'Well, it's a bit late and I'm sure you're getting ready for bed, like we are, so I won't keep you any longer. I'll give you another call tomorrow, or the day after, when I've found out a bit more about the circumstances of Giles's death.'

'Thank you, Adam. That would be kind.'

'I have been meaning to ring you for ages, but you know how it is. What with one thing and another, I just don't seem to have got round to it.'

'Don't worry, I know exactly what you mean.'

'Now, don't forget, a large glass of sherry.'

'I'll see. But before you go – is Eve all right?'

'Yes, she's fine. Well, having said that, she thinks she may have a bit of a cold coming on. She sends you her love, incidentally.'

'And my love to her, too.'

'Of course. Well, goodbye for now . . .'

A couple of days later, Adam telephoned again. 'I've finally managed to get through to Kipwell on the phone,' he announced. 'Spoke to the Vicar. It seems Giles went out in the full force of the hurricane. There will have to be a post mortem, I'm afraid. I imagine the funeral will be in a week or ten days' time, after all the formalities have been attended to. Do you want to go?'

'Goodness, I hadn't thought that far ahead. Will you be going?'

'Of course. Giles was my oldest friend.'

The following day, he rang again. 'We haven't spoken so often for years, have we? Well, the funeral's all arranged. Eleven o'clock next Wednesday at Kipwell Parish Church. Now, what I'd like to suggest is – if it's all right by you – that I come to Arundel the day before the funeral, spend the night at Rose Cottage and then, if you do decide to go to the funeral, we can go together to Kipwell the next day. And if not, it will break my journey.'

'It will be lovely to see you again,' Kitty assured him. 'Will Eve be coming too?'

Adam hesitated, then he said, 'No, she's a bit under the weather. I'm afraid you'll have to put up with just a surprised penguin . . .'

It was after Adam's calls, with their emphasis on the formal rather than the emotional aspects of Giles's death, that Kitty's mind turned towards Yondover and she wondered what would happen to it now that Giles was dead.

Presumably, since Giles must have written her out of his will after their divorce and he had no other kin to leave it to, the house would be sold. And what would happen to it then? In such a prime site, probably developers would snap it up and either demolish it or turn it into an hotel, nursing home or some kind of leisure centre. Such a notion simply did not bear contemplating.

A daring idea started to take root in her mind . . .

'But there was Yondover,' West had said, all those years ago. 'And I loved Yondover . . . I decided to turn my legacy into beautiful things – into pictures and music, flowers and trees. Money is a currency, Kitty. It shouldn't be left to grow stagnant or used simply to make more money. It should be allowed to flow – and to create beauty . . .'

How much would Yondover cost to buy and how much money did she have? Rose Cottage must be worth what – a hundred thousand? She could easily obtain a valuation from an estate agent. And then there were her savings. A quick phone call to William John would elicit that information.

In the meantime, however, the hurricane had literally become last week's news. Three days after the hurricane, on Monday 20 October – Black Monday, as it was being called – billions had been wiped off stock markets throughout the world and, during each day that followed, the value of shares was continuing to plummet, leading people to fear a repeat of the Wall Street Crash of 1929.

Every evening, the television news showed chaotic scenes at the Stock Exchanges in New York and London: young men and women screaming down two phones at once, while their computer screens danced with changing figures; the floor around them resembling a rubbish tip, strewn with crumpled paper, empty plastic coffee cups and the contents of over-flowing ashtrays.

What if her faith in William John had been misplaced? What if he had invested her royalties in stocks and shares that were now no longer worth the paper they were written on? Under almost any other circumstances that would not have mattered. In her will, drawn up years ago, she had left her entire estate to Sebastian, but he was obviously doing well enough not to need anything from her. In fact, possibly she should think about making a new will now she had met Pippa . . .

But first things first. She must find out whether, after Black Monday, she still had anything left to leave anyone – and, more importantly, anything left to spend while she herself was still alive.

Adam arrived in time for tea. While they were eating, he described his journey. The motorways and main trunk roads had been cleared of the worst debris, he told her, but the countryside was still truly terrible to behold. Houses could be repaired quite quickly, but it would be years, if

366

not decades, before new growth could repair the damage to forests, woods and hedgerows.

She knew him so well that she sensed he was talking for the sake of talking. He had something on his mind, something more than Giles's funeral the next day.

Eventually, he finished his cake, folded his napkin and pushed his plate aside. 'I have something to tell you,' he said, 'but I don't quite know where to start.'

'At the beginning?' she suggested gently.

'Normally, in the past, whenever we've met, even after a long absence, we've always seemed to pick up where we last left off. But this time, it's not so easy.' He took off his spectacles and began cleaning them on his handkerchief. 'Are you aware that Pippa came to see us last winter?'

So that was what was troubling him . . .

'Yes, indeed. Eve told her where I lived. And I'm very glad that she did, because she's been to see me several times since then. I've become tremendously fond of her – and I think she has of me.'

'I was very upset when Eve told me what she had done.'

'But why, Adam? Getting to know Pippa has been one of the nicest things ever to happen to me.'

'Did Pippa explain why she came to see us?'

For a moment she was confused, not able to remember.

'She had got hold of a photograph album,' Adam said.

'Of course! So much has happened in the meantime I had almost forgotten where it all started. Yes, I know about the album and that she's been going to see Giles.'

He replaced his spectacles on his nose. 'Well, thank the Lord for that. Because you didn't ring me, I assumed – well, to tell the truth, I have been imagining all sorts of things.'

'You could have rung me,' she pointed out.

'Yes, I know. But what with one thing and another . . . Eve hasn't been, er, too well. She keeps getting colds that she can't shake off.'

Kitty cast him a shrewd look and knew he wasn't telling the entire truth. Eve hadn't just been unwell. Eve was jealous of her – she always had been – and without any justification whatsoever . . .

'I'm sorry,' she said. 'I do hope she'll soon be quite better.'

'Oh, I'm sure she will. However, that's all by the by.' He cleared his throat. 'Does Pippa know that you and Giles were married?'

'I'm fairly sure she doesn't. I certainly haven't told her.'

'Why not?'

'Well, I think if I hadn't fallen, I might have done . . .'

'Fallen?'

'Oh, it was nothing really. I tripped down the steps into the living room and knocked myself out.'

'When was this?'

'The very first time Pippa came here. Poor girl, it must have given her quite a shock. She was very good. She stayed here until I came out of hospital.'

'You should have let me know.'

'Why? There was nothing you could do. I didn't break any bones or anything. Just shook myself up, really. Since Pippa assumed by then that we weren't related, it seemed easiest just to let her continue in that belief. In any case, I didn't know her well enough then to be sure she wouldn't tell Sebastian. And if Sebastian does ever have to know about Giles, I'd rather he didn't find out that way — from his daughter.'

'Hmm. Do you mind if I smoke?'

'Of course not. I'll find you an ashtray.'

He went through the ritual of lighting a cigar, then exhaled a stream of blue smoke towards the ceiling. 'Ah, that's better. Hmm. You know, I can understand why you didn't want Sebastian to know about Giles when he was a little boy. And I agreed with you. He had problems enough then. I remember Giles was convinced that he was his real father and wanted to spring that on him just after he came to Puddles. I had the devil of a job to persuade him not to.'

He paused. 'I've never asked you before. Whose son is Sebastian?'

Whose son was Sebastian? Ever since his birth, she had tried to convince herself that he was Leo's, but if she was truly honest with herself, she knew that no Brunnen blood flowed in his veins. Sebastian was a throwback to the Reverend Thurston Fellowes and old Samuel Lambourne.

She shrugged. 'Does it matter who his natural parents are? Is blood lineage so important? There's a Spanish proverb that goes *Yo soy yo y mis circunstancias*. I am I and my circumstances. If Sebastian is anyone's son, he is yours and Eve's. You were responsible for his upbringing.'

'In which case, he is really his own man. Which is true for all of us, I guess. Take Elliott. Now where did *he* come from? But I digress. Back to Sebastian. He's a grown man now, old enough to face the facts. Is there any reason why he shouldn't know about Giles?'

'It's probably very foolish of me, but I still live in hope that Sebastian and I may heal our differences. Particularly since we now have Pippa in common. If he finds out that I have been deceiving him all these years, it will make things worse rather than better. In any case, Giles is dead now . . .'

Adam studied the glowing tip of his cigar. 'I'm afraid Giles's death adds a new complication. What I'm about to tell you is breaking all the rules of professional etiquette, but I really think you should be forewarned. A couple of weeks ago, Giles wrote and asked me to come and see him urgently. Naturally, I went. I didn't come and see you then, because, well, it seemed best under the circumstances.

'Anyway, it transpired that he wanted to make a new will. When I arrived, he had it all written out. All I had to do was cast a legal eye over it, before witnessing it together with some chap Gurney fetched up from the village.

'Well, not to beat about the bush, Giles has left Yondover to Pippa.'

'To Pippa!' Kitty was incredulous. She sank back in her chair, the implications of Giles's bequest racing through her mind. Yet most over-whelming was a sense of relief – and, yes, joy.

'If anyone is the rightful inheritor of Yondover, it's Pippa,' she said. 'Oh, I think that's wonderful . . .'

'Mmm,' Adam murmured dubiously. 'Well, leaving aside the issue of Sebastian and his probable reaction to this news, I'm going to break the rules of legal convention yet further and tell you the other problems involved in Pippa's inheritance.

'Has she told you much about Yondover? Are you aware that Giles had allowed it to get very run down? Remembering how it used to look in West's day, I was shocked when I went there. Giles said that he and the Gurneys had recently done quite a bit of work around the house and the gardens, but it was only superficial.'

'Pippa has described it to me. And, since the hurricane, I assume it's in an even worse state.'

'Yes, it must be.' Adam sucked in his breath. 'Since Giles's death, I've

369

started to look into his affairs in order to ascertain what his estate consists of. And the answer is pitifully little. He must have been living on the breadline. Apart from Yondover, his assets appear to consist of a few hundred pounds in the bank and some shares which are pretty well worthless since Black Monday. Furthermore, Yondover wasn't insured, so the money that will be needed to repair the hurricane damage will have to be found elsewhere.'

He paused. 'Of course, I wasn't aware of any of this when I was there. I attributed the state of Yondover to eccentricity on his part, not lack of funds. Had I known, I would have insisted upon him making quite different dispositions.

'You see, together with Yondover, Pippa has to assume responsibility for Millie and Ted Gurney. Basically, they come with the house and have the right to live there, free of charge, until they die. What's more, she can't sell any of the surrounding land, for he has left that to the National Trust. So, to sum up the situation, she has no money for repairs, but, if she doesn't want to keep the house and decides to place it on the market, she will find it extremely difficult to sell, especially with two sitting tenants.'

Instead of responding directly, she said, 'There's a bottle of claret in the larder. The young man in the off licence assured me it's a good one, so I hope he was right. If you wouldn't mind opening it and pouring us both a glass, I'll get some papers I'd like you to see.'

The envelope William John had sent in response to her telephone call was in the bureau in the living room. It contained her last year's accounts, copies of her most recent building society statements and a summary of her assets. In view of recent events it was fortunate, William had written in his accompanying note, that they had resisted the temptation to be a little more adventurous with her investments. Her savings might not have yielded the same large return as they would have had they been put into stocks and shares, but at least they were intact and easily accessible.

She took the glass Adam handed her and raised it to him. 'Thank you for being so honest with me.'

'If the Law Society knew, they'd strike me off their list.'

She smiled. 'Before I show you these figures, I think I ought to tell you that, until I heard about Pippa, I was intending to buy Yondover myself.'

'You were *what*?'

'Adam, dear, I couldn't possibly allow Yondover to go to strangers.

370

Now, if you wouldn't mind looking at these. I'm so hopeless with all matters financial, but I think . . .'

Adam opened the envelope and cast an assessing eye over the figures. 'I would say that you could afford to buy two Yondovers and still have money in hand. Congratulations. I had no idea that writing was so profitable.'

'So I did understand them right. I must confess I was most surprised myself. I do appear to have done very well by the *Enchanted* books – and by my paintings. But, of course, I've had little to spend my money on. As you know, I live very simply.'

He laid the papers on the table. 'So tell me what's in your mind.'

'Isn't that obvious? I'd like to give Pippa that money.'

Adam took a very large swig at his claret. 'It isn't quite as simple as that.'

'Why not? It's my money. I can do what I like with it.'

'Yes, of course you can, but—'

'If Giles can give her Yondover, I can give her the means to keep it. She's my granddaughter. And her boyfriend is an architect. He has a penchant for old buildings.'

'Hold on a moment . . . This has to be carefully thought through. Pippa is going to have enough shocks tomorrow. Nevertheless she couldn't help but be surprised at your affection for a house which you have apparently never seen. And then there is the not inconsiderable problem of Sebastian . . .' He refilled both their glasses. 'Sebastian may just accept that Giles developed an affection for Pippa – because they shared the same name and were both photographers – and, having no family of his own, Giles decided to make her his heir. But if you become involved . . . You understand now why I asked you all those questions earlier?'

'Yes, I see what you mean. Well, there would seem to be nothing for it. I'll just have to make a clean breast of everything. But I would rather Sebastian knew about Giles before Pippa did . . .'

'Kitty, when will you stop being so impatient and impulsive? Allow me to cogitate, please.'

For a long time he was silent, gazing into some distant place beyond her shoulder. Then he said, 'Yes, that may be the way round it. I think it may be best for all concerned if you don't attend the funeral.'

'Why? I would like to see Yondover again.'

'You've waited so long, you can wait a little longer. Pippa's intending to come to the funeral. Fortunately, the Vicar told me she had rung him. If you're there, she's going to wonder why. But if you're not, there need be no reason for her to make any connection between you and Giles. After the ceremony, I'll tell her about the will. Then, when – as I'm sure she will – she tells you all about it, you can step in as fairy godmother. Yes, I can't see any flaws in that.'

'You're very good to me, Adam. I don't deserve it.'

He looked at her over his glass, his eyes blinking behind the thick lenses of his spectacles. 'I love you, Kitty. I have always loved you and I shall go on loving you through all eternity. No, don't say anything, please. I know you have never loved me and never will. But I mind that less this evening than I ever have before. Because, this evening, I have realized that my true rival for your affections has never really been another man . . .'

I was able to restore to him the one true, enduring love of his life, a love which would never fail him – Yondover. Marion McDonnell had said that, all those years ago, of West.

Adam was right, of course.

372

CHAPTER 26

Kipwell after the hurricane presented a tragic aspect. The narrow road leading to the village had been cleared but uprooted trees and jagged branches lay along the verges. Kipwell Grange, which Pippa had never seen before, stood exposed to view, the trees which had concealed its entrance toppled over. The woods belonging to Yondover lay flattened behind the barbed wire fences with their signs prohibiting trespassers. In the churchyard, a massive yew had split down its trunk and lay spread-eagled across grass and gravestones.

Feeling lonely and wishing she had taken up Chris's offer to come with her – although his company would not have been apt, since he had never met Gawaine Devere – she parked the car beside the padlocked, five-barred gate. Then, with a glance in the direction of Yondover, she passed through a small group of curious onlookers by the lychgate and up the path to the church.

Just inside the porch, Millie and Ted were standing, ill at ease in unfamiliar clothes. Millie was wearing a shapeless, dark brown coat and a woolly hat pulled down over her ears, while Ted had on a raincoat and a flat cap. He scowled, but a little smile of gratitude flickered over Millie's features and Pippa was suddenly relieved that Chris was not with her. This was not the moment to introduce another stranger into their midst.

'Oh, I'm right glad to see you, Miss Pippa,' Millie said. 'We've been through a terrible time, that I can tell you. It all come as such a shock, it did. The Vicar's been awful good to us, he and Mrs Woodford both. Ted and me, we wouldn't have known what to do, but Mr Woodford saw to all the arrangements. And after the service we're going over to the Vicarage to have some refreshments. I've been in the kitchen there all morning, making sandwiches and sausage rolls. You see, Mr Giles's lawyer is expected, too, though where he be . . .'

'Please tell me what happened,' Pippa begged.

'Well, you see, Miss Pippa, it was like this . . .' Millie went on to describe how she had been woken by the wind on the morning of the hurricane and, taking a cup of tea up to Mr Giles's room, found his bed empty.

'When I went to Ted's room, he was still asleep. How he could have slept through all that racket is beyond me. Just like in the Blitz, it were. It fair give me the willies. Anyhow, I waked him up and we searched the house for Mr Giles. But I knew what had happened. I felt it in me bones, like. As soon as it was light and all the debris had stopped flying around, we went outdoors. Lord, miss, you've never seen such a sight. A tree had come down across the stables and smashed through the roof of the dark-room. Well, we thought mebbe he might be in there. But he weren't. So then there was nothing for it but to search all the grounds. We hollered and shouted. I can tell you, I was in a right old panic. Then eventually we found him in the woods. A big oak tree had fallen right across him. Ted run down to the village. Of course, they couldn't drive an ambulance up there, so they flew in a helicopter . . .'

They settled themselves in the front pew. From time to time the church door creaked open and they turned to watch a villager or two shuffle in. 'That be old John from the Home Farm,' Millie murmured. And, 'That be Mr and Mrs Padden . . .' Then, she said, 'I know who that gentleman is. He be Mr Giles's lawyer.'

To Pippa's astonishment, Uncle Adam walked up the aisle and sat down a couple of rows behind them.

There was no opportunity for conversation. Scarcely was Adam seated than the door opened again and the Vicar entered, followed by the pall-bearers carrying the coffin.

'*I am the resurrection and the life* . . .' the Vicar intoned. '*We brought nothing into this world, and it is certain we can carry nothing out. The Lord gave and the Lord hath taken away* . . .'

There followed a spoken psalm, a collect and prayers, the voices sounding thin and pathetic in the echoing church. Pippa forgot about Adam.

Then the Vicar bade them be seated. He was a middle-aged man, with a round, goodly face. 'It is a cause of deep regret to me that I did not have the privilege of meeting Giles Gawaine Devere during his lifetime.

Naturally, since I came to Kipwell, five years ago, I could not help but be aware of his existence. The gate to Yondover was beside the church. His land bordered on the churchyard. However, the neighbourly notes I sent received no reply and I had no alternative but to respect his desire for privacy. Yet, as I have come to realize since his death, he was not as alone as I had feared. As well as Mrs Gurney and her son, he possessed other friends . . .' He paused and glanced at Pippa.

She felt tears prickling behind her eyelids and a lump forming in her throat. She clenched her fists hard so that her nails dug into the palms of her hands.

'It is very natural,' the Vicar continued, 'when somebody dies, for those who are left behind to feel guilty about the things they have left undone and the feelings they never expressed. We are afraid that the person whom we loved may have been unaware of how great our affection was for them. In the case of Giles Gawaine Devere, who shunned human contact, this is particularly true. I therefore suggest that we have a few moments' silence, during which we all say to him in our hearts the words we had no opportunity to speak. And, because his spirit is still with us, we can do this in the sure and certain hope that he will hear us.'

'Dear Mr Giles,' Pippa thought, her head bowed, her eyes squeezed shut, an image in her mind of Gawaine Devere as he was in the portrait she had taken of him, 'thank you for allowing me into your life. Thank you for sharing your little world with me. I shall never forget you as long as I live . . .'

The tears which Pippa had struggled to restrain throughout the service welled over during the burial. The Vicar's words, '*Earth to earth, ashes to ashes, dust to dust*', and the sight of Gawaine Devere's coffin being lowered into the grave in the desolate churchyard with its stricken yew tree and the heavy rainclouds overhead, filled her with a sense of the finality of death.

She felt a hand in hers and turned to find Adam beside her. Behind his spectacles, tears were glinting in his eyes, too.

After the burial, the mourners, about a dozen of them, gathered in the Vicarage sitting room, where Millie and Mrs Woodford handed round cups of tea and plates of refreshments. Pippa stood at the window, looking up towards Uffing Down. Behind her, the conversation seemed mostly to centre around the hurricane.

Gradually, having paid their respects, the other people began to disperse. Millie said she would get on with a bit of washing up and Ted announced that he'd like to be getting back to Yondover, where 'there be enough work to keep an 'ole army employed'. Adam accompanied him from the house and the two of them stood for a while at the gate, talking, after which Ted touched his cap and set off up the hillside, while Adam went to his car, returning with a briefcase.

Finally, Pippa was alone with him. 'Why are you here?' she asked.

'I was his solicitor.'

'So you did know him?'

'Yes, I first met him in 1926, when we both went up to Oxford and roomed together.'

'Then why didn't you say something, when I came to Puddles and showed you the photograph album?'

Adam sat down in an armchair to one side of the fire. 'I could lie to you,' he said. 'I could pretend that I was suffering from some temporary lapse of memory and did not connect Giles with those photographs – or something along those lines. But I'm not going to. Neither, however, am I going to answer your question. Not yet, anyway. Another day perhaps, but not today. I'm sorry, Pippa, but, believe me, I have my reasons – very good reasons. In any case, does it really matter? You met Giles yourself, which was much better than hearing me talk about him.'

'Yes, I suppose so . . .'

'Now, if you wouldn't mind sitting down, I have something far more important to tell you.'

She took the chair opposite him across the fireplace.

'For all that I was Giles's friend – probably his best friend – I saw him seldom after he became a recluse. Our friendship continued, but it was confined to correspondence. Then, a few weeks ago, he requested my presence at Yondover.

'He told me about your letter to him and your subsequent visits. He said – and these are his exact words – "Until Pippa came to Yondover, it was as if Yondover were an empty shell and the three of us just ghosts. Pippa has brought us all to life again. Now, when I die, it will be without

376

regret, for, as a result of having met Pippa, I know my life has not been in vain." '

He paused to allow her to take the implication of those words, then opened his briefcase and took out a folder, from which he extracted a document bound with a thin, green ribbon.

'This is Giles's will,' he said. 'It is dated 2 October 1987. I do not intend to read it out in its entirety. I have had a copy made so that you can read it in full later.'

He cleared his throat. 'In it, Giles has left Yondover to you.'

Pippa's mouth opened, but not a word emerged. Yondover . . . to her?

'There are two other bequests, although the first should be more strictly described as a request. It was Giles's wish that the Gurneys be allowed to continue to reside at Yondover, free of charge, for the rest of their lives. The other is that the surrounding land should be given to the National Trust as a conservation area.'

He placed the will on the arm of his chair. 'My congratulations.'

Pippa shook her head in total bewilderment. 'I don't understand . . .'

'Yondover belongs to you now,' Adam replied gently.

Her emotions were still raw from the burial ceremony. This additional shock proved too much and she simply burst into tears.

Eventually, her tears abated and she blew her nose. 'I'm sorry.'

'It's quite all right,' Adam assured her gruffly. 'Would you like me to see if the Vicar has any brandy?'

'No, I'll be fine, thank you.'

'Naturally, you will need to think this news through. But, in my capacity not only as Giles's executor but also your – shall we say "adopted"? – grandfather, I feel I really must advise you that your inheritance could be described as something of a white elephant. You see, Giles has left you the house and the garden, but he has not left you any money to repair and maintain the property. To be quite frank, he didn't have any money to leave.'

To talk about money seemed almost sacrilegious. Money was nothing. Gawaine Devere could have been a multi-millionaire and left her a huge fortune and she would not have felt nearly as deeply moved. Yondover was his home – it was a part of himself.

'He was once reasonably well off,' Adam continued, 'but over the last forty years, he dissipated his wealth. His court cases – you know about the pylons and the bypass? – cost him a pretty packet.'

It still didn't matter. 'Yes, I suppose they must have done. I'm sorry, Uncle Adam, I can't quite think straight.'

'No, of course you can't.'

'I just never expected . . . Why do you think he left Yondover to me?'

'For the reason I told you. You gave him a purpose in life.'

'But we only met three times . . .'

Adam pressed the tips of his fingers together, making a steeple of his hands, and studied them. Then he said, 'Your parents presumably know about your visits to him?'

'Yes, but . . .' She saw new complications arising. 'I don't know how Dad's going to take this at all. He thought Gawaine Devere – er, Giles – was a crank. Well, worse than that. Do you remember the pictures in the album? There were some nudes among them and Dad thought that made Giles some kind of pornographer. And because I made the mistake of telling him about Giles's campaigns to save his land, and how he and Ted went after the workmen with guns, Dad's also got it into his head that he's a potential murderer. He tried to forbid me to see him again. I was so furious that I told him about—'

She stopped, suddenly remembering the rest of their row – about Kitty – and Eve's involvement: how Eve had said Adam would be upset if he knew she had betrayed a confidence. Except that now she knew from Kitty herself why her father had been brought up by Adam and Eve, perhaps that didn't matter any more. She sighed deeply. 'It all gets horribly complicated. It shouldn't be like this. Not today. Not when Giles has done such a wonderful thing . . .'

'Would I be right in thinking that your argument with your father also concerned Kitty?' Adam asked.

'So you know?'

'Yes, I stayed at Rose Cottage last night.'

'Well, thank heavens that at least is out in the open.'

'It's always difficult trying to remain friends with two warring parties.'

'I do wish Dad would make things up with Kitty. She's such a lovely person.'

'She's very fond of you, too.'

'Are you going back to Kitty's this evening?'

'Yes, I'm not very keen on driving in the dark any more. I'll be staying with Kitty tonight and going on to Puddles in the morning.'

'Would you mind if I came too?'

Adam shook his head. 'I don't think that's a very sensible idea under the circumstances. In my opinion, you should go home now. Your parents should be the first people to learn about your inheritance.'

'What about Millie and Ted?' Pippa asked. 'I saw you talking to Ted. Do they know?'

'Not yet, but I have assured them that they will be taken care of.'

Suddenly, Pippa understood the implications of Adam's mention of money. Gawaine Devere had not only left her his home but his responsibilities. Sentiment apart, if she kept Yondover, she had to look after Millie and Ted. If she should decide not to keep it, Millie and Ted would be homeless.

Adam reached across and patted her hand. 'It's all right, Pippa. You don't have to make any decisions today. There's enough for Millie and Ted to get by on for a while. What I suggest is that you talk the whole matter through with your parents – and anyone else you trust. Then you know where I am. You can ring me at any time – or come down to Puddles. You know you're always welcome.'

Sebastian had been too concerned about the hurricane damage to Valerie's Volvo and the beating his shares had taken on Black Monday to give much thought to Gawaine Devere's death. So far as he considered the matter at all, he saw it as a heaven-sent solution to that particular problem. Understandably, in view of their previous row, Philippa had not talked about it to him, but he did know from Valerie that she was attending the funeral. Well, that was fair enough. As Valerie said, it showed respect and, afterwards, that blasted photograph album would soon be forgotten and so would Gawaine Devere.

When Philippa came home after the funeral, however, to make the startling announcement of her inheritance, his misgivings all returned. With the best will in the world, he could not help but view the news with mingled incredulity and suspicion. There was something more to all this than met the eye. No man, however eccentric, would leave his property to a young girl, upon what would appear to amount simply to a whim.

Philippa herself was overwhelmed by the whole matter and was unable

379

to provide answers to most of the questions he asked. Neither did the copy she gave him of Gawaine Devere's will help to explain the mystery. It was handwritten but seemed to contain all the necessary legal clauses. The two witnesses – Adam and a certain John Tierney, who described his occupation as farmer – testified that Gawaine Devere had been in sound mind when he had drawn up his will on 2 October.

Adam's involvement was a further confusing element. According to Philippa, Adam and Gawaine Devere had been up at Oxford together and pursued a lifetime's friendship. Why, then, since Sebastian assumed he was acquainted with all the friends of the Berkeleys, had he never met this particular one, whose name, for obvious reasons, would have stuck in his memory?

Clearly, the key to the whole extraordinary affair was Adam. But first, he decided, he would talk to Elliott.

Elliott, when he saw him next morning, was of absolutely no help. On the contrary, he found the story extremely amusing. 'So Pippa's taken a lesson from me, has she,' he laughed, 'and been doing a bit of coffin-polishing. Your words, Sebastian, not mine. Well, don't look so tragic. Death comes to all of us one day. And something has to happen to our possessions after we're gone. Far better Pippa than the Treasury.'

'Indeed,' Sebastian said sharply. 'But if you could be serious for a moment, would you mind telling me whether you have ever heard of Gawaine Devere?'

'I can categorically assure you that, until today, I had never heard the name – and it's certainly not one to be easily forgotten. Sorry, old boy, you're going to have to ask the Pater to shed some light.'

When Sebastian rang Adam, it was in the expectation that the necessary explanations could be made over the telephone. Adam, however, having stressed that the will was perfectly in order, said that the subject of Gawaine Devere was something he would prefer to discuss face to face and man to man. Unfortunately, Eve had not been at all well recently, while he was suffering from a slight attack of sciatica. Otherwise, he would gladly come up to London. So if Sebastian insisted upon knowing more about the circumstances of Pippa's legacy, he must come to Hill House. 'Tomorrow, maybe?' Adam suggested.

It was a long time since Sebastian had last been to Puddles, so long, in fact, that he had to look up the route before he left. He had married almost immediately after leaving Oxford and then, having become established as master in his own home, experienced no desire to be a guest in another, even though it was where he had passed his childhood.

When Philippa was young, Valerie had often taken her to stay with Adam and Eve, but he had been too busy earning a living to accompany them. Their family holidays had usually been spent abroad – there was nothing in the depths of Dorset to attract him. Elliott kept him abreast of news – such as it was – from Puddles. That was what tended to happen once one grew up. However fond one had been of people, one outgrew them and left the past behind . . .

Fortunately, the M3 motorway had been built in the meantime, although the last part of the journey was still along tediously crowded A-roads and, turning down the lane to Puddles, he found himself stuck for several miles behind a tractor dragging a trailer piled high with bits of tree.

Hill House, when he eventually reached it, was bigger than he remembered. In Adam's situation, he reflected, he would have sold it when he retired. Even out here in the sticks it must be worth a tidy sum. Instead of having constantly to fork out on its maintenance, he could have invested the profit. Although, of course, when he and Eve died and Elliott inherited . . .

These thoughts reminded him again of the purpose of his visit. He pulled up in front of the house, gave a toot on the horn to alert them to his arrival and switched off the engine.

The door opened and a large dog bounded out, barking threateningly. In this day and age, Sebastian supposed, it was essential to have a guard dog if one lived in the country. There was no point in having an intruder alarm if nobody else lived near enough to hear it going off.

Adam appeared on the doorstep, raising his hand in greeting and calling, 'Bertie! Come here, boy!' Once his hand had grasp of the beast's collar, Sebastian got out of the Range Rover.

'You're here bright and early,' Adam said. 'Good journey?'

'Not bad, I suppose, all things considered.'

Adam released the dog, which immediately ran over to him again and sniffed at his trousers, then made to jump up at him, its teeth bared and tongue hanging out. Sebastian drew back and Adam laughed. 'He really is the soppiest of dogs. I've often thought that if we did have the misfortune to be burgled, Bertie would probably lick the burglar, then help carry his loot. Well, come along in, Sebastian. I'm afraid Eve's still in bed. Nasty thing, this flu bug. It's really knocked the stuffing out of her. The doctor was afraid it might turn to bronchitis or pleurisy.'

Sebastian was not altogether sorry to miss seeing Eve, since she was the reason for Philippa becoming involved with his mother. Sufficient unto the day was the evil thereof and Gawaine Devere was quite enough for this particular day.

Adam led the way into the library, where a fire was burning in the hearth. 'Well, make yourself comfortable. What would you like to drink? Coffee? Or can I tempt you with something a bit stronger? How about a whisky?'

'No, I'll stick with coffee. You know what the police are like these days with drinking and driving. In any case, I can't stay all that long. I'm expecting a rather important client at the end of the afternoon.' That was not actually true, but it established an excuse not to prolong the visit.

'Yes, of course. I'll just have a word with Gladys in the kitchen.'

Had he been less preoccupied with his own thoughts, Sebastian might have noticed the strange expression that flickered in Adam's eyes before he left the room. But he was more intent on taking stock of the furniture. The library had been out of bounds when he and Elliott were boys, and now he realized there were some nice pieces here. The tub chairs to either side of the fireplace had to be Hepplewhite and so, if he wasn't mistaken, was the table. When he got back to the office, he must see if Elliott couldn't persuade Adam to part with some of this stuff. As always, they were badly in need of good stock . . .

Adam returned, bearing a tumbler of Scotch on the rocks. He was followed shortly by a plump, motherly-looking woman carrying a tray. 'Do you take cream and sugar?' she asked Sebastian.

'No, just black.'

Gladys left and Adam raised his glass. 'Cheers. If you change your mind, just say the word.'

Sebastian nodded. 'Well, I don't see any point in beating about the bush. Philippa has told me about this character Devere's will. I understand you are his executor. Obviously, what I want to know is what's behind it all.'

Adam studied the contents of his tumbler, swirling the amber liquid round the cubes of ice, then he said, 'He liked her.'

'But that's no reason to leave her his house. In any case, from what I can gather, it's a very dubious legacy. The house would seem to be in a bad state of disrepair. Furthermore, she has to take on responsibility for these Gurney characters, which effectively means that it will be very difficult for her to sell the place.'

'Has she decided to sell it then?'

'No, but I assume she will. It's no use to her. It's miles from anywhere. She could hardly commute up to London every day, even if she could afford to stay there.'

'But she hasn't actually said that she's going to sell it?'

'She hasn't actually said anything very much. She came back from the funeral and told us what had happened. Then, yesterday, she went to work as usual and was very late home, so I scarcely had an opportunity for more than a couple of words with her. And today, of course, it was the usual early morning panic.'

'She seems to take her career extremely seriously.'

'In my opinion, the amount of effort she puts into her job is disproportionate to the financial rewards.'

'Still, if she enjoys it . . .'

'I think she's being taken advantage of. She's too good-natured. She works ridiculously long hours all week, then, during the last few months, she's had some weekend job as well, photographing a building for a firm of architects.'

'That's right. I believe her boyfriend is an architect.'

'Exactly what the relationship is between them I don't know. Philippa tends not to confide in us about her personal life.'

'I was just thinking that his opinion of Yondover might be worth hearing. If he's in the property business . . .'

'My prime concern is why Gawaine Devere decided to leave Philippa the property in the first place.'

Adam placed his whisky tumbler just inside the brass fender, reached in the breast pocket of his tweed sports jacket and pulled out a cigar case. After lighting his cigar with a spill, he exhaled a cloud of smoke. Finally, he remarked, 'It's been a long while since you were here.'

Did that statement contain a hint of reproach? Was Adam taking advantage of the situation to turn it into an 'after all we have done for you' lecture?

383

'I'm sorry,' Sebastian said. 'I suppose I should have made time to come and see you more often.'

'That would have been nice.'

'Unfortunately, I lead a busy life. I seldom seem to have a minute to call my own.'

'Yes, I understand.' Adam paused. 'I don't expect you've ever given the matter a thought, but Eve and I had originally hoped to have more than one child. However, after Elliott was born, Eve was told she couldn't have any more children. Then you arrived . . .'

'And I'll always feel extremely grateful to you both for everything you did for me,' Sebastian assured him hurriedly. 'Just the other day, I was thinking . . .'

Adam held up his cigar in an admonitory manner, which took Sebastian back suddenly to his boyhood. Thus it was that Adam had used to silence him and Elliott, when they were trying to make excuses for themselves after some escapade or other.

'I could have come up to London,' Adam continued. 'Eve's quite well enough now to be left alone for a day and my sciatica is much improved. But it seemed more fitting to me that this conversation should take place here. You grew up at Hill House. After you left Austria, this was your home. This was where you were reunited with your mother after the war.'

It was an old trick of Adam's, which he had polished to perfection in the course of his legal career and mercilessly practised on the two boys when they were naughty, to extract a confession by posing a number of seemingly disconnected and confusing questions. So mild-mannered was Adam, it was easy to make the mistake of under-estimating him, to forget that behind that deceptively meek exterior lay a devious and extremely shrewd brain, which was used to analysing the minds of criminals. When, as was inevitable, either he or Elliott had given himself away by making an untruthful response, Adam had then pounced.

Suddenly, Sebastian was convinced that Adam was employing the same technique now. Every word he had spoken since his arrival had been calculated to lead them in a very specific direction. But where?

'Digressing slightly,' Adam went on, 'I gather you are aware that your mother and Pippa have met? Eve told Pippa about her. It slipped out in conversation. She wasn't thinking . . .'

But *where* was Adam heading?

'It doesn't matter,' Sebastian said. 'I must confess that I was rather annoyed when I found out. However, on reflection, I suppose the truth had to emerge at some time or other.'

'Your mother's getting old – like the rest of us. She would like to see you again and make her peace with you. Can't you let bygones be bygones, Sebastian?'

'Elliott asked me much the same thing, and I'll tell you the same as I told him. I have no desire to see her again. There's no point.'

'Do you really hate her so much?'

'I don't hate her at all. So far as I'm concerned, she's a stranger and I feel the same indifference towards her as I would to any other stranger.'

'So you refuse to accept the olive branch?'

'I can see absolutely no useful purpose being served by us meeting again. She's made her life – and I've made mine.'

'Hmm.' Adam lapsed into a ruminative silence.

'Listen, with utmost respect, the reason for my visit is to discuss Gawaine Devere. So far, we seem to have talked about everybody but him. Can we get back to the point?'

Adam studied the tip of his cigar, discovered it to have gone out and went through the rigmarole of re-lighting it. Then he said, 'Before I say any more, I want to stress that the only reason your mother is not telling you what I am about to tell you is because you have categorically refused to see her and allow her the opportunity. Now I admit that if Pippa had not met Gawaine Devere, none of this might ever have needed to emerge. But, personally, I don't think it's altogether a bad thing for you to learn the truth.'

'Adam! For God's sake, stop beating about the bush.'

Adam blinked at him from behind his spectacles. 'You have actually met Gawaine Devere. You met him here, at Puddles. He used to come and stay sometimes during the war. You and Elliott called him Uncle Giles . . .'

'Well, I don't remember him.'

'A pity, because he was extremely fond of you.' Adam leaned towards the fire and tapped the ash from his cigar into the glowing coals. 'So fond of you, in fact, that he paid for your education.'

'He did *what*?'

'He saw you through school and university.'

'But why? Are you trying to tell me that he was, in fact, my uncle?'

'Uncle? Oh, no. He wasn't your uncle . . .'

Sebastian sensed the unfinished statement. Gawaine Devere was not his uncle but his . . .

'Who was he then?'

'Your mother's husband. And he believed you to be his son.'

For a long time, Sebastian was silent. Finally, he said – and, to his dismay, he could hear a shaky note in his voice – 'Maybe I will have that Scotch after all.'

ꙮ

Rose Cottage
Pannet's Way
Arundel
12 December 1987

My dearest Sonja,

Do you remember, when we were girls, we were once sitting on the mountainside above Vevey and you told me that one needed only nine friends throughout one's lifetime? Nine friends, whom one would choose to stand around one's deathbed. No, this is not a gloomy letter – I hope to enjoy a good few years yet. But events have led me to think a lot about those nine friends recently.

When one is young, as you and I were then, one's friends tend to be those people one sees on a day-to-day basis. But as life progresses, so its paths diverge and years can pass when one never sees some of one's friends. Like you and me. But that doesn't lessen the affection in which we hold each other.

I think, at Vevey, I could not count nine friends. There was you certainly, dearest Sonja, as there still is. And, without any doubt, there was West. Then, I assume, there were the Gurneys and probably Rafe and Honey.

Well, now, at the advanced age of seventy-seven, I have finally reached nine, though some of them are dead, but I would like to think I can still include them, because on occasions they seem more real to me than some of those people who occupy the living world.

So, my nine friends. In addition to yourself and
West, who will always be the dearest friends of my soul,
there are Leo, Piers and Gebhard. From the present, there
is Adam, of whom I must tell you much more in a
moment. And there is Pippa — I do so hope you meet her
one day. She is very like me, only much more worldly-wise
and confident — how I would have liked to be.

And the eighth has to be Giles, even though he died
before we could meet again. Yet perhaps this is for the best.
We would have met again as different people and perhaps
friendship would still have eluded us. Yet before he died, he
did the most wonderful deed of his entire life. He left
Yondover to Pippa.

Before I explain all the circumstances in detail, let me
come to the ninth. This is a friendship which is only just
beginning and it may be that it will not have time to
develop very much. But at least the process of becoming
friends has started. Long years of silence have been broken
and misunderstandings explained, even if we are still very
much like strangers.

And yes, I am talking about Sebastian! You see,
miracles do sometimes happen . . .

༄

Pippa Devere aspired to be a portrait photographer long before she
discovered that her grandfather, Gawaine Devere, had been one of
London's top portrait photographers in the 1920s and 1930s. The above
portrait of her grandfather, taken just before his tragic death in last year's
hurricane, has won her an Ilford Bursary. It was shot on the original
Gandolfi camera Gawaine Devere himself used to shoot such famous
subjects as King George V, film star Howard Redmayne and composer
Leopold Brunnen. Pippa Devere's portrait of Gawaine Devere is to be
exhibited at London's National Portrait Gallery.

The British Journal of Photography, March 1988

Rose Cottage
6 April 1988

Darling Pippa,

Just a short note to congratulate you on your award for your portrait of Giles. It is, indeed, very sad that he could not live to see either the finished picture or to witness your success, but I like to think that the dead are spirits who remain with us, aware of what is taking place on earth, and that he knows.

Of course I am not shocked that you have moved in with Chris and I am glad to hear that your father has taken it so well. Poor man, he must be reeling under all the successive shocks! I think you are very wise to continue to live in London for the time being and go down to Yondover at weekends. I am looking forward to coming over to see you there during the summer and of course I will help you go through Giles's negatives and try to identify some of the subjects, though my memory is not so good as it was . . .

☞

One of the most important stretches of the South Downs has been brought under the Trust's permanent protection as the result of a most generous bequest. The land, between Uffing Down and the River Kip, belonged to former photographer, eighty-year-old Gawaine Devere, and had been in his family since the mid-1800s. It is prominent in the landscape on the northern scarp of the Downs and enjoys magnificent views over Ashdown Forest and the Weald, as well as towards the sea. It consists of uncultivated chalk grassland, home to many rare flowers and butterflies, as well as a large area of woodland which was badly damaged in the hurricane, but was the habitat of many animals and birds, including the nightingale.

Although no formal survey has yet been carried out, the large number of tumuli indicate that the site is also likely to be of important historical and archaeological interest.

It is intended to open the downland site to the public next spring, although there will be no access to the woodland until essential clearing and replanting work has been carried out.

National Trust Newsletter, East Sussex Region, Spring 1988

∾

Rose Cottage
18 August 1988

Pippa darling,

Thank you so much for a wonderful day at Yondover last weekend. You and Chris have certainly achieved miracles. I was tremendously impressed at being driven right up to the house. How incredible that the wartime concrete on the drive should have survived all these years under the turf. I sympathize that it does not look very beautiful at the moment, but I think, as it weathers, it will harmonize well enough with the white chalk.

The strangest aspect of my visit was, I think, accustoming myself to a Yondover whose rooms are illuminated by electric light bulbs. I am so glad you insisted that the Electricity Board buried the cables.

With regard to the garden, of course I will give you all the advice I can. I only wish I were able to do more of the work myself, but so much heavy digging is beyond me. I do suggest you keep a wary eye on Ted, who seems to have inherited the Gurney tendency to be rather over-enthusiastic with secateurs and saws.

Last but not least, Cherie is absolutely adorable – and so like Tabitha when she was a kitten. How wise you are to get her used to travelling in a car, so that you can take her backwards and forwards with you from London. But I don't expect she will think much of travelling pillion on Chris's motor bike!

∾

The Royal Photographic Society is staging a retrospective exhibition of images by social and war photographer Gawaine Devere, many of which have never been seen before. Gawaine Devere, who was born in 1907, retired from photography at the end of the war. The negatives were found after his death by his granddaughter, Pippa Devere, at his former home in Sussex. Pippa Devere, who is twenty-seven and following in her grandfather's footsteps as a photographer, catalogued the collection with the help of her grandmother and produced all the prints herself, using original 1930s equipment in her grandfather's darkroom.

Image, The Magazine of The Association of Fashion,
Advertising and Editorial Photographers, July 1989

೧൦

Rose Cottage
Pannet's Way
Arundel
2 December 1990

My dearest Adam,

 I was so sorry to hear your sad, sad news, although I know Eve had been very unwell for some time. Eve and I may never have been as close as you and I, but I have always been extremely fond of her and value immensely everything she did for me, not least in bringing up Sebastian as her own son — and for being responsible for my meeting Pippa.

 We shall, of course, all be coming to the funeral, but if there is anything at all I can do, now or in the future, please, please, let me know. You have been so good to me in my many times of trouble, I should like to think that there is something I could do for you in return . . .

೧൦

Rose Cottage
6 May 1991

Darling Pippa,

    I was immensely moved by your letter asking me to come and live with you and Chris when you move into Yondover. But the answer is definitely no. The last thing you need at the beginning of your married life is an old granny living with you — even in her own granny flat! But once you are fully settled in, of course I should love to come and stay with you.

    In view of the effect that the recession is having on both your jobs, I think you are undoubtedly sensible to give up your London flat and live at Yondover. As you say, lots of people do commute up to London from the Sussex coast and now you are no longer assisting full-time but building up your own client base, you can presumably organize your working hours to suit yourself rather than others. Or am I being rather optimistic? As for Chris, he strikes me as a very resilient kind of man. And possibly, if there is less demand for new buildings, there may well be more demand for the refurbishment of old ones — the type of work he most enjoys?

    Now, let us get one thing straight, once and for all. You owe me absolutely nothing. If it helps your conscience, consider that money as a gift not to yourself but to Yondover . . .

ᘓᔍ

Rose Cottage
Pannet's Way
Arundel
20 June 1991

Dearest Sonja,

    I am enclosing some photographs of Pippa's wedding last Saturday. It was quite the loveliest wedding I have ever been to and a day I never thought to experience. It took

392

place in Kipwell church, officiated over by a vicar very
different from my father! The day was June at its most
glorious, the bride looked radiant, the bridegroom extremely
smart – but you can see all that in the photographs. And
you can see the bride's proud parents and her grandmother
– I'm sorry about the hat – hats never did suit me . . .

∞

BIRTHS
MARKOWSKI – On July 2 1992, to Pippa (née Devere) and Chris, a
son (Giles Sebastian Westrup). Welcome to the world.

∞

Pippa, Chris and Giles
request the pleasure of the company of
KITTY PILGRIM
at a 'surprise' party to be held at
Yondover, Kipwell, Sussex
from noon onwards on 3 April 1993
in honour of Sebastian Devere's 60th birthday
R.S.V.P.

∞

Dearest surprised penguin,
I shall miss you more than words can say.
All my love always,
Your Kitty

∞

Dear Sebastian,

I am sorry it has taken me so long to reply to your letter, but I assure you that I would have replied quicker had I been able to. I am sure Pippa passed on my message of thanks and news of my progress. I realize I have been exceptionally lucky, especially at my age of nearly eighty-four. A warning stroke is what the doctors call it. But I have now recovered full use of the right side of my body, which is a very good omen.

I was deeply touched by your invitation to come and stay with you and Valerie to convalesce, but I think it best that I stay in my own home, with all my own familiar belongings around me and where I can take things at my own pace. My new neighbours are a young couple, who are very kind and helpful.

However, when I am quite well, I would very much enjoy coming to stay with you, maybe for a long weekend.

Isn't it wonderful news about Pippa's book? I am so pleased and thrilled for her and I am sure you are feeling immensely proud . . .

૭૭

BOOKS

Yondover by Pippa Devere, Astra, £14.99

For anyone who likes a true romance with a happy ending and who has also dreamed of restoring a neglected old house and garden to their former glory, this book is a must.

When Pippa Devere happened to acquire a 1930s photograph album, containing pictures by a photographer called Gawaine Devere, she was so impressed by the unusual imagery and intrigued by the coincidence of their names that she set out to track down the photographer, only to discover that he was her grandfather.

Upon his death in 1987, Gawaine Devere left her Yondover, his sixteenth-century farmhouse on the Sussex Downs. In the house she found negatives and photographs, taken by himself and his grandfather, showing the house and grounds as they were in their pre-war heyday. These pictorial references, together with the memories of her grandmother, Kitty Pilgrim, whose divorce from Gawaine Devere had taken place in 1940, gave her a vital starting point.

The restoration of Yondover and its grounds took Pippa Devere and her architect husband, Chris Markowski, six years to complete and throughout it she kept her own fascinating, photographic record.

∽

FOREWORD

I first saw Yondover and met its then owner, Westrup Lambourne, in 1923, when I was thirteen. Ever since, Yondover has been my one lasting passion, surviving where all other loves have failed me and enduring long after my marriage to Giles Gawaine Devere, Westrup Lambourne's grandson, broke up. I left the house in 1933 and did not see it again until 1987, after the hurricane had wreaked a fearful destruction upon it. Yet still, although it was no longer the Yondover I knew as a girl, to return to it was like coming home.

When I look at the roses clambering up the front wall and morning glory flowering in abundance over the porch, it is of the Yondover that existed in the days of Westrup Lambourne that I still think. But West's original plants have long ago died and new ones have been planted in their place, just as West himself is long dead and the first of another new generation – my great-grandson, Giles Sebastian Westrup – plays in the attic nursery where West played as a boy.

That is how it should be. A house is not merely bricks and mortar: it is a living entity, reflecting the characters of the people who inhabit it. And a garden is a growing, changing thing that should not remain static.

The story of Yondover is a book that I would have liked to write. Indeed, Pippa tried very hard to persuade me to write it, but although I made several attempts to start, I could not get much beyond the first page. I was too involved. I felt too close to describe dispassionately the intimate scenes in our old love affair. Had anyone criticized the book, it would have felt like a criticism of my innermost self, the part of me I could do nothing about. Had a publisher rejected it, it would have felt like a rejection of myself and my entire life.

Pippa, however, has succeeded in writing and illustrating my love story for me, far better than I could ever have hoped to do it. And in doing so, she has revealed aspects of Yondover and of my own self of which I was hitherto unaware.

Kitty Pilgrim
Arundel, 1994

෬

BEST-SELLERS

HARDBACKS

THIS WEEK	General	LAST WEEK	WEEKS IN TOP 10
1	**Yondover / Pippa Devere** (Astra £14.99) True story of how a photograph album led the author to the discovery of a grandfather she did not know existed and to the house of her dreams	2	4

෬

■ Her former fancies have included royals and rock stars, but now model and TV presenter Aurora Georgijev, 25, has eyes only for Kensington antiques dealer Elliott Berkeley, 38 years her senior. Berkeley's fifth marriage with the former Felicity Clements-Clarke ended six months ago. He has six children from his four previous marriages. Aurora, known to her friends as 'Princess', told me: 'He's my Prince Charming. I know I can make him happy.'

Daily Mail, Friday 13 May, 1995

EPILOGUE

The climb up Uffing Down tired Kitty more than usual, even though it was punctuated by many stops, leaning on her stick, to look at the view. Perhaps because it was such a hot August day, she kept running out of breath and her heart was pounding in a most irregular fashion. She had told nobody where she was going, but slipped away, as she had used to do when she was a girl and felt the need of being alone in a big open space.

With a little sigh of relief at having reached the top, she lowered herself on to the close-cropped turf, sweet with the scent of wild thyme, studded with scabious, harebells, yellow lady's slipper and big, purple thistles. Behind her, across several miles of rolling hills, where sheep grazed, rabbits scampered and butterflies danced, the gently undulating slopes patterned by occasional small copses and dappled by the shadows of tiny white clouds scudding across the sun, was the sea – a distant, silvery shimmer.

Ahead of her, beyond Kipwell village, a train was snaking its way towards the station. It was an electric train, quieter and cleaner if less romantic than the steam trains of her girlhood. She watched it stop, then pull out of the station again, crossing the little River Kip to continue its journey to Hastings. She shifted position slightly, so that her gaze followed the line of the Kip, meandering lazily under a hump-backed bridge and through a gap in the Downs, past the young saplings in West's wood, towards its estuary.

Finally, her glance rested on Yondover. Because the hurricane had left the house more exposed than it had used to be, she could clearly see Ted digging in his vegetable garden, Millie hanging out washing on the line, and Chris doing some repair to his motor bike. Sebastian and Valerie were sitting on deckchairs on the front lawn, and there were Giles and Pippa coming out of the back door to join them, Pippa carrying the latest addition to the family, a beautiful baby girl called Rosie.

Kitty sank back on the grass and gazed into the sky. No doubt her absence would soon be noticed and they would come looking for her. In the meantime, she had been granted a few precious moments of solitude.

Or was she really alone?

'It's grand up on Uffing Down, isn't it?' she seemed to hear West saying. 'As if you're on top of the world. I remember my father once asking me what I thought about while I was up there and caning me when I said that I didn't really think about anything. He never understood how a boy could lie on his back for hours, just looking into the clouds.'

'*J'aime les nuages . . . les nuages qui passent . . . là-bas . . . là-bas . . . les merveilleux nuages.*'

'We seem to have a lot in common, you and I.'

'Your big, round eyes remind me of a kitten's. I think I'll call you Kitty. And since we're to be friends, you can call me West.'

'I have tried to do for you what I wanted to do for my own daughter. I have wanted you to glimpse a vision of the world beyond that made by men, to be free and wild, to see, as Wordsworth described, *into the life of things*. I have wanted you to know what he called *the hour of splendour in the grass, of glory in the flower*.'

'All those stars you see are souls, keeping watch over us mortals. When you need me, Kitty-Cat, you have only to come up here to the top of Uffing Down and my spirit will be with you. At night it will be among the stars and, in the daytime, it will be flying with the gulls and singing with the skylark.'

The light suddenly became so dazzling that Kitty had to close her eyes. She lay so still in the summer sunshine that a white butterfly with orange tips to its wings, which had been flitting among the harebells, landed on her hand and closed its wings in repose.

From the grass beside her – so close that it must have been resting under the very shelter of her body – a skylark rose and soared up into the infinite blue expanse of the sky. For a while it hovered, halfway between heaven and earth, spilling out its silver song. Then it spiralled, upwards and ever upwards, into the vaulted arches of the heavens, until the bird itself could no longer be seen but was embodied only in the glorious outpouring of its rapturous melody.